BERNINI'S
ELEPHANT

ESSENTIAL PROSE SERIES 205

ONTARIO ARTS COUNCIL
CONSEIL DES ARTS DE L'ONTARIO
an Ontario government agency
un organisme du gouvernement de l'Ontario

Canada Council   Conseil des arts
for the Arts   du Canada

Guernica Editions Inc. acknowledges the support of
the Canada Council for the Arts and the Ontario Arts Council.
The Ontario Arts Council is an agency of the Government of Ontario.
We acknowledge the financial support of the Government of Canada

JANE CALLEN

BERNINI'S ELEPHANT

GUERNICA
EDITIONS
TORONTO • CHICAGO • BUFFALO • LANCASTER (U.K.)
2023

Guernica Founder: Antonio D'Alfonso

Michael Mirolla, general editor
Lindsay Brown, editor
Interior and cover design: Rafael Chimicatti
Guernica Editions Inc.
287 Templemead Drive, Hamilton, ON L8W 2W4
2250 Military Road, Tonawanda, N.Y. 14150-6000 U.S.A.
www.guernicaeditions.com

Distributors:
Independent Publishers Group (IPG)
600 North Pulaski Road, Chicago IL 60624
University of Toronto Press Distribution (UTP)
5201 Dufferin Street, Toronto (ON), Canada M3H 5T8
Gazelle Book Services, White Cross Mills
High Town, Lancaster LA1 4XS U.K.

First edition.
Printed in Canada.

Legal Deposit—First Quarter
Library of Congress Catalog Card Number: 2022947551
Library and Archives Canada Cataloguing in Publication
Title: Bernini's elephant / Jane Callen.
Names: Callen, Jane, author.
Series: Essential prose series ; 205.
Description: Series statement: Essential prose series ; 205
Identifiers: Canadiana (print) 20220443645 | Canadiana (ebook) 20220443653
ISBN 9781771837842
(softcover) | ISBN 9781771837859 (EPUB)
Classification: LCC PS8605.A4625 B47 2023 | DDC C813/.6—dc23

For Jill Robyn Fontaine

CHAPTER ONE

Pompeii

Transformed into volcanic ash, the woman clawed her way forward, her belly close to the ground. Modern science reveals a child in her womb. Kat peers between the iron bars of the warehouse at the figure in the glass coffin, then turns to glimpse the woman's killer, Mount Vesuvius.

Tourists pay 100 euros to shove buds into their ears and listen as the state-certified guide Luciana recounts the futility of the woman's flight. "Although the inhabitants of Pompeii died suddenly from a catastrophic eruption of volcanic ash in 79 AD, they were already mortally ill."

Like us, Luciana explains, they enjoyed a high standard of living.

"Their water, for instance, coursed through the city in a complex system of pipes." She kicks a remnant of piping beside a low-lying wall. "The citizens of Pompeii were dying from lead poisoning."

Like Vesuvius, the Mediterranean sun leaves its mark on every surface. Heating the stones underfoot, bleaching the colour from the brick ruins and burning the tourists' skin. Climbing into the tour bus, Kat is grateful for the blast of air conditioning and the ice-laced bottles of water Luciana hands out. She's got a throbbing headache. Pressing the bottle to her temple, Kat contemplates the Pompeiian woman in flight. Fated to die without warning from suffocating ash or suffering day after day from mounting fatigue and gut-wrenching pain. Either way, her destiny was sealed.

Kat couldn't help comparing the people on the bus with those of Pompeii. What contaminants were leaching from these plastic bottles into their systems, for instance? More chilling, could a sudden, cata-strophic act become Kat's Pompeii?

Faith adjusts her shorts before crawling over Kat's legs to settle into the seat beside the window. She frowns. "Those people were doomed."

"Aren't we all?" Faith can be naïve. Still, at times she proves herself useful.

It was Faith's idea to join a bus tour. She felt it was a safe way for two widows to travel without the company of men. Kat is unconvinced. Wedged into this coach with 50 perspiring tourists seems more daunting than facing the Italians on her own. She relented because it was easier to appease Faith than to fight her.

Faith's preparations for ten days in Italy were both admirable and annoying. With headphones permanently perched on her head and her tongue set on repeat, Faith studied the Rosetta Stone curriculum in her quest to speak the Italian language. To demonstrate her proficiency, she reads shop signs and billboards aloud and translates them for Kat's benefit.

"*Chiuso il lunedì.* That's easy, closed on Monday."

The coach shimmies into motion, then proceeds in fits and starts along the narrow streets of modern Pompeii. A gnarled, elderly man stoops over his tomato plants on a patch of dirt outside a stone cottage. He tips his flat cap at the driver as they pass. Day one and already Kat regrets not owning an iPod to drown out Faith's chatter. If Nick were here he'd be the one reading out loud, checking the written word against Italian reality. Poor Nick. Without a guidebook, a user's manual or a map, he was powerless. A gnat thrashing on the surface of a pint. Not for the first time, Kat wonders what shape her life would take with someone unafraid to make decisions, someone willing to take chances. She sur-veys her travel companions as they doze, heads lolling with the lurching of the bus. He's not here, the passionate man she likes to imagine. That's for certain.

A burly guy at the back breaks into a version of *Volare* amid frag-ments of laughter. He takes this as encouragement and he's correct. They join him on the refrain. "Volare, oh, oh." It never ends, intrusions of others. If Kat had her way, the passengers would swear a vow of silence. If she were the woman of Pompeii, she wouldn't have tried to escape. No, she'd cross her arms over her breasts and shut her eyes. Welcome the silence after the thunder of Vesuvius' wrath.

* * *

Nick asked her to join him on his forage for woodland mushrooms. He joked that instead of a romantic outing it would be an aromatic one. Quoting from his guidebook, he informed her that mushrooms have microbial relationships with tree roots. Chanterelles need Douglas fir, while oysters require alder deadwood. He pushed that errant lock of dull brown hair back from his face and grinned. Come on, Kat. Let's unearth a few local specimens. They'll make for a delicious meal. She could imagine nothing less engaging than tromping through scrubby bush, head down, looking for fungi. She begged off, said she had a kick-boxing class she couldn't miss. That was the last time she saw Nick alive, but how easy it is to conjure him up in her mind's eye. Nick heading out the kitchen door with his mushroom guide in his left hand. The clomping of his Wellingtons on the pea stone drive. He was a heavy-footed man. The thud as he slammed the door of the SUV and revved the engine. Then the spit of gravel as he raced away. These sounds play on Kat's internal iPod in a perpetual loop.

Her kick-boxing partner failed to show. With Nick hiking through Capilano Canyon, Kat decided to head to West Vancouver to do a bit of shopping. She found a classic black pantsuit, purchased for the boardroom or dining with clients at the Vancouver Club. It made its debut at Nick's funeral.

Getting into her car that day, she noticed Faith had left a message on her cell. Nick's foraging had been a success. There'd be a fungus feast tonight. Faith was already mincing and chopping the mushrooms and shallots. Faith as *sous-chef*. It's what she did now as their permanent houseguest. Kat headed home.

* * *

The Roman sunset wraps around the rooftop garden of the Hotel Grand Minerva. Striations of pink and gold illuminate the red tile roofs but Saint Peter's Dome dominates the night sky. Tonight belongs to Peter, the first fisherman, but tomorrow the tour group will explore the Pantheon, the pagan temple of his predecessors. Kat sees that dome too. Said to be the oldest sacred space in the eternal city, it casts its shadow onto the piazza in front of the hotel.

Choosing a corner table away from their group, Kat sips her chilled white. Faith joins the others. Without the pianist's permission, their ragged voices accompany his medley. This isn't a beery sing-along bar.

Tables set with pressed white linens, polished cutlery and fragile orchid arrangements exude subtle elegance under the stars. No matter. *Arrivederci Roma, Three Coins in the Fountain* and *Volare*. Out of key, careless with the melody. Tourists making a spectacle. Kat cringes. She hopes they at least leave a healthy tip.

Faith runs fingers through her wash-and-wear hair. In preparation for their trip, she changed her style, cutting back her salt and pepper bob to an implausible blonde crew cut. And in Kat's opinion, Faith wears questionably short skirts for a woman in her fifties. She fits in with the group, whereas Kat goes out of her way to maintain distance. As Faith belts out a solo, Kat drains her glass and signals the waiter.

* * *

Road construction on a Saturday afternoon in West Vancouver. Traffic on the Upper Levels Highway backed up well past Capilano Road. It was after six by the time Kat fought her way through the detours. Expecting a chilled Pinot Grigio and the twosome fussing over the sautéed fungi, she found instead a deserted house.

Greasy fry pans and food-encrusted utensils filled the sink; a carton of Nick's favourite free range eggs sat open on the counter. Under a small white pebble, she found a note scrawled in Faith's spidery handwriting.

The parking lot at St. Paul's Hospital was full. Kat drove round the neighbouring streets in ever larger circles looking for a space. When she reached the entrance to Emergency her head was pounding and her gut roiling. A doctor, whose face she cannot recall, took her arm and led her to a cubicle, where he insisted she sit down. As she stared at the medical equipment dangling off the opposite wall, she learned that Nick had succumbed *en route*. After some confusion, she located Faith behind a drawn curtain, keeping vigil over his body. Anguish washed over her as Kat manoeuvred Faith out of the way. My husband, not yours. She held Nick's open hand in her own. Already his was heavier, waxier than human flesh. Whatever electrical spark ignited living beings, Nick's was gone.

Her husband's eyes were closed. They would never open again to give her that questioning look she'd come to hate. Leaning over his corpse, Kat whispered into his now-deaf ear. "I know I kept you out. I never gave you a chance." Bowing her head, she rested her cheek over his stilled heart. "None of it was your fault, Nicky. It was mine. I'm sorry."

Death Cap is the common name of the mushroom that did Nick in. Three grams of the deadly fungus will kill. The pathologist's report stated it could easily be mistaken for an edible mushroom known as the Paddy Straw. Nick thought he had the Paddy Straw in his omelette, an honest error, but Kat wonders how his *sous-chef* managed to escape unharmed. Didn't Faith taste the mushrooms as she sautéed, added butter and herbs?

* * *

Luciana flashes her plastic-coated credentials at a man behind a glass partition as they enter the Pantheon. In response, he bellows into the address system that they were in a house of worship and voices should be kept low. Luciana recounts the building's history into her microphone which the group hears on the wireless gizmos plugged into their ears.

"A temple to honour pagan gods, the Pantheon was built by Marcus Agrippa whose name remains on the exterior façade. The original wooden structure burnt to the ground in 80 AD. All that remains are the bronze doors, once covered in gold." The group joins other tourists as they gawk skyward.

Luciana continues. "The present-day Pantheon was resurrected in 118 AD. Seized by Christians in 608 AD, it's been an active place of worship ever since. Even during World War Two."

Shoulder to shoulder, Kat and Faith take in the gilded dome and the tombs of the artist Raphael and Italy's first king, Emmanuel. Circling the rotunda, their necks arch to view the light streaming through the *oculus*, the largest in Rome. They scan the floor of marble tile, which Luciana notes is convex to allow rain to flow into ancient Roman drains.

"Genius," she proclaims. "The architecture, the mathematics, the workmanship. *E italiano!*"

Overhead are the vacant alcoves which previously housed pagan deities. Their roles were usurped by statues of Christian saints who now keep watch at floor level. It strikes Kat that this sacred space, stripped of its original meaning and occupied by interlopers, still belongs to those pagan gods for whom it was created. No different than it was in Provence where evil permeated the ruins of the Château de Sade long after the Marquis was dead. She felt his power there. Only fools believe they can destroy energy. They cannot, neither the sacred nor the malevolent. This Kat knows.

* * *

Reaching their destination, a medieval French town of narrow winding streets held together by gothic arches, they discovered they were lost. Lacoste lacked signposts. Nick couldn't figure out where to park, so he abandoned their rented Peugeot along the side of the road. The foursome made the steady upward trek, some 40 minutes to reach the pinnacle and the remnants of the Château de Sade. Nick and Gerhard summited first but Kat and Faith weren't far behind. Lacoste didn't cater to tourists back then and nothing on the winding route held their attention beyond a solitary café.

As they entered the ruins of the home of the Marquis, a chilly mistral raced through the structure, kicking up dust on its way. Nick was focused on his travelogue, relating that de Sade poisoned his young victims if they didn't acquiesce to his sexual demands. This information made no impression and he decided to explore the tangled forest below the ruin, while Gerhard exclaimed his gratitude that there was no fee to see this "pile of rubble". Ordering Faith to meet him in an hour at the café, he stomped off. Kat remembers thinking that his choice of knee-length pants did not flatter his cigar-stub legs.

The women stood in the vestiges of de Sade's sanctum. Kat watched Nick's progress into the grove where the Marquis forced his victims to wander blindfold. He terrorized souls just feet from where her husband roamed.

"Poison, de Sade used poison." That's what Faith said. Her thoughts were already contaminated by the malignant energy in that space.

"He was a murderer, Kat. His evil's still here." Faith folded her arms across her chest. "Don't you feel it?"

"I feel …" Kat placed her palms flat along a remnant of château wall. An electric charge emanated from the stone; a force so strong that she pulled her hands away. She shivered in the sunshine.

"Kat, you alright?" Faith's voice filled with alarm.

Kat kicked the rubble at her feet. A coin-sized white stone rolled toward her. Reaching for the pebble, she held it up. "Memento."

"No, it's bad luck." Faith moved away, toward the falling down exit. "Leave his energy here."

"Memento … or inspiration." Kat stroked the smooth stone and slipped it into her pocket.

* * *

Shuffling feet on marble. "Quiet please, people!" belting out over the public address. Luciana holds the blue scarf tied to her umbrella high above her head. The tour group follows it to the exit into the blistering Roman heat. They're heading to the Trevi Fountain, where tourists are encouraged to turn their backs on the monument and throw a coin over their left shoulder. A guarantee of a return visit to Rome. In anticipation, the crooner, now known as George from Edmonton, breaks into song, "Three Coins in the Fountain." The others join in as they trail Luciana's blue scarf fluttering above the crowd and over the uneven cobblestones. Kat hangs back, putting distance between herself and the scarf. At first Faith keeps pace with her but soon speeds up to join the singers.

The unending stream of tourists fills the growing gap between Kat and the singing. Slipping past the gawkers lining its circumference, Kat re-enters the Pantheon and settles on a wooden bench reserved for modern day worshippers. Ignoring the Christian statuary, she closes her eyes, allows her thoughts to focus on the ancient gods to whom this sacred space first belonged.

All she hears is the shuffle of humanity on ancient marble. An echo from times past.

Yesterday, Luciana had recounted how Vesuvius annihilated Pompeii's inhabitants in 79 AD. Today she shared that the first temple built here burned to the ground the following year. The original residents of the Pantheon, those ancient gods, were ruthless. In a world where anything goes, Kat finds comfort in that thought.

At dusk, the waves of tourists in the piazza give way to ordinary Romans engaging in their evening *passeggiata*, the social stroll before a late dinner. The elderly sip wine in the cafés and discuss events of the day. Mimicking the locals, the tourists calm down and move about in a more leisurely fashion.

Poised at the edge of the cobbled square, Kat surveys the cafés and bars. In the centre, Roman schoolgirls and their admirers settle on the fountain steps for the evening's socializing. Next to the fountain, a woman with a mess of yellow hair sets up her guitar and music stand. Rossana introduces herself in Italian, announcing that she'll sing both French and Italian this evening. Kat chooses a table facing the singer and the Italians on their *passeggiata*. Faith's chair scrapes on the cobbles as she settles in next to Kat. Listening to Faith's description of the attractions they'd covered today—Trevi Fountain, Spanish Steps and the Colosseum—Kat's glad she'd stayed behind.

The crisp-shirted waiter places a serving of Marsala *di vitello* before Faith who leans in to inhale its savoury promise. Kat re-arranges her cutlery and water glass to accommodate an over-sized bowl of Osso Bucco. The veal's juices run red under the candlelight. Topping up their wine, the waiter makes a slight bow and disappears into the café. Rossana works her way through her repertoire, stopping every now and then to sell her homemade CDs. The crowd of young Italians on the fountain steps grows, their chatter competing with the singer's song. Kat follows the path of moon in the inky sky. Yellow and almost full, it hangs low over the apartments above the cafés.

"Why didn't you taste the mushrooms Nick brought home?" Kat's question catches Faith's forkful of veal and mushrooms on its way to her mouth. "Isn't that what a *sous-chef* does, season and taste?"

Faith lays down her fork to meet Kat's question full on. Her blue eyes look naked with most of her hair gone.

"You *know* why." She swallows an oversized gulp of wine and resumes eating. Every morsel. All that remains is the sheen of Marsala glaze on the empty plate. Kat has less appetite, coasts on wine instead. She remembers de Sade's white stone anchoring Faith's message on the kitchen counter the day Nick died. Kat does know why, now.

"I've decided to sell the house. Thought I'd warn you." Kat glances at her dinner partner. They've played the grief-stricken widows long enough. Faith re-folds her linen napkin. Has she even heard what Kat said?

Rossana begins a new set with *Je ne regrette rien*. The familiar song sends Kat's memory back to Provence and a young chanteuse performing the Piaf favourite under the shelter of a planetree in Roussillon. An elderly guitarist in a dusty tuxedo accompanied the singer, who Kat thought too young to have done anything worthy of regret. The girl's nerves betrayed her as she draped and re-draped her filmy scarf while she sang. Nick had pointed out the upturned cap on the dirt in front of the performers. Empty, Kat remembers. Reaching into his pocket, Nick flung what coins he had into the hat. Gerhard scoffed. *We didn't ask her to sing, so why should we pay her?*

"We could pool our resources." Kat watches Faith count out 50 euros in the dying candlelight and tuck them under her empty wine glass. "Buy a condo together, maybe downtown near Coal Harbour?" The naked eyes now burn a fierce blue. "Think about it, Kat." Faith gets to her feet, stretches her arms above her head. "We leave for Florence at nine, unless you aren't coming?"

Kat meets Faith's stare for a moment, then turns away to follow Rossana's song. *Je ne regrette rien.* In the shadow of the Pantheon, the singer's cigarette-strained voice lends authenticity to the words.

"Suit yourself then." Faith's heels click across the square. Her crystal earrings are gaudy in the moonlight.

* * *

How many years had passed since Faith had abandoned her Vancouver roots and moved to Seattle to marry that rotund and balding man? Ten at least. She was well past 40, Kat remembers that much. When Faith contacted Kat on LinkedIn to suggest they share a vacation farmhouse in France, Kat's first thought was to press delete. Once flatmates, their friendship had gone stale long before Faith moved away. Still, holidays with Nick had become excruciating in their blandness. When she offered him the opportunity to meet up with a flower arranger and a financier at a farmhouse in Provence, Nick's initial response was: "Not a farmhouse, Kat. *Gite.* The correct terminology for the stone building in the middle of a terraced vineyard is *gite.*"

The husbands, it turned out, had similar taste in apparel. Baseball caps to cover thinning hair, tan golf shirts and beige slacks, sandals with socks for comfort. But their personalities were distinct. While Nick struggled to capture the authentic Roussillon with his brand-new Nikon camera, Gerhard kept his finger on the button of his battered video cam. Indiscriminately, he filmed everything and anything.

What Kat remembers most clearly was that, despite the glare of the Mediterranean light, Faith removed her sunglasses. She cupped her hand over her left eye and confessed to taking a tumble in the bathroom the previous evening. The eye was swollen and bruised, but Kat wondered about the purple shadow encircling her upper arm.

* * *

Kat drains her glass. Both men are gone. Gerhard died on an August evening shortly after dining on Nick's *Coq au vin* at the *gite.* Poor Nick, he'd followed Julia Child's recipe to the letter. Already Nick's eager *sous chef*, Faith chopped and sliced. She shooed Kat away from their cast iron pot but Kat was tenacious.

Saint Émilion was her accomplice. Kat dragged the wooden casket across the terra cotta tiles into the dining room and lined up half a dozen bottles of red wine at the far end of the table. Then, she set out four tumblers and a corkscrew.

"Nicky, it's time to open the Bordeaux. Such a fine vintage needs your expert touch."

Nick protested. According to Julia Child, the *Coq au vin* required another 15 minutes. Kat insisted their palates needed to be ready too. Ever willing to please, Nick made a show of opening the Bordeaux bought that morning. He poured generous portions. As Gerhard joined his wife in sniffing and swirling the pricey red, Kat backed into the kitchen. She only needed a few seconds to pour the colourless liquid into the pot and stir.

Gerhard's official cause of death was organ failure due to environmental misadventure, etiology unknown. His widow never mentioned his allergy to clams or their juices. In the days after Nick hurled Gerhard's ashes off the cliff above Roussillon, Faith's clumsiness disappeared, along with her bruises.

* * *

The moon ascends in the midnight sky and the piazza empties. Comfortable in her alcoholic haze, Kat almost forgets the decisions that brought her to be a widow in Italy. *Non, je regrette rien.*

It's a short distance to the hotel in the Piazza della Minerva behind the Pantheon. Kat keeps her eyes on the cobbles. They're precarious enough in the daylight, sober. A lone figure crouches next to the statue of *Bernini's Elephant* in front of the hotel. A young male with a head of tousled curls. Moving closer she sees his paints spread on a folding stool and the easel propped at the base of the elephant. His eyes move from canvas to statue and back. Unnoticed, Kat watches him from the shadow of a lamp at the entrance to the square. Bernini's porcine elephant. The ancient dome of the Pantheon. The failing light. Even from where she's standing, it's clear the young painter has captured a postcard-perfect Roman scene.

"Finished, *fini, finito?*" She moves closer and struggles for a word that will work.

Ignoring her, the boy adds a sliver of yellow to the edge of the elephant's silhouette, which changes everything. The perspective shifts, clarifies. He turns and smiles. "*Si.*"

"For sale?" She rushes on, not wanting to give him a chance to refuse her. "*Quanto costa*? I'll take it to Canada. You'll be famous." Kat's raw laughter reminds her of how much alcohol she's consumed.

Seventy-five euros. It is Franco Ghibellini's first commission since obtaining his Fine Arts Baccalaureate from the university. As the last of the light dies, the painter in a worn blue shirt and ragged jeans introduces himself to the stranger who's agreed to purchase his work for this substantial sum. Franco's family has a vineyard in San Gimignano, in Tuscany. As the only son, he's expected to join the business but doesn't wish to be a farmer. He shrugs. His dream is to paint. And so, he does. Kat discovers the work is not on canvas, but on the cardboard backing of a sketch book. The ragged notches, where the backing was ripped from its spiral ring, rim the top of the painting.

Holding the elephant by the edges, she asks how many days it will take to dry.

"*Cinque.*" He holds up five fingers. Concern crosses Franco's face. "Is not dry …" He gestures broadly, forecasting disaster. Kat isn't paying attention, noticing instead the elegance of his hands, the finely-tapered fingers smeared with colour.

"Five days is not a problem." She assures her painter. "*Grazie.*"

It's decided. Kat isn't leaving Rome. Yet.

CHAPTER TWO

Rome

It's proving difficult to find Franco. Kat imagines he moves from one monument to another, painting scenes where tourists gather, where someone might purchase his work. Consulting the guidebook Faith left behind, she decides to check out the most obvious locations.

Another searing Roman day under a cloudless cerulean sky. In Piazza Navona, a stadium repurposed over the centuries, the foot traffic streams past Kat as she makes her way to Bernini's *Fountain of Four Rivers*. She scans the artists on folding chairs or leaning against a railing as they sketch. Franco's not among them. Ignoring the sweat trailing down her back, she trudges along the cobbled streets and elbows her way through the crowds in Piazza di Pietra. Fetid, her armpits stink as she continues to the base of the Trevi Fountain.

Here, eager tourists wishing to toss their coins push past Kat. Franco's not among this human chaos. She makes her way to the Spanish Steps with its hideous boat-like fountain designed by Bernini's father. The tourists thin out. No Franco. Day three, the paint on Bernini's elephant is almost dry but her artist is nowhere in sight. It isn't lost on Kat that she's covered more tourist sites searching for Franco than Faith managed on her Roman tour.

Back in the Grand Hotel Minerva, Kat leans against the ornate grate on her windows and stares down at *Bernini's Elephant*. Local children play hide 'n' seek at the statue's base. Shrieks of laughter as they tag the unsuspecting runner. Music drifts up from the Piazza della Rotunda.

An accordion player this time. Kat is deaf to the music or the joy of the children. She remembers the curly-haired painter instead. Elegant hands coated in paint gesturing concern over his painting.

The painting leans against the desk lamp. It's almost dry, Franco. In daylight and sober, she assesses the work. Years of developing high-end marketing material to sell everything from fast cars to even faster computers taught Kat to appreciate a balanced composition and innovative use of colour, to discern the tone and emotion of graphics. She revisits the manner in which the painter added a sliver of yellow to the elephant, how this changed the perspective. He gave the porcine creature presence, permission to inhabit the piazza. This man, Franco Ghibellini, has talent.

Kat wants to learn more about the painter. A crazy idea perhaps but Nick's not around to rein in her impulsiveness with a raised brow or wisecrack. Nor is Faith. She's on her way to Venice by now. Kat's alone in Rome and she's going to find the artist. But where?

She riffles through the guidebook again. Perhaps Franco follows Bernini, not the tourists. The guidebook describes Bernini as prolific. His art embellishes fountains, churches and piazzas. The Museo Borghese houses a significant number of his works. That's as good a place to begin as any other. Kat pulls on her linen jacket, tosses her purse over her shoulder and heads to the lobby to order yet another taxi.

Villa Borghese Parco in the centre of Rome offers her citizens refuge from second-hand smoke and polluting Fiats. Over two hundred acres of tree-lined avenues leading to all things Italian: secret fountains, formal gardens, larger than life sculptures and hidden grottoes; even a zoo. Late on this Sunday morning, the sole inhabitant is a lean woman in a tan silk sheath and oversized sunglasses who calls out from a pathway: "Flori!"

An Irish Setter skitters across the lawn, landing in a red rush at Kat's feet. The woman snaps a leash to the dog's collar as her pet licks a circle around Kat's ankle with its narrow tongue. The woman addresses Kat in rapid Italian, an apology perhaps and strides away. The crunch of pea stone under her well-heeled feet sets off memories of Nick walking down the driveway the last time Kat saw him. Nick returns to her often. Perhaps he'll never leave for good.

She's lightheaded in the noon heat. Even filtered through the umbrella pines, the Mediterranean sunlight is punishing. She pushes thoughts of Nick away. He doesn't belong here. He'd never understand what's on Kat's mind. Not by-the-book Nick.

Under duress, Camillo Borghese sold the most precious works in his collection to his brother-in-law, the emperor Napoleon. Today, art aficionados admire them at the Louvre. Robbed of its heritage, the Galleria Borghese displays later masterpieces instead. Among the most valued are those by Bernini and Caravaggio. If Franco follows Bernini, then this is where she may find him. Kat climbs the marble steps of the Galleria and turns left for the ticket office.

In the first room off the central salon stands a life-sized god. Apollo, in mid-flight, reaches for the object of his carnal passions, the wood nymph Daphne. His beloved wants none of her destiny and escapes by turning into a laurel tree. Bay leaves sprout from her outstretched fingers, roots grow from her toes and rough bark enfolds her smooth body as she shapeshifts. Kat circles the massive tableau, wonders if Daphne's leafy fate was preferable to submitting to Apollo's demands. Perhaps this is Bernini's message. Beware the consequences of a willful shift in destiny.

In an out-of-the-way corner, she spies Franco perched on his folding stool. Head bowed, he sketches on a pad similar to the one he used for Kat's elephant. She recognizes the blue shirt. Today he wears it as a jacket over a white tee. His jeans, although clean, are paint-stained. Tucked under the stool, his only extravagance, those sleek and ridiculously expensive sneakers that all Italian men seem to wear. Kat notices the prominence of his collar bone above his tee shirt and bets that surviving as an artist is a struggle, especially if one has a penchant for finery.

At first, he doesn't notice her. She's just another middle-aged tourist milling about. He's probably used to tuning people out. When Kat calls his name, Franco tilts his head and gazes her way but he doesn't recognize her. His brow furrows as he tries to figure where they've met and then a flush of colour lights his face as he offers a ready handshake. *L'Elefante*. He offers her his sketch pad. Unlike the painting, which is impressionistic in style, the pencil sketch is fine-lined and detailed. He did not misrepresent his credentials. Franco is a classically trained artist.

When Kat invites him to lunch, he's quick to gather his belongings. She suggests the cafeteria she noticed on her way in but Franco shakes his head. There's a trattoria nearby, he'll show her where. As she follows his lean frame down the expanse of stairs and out of the galleria, Kat wonders if her artist's quick acceptance speaks to his hunger or to the fact that he's accustomed to being fed by strangers.

Franco perches on the edge of the straight back chair opposite Kat at *Fiore di Zucca*, a modest bistro five minutes from the Borghese. Kat picks up the multilingual plastic-coated menu.

"*Io.*" He points to his chest. She gets the message. Franco will order their meal. His easy banter with the waiter in Italian is incomprehensible to Kat. These two know each other. Is this where the artist brings all his customers? Kat attempts to find a comfortable position on the unforgiving wood chair. Franco completes his order.

She adds, "*Pinot Grigio per me, Franco per te*?" Kat's command of the Italian language extends as far as getting the next meal or the next drink.

"*Non.*" His eyes, intense as black chocolate, fix on Kat. "*A Roma, Frascati.*" He turns to the waiter. "*Un bottiglia di Casale Marchese.*" His attention returns to Kat. "*Scusa.* I make the choice because I am Italian. I know what we need." He shrugs as an afterthought.

Her artist is not timid. If Nick had presumed to order her meal without consultation, there'd have been a row, but in this noisy trattoria Kat merely notices the painter's full lower lip as he returns her smile.

"Where did you learn English?" Surely not in a Tuscan hill town.

Franco explains that his first year at university he enrolled in business administration. He was preparing to oversee the farm and the winery. In that program English is a mandatory course because it's the international language of commerce.

"Then you changed to fine arts?"

The artist nods. "Papa died that year, so I was free to change my studies. The farm was his passion, not mine."

How different his life would be if he'd continued his business studies. He'd be an entrepreneur heading up a family business. Instead, he's bumming lunch off a stranger who purchased a piece of his work painted on cardboard torn from his sketch pad.

The waiter returns with a chilled bottle. Franco takes a generous swig of wine and closes his eyes, holds the fluid in his mouth and swallows. His Adam's apple skids up and down in his slender neck. Then he grasps the bottle by its neck and pours a small amount in Kat's glass. "You like?" Intent eyes watch her sip.

The wine is subtle, dry and cold. She nods her approval and holds out her glass. Franco laughs and fills it two-thirds full and then tops up his own.

"These are the grapes of the Lazio, the Roman *terroir*. My family, we grow the Trebbiano and others. You sure you like?"

Kat reassures her lunch guest that she does indeed like his choice in wine, sensing her approval means more to him than mere politeness.

The waiter returns. He sets a half dozen platters in the middle of the table. As plates and cutlery are distributed, Franco names the dishes.

Fiori di zucca fritti in pastella or batter-fried pumpkin flowers. The house specialty, he notes.

Stinco de maiale or pork shank slow cooked over a grand open fire. You will like, he promises.

Tartaro di Salmone, tartar of salmon. *Bruschetta al brie e alle noci tostata* or Brie and walnut toast. He makes a back and forth motion with his hand. Kat deciphers that these could go either way.

Finally, *Spaghetti con tartufo rasato* or spaghetti with shaved truffles. This one she knows she will enjoy.

Where to begin? Competing odours. Array of colours and textures. Hesitant, she sips. Franco suggests she taste everything and then make her choices. Obedient, Kat dishes out her food a spoonful at a time. Franco nods approval and adds his opinions about the dishes.

"*Le zucche sono fantastica*. Take two, signora."

When she's finished, he piles healthy portions onto his own plate. He already knows what he likes.

"You're familiar with the menu. Do you come here often?"

"You could say that. When I'm not painting or sketching, I am here. I work in the kitchen, signora. It's good because they feed me." He grins. His teeth are straight and toothpaste-commercial white. Fresh cow's milk from the farm has contributed to that smile.

"My name is Kat. I would like you to call me Kat."

He cocks his head to one side and frowns. "That is a name?" He makes a meow sound. "Strange."

Kat's chokes on a crust of bruschetta and reaches for her glass. Franco rises in alarm, but she waves him off as the wine dislodges the crust. She tries again. "My name is Katherine, with a K not a C as in Italian and there is no meowing involved. I prefer to be called Kat." She isn't smiling as she spells it out. "K-A-T."

"*Capisco. Kappa-ah-te.* Franco's eyes meet hers. "Is very interesting this name. Kat." This time he does not meow.

They meet daily. She's greedy for more of this painter's life. Franco appears to enjoy her company. The hotel asks Kat how much longer she wishes to extend her stay. She replies that her departure date is unknown. A nod from the front desk manager but Kat knows he will raise his brows once she turns her back.

She shares the midday or evening meal with Franco and then a *passeggiata* through the nearby neighbourhood. He has five sisters, all older. Their mother died giving birth to him and the eldest, Mariola, raised him beside her own infant son. "My nephew is older than me but we are brothers."

As an only child from a nuclear family, Kat struggles to imagine the childhood Franco describes. Sister as mother, nephew as brother. Traditional roles blending or morphing as the situation demanded.

"It's hard, Kat." He stops, takes in the cars and *motorini* that speed around Piazza Venezia. "I owe my family for everything." He turns to her. "Now, because I choose to paint, they tell me *sono un traditore*, that I betray them." Tears well in those dark eyes. Kat follows instinct and wraps her arms around the boy. She whispers into his ear that he must be brave. Smells for the first time the sweetness of his flesh.

"You're an artist, Franco. They don't realize your gift, that's all." She feels the heat of him through his thin shirt. He pulls her deeper into his arms. She's surrounded by a strength which belies his slim build. They remain like this until he releases her. *Grazie.* That's all he says as he takes her elbow and they continue their *passeggiata*.

Vancouver is a city forged of glass and steel, infused with light and surrounded by mountains, rainforest and sea. Most people speak English and there is a significant Asian population. Some Italians too. This she says to Franco on a Wednesday afternoon as they shop for men's wear. Franco knows what he wants and where to find the designer jeans, cashmere sweaters and a calfskin leather jacket. Kat offers her credit card. The clerk gives the artist a quizzical once-over and proceeds with the transaction. As they head back into the street Kat asks, how old are you, Franco? Twenty-four, he replies.

She glimpses her image in the store front window. A middle-aged stranger stares back. Laughing broadly, the woman in the glass links arms with the curly-haired boy who could be her son. Clutching stuffed shopping bags, the two meander along the cobblestones.

"What will you do when you return to Vancouver?"

"I don't know." All traces of laughter leave her. "I had a high-powered marketing career, but there's no need for it now. My husband's estate provides for my needs."

"But without work or a family, won't you be lonely?" A question coloured with puzzlement.

Kat hesitates, and then says out loud what's been on her mind since she first saw the artist bent over *L'Elefante* in the piazza.

"Not if you come with me, Franco. Then I wouldn't be lonely at all."

He's travelled to Southern France and even worked for a season in a vineyard on the Rhine. But Franco's never needed a passport. He shrugs, Italy is part of the Eurozone.

Together, they arrive at the nearest Stazioni dei Carabinieri where Kat counts out 42 euros for the biometric passport. An additional fee ensures the document will be ready in 48 hours. At a travel agency she purchases one-way tickets to Vancouver. They leave in seven days. Franco's eyes grow wide when he reads that they're flying business class.

Exchanging kisses on both cheeks, Franco takes his leave of her. He's working the evening shift at *Fiore di Zucca*, as a dishwasher and dogsbody for the kitchen crew. He will tell them of his plans tonight. Kat follows his slim frame until he is lost from sight. Soon, Kat. She feels giddy with anticipation of their life together in Vancouver.

Before they leave Rome Franco wishes to introduce her to his uncle. A good idea, as Kat wants to assure him of her motives. When Franco abandoned the farm, it was his maternal uncle who offered the art student a room in his apartment in central Rome. Franco pushes open the massive wooden door. Inside, Kat is surprised to find no elevator and a significant climb to the sixth-floor apartment. Franco promises the view of the red-tiled skyline will be worth the effort. Ninety-six steps. Kat's not convinced but climbs steadily, careful to breathe evenly and not show her age. Franco bounds up two stairs at a time to the landing and waits for her to catch up.

"*Avanti, avanti.*" A raspy voice calls from the interior. She hears the uncle's carpet slippers shuffling toward the doorway. Stooped and grey, he speaks no English. Kat imagines the ancient to be well into his eighties. He gestures for Kat to enter the threadbare sitting room. Hesitating, he decides she should take the grey velvet armchair by an open hearth.

The uncle sits across from Kat, their knees touching in the tiny parlour. Kat rearranges herself at an angle. Franco stands behind his uncle's chair and rests his hand on the man's shoulder. He interprets Kat's words as she explains that Franco will accompany her to Vancouver where he will continue his studies at Emily Carr University.

"Tell him it's an internationally respected institution for its Master level studies in applied arts, Franco." Kat leans forward in her chair, anxious that the uncle understand what she has convinced the artist to do. "And mention how we forwarded a digital portfolio from your undergraduate studies, which blew them away."

Franco's cheeks flame as he recounts Kat's words. He adds that he has been accepted as an international master's candidate. It is a two-year program and Kat is supporting him financially. She is my patron, he says.

His frayed-at-the-edges uncle peers into Kat's eyes. She feels he's searching for a sign, something to indicate her words are true. She holds his gaze and nods. After a moment he raises himself to standing and embraces Franco. Patting his nephew's back, he whispers. There's a catch in the old man's voice. He wipes away his tears with a trembling hand and Franco bows his head to kiss the old man's cheek.

The men decide to make a small celebration. A platter of fragrant antipasti and cheese appears from the kitchen and then the uncle opens a reserve vintage from the Ghibellini Winery. She remembers Nick in the café near the château of the Marquis de Sade. They had toasted "*cin cin!*" as she fingered the white pebble in her pocket.

Franco packs an oversized leather valise, on loan from his uncle. It overflows with old and new gear, sketch pads and sundries. Kat leans against the doorjamb of the nook he calls his bed chamber, watches as he slides a black bead rosary into a side pocket and clamps the fine-grained bag shut. Clear brown eyes ask her, what's next? Her painter's only 24 and he's never been off the continent.

Does she know what she's doing? Delete. Don't ask questions if you aren't prepared for the answers, she reminds herself.

"It's time to go." Kat taps her watch.

"*Andiamo!*" The shout, accompanied by a fist pump, reverberates throughout the attic apartment. Kat's laughter is just as loud. Franco's ready for his journey to the new world.

CHAPTER THREE

False Creek

As the winds whip through the waterway, the cobalt-blue houseboat nudges in its moorings at False Creek Marina. Franco will arrive any minute now. Kat's edgy with anticipation. What did he experience today? Everything registers with the wide-eyed artist accustomed to the warm colour palette of Rome. Vancouver is a city of glass, water and light. A city that eludes Franco's attempts to capture its elements with his paint.

Faith was stone-faced when Kat arrived in Vancouver with Franco. She circled him like a wildcat, sussing him out with kohl-rimmed eyes.

"What the fuck!" is all she could manage to spit out as Kat revealed that she'd rented a houseboat in False Creek.

"How are we all meant to live in such cramped quarters?" This, with her hands on her hips, tapping her stilettoed heel repeatedly. "Well, how, Kat?"

"I wasn't planning on three of us." Kat's goal is to have her protégé live in close proximity to the university on Granville Island. Give Franco ample opportunity to immerse himself in the False Creek arts community. But she read her artist wrong. Franco is content to stay close by her side. Perhaps the change in continents and cultures presents more challenges than she anticipated.

Realizing she'd been ditched, Faith changed tactics. She offered to take care of the water-bound household just as she managed their home in North Vancouver.

"Like before, Kat. You look after this kid and I'll take care of the day to day. That way no one will starve." Batting her sapphire-tinted eyelashes. "Makes sense, doesn't it?"

So, Faith is in the galley, gutting trout, seasoning rice, tossing greens. Kat watches her from the stairwell. Faith agreed to pay half the rent for the houseboat once Kat put the house in North Vancouver on the market. When Franco's studies are over, she and Faith will part ways for good. Besides, now that George has relocated here from Edmonton, it may not be long until Faith and her skinny jeans want out of the lease. That's what Kat's counting on. There are three separate berths on the lower level, but the toilet and shower are shared. It's claustrophobic when all four are in residence.

George snores. Franco confides to Kat that he bets *il Vecchio,* the old one, *frightens all the fish out of the creek.* And the amount of flesh they've all glimpsed as they navigate their daily toilette is almost comical. Faith never bothers to tie her robe, preferring to let it act as a cape as she flits from shower to berth. George's beet-red genitals routinely find a way to poke out from beneath his towel. They're all guilty of an extra peek when Franco comes out of the shower. Michelangelo's David with his towel knotted below hip level.

Aside from their quirky living arrangement, Franco assures Kat that his studies at Emily Carr are going well. Kat's troubled that he's made no friends but at least he enjoys time spent at the Italian Cultural Centre across town in East Vancouver. Perhaps his limited English is a barrier but she fears his devotion to her is the real impediment. She can't convince him that he doesn't need to look after the houseboat, fetch groceries, gas up her car or any of the myriad tasks he undertakes. *Stop acting like a husband.* She wishes he'd go be a boy.

Tonight, Franco has news. His hands slip as he opens the Prosecco. With a self-deprecating grin, he announces that the Italian Cultural Centre has agreed to hire him as curator for their *museo e galleria.* This internship is a key to fulfilling his thesis requirements. He relates in a mix of Italian and English the possibilities of bringing exhibits from Italy to the west coast. And to make some solid contacts there, Kat surmises. When his studies are done, he will return home and be lost to her. A memory soon enough.

Franco hands Kat a flute of sparkling wine. His eyes glow with genuine enthusiasm.

"Bravo." Kat raises her glass. "I'm so very proud of you, *caro*."

"I need your assistance, Kat." Faith, with her hair gelled in spikes, stands in the galley, hands on hips. "I need an investor for my Wild Things venture."

Faith, with George's encouragement, dreams of creating a floral service with a difference. Drawing on Vancouverites' love of the rainforest, she'll design bouquets and centrepieces from Indigenous plantings. Salal, salmonberry and evergreens. George drew up the business plan, spending his days sourcing suppliers in rural communities surrounding the city who are keen to rid their property of nuisance vegetation. Funding is proving problematic. The banks aren't buying Wild Things.

"I need 90K, 100 would be better. I need a silent partner, Kat." Blue eyes rimmed in navy kohl focus on Kat, whose face is devoid of makeup.

Has Faith lost her mind?

"No way, not me." *If she were to invest in any venture it would be one Franco proposed, not Faith's eco-dream.*

"You've no choice …" Faith hesitates. "Look, the American government took what money he left …" She twists her cherry-red mouth as if she'd just tasted something foul. "Given your part in Gerhard's death… you owe me."

Kat steps backwards, banging her head against the wooden doorjamb. *There it is. Faith as blackmailer.*

"No!" A wave of heat envelops her, she needs to escape. "Nick died here, remember? On Canadian soil. Back off." Blood thunders through her ears as she clambers off the houseboat and momentarily loses her balance on the damp wharf. She doesn't hear Franco's footsteps on the stairs as he ascends from below deck.

Seven shopping days before Christmas and False Creek is aglow in white twinkling lights. They hang from eaves, line windowpanes and blink from the branches of potted evergreens beside the houseboats. Granville Island is overrun with gift-givers looking for that special artisanal piece. Even the pouting Faith is feeling festive. She scours the market for delicacies to make their Christmas dinner unforgettable. She's backed off her bold demand for now but there's been a shift in her attitude. She glares at Kat but rarely speaks to her. For her part, Kat wonders if Faith has so quickly forgotten the purple bruises, her midnight falls. It was a mistake allowing Faith to move in but the woman is a loose cannon. Their shared secret makes Faith dangerous. Keep your enemies close.

George arrives for dinner almost every evening, stays over almost every night. Kat wishes they'd go to his apartment, give her respite from the adolescent displays of affection. It's a small vessel. What must Franco think? He understands that things are strained between herself and Faith. Calls her *la puttana,* whore, when they're out of earshot. Yet he appears to tolerate their living situation but how could she know for certain? On the houseboat he speaks only when spoken to, which means he's mostly silent.

When he and Kat are alone, it's a different story. Arm in arm, they make their nightly *passeggiata* as they did in Rome. Only now they walk the empty perimeter of Granville Island instead of the amber-lit streets of Rome. No longer in a crowd, they relax into each other's company.

"They don't understand, none of them." Franco struggles with the modern aesthetic of his classmates and their under-appreciation of his classical style. "They've never heard of the *chiaroscuro* or its master, Caravaggio. They have no appreciation for the emotion of *la tradizione barocca.* They know none of it." Punctuating his words with hand gestures, he says: "*Sono dei cinghiali.* They're boars."

"But the instructors, do they not recognize your talent? Surely …"

Franco untangles his arm from hers. He punches the darkness in desperation. "They're the worst. They talk of this Group of Seven who became a political force for Canada. The university has a mandate to produce a new generation of artists who will translate this country to the world." Franco's yelling, pacing in circles. His frustrations bellowed into the night. "I must interpret a country I do not know? How Kat?" He stops pacing, stares at her.

He tells her that he grapples with old and new techniques in his attempt to portray this northern light. The architecture of steel and glass. "But I cannot. *Spazzatura.* I make trash." Kat remembers how he captured the Mediterranean light so elegantly on *Bernini's Elephant.* Has the change of latitude threatened Franco's art?

"What about the work with the Cultural Centre? You still enjoy that?"

He nods and they resume their walking. "There will be a minor exhibit in the coming year. February." He thinks. "You will come?"

Kat smiles in the affirmative as she circles her arm around his waist. Franco calms at her touch. He's small-boned, not like Nick, who was beefy.

"What if you paint the night sky?" Kat nods towards the ice-white moon illuminating the corrugated metal roofs of the Granville Island ateliers. "The vista is different here, but the sky has much in common with the Mediterranean night."

Franco surveys the heavens, taking in her suggestion. Without warning, he pulls her hip to hip. Franco's sweat mixed with turpentine, the warmth of his mouth and his hand resting on her thigh. Kat freezes. *No Franco, I can't, won't cross that line.*

Acknowledging her resistance, he retreats.

Mi dispiace. I'm sorry, Kat." Wipes his mouth on the back of his palm. "Your idea is a good one. I will try to paint the night. *Grazie.*"

Linking arms, they resume their *passeggiata.*

Tonight, the houseboat community association hosts a party on the largest vessel moored at False Creek. It's a bring-your-own-food and drink affair. Faith stuffs seafood into portobello mushrooms she acquires at the market. George supplies two magnums of sparkling wine. Kat isn't going. She's looking forward to an evening by herself. Franco isn't going either. He has a late class, a guest artist from the MoMA in New York. A presentation, time for Q &A and then the mandatory socializing afterwards. He scoffs at these attempts to network. Just an excuse to grab free pizza and beer. It's not good pizza, Kat. He expects he'll be home by midnight.

Alone, but the laughter and chatter of the partygoers carry on the night air. The music too. Rock and roll from the sixties, Nick's kind of party. He loved to dance. Come on baby, let's do the twist. The words travel down the wharf. She remembers Nicky's awkward gyrations as he sang along. It was his enthusiasm, not his prowess, that made him popular.

Despite the noise, Kat's thankful for this time alone. Shuts out the lights on the main deck save the one at the entrance, descends into the hold and readies for bed. The luxury of solitude wraps round her, gives her space to breathe and she falls asleep despite the cacophony continuing further down the dock.

She must be dreaming. Nick's mouth on hers. His hands on her breasts. Oh Nicky, I do miss you. A crack of lightning, she opens her eyes and it's not a dream. It's Franco who lies naked beside her. Seeing her wake, he straddles her torso and without permission or a single word spoken, enters her. *Franco, what?* She pushes his shoulders away, attempts to extricate herself from this sudden intimacy.

"*Ti amo,* Kat." Blind to her reaction, he grabs her ass, draws her inward. "*Ti amo, ti amo.*" Not words of love, instead a wounded cry.

A pivot shifts. The universe tears open. Kat loses herself to his anguish, the intensity of it, to her growing need to comfort him and then to the pleasure of their tangled limbs.

And when they're done, he falls away and whispers: "*Ti proteggerò sempre, mia donna.*" I will protect you always my lady.

Staring into the blackness of the hold, Kat's unable to make sense of their act. She calms herself by listening as they breathe in tandem.

It's not yet dawn when there's pounding at the entrance of the houseboat. Faith's too drunk to unlock the door or forgot to take her key. Pulling on her robe, Kat climbs the cramped stairwell in the dark. On the other side of the door a male voice identifies himself as a police officer. The hairs on Kat's arms stand erect, she trembles. Through the peephole she sees the outline of two men and one RCMP badge.

The officer across the kitchen table explains that Faith is dead. Found in the creek by a fellow reveller, there's massive trauma to the back of her skull. It's possible that she was attacked, then pushed into the water. An autopsy will reveal whether the trauma occurred before or after she fell into the creek. Either way, it appears that she drowned. No heartbeat, no pulse. All efforts to resuscitate her failed.

Faith, dead in the winter waters of False Creek. Icy cold shivers travel down her spine. Her hands shake. Where's Franco? She senses his presence on the stairwell, marks his progress by the creaking of the boards.

"What about George? He's her partner." Isn't that who the cops look at first, the significant other of the dead? Kat shoves her hands under the table, hoping to hide her tremors.

The officer, a sturdy Nordic thirty-something, says George was on the party boat when she was found. He identified her body. "Did they have a good relationship?"

Kat looks beyond him. The galley where Faith did her chopping and dicing is shrouded in darkness.

"I guess so." The stairs have stopped creaking. Franco is close by.

"Do you mind telling me where you were this evening?"

Kat pulls her robe tight. Semen seeps between her thighs. She's about to confess that she was in bed with a boy half her age, her protégé, when Franco appears. He's barefoot and wearing only his jeans. His nakedness is accented in the half-light by the black swirls of hair on his chest and the unruly tuffs sprouting out from his armpits. Next to the sleek, uniformed officer, he's diminutive and raw.

"We were together." Franco, behind her, his hands on Kat's shoulders.

She feels the heat of his palms through her robe. Steady. The cop gives them a long hard look. Franco's words hang in the silence.

"Franco lives with me. We were together." With this admonition comes the realization that last night changed everything. Vesuvius erupted. And just like the woman in Pompeii, she didn't see it coming.

Closing the door behind the officers, she turns the deadbolt. Her thoughts run fast. What if Faith divulged their past relationship to George, shared the reason Faith felt entitled to Kat's money? If George took that information to the police, they'd have the motive. Without Franco to corroborate her whereabouts she could be charged with Faith's murder, but Franco can't stay, can't be her alibi. If the police nose around who knows what Franco might say. He's not safe here. She can't think of her own situation, she needs to get him back home.

"Pack!" She yells in Franco's direction as soon as the black-and-white cop car pulls away. Scrambling down the stairs to her berth, she turns on her laptop. There's a flight on KLM through to Rome in the early morning. She books it. The Italians will never allow one of their sons to be extradited. Of that she's fairly certain.

Franco wants none of this, begs her to come with him. Everything he did was for her.

"We must be together, Kat. I will protect you always." His face wet with tears, he gesticulates wildly, and then grabs at the steering wheel as she merges onto Marine Drive.

"Calm down." Shouted. "You'll kill us too." Kat inhales ragged breaths. "*Tranquillo per favore.*"

But Franco isn't listening. To drown out his pleas, to keep herself strong, she barks commands. Don't draw attention to yourself on the flight. Say nothing to no one. Go straight to your uncle and wait, I'll contact you there.

He howls, abandoning his English. "*La cagna voleva farti del male.*" What's he's saying? She can't concentrate enough to translate.

At the entrance to the security lineup, the artist, barely a man, places a small pebble in her palm. It's the white stone from de Sade's chateau.

"Where did you get this?" Hissed. Don't make a commotion, nothing that anyone will remember.

"Faith gave it to me the night we arrived. She said for luck."

Faith, you cursed him! Cupping the stone, she still feels its energy. She wants to hurl de Sade's evil into the night, but Franco's eyes are on her, so she pockets the stone instead. Her painter thought he held good fortune, but the evil energy wasn't confused. Franco was its pawn.

And what about you, Kat? It was you who put him in harm's way. She can't think about that right now.

"Go!" she commands Franco as she turns away. Walk slowly. Look normal. *And don't turn back, Kat. Don't look at him again.*

It's begun to rain. The drive from the airport is typical stop-and-go traffic as early risers clog Granville Street. Reaching the island, she walks towards the art school, disregarding the puddles on the uneven pavement. A thick swath of rain obliterates the surrounding buildings, but she stops at a bench in the open anyway. It's where she would meet up with Franco. The force of the rain washes away her energy. There's nothing left. He's gone.

Soaked, she should return to the boathouse and avoid drawing attention to herself. Franco's plane is in the air by now. *Pray Kat, pray for him.* For Kat the only gods she knows are those of ancient Rome, so she pleads with the lost residents of the Pantheon. Fingering the pebble in her pocket, she begs. Give him time. Franco needs 12 hours to make it home.

CHAPTER FOUR

Genoa

They never came back. Kat waited four years to hear the knock on the door, but the police never came back. George did. He picked up Faith's belongings. Kat didn't ask what he planned to do with them, nor does she know what happened to Faith's estate. After George left, Kat was alone. Nothing remained to say Faith had lived here, not even a notice in the mail reminding her of a lapsed magazine subscription or a flyer touting discount deals for her next flight to Italy. Her death was never mentioned in the local media. Neither Kat nor George saw a need to write an obituary. It was as if she'd never existed.

The same could be said for Franco, although Kat imagined his life every day and most nights. She called him just once, two days after he flew home. She needed to know he was safe. His voice was soft and low. He said he was returning to San Gimignano. To paint, she asked. *No lo so*, he responded. I don't know. She told him he mustn't contact her. She said it was to protect her. In fact, it was Franco who needed protection. Break the connection, Kat. Murder undetected is still murder.

She measured her activities through the lens of an attentive detective. When the lease on the houseboat expired, she thought it safe to move. An innocent woman would move when a lease was up, wouldn't she? But where might she go?

Alone and rudderless, with no need for employment, she chooses to disappear. On Vancouver Island. She sells her BMW ragtop to a dealership in Victoria, buys a beater Honda Civic off Craigslist. It's a dirty grey with rust eating the undercarriage. With no destination in mind, she drives up the coast of Vancouver Island, stays in short term rentals in seaside towns with names like Courtenay, Tofino and Port Renfrew. Perched on wide swaths of beach, these fishing villages attempt to draw revenue from eco-tourism. Transients are a part of daily life, so Kat moves about unnoticed. She figures if enough time passes the cops will forget about Faith's death, whether it was an accident or a murder, move her to the inactive files. She decides her best chance to remain undetected is to hide in plain sight.

Surveying the locals from a picnic bench at the side of the highway 4A outside Coombs, she decides to emulate them. Like Daphne escaping her fate, Kat will shapeshift. Growing her hair to her waist, she lets it grey, and weaves it into a braid. Hauling on the worn-out jeans and faded tee shirts she finds in second-hand shops, she blends with the rough-edged citizens who inhabit these remote island communities.

Time and seasons pass. Her itinerant life takes on a pattern. Kat rents battered vacation cottages, remote from the coastal towns. Places where she can pay cash, stay for three months and move on. I'm a photographer, she says by way of explanation. No questions are asked, no eyebrows raised.

The Honda's low on gas and her fridge is down to butter and ketchup, so Kat risks a drive into Tofino. It's mid-morning. The co-op store's open, but Main Street's empty; most of the town's still on their first coffee of the day. She passes knots of tourists lingering over breakfast on the verandah of the waterfront pub. No one pays attention to the scrawny stranger pushing a shopping cart through the co-op's double doors. If she's quick she can slip in and out of town unnoticed.

Her cart piled high with groceries, Kat rounds the aisle toward the check out. The sole cashier kibitzes with two RCMP officers. A male and female in those pale blue shirts and navy pants with that thick yellow strip, they're wearing body vests with the word POLICE printed across them. Armed, they're on duty.

What if George has finally made sense of Faith's chatter, figured out that she was blackmailing Kat. Has he gone to the police? Has Kat's photo been featured on Vancouver television news? Highlighted on *Crime Watch* as a person of interest, the code word for a suspect? Kat retreats, trembling and stumbles over a display of tinned tomatoes. Litre-sized cans topple to the concrete floor and splay across the aisle.

"Hey! What's going on there?" The crash catches the cashier's attention.

The cops move forward, stare at the jumble of cans. She waves her hand to say she's taking care of business.

"Sorry, I'll fix it." She crouches low, her back to the cops and rebuilds the tin pyramid. Her heart pushes against her chest wall. Are the cops coming her way? She listens, but no footsteps approach. She's having trouble stacking the tins, their edges waver in the dimly lit store. Heat rushes down her limbs, Kat drops to her knees. Her chest feels too full.

Using the cart for ballast, she pulls herself to her feet. Abandoning the thought of buying groceries, Kat sneaks down the aisle adjacent to the exit and then bolts through the automatic door. The gassed up Honda starts on the first turn of the ignition. She checks. No blue in her rear-view mirror. No sirens either.

Stowing her few belongings and Nick's camera in the trunk, Kat waits for nightfall and then guns the Honda until she's put enough miles between herself and Tofino, until her heart stops thrumming in her ears. Just outside Port Renfrew, she turns down an abandoned gravel road and parks close to the brush. Crawling into the back seat, Kat sleeps. She'll search for a place to stay in the morning.

Close to the shoreline at Point No Point, she bends over a crop of black rocks slick with ocean spray. At their centre is a tide pool inhabited by purple mussels and powder-pink sea anemone, but it's the translucent clingfish Kat watches as they dart about the microcosm. Picking up a pebble, she drops it into the pool; the yellow slivers flit and disappear. Just like us, she thinks. A stone fell and we were gone.

Because of that one act by Franco, she subsists on the edges of society, but this doesn't colour her thoughts of him. It was Kat who set their destiny in motion. He was an innocent. She perceives life differently, having known him. She imagines that she views the world through his painter's eyes. The world of light and shadow. She attempts to capture what she sees with Nick's Epson camera. Sometimes she envisions discussing her photos with Franco. Teases out what she hoped to reveal and how he might interpret the same vista. Sometimes she looks in the mirror and sees a sinewy old woman. Then, she lays her camera aside and weeps.

Fearful of the attention of strangers, she wanders along the coastline at dawn, becomes expert at predicting weather patterns at sunrise. She prefers to drive beyond the logging roads to Point No Point which is often uninhabited, especially early in the day. Kat photographs the driftwood, captures its shadows, the damp and the desiccation on the long logs thrown onto this wilderness shore. Winds blast the coastline on the southwestern edge of Vancouver Island. Tides are swift and noisy. You can't hear feet on sand and stone out here. You can't hear Nick or even the living when they pass by.

Crouched, framing the snail-encrusted woodpile on Nick's Epson, Kat is oblivious to the stranger running along the beach. She's unaware that he's fallen until she stands and gazes at the waterline.

Not certain what she's looking at, she inches toward a heap of clothing and realizes it's a man. Letting the camera dangle from a leather strap around her neck, she reaches out to the stranger. Rolls him off the rock. No response, but his breath feels moist when she leans in close to his mouth, where spittle leaks into his blond beard. Arranging the unconscious man on his side, she plans to run for help at one of the cottages on the bluff, but the waves are lapping close. If she leaves him, he'll soon be engulfed. He's too heavy to lift, so she removes her fleece jacket, wraps it around his head for protection and rolls him away from the shore. It's a piecemeal process. His upper torso, his middle and then his legs. He's not a small man and Kat feels the strain in her back but she's making more progress than the tide. The camera's in her way, so she flings it further up shore and returns to the stranger.

When they reach the spine of the bluff, she unwraps his head. He's unconscious but he's breathing. Young, mid-thirties. The tide's several minutes away but it thunders forward. Her lower back knots as she reaches down, balls her fleece and places it under his skull. If the tide comes this far at least his head is on higher ground. Kat scrambles up the gravel path toward the cottages, yelling for help.

The battered kettle whistles atop the wood burning stove. Kat is halfway across the cabin when there's a rap of knuckles on the door. She freezes. Other than her landlord who drops off a cord of firewood now and then, she has no visitors. He never even knocks, just waves from the window as he piles the wood along the back wall of the cabin. Perhaps they'll go away. She waits. Another rap, more forceful.

There's no peephole, so Kat calls out. A male voice, strong and clear, answers.

"I'm looking for Katherine. My name is Laurie. She rescued me on the beach last week. I want to thank her."

Kat opens the door, comes face to face with the man she found at Point No Point. It turns out his eyes are watercolour blue.

"Ah! Are you Katherine?" Kat nods. "I want to thank you, then." Laurie extends his hand. His handshake is firm and Kat realizes it is she who has the rougher skin. "May I come in for a moment?" He glances over her shoulder and Kat suddenly sees what he sees.

A cabin with a bed and bath tucked away at the far end. Walls of unfinished cedar. The stove is wood fired, the fridge is a junked castoff, but it functions. The lone window above the Arborite table overlooks the woods. Three chairs, mismatched. Kat uses the table as a desk. A rumpled couch and a shadeless lamp occupy one corner. Several paperbacks lie scattered on the low slung coffee table, its surface ringed in watermarks from countless coffee cups.

He's seen enough of her life. Kat wishes to end this encounter but Laurie asks what brought her at such an early hour to the desolate beach where he suffered a seizure and fell … concussed. Without her intervention he would have drowned. Surely fate put her there to rescue him.

Kat explains that she's developed the habit of photographing the seacoast at dawn. Leaves out, of course, the fact that she's avoiding the police or anyone who might identify her. And that dawn is the only time she feels safe outside her cabin. Laurie fingers his beard and asks: "Might I see some of your photos? I have a special interest in the ecosystem of our coastal waters."

Surprised, she nevertheless boots up her laptop and pulls out a box of USB sticks from the drawer usually reserved for cutlery.

"They're numbered by year and month," she explains. While Kat brews some Earl Grey, Laurie pores over her work, which by now is likely as prolific as Bernini's. Sipping her tea, Kat wanders about the room, curious about the blonde-haired man hunched over her laptop, engrossed by her work.

"This batch"—Laurie looks up—"they're impressive. Where did you shoot these?"

Kat peers over his shoulder at the photos she took in Ucluelet the previous summer before the sea was overrun by surfers. Before she moved on to Point No Point.

"You capture images no one normally sees. The attention to detail and the colours. Spellbinding."

"I'm self-taught," Kat says. "Nature is photogenic in her own right."

"Nonetheless, this collection is a treasure, Katherine." Laurie grins, genuine appreciation in his voice.

"Please call me Kat." Her shoulders relax. She feels at ease with this man. After all, she did rescue him from drowning.

Laurie explains that he's the president of a foundation that educates the public on the value of the ecosystem of the coastal waters surrounding Vancouver Island.

"The foundation is about to mount a fund-raiser with global reach. We have a couple of heavy hitters backing us. The Cousteau Foundation among others." He scrolls through several more screens. "Your photos would make compelling visuals for our campaign." He surveys the tumble-down interior of the cabin and rests his pale blue eyes on Kat. "There's no money, but full photographic credit." A moment's hesitation and then: "Would you consider joining us, Kat?"

How? She paces the bedroom which houses a mismatched double bed and chest of drawers. How can she accept this incredulous offer? A Walmart-stickered mirror leans against the wall. She peers into the glass and sees what Laurie saw.

Oversized and shapeless tee shirt, threadbare jeans. *You are unacceptable.* Ripping off her top, stepping out of her jeans, she tears off her ragged bra and panties and stands naked before her reflection. A 56-year-old woman, spare and muscled, stares back. A woman with callouses on her hands and feet; a body that has not received any care. A woman with an unkempt, brinded braid hanging down her back. *You must go!* She bellows the command throughout the cabin.

She rifles through the junk drawer in the kitchen, laying her hand on the only utensil with a cutting edge. Holding the braid above her head, she saws at it with the boning knife until she manages to slash all the way through. She swings it back and forth as she approaches the stove and tosses the offending plait into the fire. It crackles and sizzles as it catches the flame. Kat watches until the hair is fully aflame and slams the cast-iron door.

Kat picks up the cardboard backing from a sketchbook leaning against the wall. Presses her lips to the image of *L'Elefante*. *It's time for us to go.* Her voice a whispered caress.

What does it cost to change a person's appearance? That's what Kat asks herself as she navigates the Honda on the tortuous road to Victoria. She needs to ditch the weathered hippie Laurie met in Port Renfrew.

Registering at the classy Empress Hotel, Kat puts herself in the hands of its spa staff. She figures if anyone understands what is current and professional, it's this lot and she gives them free rein. After four years in the wilds, she has no sense of what she should look like.

Scrubbed, exfoliated and polished, Kat's fine skin emerges from the damage done by the sea winds and weather. Her hair, cut chin length, shines like waxed mahogany. A gel manicure—guaranteed as long-lasting—and a pedicure with paraffin. From beneath calloused hands and chapped feet there emerges smooth skin. A personal shopper pieces together a wardrobe appropriate for a wildlife photographer meeting a marketing team—no beige safari jackets are welcome, thank you. A make-up artist conjures up a stranger's polished face. The final tally approaches $3,000 but, when she catches her reflection in the chrome of the elevator door, she thinks Nick would recognize this Kat. So would Franco.

Clutching a sleek leather portfolio, Kat steps off the elevator at the fourth floor and checks the signage. She finds Laurie's organization at the end of the grubby hallway and tries the faux-teak door. Inside, floor-to-ceiling windows line an immense space housing low-walled cubicles where she can hear the hum of workers busy at their workstations. Two rectangular tables anchor the centre. Some workers are gathered at the nearest table. Laurie, his back to her, addresses them. All eyes turn to Kat as she shuts the door. She's over-dressed in navy trousers and jacket for this vintage tee and ripped jeans crowd.

"May I help you?" Laurie turns to greet Kat. Doesn't recognize her.

"Laurie, it's Kat. I hope I haven't kept you waiting." She shifts her portfolio in front of her, forcing a smile.

Laurie's face travels from disbelief to confusion. Taking her hand, he stares at her and frowns. "I'm flummoxed, Katherine." A second, harder stare. "You're quite the chameleon, I think." Turning to the table he announces: "This is Katherine who likes to be known as Kat." She nods in agreement. "I'm hoping she will join us as the photographer on the campaign. We're going to view some of her photos today to give you a sense of the treasure I found on Point No Point." He pulls out a chair and offers it to Kat, settles in beside her.

The team makes welcoming noises and some lean over to shake her hand. Kat offers her own with nails lacquered the colour of blood oranges. She unzips her portfolio, offers Laurie the memory stick he liked from last summer in Ucluelet.

Elegant. Honest. Challenging. Intricate. These are the initial responses to her photos. As they work together, she thrills at the beauty of the messages the marketing team attach to the images, with a rush of memory and emotion. She once derived pleasure from this creative process. How is it that she took it all for granted? Working with Laurie's team, she glimpses the Kat she'd abandoned.

She toys with the thought of resuming a marketing career in Vancouver. Could she cut it? It's been four years, several lifetimes in the business of image-making for marketing. Still, the idea is tantalizing. What if she managed a re-birth, if she became a name again? She savours the what-ifs of living in Vancouver, then stops herself. Forget it, Kat. Resurrecting that career is as likely as the woman of Pompeii crawling out of the ashes. Besides, what if Faith's case isn't buried deep enough in the inactive files yet? Better to remain in a backwater and embrace this new persona Laurie has thrust upon her. Better to take no chances.

While Kat busies herself settling into a micro-loft overlooking the Upper Harbour, her photos are published in both paper and digital format. They start popping up around town. Posters decorate kiosks in Uptown Mall and add colour to bus shelters on Blanshard Street. She's lost track of the number of internet sites that broadcast her digital images. Kat's solitary work is reaching across the globe. She's K. Black, marine photographer. Her new persona calms the terrors of the last four years.

Laurie stops by the cubicle Kat uses when she's in the foundation's office. "Enjoying yourself?" He's drinking a cup of the gut-rotting fair trade coffee they brew every morning. Kat nods, waits for whatever he has on his mind. She gets along with Laurie, enjoying his straightforward manner, but some things don't change. She's as protective of her interior world with him and the others as she was with Nick and Faith, even with Franco. Laurie, for his part, knows he's only scratched the surface of Kat's façade and is frustrated by the fact that he can't read her. He says so, when her taciturn responses don't give him what he wishes to know.

"Genoa, that's the seaport made famous by Christopher Columbus." Yes, Kat knows this piece of trivia too. "An impressive aquarium biosphere and conference centre was opened up last year. Next month they'll host the International Marine Conservation Convention." Gulping the last of his coffee, Laurie places the cup on the corner of her desk. "Ever been to Italy, Kat?"

Returning to Italian soil, even in conversation, makes her chest grow tight. To be in Franco's homeland. No. Too many buried emotions. Kat fears their unearthing. The ash on her Vesuvius is cold.

"I'm an amateur, Laurie. I have no formal background, not academic nor as a photographer. I don't belong with you and the other specialists. You've been at this project for years." Kat is not going.

"So have you, Kat. There are hundreds of hours of work behind your images." He places both hands on the desk, leans forward. "Besides, your point is moot. I 've already entered your campaign photos as part of our submission."

No. She will not return to Italy.

"You don't understand, I've been to Italia and I prefer not to return."

He cocks his head and eyes her with the cool blue eyes she's come to know. "*Italia* is it? It's not that simple." Laurie rubs his beard. "Katherine, we need you to represent your images, not just those we sent but others. They're scientifically significant. I want you to speak to where the images were shot, your experiences in capturing the marine world of the west coast." He's almost nose-to-nose with her. His affable grin thins. "Now unless the Italians have banned you from Genoa, I have only one question: Aisle or window seat?"

* * *

The Italians offer a perfect location for the convention. *Acquario di Genova*, touted as the largest display of aquatic biodiversity in Europe, features wall-sized displays of diverse marine environment. The colours startle in their intensity. Cadmium red to exotic vermillion. Kat's accustomed to pink and chartreuse in the sea life she photographs, but some shades here defy description. Dense hues meld with pallid tints. A painter's dream palette.

As Kat anticipated, her photographs are exposed to an international circle of professional artists with strong technical backgrounds. Photographers, videographers and graphic designers discuss their goals, techniques and challenges. Laurie was wrong to push this upon her. She's too far from shore, tires of trying to keep up with their expert expositions. Is unconvinced that either she or her images belong at all until a videographer from Norway comments on her work.

"There's a simplicity, a clarity in your images that's faithful to the nature of the ecosystems we wish to save. You capture the northern light authentically." Spontaneous applause breaks out among the professional photographers. Kat bows her head, feels the heat flush her cheeks.

You capture the northern light authentically. Kat turns this phrase over in her mind. The Norwegian understands what Kat did not when she brought her painter to Canada. Southern artists are exposed to a different colour spectrum than those in the north. No wonder Franco had difficulty adjusting his eye, failing to interpret the northern city of metal and glass. *Mi dispiace,* I am sorry, Franco.

The convention winds down, the hotel next to the marina empties and the Canadians head to the airport, but Kat stays a bit longer. In the morning, she'll fly to Avignon. Set right a wrong before returning to Canada. She's grateful Laurie railroaded her after all. Exuberance and terror were her companions, but she's earned her credentials as a marine photographer. For now, it feels good to rest.

The southern sun warms the stones of the marina patio and melts the tension in her shoulders. Sipping a *caffè Americano*, she closes her eyes, content to listen as the water laps against the elegant yachts in their slips; is reminded of another marina where a navy-blue houseboat pulled at its moorings in the northern winds.

"Kat. Kat." A low male voice, accented.

She shields her eyes from mid-day glare as she turns toward the voice. A dark and curly-haired man stands in silhouette before her. After repeating her name, he takes her hands which are on their way to her face in disbelief.

Franco, four years older, grown into his manhood, but still Franco. His hair tamer, his shoulders and midriff maturing, he's dressed in a business suit. Pulling a chair up beside her, he's quick to tell her that a poster for the convention caught his eye at the University of Firenze. When he saw the photographer's credit, he googled her name and discovered the fundraising campaign. Hoping she'd come to Genoa he registered for the public sessions. Kat takes in his words but it's his face that holds her attention. Those liquid eyes, their intensity.

"I could not find you, Kat. You did not attend the public lectures." He gestures his discouragement. "I was mistaken, you were not in Genova, but your name was on the program." His words tumble out. "*Grazie Dio,* the concierge located you for me today." She'd forgotten about his heavy accent. She must listen hard to every word to understand him. How old he is now? *Ventotto.* He's 28. She reminds herself that she's now closer to 60.

Again, Franco reaches for her hands in his own. His palms are warm, just as she remembers. He's wearing a broad gold wedding band. Kissing her fingertips, he entreats: "Come with me to Firenze." Noticing that she's seen his ring, he adds: "I wish you to meet my family."

Franco appears to have prospered, yet despite the passing of time and changes in circumstance his yearning for her remains. Why, as she prepares to leave her past in France, has her painter appeared? She's found a different destiny, but Franco's found his way back into her life.

"You will come, Kat?" She wants so much to trace the curve of his upper lip with her finger.

For Kat, there's only one response.

CHAPTER FIVE

Florence

Franco insists on paying for their first-class tickets on La Freccia-bianca, the high-speed train that joins Genoa to Florence. *You are my guest, Kat.* Perfect white teeth against smooth brown skin. As the train flies through the countryside at 145 km an hour, he explains his present situation.

He's the curator of Il Museo Moderno at the University. "It is a modest collection," he says. "And I have a studio in the apartment. The light is *magnifico*." Head down, he searches for the words and blurts out: "I marry Chiara Alighieri three years ago. We meet at the university. She studied art also. We have a son, Antonio." Franco's face softens as he mentions his child. "Chiara's pregnant, *un bambino presto*." Soon. Kat nods a mute response to every revelation. Reminds herself that three years ago she was in Courtenay, growing her hair, still fearful the police might knock on her door.

His hand on her elbow, Franco guides her through Santa Maria Novella, the train station thick with travellers, to a taxi. *Numero sei,* Piazza della Repubblica, he informs the driver with a confident tone that's new to Kat. It's a quick ride under a triumphal arch into an elegant square. Franco waves off the driver and removes her luggage from the trunk. Kat tips the driver, knowing it's unnecessary in Italy, but habits die hard. Number six is a grey stone building covering the entire north side of the square, anchored at either end by cafés with decorative ivory awnings. "Caffè Gilli," Franco points to his right, "famous for writers and artists meeting since the 1800s." As an afterthought: "The coffee's good too."

Massive mahogany doors swing open when Franco keys in a code on the brass pad embedded in the stone wall. Kat's eyes need time to adjust to the muted lighting. She makes out a broad marble staircase leading to the mezzanine level where a glass-walled elevator addresses them in hushed tones. Franco presses PH. How can he afford a home in such a luxurious space? She doubts that, even with the money inherited from Nick, could she assume residence here.

The elevator door opens without making a sound, but their presence is detected by sensors in the corridor. Light after light flicks on as they climb a short flight of stairs to a vestibule. A mural of Tuscan countryside, rolling hills and Cypress trees adorns the walls. "Your work?" He smiles. To the left there's an ebony door with a brass knocker in the shape of a lion's head. Franco inserts an old-fashioned bronze key into the lock, turns the oversized knob and with the curve of his arm gestures for Kat to enter.

The apartment occupies the entire top floor. Black marble counters with steel appliances in the open kitchen, white leather sofas in the living area and a dining table of glass and metal. Following Franco beyond the living room, she steps out onto a wood-planked terrace. They're surrounded by clay rooftops with the dome of the cathedral as their nearest neighbour. Kat puts out her hand, feeling like she could touch the dome from where she stands. Bells begin to chime. First, the sonorous clang of the Duomo and then the lighter tones of the lesser churches until the whole city is ringing. Franco grins as he takes in her pleasure.

Taking Kat's hand, he leads her to the sleeping quarters. There are two massive bedrooms outfitted with king-sized beds but it's the cavernous space on the opposite side of the hall that he invites her to enter. Franco's studio. The warm Mediterranean light streams through a trio of windows. A messy cot in the corner is the only furniture. Franco has three easels in progress; paints and brushes crowd a long worktable covered in drop cloths. Turpentine and paints. The smells that clung to her painter after a day in class in False Creek. Time rips away and Kat is on that houseboat but Franco's gone. Emptiness sweeps through her like the waves of Point No Point. An undertow of anguish threatens to overwhelm her. She mustn't let him see her like this and turns away.

But Franco has seen. Wrapping his arms around her, he holds her so close she feels his heart.

"That is why I bring you here. Stay, Kat." His mouth on her ear. "My wife knows of you. I tell her right away." Warm breath, not a kiss. "I want you in my family."

On the far side of the apartment the ebony door opens and a soprano *"Buongiorno!"* announces the arrival of Franco's wife. Antonio, Franco's two-year-old, toddles toward his father. Without a trace of shyness his baby arms reach for Kat instead. He so resembles Franco that Kat, though unfamiliar with children, feels at ease lifting him into her arms. Behind her son is Chiara, a slender woman whose belly is distended to the point where Kat wonders how she can walk at all in those stilettos. Blonde curls frame her finely-chiselled features. She welcomes Kat with a kiss on both cheeks and a handshake with a cool, smooth hand, the nails a perfect pink. She smells of exotic flowers whose scent Kat's never had the privilege to know.

Chiara asks if the guest chamber is to her liking. It seems her Papa, the director at the university and Franco's employer, offered them the use of the flat on the occasion of their marriage. They have tried to think of everything to make Kat comfortable but if changes are needed her father will be pleased to comply. Chiara delivers her greeting in Italian and Franco translates for his wife, who speaks no English.

Her painter's new world shifts into focus. Franco became a *de facto* prince because he married the princess. Remembering his mouth on her ear just moments before she wonders if he realizes that the father who gives can also rescind his generosity. *Be prudent, my painter. Bringing me here seems foolhardy when your fortune and misfortune are so delicately aligned.*

Through the half-open door Kat glimpses the artist as he paces and gives direction to his model. She inches closer. Naked, Chiara poses on a chair draped in blue cloth. Her body resembles unblemished ivory. Her eyes are the colour of slate. The newborn suckles on her reddened teat, a babe so tiny its head fits in her palm. This image is punctuated by the light streaming through the window and a silhouette of Brunelleschi's red-roofed dome. Franco arranges Chiara's limbs, her hair and the angle of her jawline. Kat moves into the doorway. Franco turns, the artist and his model become aware of her presence.

The strokes on Franco's canvas are rudimentary. How long does he imagine the newly-delivered mother and child will pose, feed his desire to capture a 21st century Florentine Madonna? While their fragility might appeal to the artist, where is the husband's caring? Kat quietly fetches her camera.

Without asking his permission, she begins with long shots. "Let's capture your Madonna digitally, Franco." If the artist wishes to protest, he thinks better of it. Instead he watches Kat as she shoots. The model remains frozen in place.

"Close-up. I need detail." Franco points to the curve of Chiara's arm, the shadows in the creases of cloth, the wisps of hair against her neck.

Kat snaps each shot as he directs. They work together for almost an hour. The baby wakes and mewls.

"Enough to start. You can blow them up." Kat nods toward the flat screen hanging from the far wall. "Besides, your Madonna's getting chilled." Kat retrieves Chiara's robe from the cot in the corner and wraps it around her shoulders. The model's skin is pebbled with gooseflesh. "I'll load the images onto my laptop and you can choose the ones you want."

Kat downloads the photos onto a USB stick, taking time to organize them, but she needn't hurry. Franco's otherwise engaged with his wife behind closed doors in the bedroom on the other side of the wall. Closing her laptop, she listens for sounds. There are none. Laying her cheek against the plaster surface beyond which lies the matrimonial bed, she closes her eyes and whispers his name.

At two months of age, Katerina Sofia is fêted at Fattoria Ghibellini, the family farm that Franco abandoned when he became a painter. Three generations of Ghibellini busy themselves cooking and sharing platters of handmade pasta and farm-grown vegetables, an endless supply of the family varietals, and pieces of a freshly killed pig roasting on a spit. Chiara, sleek and showing no signs of childbearing beyond her abundant lactating breasts, moves through the gathering greeting family members with cheek kisses and accepting their adoration. Laughter rides the breezes that pass through the colonnade where a dozen long tables are readied for *la festa*. The towers of the medieval city of San Gimignano rim the horizon. For Kat, this is an alternate universe. Not only is she here with Franco, his wife and his extended family, but she's a guest of honour. Franco insists she be godmother to his daughter, whom he made her namesake.

When he asked her if she was Catholic, Kat said yes, with no hesitation. That she had no religious affiliation whatsoever seemed less important than disappointing her artist. If Franco thinks all the world is Catholic, then for his sake, it is. Besides, she has a belief. Her gods are the gods of ancient Rome, the predecessors to Franco's God, who heard her prayers. They saved her painter.

Franco's uncle, the one from Rome who sent his nephew off with the stranger, is given the role of chaperone. His English is no better than Kat's Italian. He eyes her with quick glances. Kat wonders if Franco had made a scene when he returned to his uncle's apartment. His voice was distant and subdued the one time they spoke. She's relieved the old man can't ask her why his nephew returned so abruptly. Taking her elbow, Franco guides her from one cluster of family to another where introductions are made, and after a disinterested sharing of a sip of wine or two, they move on. The Ghibellini are polite but show no interest in the *Canadese*. Until she is introduced to Brigitta. Franco's sister, the one closest to him in age, who resembles her brother. Same dark eyes, bronzed-by-the-sun complexion, but her hair's finer than Franco's and as straight as Kat's.

"Call me Bri. Franco calls me this since a boy. It stuck." She shrugs. Halting phrases. "We were surprised you come back. That you are living with Franco after …" Like her brother she searches for her words. "… his studies in Vancouver ended not so good." Ebony eyes drill through Kat's guarded persona.

"I didn't return to Italy for Franco. I was attending a conference in Genoa and your brother found me." Kat hears the edge in her voice, feels her jaw tighten. Franco convinced her she'd be well received by his family. How foolish to believe him. Of course, it would be like this. He returned to the farm two weeks after he fled Canada. How did he explain himself? What do they know? What does this one know?

"And now you are here. My brother make you Katerina's godmother." Pauses again, surveys the festivities. Her voice goes cold. "*Complimenti.* Enjoy the *festa.* I am needed in the kitchen." Turning away, she hustles through the maze of partying Ghibellini.

The uncle from Rome has disappeared too. Kat finds herself alone, stinging from Bri's unspoken thoughts.

"It appears your escort has deserted you." The lean and bony man exhales the last of his cigarette before introducing himself.

Chiara's father speaks impeccable English but with a stress on con- sonants, as if he were pronouncing Italian words. Slim and attired in an elegant pin-striped suit, he stands soldier-straight by the gravel path leading to the fields of terraced grapes. His eyes are the same icy hue as his daughter's. Perhaps the newborn Katerina will take after her mother's family in the same way Antonio favours his father's. *Franco's father-in-law is charming, in the calculated way of men who mete out their time. You receive the portion due your station. How much time will he grant to Kat, as godmother?*

He recounts his fondness *per l'artista e la sua famiglia*, sweeping his arm to indicate the immensity of the vineyards and the farmland beyond as much as the family around them.

"I am pleased that we meet, Katerina. Franco was beside himself with anticipation of your arrival. Now he can focus on his work again." Ice blue eyes underline his message. "Will you be helping Agnes with the children? Give Chiara opportunity to resume her art studies?" The eyes darken as he calculates the effect of his words.

Kat turns to the rolling hills below San Gimignano. "Tell me about that town. It's so different from anything in my world," is all she offers in response.

With a sigh, he pulls another cigarette from a silver case tucked into the silk lining of his jacket, lights it with an equally fine silver lighter and with his first exhalation begins a detailed account of the medieval history of the Guelfi and the Ghibellini. Kat listens with interest to the history behind Franco's family. Kat cares for Franco's son in the haphazard way of someone who is uncomfortable around children. Passes him the *pane* when it is out of his reach from his highchair. Keeps watch as he climbs onto the chaise at the edge of the terrace. He calls her *nonna*, grandmother. Chiara's idea. A cheap shot that Kat thinks reveals Chiara's true attitude toward her husband's guest.

Kat makes no contribution to the household. She's tried to pay her share but husband and wife consistently refuse her offers. There's no need to assist Chiara with the cooking, cleaning or laundry. The no-nonsense Agnes arrives every morning, rolls up her sleeves and works until the household is spotless and the evening meal is ready.

Franco suggests she shop for the produce at the market, *il Mercato Centrale*, using this task as an opportunity to improve her Italian. To please him, Kat heads out three times a week, with a shopping list from Agnes in hand. She makes her way along the cobbles, skirting potholes filled with asphalt which eventually breaks down into treacherous terrain. The tourists thin out the further north she travels. Kat loathes these noisy swarms who make the narrow road impassable. Dumb followers of tour guides who hold umbrellas or glossy signs, sometimes just a number, above their heads. The same number's stickered on their chests to remind them who to follow. Multiple languages assault her ears, but Kat focuses on the items written in Agnes' cursive script. Via Sant'Antonino leads to the piazza in front of Mercato di San Lorenzo. Franco informs Kat that it was designed by Mengoni, the architect who created the celebrated glass arcade in Milano. Rimming the building of steel and glass, migrant workers set up portable stalls each morning in hopes of selling their leather goods and silk or cotton scarves. Loud claims of "made in Italy!" greet each potential customer but the goods often bear import stamps from China. Street vendors are aggressive. *Signora*, they shout. A command for Kat to stop. Often, they block her path, shove a scarf into her hand. She knows the game. Don't interact or you'll be there until you purchase the scarf made of viscose and twice the price of its department store clone. She's careful to keep her eyes on her destination, slices the air with her hand if a vendor gets too close. It's a relief to climb the stairs and enter the market proper. Here the sellers are pinned behind their stalls or are gentle in their invitations to sample their truffles and honey.

Kat scans the list. *Pomodori, cipolle, basilico, miele, pere.* No surprises like the one last week when a roasting chicken was added to the list. How was she to pick the right bird? Nick would have been in his element here, but to Kat they all looked like roadkill.

She's worked a deal with a farmer. He's there behind his stall. Signor Morelli acknowledges her with a wave and mentions to his son that *La Signora e qui.* Franco's satisfied that Kat's picking up a good vocabulary, at least where fruits and vegetables are concerned. He isn't here in the market, doesn't know that she hands the list to the farmer who fills the order from his own produce and purchases everything else from others. Signor Morelli bags her goods himself. Nor does her painter know that Kat adds five euros to the bill for the farmer's service. In reality, she figures that she and Antonio have a similar comprehension of the Italian language but the two-year-old's gaining on her.

Franco's at the university all day and paints in his studio most evenings. Kat wanders the streets around Piazza Repubblica in ever-widening circles, seeking unique vistas to photograph when there's a break in the crowds. Capturing ancient architecture in the southern light seems as difficult as Franco's attempts to interpret the cool blues of Vancouver.

Tourists mill around her. Kat feels disconnected. She's not a day-tripper or wide-eyed visitor. She knows more of the day-to-day life of an

Italian family than these people would care to, but she's not a local either. She is a guest, a foreigner. She has her set place in Franco's household. It's a solitary life not much different from the one she led on Vancouver Island, with one exception. Sometimes, more often lately, Franco comes to her bed after he finishes his evening of painting. Chiara understands, is all he will say. Is Chiara even aware of Franco's need of her and that she returns that desire? To Kat, those slate-blue eyes across the colonnade do not agree to what transpires in her household.

If Kat was simply an assistant to Agnes, she'd extricate herself from the Ghibellini household. Despite Franco's protests, she'd return to Canada. A life waits for her there. She can morph into the marine photographer Laurie imagines. His anxious emails asking for her return date are piling up. Instead, Kat chooses to be Katerina's godmother at the Fattoria Ghibellini, the role Franco has offered her. Peering at the distant medieval skyline, she puts Chiara aside. Instead, Kat wonders if her painter will come to her tonight.

CHAPTER SIX

Lacoste

Franco lies across her bed quizzical eyes taking in her every movement. "I must do this if I'm to be free." Unzipping the weekend satchel Franco insists she borrow, Kat packs clothes for two days. She promises she will be away only as long as it takes to do what needs to be done. Still, Franco's dead against her leaving but he can't understand that, while the white pebble is in her possession, she can't rest. It's not possible to toss it away. It belongs in Lacoste, in that deserted wreck, where its evil energy can hurt no one.

She chose the Hotel Mirande for its proximity to the train station in Avignon. Her room is the antithesis of Franco's ultra-modern apartment. Hand-painted wallpaper, peeling in the corners, depicting bucolic meadows which the painter would despise. A carved marble hearth dominates the modest room and the French provincial furnishings are chosen for form not function. There's a decent view overlooking Le Palais des Papes but it's already autumn and the sky's dark with rain. Below her window, the cafés in the square are empty, the umbrellas tucked away until the first rush of spring tourists. She's drained from her journey. First a train to Rome and then a transfer to a different line into France. Unable to gather sufficient energy to dine in public, Kat takes her evening meal at a marble side table teetering in front of the fire.

The single-paned window shimmies against the winds and driving rain but inside this decorous retreat the heat of the fireplace warms her. Crawling onto the king-sized bed, Kat leans back into plump pillows, watches the flames ebb and die. Tonight no one and nothing can touch her. Franco, with his persuasive hands and hot breath, waits in Florence and de Sade's evil is stored in the glove compartment of the rental car parked on the street below. In the morning she'll complete the task interrupted by Franco's appearance in Genoa. She'll return the white pebble to de Sade.

Before, Nick did all the driving. Now, it feels good to be at the wheel of the rented Citroën, navigating the stone-lined road to Lacoste. She glances at the bag on the passenger seat. Soon. The road ahead is clear but she slows while passing the villages along the route. Cavaillon, Menerbe and then Lacoste. She takes time to remember.

Parking the Citroën near the entrance of the old town, Kat slings her bag over her shoulder and starts the steep climb. The rains have not yet begun but storm clouds lie low in the darkening sky. Her scarf whips at her face as the winds close in. Ignoring the turn in the weather, Kat climbs on. Lost in memories, she re-traces the footsteps of another time, the footsteps of Nick, Faith and Gerhard.

As Kat reaches the summit the winds twist and gust, the rains pelt down. Entering the ruin of Château de Sade, she turns in a careful circle, taking in the space. Nothing has changed in five years. The stone walls continue their descent into decay. De Sade's victims still scream without making a sound. As Faith said, the place still holds his evil.

Rooting in her bag, Kat's fingers find the suede pouch and loosen the drawstring. Inside is the diminutive white stone. Placing the pebble in her open palm, she offers it to the only source she believes in, the gods of ancient Rome.

I admit to making a terrible mistake in taking this stone. Contain its evil in this place, for the sake of the innocent ones.

Her thoughts go to Franco, to the anguish of the night he murdered Faith.

He was an innocent. He needs forgiveness.

Kat flings the stone onto a pile of rubble, where it becomes indistinguishable from the rest. The rains descend across the Vaucluse, beating down on her. Turning her back on de Sade's ruin, she retraces her steps through the town. The route is slippery and she loses her balance, falling onto her hands and knees. Struggling on the muddy incline, she secures her footing and continues her descent.

Soaked, her jacket hangs limply from her shoulders. She wipes her face. Aubergine pigment stains her palm. Reaching the Citroën, she dials up the heat in the old car, shivers. It's almost done. An hour's drive back to Avignon to dry clothing and a warm fire. Tomorrow, she'll leave it all behind.

Outside number six in Piazza della Repubblica, Kat presses the gold button for the roof-top apartment. The massive door swings open. Before she reaches the elevator Franco appears from the stairwell. Barefoot and dishevelled, he sports a two-day beard and knotted, uncombed hair. Weeping, he pulls her into his arms. *Non lasciarmi,* Kat. He pleads. Don't leave me again. Kat kisses his cheek, tastes the bitterness of his tears.

CHAPTER SEVEN

Piazza della Repubblica

As he fleshes out his Madonna and child on canvas, the painter's sense of urgency heightens. Details matter, he moans. The way the light plays off Chiara's hair, the *ombré* creases in the blue cloth. As his wife goes about her daily life, he asks that Kat's camera capture the curve of her breast, the muscularity of her thigh and the shape of her bare foot on hardwood. When Kat observes him holding his infant daughter to the light; first this angle, then that, she worries that Franco's vision and his ambition are marring his judgment. Not that he's unpleasant or in any way nasty, rather that his sole focus is his work. It seems to Kat that the only time he's not conjuring his masterpiece is when he visits her bed. Then, his emotions break free and wash over them both. Kat holds fast to his shuddering torso, whispers that he will find his way, will make his vision whole. As the days go by, Franco's focus becomes more intense. How can he create under such self-inflicted pressure? Kat's having her doubts.

When he isn't working on his own Madonna, Franco studies those painted by others. Often, he asks Kat to accompany him. Without the yokes of husband, father or job, his shoulders loosen and the furrows on his brow disappear. Linking arms, they make their way through the cobbled streets and she's reminded of their beginning in Rome. Franco becomes her painter again, the humble artist she discovered in the Piazza Minerva.

They spend hours at the Uffizi Gallery where the population of Madonne gives historical context to this iconic art form. The earliest artifacts were found in the catacombs of Rome. Mary was especially beloved by Italian painters from the Byzantine to the Renaissance eras but there are Madonna traditions in the Netherlands and Germanic countries too. Franco doesn't limit himself to the Italians, devotes himself to other schools too.

They acquire annual passes to avoid the lines of tourists that snake around the museums and galleries. Franco strides past the crowds and through the security check, going directly to the salon of the Madonna he wishes to study. Kat follows behind. Today's subject, *Madonna with Child and Two Angels,* painted in 1465 by Fra Filippo Lippi, has a modern intimacy about it. Franco points out that the subject for the Madonna was the painter's lover, a scandalous situation for a Friar and a nun. He approves of the natural manner in which the friar depicted his muse's hair, blonde strands entwined with pearls and a diaphanous scarf. So real we want to touch it but too fussy for my Madonna, Franco decides. He motions Kat to photograph the painting. She's careful to avoid glare from the overhead lights which will distort the rich coloration. Satisfied with her photos, her painter busies himself creating annotated sketches for later reference. Abandoned by her painter in Salon Eight, surrounded by the gold and glitter of ornately-framed Renaissance Madonne, Kat is left to study the collection on her own.

What she learns is that wealthy patrons commissioned painters to depict the Holy Mother. The works graced private chapels or were donated to churches. They were an artistic penance assuring the patron's path to heaven was unimpeded. The subject matter was sacred but human conceits played out in many of the portraits. Not all women made as fine a Madonna as Fra Lippo Lippi's Mary. Kat finds the unexpected choices the most captivating. A fishmonger's scrappy daughter takes time away from a street fight to be portrayed as saint. The bruises can always be painted out.

Another conceit. Once past the 13th century, Italians preferred the familiar over celestial backgrounds. Less gold, more trees. If these works are taken as literal, the Mother of God was frequently surrounded by elegant Tuscan vegetation with a glimpse of the patron's fine palazzo just over the horizon.

Then there's the language of the garments to consider. The red sheath and blue cloak, the optional halo of diamonds or stars. None of the Madonne at the Uffizi are nursing mothers as Franco portrays Chiara, but such Mary portraits exist. In Rome, a mosaic *Madonna Lactans* adorns the façade of the Basilica Santa Maria in Trastevere. Franco studied her as a student, knew someday he would create his own. To produce your own Madonna is an Italian artist's rite of passage, Kat learns.

As much as she wishes to understand the tradition of Madonne that captures her painter's imagination, Kat finds herself drawn to the gods and goddesses. She wanders from salon to salon, curious to learn which goddesses hold place here. Were they also resident in the Pantheon? She finds that the Goddess of Charity is often depicted with a child nursing at her breast. In one painting she offers her breast to an ailing man. She must remember to mention this to Franco. These women may be of interest to her painter. Personally, Kat favours Titian's *The Venus of Urbino*. Lazing seductively on her divan, she stares boldly at the spectators, her sexuality on display. Kat feels her heat, is reminded of her nights with Franco. She's come to know *la passione* that flavours Italian life and compares it to Nick's by-the-book mentality which determined their nights in Vancouver.

It occurs to Kat that gods and goddesses are depicted naked, but the Madonne are clothed in iconic vestments. Except for Franco's Madonna. How will his painting be received? Kat's scant knowledge of Italian society offers few clues. Will her painter be lauded or condemned?

Sometime after eight in the evening, when the children's stomachs are full and their eyelids droop, Chiara taps her manicured hand on the door of her husband's studio. Her soprano *"La cena è pronta"* advises her husband that the evening meal is ready.

To be useful, Kat sets the table, chills the wine flutes and then arranges the platters piled high with the pasta and salad that Agnes prepared that morning. Nearby, Antonio crawls amidst bright and noisy toys spread across the hardwood. His sister clutches the pink blanket crocheted by Brigitte for her christening and naps on the white leather sofa.

Franco rounds the corner barefoot. He wears a particular uniform when he paints. Sleeveless tee shirt, jeans or shorts splattered by paint and a pair of sneakers that remain in the studio so he doesn't track the paint throughout the apartment. Pausing, he nods to the women. Kat locks eyes with him before remembering they're not alone, masking further glances at his lean, muscled arms and thatches of black hair escaping the tee.

Just as they did on the houseboat, Franco takes a chilled bottle of Prosecco from the fridge and turns to Kat, who retrieves the flutes from the freezer. As he fills Chiara's glass, she blurts a staccato phrase. Franco stops pouring, peers at his wife and grins. Then he kisses her full on the mouth. At the other end of the table, Kat stares. Franco's careful not to show affection to Chiara in her presence. Usually.

"Magnificent news, Kat." Franco offers her a flute, then lifts his glass and smiles towards Chiara.

"*Numero tre.*" Franco takes a long swallow of wine and then fixes his gaze on Kat as he delivers the message. "Chiara's pregnant."

Another child. Proof that the husband and wife are intimate behind that shared wall even though he climbs into Kat's bed, even though he moans his need of her as he caresses her breasts. She challenges her painter's expression. Everything is the same, he replies. Maybe for Franco, but for Kat this arrangement is too crowded. This apartment too. She needs out of this kitchen of chrome and glass; she needs to abandon her painter. Raw anger roars through her. So much has passed between them yet the futility of the woman of Pompeii is still hers.

Passing the platters between himself and the women, Franco settles into his meal as though it were any other night. He converses with Chiara in Italian and in English with Kat. He prefers topics of little consequence—how the soccer league is faring, will Berlusconi be arrested or return to former glory, that it may rain tomorrow evening. Chiara answers him absently, eats sparingly. Perhaps her morning sickness is a day-long affliction. When Antonio climbs on her lap, she shares her *insalata* with him. Kat pushes her food around her plate, ignores Franco's attempts to engage her and then gives up any pretense of eating. He shrugs and concentrates on his *scialatielli*. Head down, he forks the pasta into his mouth, reminding Kat of the schoolboys she passes in Piazza di San Lorenzo on her way to the market.

Kat's having none of this charade. They won't be exchanging kisses, his hand caressing her thigh, as he waits for his coffee to brew tonight. Rising from the table she thinks only of escape. Her ribcage feels crowded, she might faint. Her heartbeat thunders in her ears. Franco grabs for her wrist, then thinks better of it as she shouts the words that ricochet inside her head: "No, Franco, *basta!*"

Striding out of the room, she doesn't slam the door or shut it behind her. Unwilling to wait for the elevator she tears down four floors of stairs. Using both hands she shoves open the storey-high *portone*. The din of bistro diners reaches her ears. It's past ten. Twilight descends on the eateries lining the piazza. Only persistent tourists dine among the locals in October. Transparent vinyl walls have been lowered around the cafés and towering space heaters keep the diners warm. Adrenaline pushes her past them. She turns right and hurries toward the Arno. Foot-traffic thins as she makes her way beyond the storefronts to the Ponte Vecchio. The magnificent old bridge houses glittering jewellery shops but their medieval wood shutters are drawn for the night. The Ponte Vecchio is a gathering spot for lovers. A street singer strums an acoustic guitar and persuades passers-by to stop and listen, perhaps buy a CD or give up a euro or two in appreciation.

She presses past the crowd to the Oltrarno district on the far side of the river and turns onto Via De Barbadori, the street of the artisans. Here too the shops have been secured, this time with metal grates. Kat's alone as she walks down the centre of the narrow *via*, making her way to the gallery where Franco sells his line drawings. *Chiusa, closed.* Peering into the space, it's impossible to make out his work from the street. She'll come back tomorrow, purchase some of his sketches before she leaves.

She wants more of Franco than *L'Elefante*. She wants more of Franco than she has right to. More than he is free to give her. Another child—a physical betrayal of the words whispered in her bed. "We are one, Kat."

Her adrenaline subsides, taking her anger with it. Leaving her hollow. Crossing the Ponte Santa Trinita back over the river, she's jostled by pedestrians from the opposite direction. She inches close to the stone wall that lines the Arno's edge. Overhead, the lush ebony sky shuts out the day but the reflections of the streetlamps flicker on the water's surface. Rain spits into the river. Franco was wrong. Not tomorrow, it rains tonight.

A hand at the small of her back. Kat knows it's him. Her impulse is to bolt but his hands glide along her waist and grasp the wall, holding her in place. He knows her too well.

"The child's a surprise." His exhalation on her neck sends shivers down her spine, and further.

"A surprise! You're telling me God fucked your Madonna too?" Hissed between clenched teeth. "Well, that's a miracle!"

"*Gesu Cristo!*" He rests his forehead on her shoulder. "Let me explain …"

"No, you let me explain. I'm an interloper, Franco." Thinking he won't understand that word, she says: "A stranger in the bed next door whom you enjoy fucking when you're finished with your wife. But the stranger has overstayed her welcome." She chafes at his tight grip and turns to face him, to loosen his hold on her. "*Tre.* You said it yourself. You and Chiara have three children together."

"In Italia, un bambino belongs to everyone. To friends who give him kisses, to priests who pray for him, to his teachers. *A tutti*, for all!" Franco throws his hands wide, releasing her. "Antonio calls you *nonna* and I make you Katerina's godmother in the church. *Tu sei la mia famiglia*." He moves closer until she feels him pressing against her belly, his mouth to her ear. "You're no stranger, Kat." He smells of basil and stale booze. "Come home, *prego*, I beg of you."

It's been five months since Laurie read her text message: "Remaining in Italy longer than planned." He's sent a stream of emails in reply. When are you returning? Kat's responses were vague. Soon. Not sure. I don't know.

His latest email is different, however. No questions about coming home. He wants her help and her photos.

The recent oceanic exhibit garnered significant success across Canada, long lines of interested public, well-attended lectures. To his surprise, the exhibition turned a profit, enough to fund a modest European tour. Genoa's a natural, and they'll hit Marseille, but since Kat is in Florence he'd like to try there too. Could she arrange a contact? Florence isn't a port city but she's glad Laurie's decided to come. It will be good to see his familiar face, hear unaccented English and perhaps, with his help, make her way back to Canada. She'll find him a venue but she wants a favour as well. Franco's first sale, her elephant, should be part of his inaugural show but it's in storage. If Laurie agrees to retrieve it, she'll locate a venue.

A petite woman in an ironed white shirt and black pencil skirt leads the way along the corridor to the Director's office. Chiara's father has made time on his busy calendar to meet with Kat.

Rising from his desk, which like the apartment is modern glass and chrome, he meets Kat halfway as she crosses the room. Papa, whose Christian name is Massimo, offers a two-pump handshake and almost as an afterthought the perfunctory air kiss to each cheek. Does she wish some *caffè*? Switching from precise English to Italian he instructs the woman in the pencil skirt to bring two espressos.

"A lovely work space." Kat notices that although there's art on the walls none of it is by Franco.

"Local designers, artists. Important to encourage, be a patron. Like yourself." The Director takes the diminutive tray from his assistant, pours the muddy brown espresso into demitasses and sets them on the desk.

"*Prego* Katerina, enjoy." His ice-cold eyes fix on her as she puts the cup to her lips.

"You may call me Kat, everyone does." *As you've noted, Massimo, I'm Franco's patron and as you may have guessed, his lover. Indeed, even more worrisome but unknown to you, I'm his accomplice to murder.* Kat sips the espresso. It's stronger than she likes it.

"Then you must call me Max." He drains his cup. "My son-in-law speaks highly of you."

It occurs to Kat that Franco's in this building conducting his day job as *curio*. "Perhaps we can drop by Franco's space before I leave."

A thin smile and a shadow of a nod. "What brings you here? I mean to Florence, to live with my daughter's family."

She's rehearsed a version of her life for him. A widow in Rome with an appreciation for the arts meets Franco, has a desire to assist in his education. Kat dwells on this part of the story, but Massimo moves her forward.

"Still, that was four years ago and you are here now." He sets his cup on the tray and leans back in his Lucite chair, fingers steepled.

"Photography." She pauses, gauges Max's confusion. "After my husband died, his estate made the need to work unnecessary." *And your curiosity around my finances can rest.* "I developed a hobby that became a passion. I have earned a bit of a reputation, internationally." Kat looks away, hoping her demeanour comes across as self-effacing. "I photograph nature, coastal shorelines and the weather. Photography was my late husband's hobby. I prefer to use his camera, to feel close to him when I work." Kat pauses and fixes her eyes on Max's. She wants him to understand that being in Florence was not her idea. "I participated in the International Convention in Genoa. Franco saw a poster advertising my work here at the university. That's how we re-connected. He convinced me to stay with him and Chiara, help out with the babies." *So many babies, Massimo.* The Director nods. He's heard the story before and she's not sure how much he believes, although most of it is factual.

"My colleague in Canada is planning his second international tour and needs a venue in Florence to exhibit a collection of marine photography. When he contacted me, I thought of you. An aficionado of art and beauty, you'd be a helpful connection for the President of the Pacific Northwest Oceanic Society." Kat sits back and folds her hands in her lap.

Rising from his chair, Massimo walks to the window on the far side of his office, clasping his hands behind him. Though casually dressed, his outfit is impeccable. The shoes alone must cost 800 euros.

In a voice so low that Kat struggles to make out the words, he asks: "Is your work part of this exhibition, Katerina?" He turns, a lukewarm smile pasted across his face.

"I have a role to play." *A smile or a sneer?*

"Ah, then. The person you want is my counterpart in environmental studies. I'll set up a meeting. You have a mobile?" Massimo jots down Kat's cell number and pushes his business card across the desk to her. "When's this exhibit coming to Florence?"

"March. Laurie has some flexibility in the schedule once they're on the continent." Kat rises from the plastic chair, glad she isn't bare-legged. Max gives her a two-finger shake, two air kisses. In the corridor she asks where she might find Franco. He points to the elevator at the end of the hall. Two floors down and to the left. And then without a word he turns and shuts the door. *Your allotted time is up, Kat.*

The Picci family carousel in the Piazza della Repubblica whirls around morning to dusk from March until December. The steeds have welcomed riders for more than a century. At night the carousel wears a crown of light, but even by day the ancient round-about entices riders of all ages to climb on their chosen beast. As the colourful ponies dance, Kat wishes she had the courage to enjoy a ride. Even though other adults mount the horses, Kat reminds herself she's closing in on 60, that she'd feel silly on a painted horse. She decides to treat Antonio and Katerina instead.

For Kat, it's a constant surprise how quickly the children grow and change. Sometimes they remind her of their father and other times she sees Massimo in them both. She's taken aback by Antonio's never-ending energy. He was banned from Franco's studio after knocking over a wet canvas and because Chiara worries that he might get into the toxic substances that sit open. Antonio calls her *nonna*, grandmother, as his mother teaches him. Chiara's dig at Kat's age. Like his father, Antonio finds his way into Kat's bed. He crawls into her arms, applying wet kisses to her cheek. She doesn't tell Franco that sometimes she wakes to find the child nursing on her empty breast.

At seven months, her namesake is as unknowable to Kat as her mother. Katerina's eyes dominate her face and follow everyone, especially her brother and mother. She's teething and drooling. She nurses on demand. Chiara carries Katerina on her hip as she saunters through the apartment, her blouse unbuttoned, the child's mouth clamped on her nipple. Antonio, who suckled until he was usurped, begs for a share of his mother's breast. Chiara obliges. Kat understands the mother's generosity; when the boy suckles on her own breast there's a sense of intimacy unlike anything she's experienced. Stroking his black curls, she wonders about her decision to be childless. Would young Kat have made that choice if she'd held a baby like Antonio?

Strapping Franco's offspring into the double stroller, Kat descends the marble stairs awaiting them after the elevator ride. The children stare wide-eyed and silent. Perhaps they wonder if *nonna* can get them out of the building safely. She knows she does. As she rolls up to the merry-go-round, their noisy selves return. The old man from the ticket booth hoists the cumbersome stroller onto the platform. Kat unstraps Antonio, who immediately escapes into the forest of painted legs. Katerina kicks her pink leather booties, straining after her brother. Two school-age boys rush onto the platform and climb their chosen mounts. Remembering to put the brake on the stroller, Kat's about to chase after Antonio when he runs into her arms. Bending low, she kisses his cheek. He smells like honey.

The carousel hums, begins its unending route. Kat lifts Franco's son onto a pony with golden riding tack and a cherry red plume on its head. He grabs the leather reins with a child's version of the painter's hands and Kat holds fast to the back of his trousers. Katerina's eyes never leave her brother as he glides up and down.

Kat pays for two more rides. During the second one Antonio finds his balance, so she lets go, but rests her hand on the back of his steed just in case. Be watchful, she tells herself. You're not a *nonna*. This is new to you. The piazza whirls past them again and again. Out of focus and out of reach. Kat wishes it would whirl forever. When ponies go still, she lifts the boy off his steed. Caught up in the excitement of the moment, he doesn't protest. Neither does Katerina. The throb of the carousel has lulled her to sleep.

By the time Kat hauls the stroller up the second marble staircase, her arms ache and both children are slumped in sleep. Unlocking the shiny black door, she's greeted by silence. Where's Chiara? Even Franco should be home by now. No one in the studio or the great room. Kat listens and then knocks on the couple's bedroom door. A muffled cry. Kat hesitates but turns the knob.

Light creeps past the edges of the carelessly drawn curtains to reveal the massive king-sized bed covered in a mess of ivory linens. At its foot is the baby's crib. A life-size nude of Chiara crowned with a bridal veil hangs on the opposite wall. One of Franco's early works, Kat gathers.

"Chiara?"

Movement under the linens. Approaching the marital bed, she finds Franco's wife sobbing. She's lying naked on her side, knees pulled up to her chest. There are smears of blood on her thighs and on the bedsheet.

"What …?"

Chiara raises her arm. In her hand is a pencil thin paint brush, one of Franco's finishing brushes. The handle's coated with clotted blood.

"What the fuck have you done?" Kat grabs her wrist. Chiara winces as she releases the bloodied brush onto the bedding. Franco's wife rolls away, exposing more of her blood-streaked haunch. She moans. *"Non lo voglio. Non un bambino.* I don't want it. Not a baby."

Kat's confused, unsure what's going on. If she doesn't want this pregnancy, don't they have clinics in Italy? Why is this wealthy woman resorting to self-mutilation? Why this pregnancy? Then, Kat's aware that they're not alone. Franco appears in the doorway.

Chiara forbids Franco from calling her father to ask for the limo, unwilling to leave her bloody bed. Tears streaming down his face, Franco bundles his uncooperative wife into a woolen blanket Kat grabs from the wardrobe. He carries her to the elevator and into the waiting taxi. The ride to the emergency at the Ospedale Santa Maria Nuova is about 15 minutes, he shouts back to Kat.

She wraps the bloodied paintbrush in a rag from Franco's studio. The children are still asleep, so she tears down the stairwell and out the massive front door into the piazza. Kat is oblivious to the din of foot traffic, street singers and bistro diners. Keeping the rag-wrapped paint brush close, she passes the carousel and heads into Via di Pecori. Here, in one of a row of municipal trash bins, she disposes of the instrument Chiara chose to terminate her child's existence. Racing back up the four floors, she arrives as the children are waking. Later, Kat cannot remember if anyone in the crowded piazza noticed her disposing of the bloody rag.

Antonio stands in front of the fridge and points, but Katerina screams and twists her body out of reach when Kat tries to pick her up. They're hungry. Kat remembers the pasta salad Agnes prepared earlier. She sits Antonio in his multi-coloured highchair and dumps some of the *fusilli con pesto* on the tray. He clutches the pasta twirls with his fingers. Katerina poses more of a challenge. Kat's not clear on what the child eats when she isn't at her mother's teat. Surveying the fridge, she finds bowls of what look to be puréed vegetables. One orange, one green. Heating them in the microwave, she pulls Franco's daughter onto her lap against the child's will and attempts to feed her. It goes well until the baby sneezes and green goop flies out of her mouth onto Kat's beige linen trousers. Seeing Kat's look of dismay, Antonio clamps his pesto-dipped hands on his forehead. Katerina begins to scream again. At this point Franco returns. He grins, finding the scene amusing. Oh well, Kat's glad. At least she gave him some comic relief on this awful night.

As fate would have it, all Chiara managed was a superficial tear to her cervix and the pregnancy continues. She remains in hospital overnight for observation, but barring any change, it appears that antibiotics and the care of her midwife will suffice. Franco shrugs, his every movement sagging with fatigue. *"No lo so.* I don't know." He shrugs. "I take a shower, Kat." Leaving her to the feeding experiment, Franco disappears into the bedroom.

But Kat can't let go of the image of Chiara holding the bloodied paintbrush. Can't shake the feeling that something's still wrong, that Chiara might try again. Kat fears that the life Chiara wished to end was her own. That the unborn child was simply the means.

Franco's shocked out of his single-minded focus on his painting. He hovers around his wife until she slaps him away. With Kat's help, they feed and bathe the children. Franco encourages Chiara to rest and to sketch. He offers to display her work at the artisan shop in the Oltrarno. *Vai, vai,* go away, she replies and closes her eyes.

The mid-wife visits on Tuesday and Thursday afternoons. Agnes prepares a pot of chamomile tea, which Chiara and the midwife share, chatting at the dining table until they drain the pot. Franco explains to Kat that Italians only drink tea when they are ill.

Perhaps they're doing enough but Kat doesn't think so. Neither does Franco. She catches him studying his wife's face, not as a painter but as a father seeking to know the motive behind her violence. His wife is his intimate, but her inner thoughts are unknowable, even to him. Her fine features dissemble whatever darkness lies within. Kat doubts any amount of chamomile tea will change this.

Kat scans the floor-to-ceiling library in the great room. Art tomes of course, scholastic treatises probably belonging to Massimo, and somewhere the book she seeks. She examines the shelves, spine by spine. There it is. Dragging the rolling ladder to the centre wall, she kicks off her shoes and climbs halfway. It's a heavy book and the spine's broken. Probably a family Bible. Ghibellini or Alighieri?

Antonio's perched in his highchair intent on eating spaghetti with his utensil of choice, his fingers. There's more pasta on the tray and in his hair than he manages to put in his mouth. At the table Chiara monitors his progress, with Katerina nursing on her lap. Kat's namesake's almost nine months old.

They're alone in the apartment. Approaching from behind, Kat rests her palms on the mother's narrow shoulders. Kat feels the outline of her clavicle. Her delicate bones remind Kat of a bird carcass, the easy-to-crack wishbones of Christmases past. As though reading Kat's thoughts, Chiara flinches. Placing the Bible on the table, Kat wraps her fingers around Chiara's narrow wrist and lifts her hand to rest on the book. She places Chiara's other hand on the crown of Katerina's head. The child's eyes flicker under blonde lashes as she continues to suckle.

"Promise that you will never harm Franco's children. Swear it."

Chiara's face pales but she remains mute. Does she understand what Kat's asking?

"Say it, Chiara. I will never harm Katerina." Kat moves behind Franco's wife again, places her hands on Chiara's shoulders and presses down hard. In a rush of anger. "*Ripetere,* repeat!"

The mother repeats Kat's words, then places her hand on her son's head and gives the oath as Kat directs. Antonio watches his mother with interest. Lastly, Kat directs Chiara to lay her palm on her belly.

"I will never harm Franco's children born and unborn," Kat whispers, but her words sound more like a hiss. "*Lo dici.* Say it."

Fear in her eyes, she complies.

Kat nods. "Now make the sign."

Confused, Chiara plucks at the trim on Katerina's shirt. The child stirs, the nipple drops from her mouth. Kat spits into Chiara's ear: "The sign the priest makes."

Comprehending, Chiara makes the sign of the cross and then reaches past her daughter to caress the leather-bound Bible. She whispers her own amen.

CHAPTER EIGHT

Via San Pier Maggiore

Stretching until her toes hit the footboard, Kat hitches closer to the top of the bed and stretches again. Her calves ache, unused to standing for hours at a time on a concrete surface. The Marine exhibit was a modest success. Laurie says they had a better run in Genoa. In the massive entrance hall of the aquarium a steady stream of tourists passed by. In Florence, the exhibit was tucked in a room off the Botanical Gardens maintenance shed. Locals attended. Academics, students and Massimo's invited guests. No matter, Laurie's pleased with the outcome. The connections are made and, of course, there's the opportunity to see Kat again.

The air in the apartment hangs warm and still, even with the windows ajar. Cathedral bells begin their vesper pealing. Kat loves the erratic participation of the churches across the city. A daily reminder that she is in Italy, in Florence, with her painter. From her bed, she makes out *L'Elefante* propped against the middle shelf of the bookcase. She won't frame it, enjoys seeing the ragged edge where Franco tore the backing from a spiral sketching pad to paint his first commissioned work. No longer a street artist, nowadays he sells his pencil sketches of Florentine architecture through a dealer on *via de* Barbadori. Each piece an original but not that difficult to produce. Because this is Florence and the architecture is elegant, the drawings fetch a reasonable price. They are purchased by tourists, buyers unaware of the calibre of the work but impressed with the decor of the ancient art gallery, the subject matter and the delicate manner in which the vendor packages their acquisitions in parchment, bound with scarlet twine.

The bedroom door opens and he appears. She inhales the paint and turpentine mixed with his own scent as he sheds his work clothes.

"Who is this man, this Laurie?" Franco's arm rests across her breasts, his leg between hers. So easy to move to him, get lost in his touch.

"You know the answer. He's the marine biologist who discovered my pictures." She turns towards him, makes out his face in the shadows.

"Your patron?" His palm, warm and smooth, on the small of her back.

"Yes, but not how you imagine that word. He wasn't my lover, ever. He's a colleague." Pressing her belly against his, she wishes he'd give up this preoccupation with their years apart. She's ashamed that her life went so badly on Vancouver Island, while in Florence Franco managed to create such an elegant one for himself. She hopes he never learns the whole truth; that she clung to the edges of society, sometimes to the edges of her sanity.

"You didn't take pictures in Vancouver. Then you take hundreds ..." His fingertips trace circles on her skin. "*Perche*?"

Kat remembers why. After a night like this, lying with him, she'd had to send him away. Photography was how she kept Franco with her.

"Because of you."

Franco raises his head off the pillow, looks down at her as if distance will make things clearer.

"Our talks. I learned to view the world through an artist's eyes, through your eyes." She follows the outline of his lips with her index finger. "I remembered your words, tried to capture them in my photos." Tears, where did they come from?

"Kat, Kat. *Cara mia*, I understand. *Mi dispiace*. I am sorry."

"These." Laurie refers to Kat's photos enlarged, vivid in colour and fine in detail. They stand surrounded by Kat's work on three sides. "They're spellbinding. Your work. Your talent." His face searches for a connection. "What you did has value, Kat. What do you photograph in Florence? Grubby architectural ruins?" He examines a pink and orange close-up of a tidal pool on the beach where she found him. "I hear food-porn artists are the rage in Europe."

"I'd probably make good money selling food shots," she says. "Especially Italian fare."

"*Touché*."

The outdoor patio at *I Ghibellini Bistro* has been dismantled until spring, so the farewell luncheon for Laurie and his team has been set up around a long table pressed against the interior wall close to the kitchen. The Director footed the bill and Franco, under his direction, organized the event.

"It's where I work when I first come to Firenze. My cousins make me a waiter though. I didn't have to wash dishes here." Franco grins and disappears into the kitchen.

As he enters, Laurie shouts her name. Patrons lift their heads from their plates as the compact man in bulky jeans and hiking boots strides across the terra cotta floor to Kat's out-stretched arms. They exchange a heart-felt hug unlike anything that passes for social contact in Florence. No air kisses or two-finger handshakes here.

"This won't do." Laurie directs his team to move the table away from the wall and the Canadians cluster along each side. Only the red-headed tech guy is familiar to Kat. Laurie pulls up a chair across from her and when Franco re-appears he makes a beeline to the chair beside her. Draping his suit jacket over the back of his chair, Franco rolls up his sleeves and loosens his tie. His lips touch Kat's cheeks and then the painter's slim hand extends across the table to Laurie. This is the first time the two have met.

"*Sono* Francesco Ghibellini—"

Laurie accepts the outstretched hand but interrupts Franco's introduction. "I know who you are. You're Kat's painter." Handshake complete, the attention of both men settle on her, but it's the Director seated to their right that Kat notices. Massimo, his lips in a thin sneer, glares at the men. Clearing his throat with a staged cough, he re-introduces Kat's "painter".

"Francesco Ghibellini is related to the family that own this bistro and he is my son-in-law."

Massimo has made a brief appearance to open the exhibition, welcoming Laurie and the rest of the Canadians. He's reminding them who's in charge. "Francesco is a skilled artist, holding his inaugural exhibition next week, also at the university." With a nod of his patrician nose, Massimo turns his attention to his mobile.

Unmoved, Laurie leans back, folds his arms across his chest and asks for advice on the menu. Eager to showcase his family's fare, Franco rhymes off the Ghibellini Tuscan selections. He stresses that the food is hand-crafted on the premises and locally sourced.

"Choose, Franco. I trust your judgment." Laurie flashes a row of perfect teeth above his bushy, golden beard. The painter morphs into the familiar role as waiter and disappears through the swinging doors into the kitchen. Massimo mutters: "Next, he'll be wearing an apron." He heads outside for a smoke.

Kat had hoped for time alone with Laurie. The interrupted moments at the exhibit were not enough. She enjoys listening to his unaccented English seasoned with his forthright point of view. He's made it clear that he doesn't understand the hold this painter has over her.

"Good, that got rid of them for a while." Laurie chuckles, but Kat doesn't join in, refusing to make Franco a joke. Massimo can be nasty but she's accustomed to giving him the respect his station commands in Italy. To Kat's ear Laurie sounds a bit rough around the edges.

"Serious question, Kat. When are you returning to Victoria? Or do I need to recruit another photographer? Where would I find someone with your body of work, I don't know." Laurie leans forward and lifts her hand onto his square palm. "Tell me young da Vinci isn't the reason you stay. He can't be that fucking good an artist …" His countenance darkens. "Or is it that he's that good at fucking?" Kat withdraws her hand, feels her face burn. She's grateful that the other Canadians are chatting up the teenage waitress filling the water glasses instead of following the conversation.

"He is a talented painter and I support him." How to explain their tangled story to a marine scientist. "I photograph images for his reference. Still-life scenarios he wishes to consider, including arms, legs, and breasts. Anything he needs." Her explanation peters out but she adds: "I'm not going back, Laurie. Best to find another photographer." Placing her hand back on Laurie's broad palm, she says: "It's difficult to explain my feelings for him."

Laurie stares at her hand. "I *knew* it. The Italian's fucking you, that's why you followed him to Florence. It's what women do. Confuse lust with love." He squints. "Just be careful that he isn't fucking you over, Kat."

Massimo re-enters the bistro and returns to his seat. Franco sweeps through the swinging kitchen doors with a smile on his lips and the young waitress uses that moment to escape the grasp of the over-friendly Canadians.

The Prosecco pours freely from jugs at *Ghibellini's*. The hand-cut ravioli stuffed with truffles and covered with wild boar sauce is plated on authentic Majolica platters. Abundance. Tomorrow the Canadians embark on the next leg of their tour—the port city of Marseilles. Today they relax as their self-deprecating humour colours the air. Just as he did on the houseboat, Franco takes in their conversations, speaks only if he's addressed. Kat wonders if this is his natural way in social situations or just when the language is not his own. And then he surprises her. "Laurie, how did you come to meet Kat?" Franco re-fills his glass. Laurie's had a fair amount to drink, as have they all, except for Massimo who busies himself on his cell phone, eating little of the pasta in front of him and ignoring his wine glass.

"The first time we met, I was unconscious." This brings ribald commentary from the Canadians but leaves Franco and Massimo blank-faced. Laurie shakes his head at his team. "Nothing like this bunch imagines. I wasn't drunk. I was literally unconscious."

Laurie sets the scene in such detail that Kat finds herself back at Point No Point. He explains that he wasn't feeling well and thought a run would clear his head. Instead, he had a seizure, fell on a rocky outcropping and slipped into unconsciousness. "Kat can tell you what happened next better than I can."

All faces turn to her, but Kat meets only Franco's glance. He remembers an unconscious person and a rock under different circumstances. Kat turns away. Matter-of-factly she recounts in a few words how she saved a man's life. She wants to explain how he in turn saved hers, but Laurie interrupts.

"I wondered why this woman was on such a remote beach at dawn. Imagine my surprise when she showed me her photographs. Four years of photos catalogued along both the east and west coasts of Vancouver Island. All taken at dawn." He pauses, scans his audience, and asks: "Do you know how significant that is to our work?" Resting his gaze on Kat. "An amazing discovery. One I knew needed to be shared with the world."

The Canadians already appreciate Kat's photography. Massimo seems to measure the weight of the message. Franco leans toward Kat and kisses her cheek, whispers: "*Brava*."

"Kat saved my life. The paramedic said if she hadn't moved me to safety and sought help, I would have surely drowned." Laurie strokes his yellow beard and then addresses himself to the Italians. "You have an extraordinary woman in your company. I hope you realize that." Raising his wine glass, he gestures to Kat. "Safe journey until we meet again, my friend."

The painter lowers his head, stares into his empty glass and murmurs: "I'm sorry, Kat. Forgive me."

CHAPTER NINE

L'Oltrarno, Florence

Franco and Chiara's apartment stands in the shadows of Brunelleschi's red brick dome, the Cathedral Santa Maria del Fiore and Giotto's ivory marble bell tower. Together they're known as Il Duomo di Firenze, architecture that dominates the Florentine skyline. Franco paints his Madonna in front of this iconic landmark, although in reality the wall of the apartment hides the view of the Duomo.

Standing on the rooftop terrace, Kat stretches her arms out straight, imagines she can touch the majestic structure. The terrace is Kat's refuge from the family. Late October and the evening air is still warm. It's almost midnight and a perfect moon traces its way across the inky sky, appearing to pause beside the dome, which is highlighted by a ring of white lights. My painter should capture this, she muses.

"Kat, Kat. Come, I want to show you." Franco is tousle-haired, a day's growth darkens his face. He's been holed up in the studio organizing his portfolio. Tomorrow, he transports his body of work to the university's gallery. Two days later his inaugural exhibition begins and he will be revealed.

The women have been banned from the studio for the past week, although access to Franco's work has always been by invitation only. When Franco opens the door, Kat doesn't know what to expect. Three rectangular worktables form a U-shaped exhibition space. Franco points to the table closest to the door. "Start here."

Kat takes her time with the works. Franco explains that the gallery will organize his papers and painting in a different configuration. This set-up was a way for him to determine what he would offer Massimo. The initial grouping is his student years, sketch books like the one he carried at the Museo Borghese when Kat found him. He flips open one of the books and asks her if she remembers the sketch. Of course, she does. It's his Apollo and Daphne. The wood nymph morphing to escape her fate, just as Kat wished to disappear and change her own. Then, the early paintings. *Il Elefante*, the first commission. A series of eight by tens, more abstract than Kat's painting, but the subject matter familiar to her. The Vancouver skyline, Granville Island market, the marina and the blue houseboat.

"Franco, I didn't know these existed. You didn't take them with you, so how?" Kat can barely ask her question, wanting to blot out that terrible time, but she needs to know how they are here now.

"They were at Emily Carr. I wrote the university and asked for them. Massimo said I should."

While she was intent on disappearing on the island, Franco led a trail to his door. But her only response is: "I'm glad they arrived safely." Kat thinks the paintings are cold and oblique. Too much of that awful time. She moves on.

There's a set of pastoral scenes at the Ghibellini farm and winery. Painted in a soft palette, they're nostalgic of another era and she doesn't recognize them as Franco's.

"These, when you first came back, when you stayed with your family?"

Franco nods. "They're okay. No, they're not good. Massimo will decide." He shrugs. Kat finds them flat, uninspired. *Yes, Max will decide.*

A trio of pencil sketches of Florentine architecture is mounted on table easels. These are the drawings Franco sells through the art gallery, the commercial work.

Scenes of Florence are next: The Ponte Vecchio, the Duomo, Via Strozzi, the Arno. But unlike the paintings sold by artists in the streets outside the Uffizi, these have unique perspectives, as if the artist were a mouse or a bird.

"They're riveting Franco, unique."

Franco grins, pulls her close. "Massimo's idea. He says I follow my training too much; he wants me to break from convention. I try."

Kat begins to understand. Massimo has been influencing his-son-in-law's career since his return to Italy.

There are two paintings left. Both covered by cotton sheeting.

Franco moves to the small painting on the table easel. Biting his lower lip, he removes the drape. He calls the painting *La Donna al Chiaro di Luna*, *The Woman by Moonlight*.

Kat moves in to get a better view because from where she's standing she could swear that she is the woman in the painting. With the Duomo backlit by moonlight, there's a woman in a black robe, her leg revealed through the opening of her gown, holding a book and gazing outward. There's a sense of sadness in her bearing. Then Kat recognizes the garnet drop earrings that Nick gave her on their tenth anniversary.

Whispers: "Franco, this is me." Her hands fly to her mouth. Embracing her painter, she whispers: "*Mio tesoro*, my darling, *grazie*."

Franco hesitates before revealing his final work. The star of the portfolio, *La Madonna di Levi*, named after the apartment building in which she was painted.

Chiara, six feet high and four feet across. Naked and in frank detail. Her breasts, her pubis, her ankles. To Kat, he's stripped Chiara raw and called her Madonna—the woman who gives birth, the woman who makes the future. Franco wants the world to remember she's human. With breast and pubic mound, she is not a goddess, she is mortal. The artist, true to his nature, obeys the iconic rules. Blue and red linens fall from Chiara's pale shoulders, pool at her feet, and a circle of lights dance above her head. Katerina, the naked Christ, suckles at her mother's breast. And the backdrop is the Duomo, a Papal blessing.

This picture, it's the fireworks of an otherwise pedestrian exhibit. When you reveal your Madonna, your world will tilt, Franco. Watch out, my painter.

She's to meet him at a jazz club in the Oltrarno district just beyond the Ponte Vecchio. Why he decided on this place of dim lights and sensual music is beyond Kat. It's perfect for a romantic assignation but a meeting with Massimo is never that.

At dusk the cobbled streets give way to local traffic. There's room to breathe. Kat passes lovers kissing near the gate of locks on the bridge. It's what the young do here to show their commitment, lock a padlock onto the rail and toss the key into the river. Permanence, at least until the city saws the locks off on the first Monday of the month. Her artist didn't hang a cheap lock on a railing. No, Kat's artist declared himself on canvas.

Franco's world did go haywire when his exhibit opened. Massimo was careful to have local media present, promising it wouldn't be a waste of their time covering a university art show. *Madonna di Levi* made the evening news on RAI, the Italian television network, and the front page of *La Nazionne*, the city's newspaper. The stories and pictures were picked up nationally and then across Europe. Yesterday, Franco returned from the newsstand with copies of *USA Today* and *The Daily Telegraph*.

"They read about us in the England and America!" he shouted to his wife as she lounged on the sofa with Katerina at her breast, her pregnant belly growing ovoid.

Opinions are divided. Either the *Madonna di Levi* is a work of genius with a modern play off archetypical symbols, or a frivolous desecration of all things sacred. Franco's a Warhol or a fool. Either way, he's noticed and his name is on the lips of collectors, critics and the vendor who hawks fake serigraphs in the Piazza della Repubblica.

But there's scant peace in the household as Chiara's fame threatens to upstage and outlast Franco's. In an age when posing pregnant and naked on a magazine cover sells copies, *La Madonna di Levi* is the sought-after story for glossies that make their living documenting avant-garde lifestyles. The French magazine *Closer*, infamous for publishing shots of topless royalty, is first to approach Chiara. Then the Italian magazine *Chi* offers a hefty sum for a photo of a naked Chiara posing next to the painting. This request sends Franco into a tirade of Italian from which Kat can only make out the profanities. Chiara simply smiles. Now, *Vogue Italia* wants a pictorial spread on the artist and his Madonna. A more reasonable request. One Massimo thinks they should entertain. Chiara revels in the notoriety the *Madonna di Levi* brings. She's unconcerned that a depiction of her naked body has travelled around the globe. Meanwhile, Franco bristles every time attention shifts from his art to his wife's naked body.

The club is dark, lit mainly by candles, but she spots Massimo at a table overlooking the Arno. The epitome of Italian style, he wears a blue pinstriped shirt open at the collar, beige trousers, oxblood red belt. His black linen jacket drapes over the back of a neighbouring chair next to his shoulder bag. He rises, ignores her outstretched hand and kisses her on both cheeks. Then he pulls her into a firm embrace. He chose a lemony cologne.

After ordering their drinks and antipasti, he asks if she minds if he lights up. It's Europe and smoking is ubiquitous so Kat humours him although she despises second-hand smoke. He draws a cigarette from the silver packet of British Dunhill in his leather bag.

"The show went well, reactions as I expected." He checks Kat's response.

She has none, having had no expectation or experience against which to measure Franco's work.

"Do you imagine there's staying power in all this publicity?"

"Some for a serious painter, this is simply a debut. Recognition, a bit of controversy, a beautiful wife stripped naked." Massimo pulls on his smoke, laughing as he exhales. "My daughter's quite the Madonna."

"It seems to me that Chiara's notoriety threatens to outstrip interest in Franco's talent. Already it's generated jealousy between them—"

Massimo cuts her off.

"Damage to that relationship came long before now, Katerina. You, of all people, know that." Grinding his cigarette into the ashtray, Massimo empties his wine glass in one swallow. "That's why I invited you here tonight. You're the one person who can resolve their dilemma."

Kat raises her hands in protest. She wants no further role in manipulating their relationship. She's done enough. But Massimo plows forward.

"You see, my daughter wants a divorce. She's tired of being a painter's wife, tired of so many pregnancies … tired of your continued presence. Chiara's a beautiful woman, but one who cannot deny herself. She has little impulse control." He shrugs. "I guess you could lay that at my door but …" He signals the waiter to pour the wine. "I've convinced her that she needs not divorce, but to live apart from Franco. At first this infuriated her, but now that she's *La Madonna di Levi* she's amenable to my proposal."

Kat sips her Prosecco. This conversation is going somewhere dark.

Massimo steeples his hands as she has seen him do when he's about to make a rebuke or demand the impossible. "This is what I propose, Kat."

It seems Massimo has a home on Torcello, a far-off island of the Veneto, one of the 20 regions of Italy.

"In the northeast, two hours by rail."

Kat cocks her head, listening. The townhouse is located by a canal and can accommodate two people comfortably. The second floor boasts a sunroom with views of the pre-medieval village, a respectable-enough basilica and the marshy farmlands beyond.

"They're painter vistas, Kat. A studio for Franco." Max takes a long pull on a new cigarette and Kat feels nauseous.

"The property's maintained by a caretaker and a housekeeper. Of course, there's an outboard for transport along the nearby canals, but

Vittorio looks after that." Kat's mouth tastes of stone. She reaches for water. Canals? Water transport? Massimo continues. The couple lives in a secondary suite next door, close enough to respond to her needs. *Close enough to report back to you, Max.* There's even a micro-vineyard should Franco get lonesome for his heritage. A broad grimace stretches those thin lips. Massimo enjoys his own wit.

"Why not just divorce if that's what they want?" Kat's chest hurts. The cigarette smoke cuts her breath. *What does Franco think? He's made no mention of this to Kat. Maybe he wants his marriage. Max doesn't know everything.*

"Katerina, I will be frank with you. My daughter married Franco because she couldn't say no to his sexual advances, which resulted in an untimely pregnancy. When she came to me, I did a bit of investigating and found that he comes from a reasonably established family. They're farmers and food purveyors, but I knew that wasn't the lifestyle Franco desired. I offered him a dowry I knew he wouldn't refuse; the lifestyle you now enjoy." Eyes hard and implacable. "More important, I took him under my tutelage. You see, my daughter will never be more than *La Madonna di Levi*, but Franco will be a great painter someday, perhaps the greatest his generation produces. Only if he is groomed, if his art is nurtured." Massimo lights another smoke, ponders the shadowy Arno as he inhales. "Kat, any man can be a husband or a father. For Franco there is more." He turns to her as he exhales, the smoke narrowly missing her face.

"I want you to accompany him to Torcello. He can paint undisturbed by the messiness of domestic life. Of course, you will do whatever it is that makes him content. Something you are very accomplished at, Katerina." Massimo pauses, gulps more wine and eyes lidded, stares at her through the cigarette haze between them. "Franco will see his children and his wife on family occasions. Chiara will have her freedom and her status. To the world, nothing has changed." The waiter refills his glass. Max empties it. He's a man with a thirst. "And you will finally have what you want, Kat."

Her mind spins, so many reasons to say no to this man. He puts Franco's career ahead of the children's future. He cares not that he's setting his daughter up for a life of empty choices. And what of Franco? What does he want? What sacrifices is he willing to make?

"I can't be part of this, Max. The choices they make are theirs, not mine." She pushes her full glass away. It's time to get out of here, to clear her head.

Massimo grabs her forearm and presses it hard on the table. He's hurting her but Kate senses that to protest is to further provoke him.

"Listen to me. There's only one decent picture in that whole show and I've already had serious collectors inquire about it. Do you know which painting that is, Katerina?"

Kat shakes her head. If not the Madonna, then which one?

"*La Donna al Chiaro di Luna*. The *capolavoro*, they're calling it a masterpiece. It's Franco's future. And we both know it's his portrait of you. Don't play coy with me." Flickering candlelight throws shadow on Massimo's face as his grasp tightens, burning her forearm. "Help me, Kat. Help Franco fulfill his destiny."

"You love your wife?" The question that needs answering. Franco stares up at her, unblinking, but his brow furrows. "How can you ask me this from your position?"

"Fair enough." Kat rolls off Franco's naked torso and onto her back. She stares into the blackness. The light bleeds from the edges of the window blinds. She asks again. "You love Chiara? You made three babies together, after all."

"Massimo thinks this arrangement best for everyone. We go to Torcello and I paint." Franco faces her, draws circles with his fingertips around her navel. "Chiara desires her freedom. She does not like living here at the apartment anymore."

"Forget Massimo. What do you want, Franco? You're not only a painter, but you're also a father and a husband." Rising on one elbow she looks down at him. "Perhaps you're not being fair to Chiara or the children. Or yourself."

Franco shoves his arm behind his head. The only sound in the darkened room is his prolonged exhalation.

"An honourable man doesn't leave his pregnant wife. *The painter doesn't abandon a Madonna with child*. Wait." There, she's said it. The words that have drowned out all other thought since meeting Massimo in the jazz club. Kat will travel to Torcello alone.

"Three months. What do I do for three months?" His voice sounds young and petulant in the dark.

"Massimo's scheduled a travelling exhibition for the Madonna. Don't you show up for the openings?"

The painter grunts in agreement.

"Then attend the openings with Max. I'll send you photos from Torcello. If you find what you want to paint, when the time is right, you'll join me."

"How will I know the time?" A low, wounded voice.

"You'll know, Franco. When you and Chiara decide that it's time to part, I'll be waiting in Torcello."

"Have it your way, Kat ..." His mouth opens with intention. White-hot breath on her skin. Grabbing her ass, he pulls her closer. Kat moans in the darkness. Captures her pleasure in primal memory. On the windowsill a one-way ticket on *La Frecciarossa* flutters in the breeze.

CHAPTER TEN

Torcello

Kat's unprepared for the assault on her senses that is Venice. Walking through the train station, there's the usual foot traffic, noise and chaos but no warning of what's to come. On the terrace outside, at the top of an expanse of concrete stairs leading down to the canal, she startles. A steady stream of people make their way down to the canal's edge, their rolling luggage echoing on every step. Languages assault her ears: French, German and Spanish. Or is that Italian? Other phrases are shouted in Asian dialects. Kat knows that throughout history Venice was known as the meeting place of East and West. She supposes it still is.

Below, canal boats grand or utilitarian bob and yank on their tethers as the captains wait for clients. Earnest hand gestures vie for the attention of water taxi drivers. The air's thick with moisture but not the stench that Chiara predicted. No, Kat's familiar with the foulness of a low tide in sea towns, from the island. There too the scent of brine nibbles at your nostrils, announces that maritime waters are nearby.

Beyond the canal looms a green domed cathedral. The plain exterior lacks the decorative charm of Franco's Duomo in Florence. She doubts he'd care to paint it. To the left a bridge arches over the waterway, leading to a narrow street crowded with tourists dragging their luggage. A man jostles Kat's hip, gestures that she needs to move. In gruff Italian, he complains that she's in the way. That she understands.

Moving out of the direct flow of traffic, she scans the vessels, searching for a man with a cardboard sign bearing her name, but he's nowhere to be seen. Fifteen minutes past the time Vittorio agreed to show up.

Fishing her cell out of her purse, she feels for the paper with his number on it in her jacket pocket. She'll call him even though she's still anxious using the Italian phone system. She doesn't understand enough of what is being said and her vocabulary fails her. Max said the keepers speak English, though.

She's keying in the last of the ten-digit number when she hears a muffled voice behind her inquire: "Signora Katerina?"

Kat turns to find a stove-pipe silhouette in black tee shirt and jeans. "*Sono Katerina … Kat.*"

On hearing her speak, the man grins. "*Sono Vittorio. Da questa via per favore.*" He gestures towards the canal and picks up her suitcase. Kat follows close behind, fearful of losing sight of him in the throng.

Taller than Franco, Kat guesses that Vittorio is in his late forties. He's dark-skinned with close-cropped greying hair. Overtly masculine, he's attractive in a manner quite different from her painter. He says they'll travel the length of the Grand Canal before hitting the open waters of the lagoon. Tourists pay many euros for this famous ride. He motions Kat to the seat beside him and guns the throttle.

Again, she's unprepared for Venice. This time it's the dazzle of water and light, the unending façades of Moorish and Gothic architecture. Pink, ivory, salmon and flashes of gold. The buildings are low to the water, three or four storeys, some with frilly balconies and colourful awnings, others with colonnades at sea level that Vittorio says are gates for the boats. Narrow waterways branch off on either side of the canal, allowing a glimpse into ordinary Venetian life. Kat reads the names painted on the corners of buildings. Rio di San Marcuola, then Rio San Stae. The water sways beneath them, slaps against mooring posts as the traffic, dominated by the public water buses, the *vaporetto*, making their way up and down the canal. Water taxis, a diverse fleet of delivery boats and the dramatic black gondolas tarted up for tourists compete for right of way. A roar of mechanical and human noise assaults her ears, but Vittorio, unperturbed, manoeuvres his craft as Kat might drive along West Georgia at rush hour. When Kat compliments him on his navigation skills, he admits he's been sailing on these waters since he was a child. When he smiles, he reveals a set of perfect teeth.

They pass under two bridges which Vittorio informs her are the Rialto and Accademia. The white-marbled Rialto is familiar, an oft-photographed icon of Venice. The Accademia is a wooden structure which reason would tell you should be falling down from decay. Beyond the bridge Kat spies a building featuring brightly-coloured frescoes with accents of gold, the Palazzo Barbarigo. Glimmer and arches. Outrageous beauty. Vittorio slows the engine while Kat snaps photos of the Klimt-like image.

The canal widens to open water. Her eye is caught by an ivory stone building backing into a thicket of trees. Straight lines, one storey, so different from its neighbours. Pointing toward the structure, this one? A look of distaste crosses Vittorio's face as he revs the engine. The Palazzo Venier dei Leoni. Americans.

They skim the chop produced by the winds and sea traffic of the lagoon. Venice drops back into an inky scrawl on the horizon. The boat moves steadily past the red brick *fornace*, the glass blowing furnaces rimming the island of Murano, toward the crayon colours of Burano's fisher cottages. Vittorio follows a route marked only by rows of steepled poles. Now, the only sounds are the motor and the rhythmic bumps of the waves against the hull. They've been on open water for 20 minutes or more. How much longer? Alongside Burano, Vittorio cuts left and nods toward the distant bell tower. The red brick silhouette shoots skyward above the farmland. Torcello's *campanile*. Her bell tower.

"*Quasi lì.*" Vittoria points to the entrance of a channel beside a *vaporetto* stop. Torcello is stamped in black under the eaves of the hut on the dock. As he slows the boat and enters the smaller waterway, Kat's struck by the rapid change in sound. They are surrounded by farms and woodland. The only noise beyond the engine is a trill of a songbird.

Sixty people reside on Torcello. She and Franco will make sixty-two. This will take some getting used to. Even Venice seems far away. What is Max's true intention in shunting them off to this silent place?

Vittorio cuts the motor and they drift. The *Canale Maggiore* is a couple of boat-widths across. Shrubs and bushes crowd the right bank, while on the left a herringbone path of pink brick paves the way for tourists. They travel for a minute or two before Vittorio kills the engine altogether and moors the boat on a post beside the canal wall. "*Siamo qui.* This is Torcello."

He points to the brick arch just ahead. "*Ponte del diavolo*, the Devil's Bridge. No parapet. The old people say that, when you cross, the devil takes your soul in return for safe passage." Kat accepts his arm as she hikes herself up onto the canal's edge. He has the solid strength of someone accustomed to physical labour.

"Do you believe the superstition?"

"*E antico*, from the 13th century." Tilting his head, he considers the bridge and says: "They say if you hold your breath, *il diavolo* can't harm you." Vittorio leaps out of the boat, grabs the handle of her suitcase and hoists it onto the path. Without further explanation he strides across the bridge, leaving Kat to hold her breath and follow him to the other side of the canal.

Kat thinks they could be blood relatives. Anna shares Vittorio's height and colouring, even his fine teeth. The slowness of their cadence in English leaves Kat completing their thoughts long before they articulate them. A drawn-out pronunciation of every consonant and vowel. Of course, when they speak to each other she's lost. The dialect is a slur of vowels combined with clipped consonants, incomprehensible next to the rudimentary Italian she's picked up in Florence. The rapidity of their speech makes her mind go numb.

Anna reveals that the remodelling of the second floor was completed the previous month in a rush so that the painter would have a studio. They were expecting him to arrive today. Is he joining Kat soon? Her dark eyes survey Kat's face for the answer.

Soon? *Non lo so.* I don't know. Kat turns away. Climbs the worn wood stairs to the second floor which creak with her weight. Again, Kat is taken off guard. Nothing in this place is as she's imagined it. The second floor has been re-structured into a single space with windows on every side. There are views of salt marshes next to fallow fields, meandering canals cutting through wild meadows, the dusty clay roofs of the village clustered beside the crumbling basilica. This is what Max saw. Potential for their painter.

The walls are whitewashed to maximize light. Flat plank floorboards make for practical footing. In her mind's eye, she imagines the traces of paint smeared here and there, the drop cloth arranged under the massive easel in the centre of the studio and Franco's broad swathes of colour as he begins his work. Max has thought of everything. The worktables, easels, pots of paint, brushes and canvasses. All is in waiting. All that's required is Kat's painter.

Is he joining you soon, Kat? Non lo so.

Throughout the day the *vaporetto* brings tourists along the dusty walkway outside her door, leading to the centre of the village where they snap photos destined for Facebook or videos to debut on YouTube. The

Byzantine cathedral, Santa Maria Dell'Assunta, features medieval mosaics which rival San Marco's in Venice. Torcello's *Madonna* bathes in golden light. The trek up the Bell Tower is worth the sweat for the spectacular vistas, according to Vittorio. Of course, he adds, so are the views from the studio.

Kat prefers to walk along grassy paths toward the outreaches of the island where overgrown meadows offer silence from multilingual chatter. Here, Kat understands why Massimo wants his son-in-law to paint at Torcello. The light of the Veneto tints the lagoon silver. The long horizon tricks the eye into believing that sea and sky merge into a luminous oneness. As the day progresses the quality of light shifts. Kat's lost in thought, at the centre of a translucent sphere. It's this light that Canaletto so famously brought to the world of art. Kat now knows it's what Massimo wants Franco to capture; it's where Massimo imagines he'll paint his masterpieces. If he was here.

As promised, she sends him photos, explains that her camera doesn't do justice to the countryside. His only response a curt *grazie*. Does life in Florence capture his full attention? Or is it simply that his written English is rudimentary? They've never communicated in writing, so Kat doesn't know which is true.

Frustrated, she emails Massimo. Updates him on her progress, gives him details on the venues she's photographing. Are there others she's missed? How is the roadshow going? She can't bring herself to ask how Franco is doing, doesn't want to admit she doesn't know. She hopes that Chiara's pregnancy is progressing well. By the way, when's she due?

As she imagined he would, Massimo reads the subtext. He responds with a list of places to document that she should send to the painter. Venice is an ancient city and Franco is at home in urban areas, so shoot Venice, he instructs. And Burano, a graphically vivid village, shoot Burano. The roadshow suits Massimo's purposes: Franco's been alternately mauled like a rock star and mistaken for a trespasser. He's thrown himself into painting a follow-up Madonna, more outrageous than the first. The sooner he gets to Torcello, the better. Another two months, Massimo's daughter will give birth, sometime during the Advent season. That should add some media interest, he says.

A new Madonna. Naked no doubt. Kat's stomach wrenches; she might throw up. Opening a bottle of Prosecco, she grasps its neck in one hand and a wine glass in the other. She throws herself onto the chaise beside the snapping fire set by Vittorio in the fieldstone hearth just minutes before. Kat pours until the bottle is almost empty and over-flows the glass.

Following Massimo's directions, Kat returns to Venice and photographs the sites she hopes will entice Franco. The Piazza San Marco, the Duomo, Rialto Bridge, the Grand Canal. At the Duomo she crosses the Bridge of Sighs where convicted criminals caught their last glimpse of the harbour, of freedom, before imprisonment. To her, The Devil's Bridge is Kat's own bridge of sighs.

She'd no intention of falling in love with Franco, especially after Faith's ugly end. She made the right decision, chose rational action over Franco's emotional pleas. She forced him to return to Italy and turned her back on their relationship. Peering out the studio window at the mud flats beyond the artichoke fields, she no longer feels capable of making that decision a second time. Where is he? What's he doing? Her soul craves his return to her. She's empty without him. Vittorio and Anna stare at her, speaking in low tones. What does Massimo tell them? She knows they question why she's the one in the studio peering out at the winterscape, why they're still waiting for the painter.

In late December, the tourists recede, replaced by the rains. Anna busies herself preparing *un buon natale festa* for her extended family, arriving tomorrow. Vittorio insists Kat join them. The last thing Kat wants is to be stranded among cheery strangers speaking the Venetian dialect which she cannot grasp no matter how she tries. But she agrees. It'd be awkward eating the meal they prepare on the other side of their shared wall. No email from Franco since his acknowledgment of the Venice photos two weeks before. Massimo's silent as well. Life in Florence occupies them both. She's been forgotten.

Vittorio glides the launch into a private stall along Riva degli Schia-voni on the Canale di San Marco. Kat climbs out of the boat in one fluid motion, accustomed now to this form of travel. She strides across the *piazzetta*, empty except for stacks of *passeralle*, the wooden cat-walks ready to make a foot path when the high tides of the *Acqua Alta* flood the island. Dominated by the Duomo with its arches of glinting mosaic on gold, animated by the dancing Archangel atop the bell tower and protected by the marble colonnades around the periphery, the piazza reminds Kat of a theatrical stage in waiting. Come April, when the tour-ists, not the sea water, flood the piazza, the local citizenry will argue over what is to be done with the throngs. All the while, they will allow the cruise ships to travel the delicate waterways and accept the day-tripper euros. Venetians don't fool anyone. They wish to save their fragile city but aren't willing to pay the price in lost tourist revenue. Today in San Marco, there are few tourists and even fewer Venetians since they are retreating to homes on the mainland in increasing numbers. Venice is too expensive for everyone now.

Kat chooses to shop in streets that snake behind the Piazza rather than in the colonnades which cater to the tourists and their willingness to pay the absurd prices. For Anna, she will purchase a tart called *panforte*. It's a chewy version of fruit cake with additional honey, nuts and spices. Anna likes a slender slice with her morning espresso or after a day of cleaning and meal preparation for Kat. Vittorio is another matter. Perhaps a bottle of *grappa* or better still, the liqueur Montenegro which he sometimes buys when he picks up Kat's wine on the Island of Lido.

She's left her map in Torcello and wanders the narrow *via* without guidance. Reaching a dead end, she backtracks and tries a different turn. She spies *Pasticceria Marchini* with an assortment of Christmas cakes in the window. She'll get the *panforte* here.

Her purchase, wrapped in paper printed with golden stylized lions and tied with blue twine, is so pretty it needs no further Christmas wrapping. Kat rounds the corner of Calle dei Specchieri where a grainy photo on the newsstand catches her eye. Moving closer, she picks up a copy of *La Repubblica*. *La Madonna di Levi* dominates the front page. Chiara cradles a newborn, a boy, apparently. The painter stands behind her, his hand over hers. A child is born, shouts the headline to the world. No one thought to mention the birth to Kat. Not Massimo and certainly not Franco. Not even Vittorio or Anna, who surely must know. She's been shut out. Kat drops the newspaper and a gruff voice reprimands her from behind the stand. She ignores the seller and the pages that flutter and drift in the wind. The rain begins to spit.

Kat dashes blindly down the route in front of her, becoming lost in the complex pattern of *calle*. One wrong turn after another. Lightning streaks across the sky and finds its way to ground. The rain is heavy. The streets empty. The stores close. Restaurants too. Italians are notorious for their dislike of rainy weather, fear getting wet and possibly sick. Never go out with a damp head. Always wear a scarf to protect the neck. That is what the mamas say and everyone obeys.

The water runs deep over the cobblestones. Her shoes are soaked. Kat's aware of an ancient war siren screaming overhead. It's the warning sounded in old war movies when the enemy bombers were approaching. Then come the tones. She counts them. One. Two. Three. The alert that the *Acqua Alta* is expected to be a three-level flood. That's serious. Where is she? The sirens continue their warning. In the darkness Kat panics, runs down the dark *calle* until she stumbles out onto Piazza San Marco and realizes she's back where she started.

She won't trouble Vittorio to bring the launch in this weather, but Torcello seems an impossible destination. The waters chop beyond the *fermata* San Zaccaria, the stop where Kat's to board the ferry. The wharf dips under the weight of the sea and then jolts upward, causing bystanders to buckle at the knees. The sky over the lagoon turns black. The rains are relentless and she's soaked through. Boarding the number 5.1, she huddles in a slick seat and shivers, peering out the steamy windows into the shadows. The engine labours as the boat churns its way through the chop. Standing passengers lurch as they grab for rails. The *vaporetto* stops in one *sestiere* after another. Castello, Dorosoduro, Santa Croce and Cannareggio. On a fine day this would be an opportunity to enjoy the diverse quarters of Venice, but tonight it's a voyage to be endured. Finally, the *vaporetto* arrives at its terminus. Kat disembarks. The sea's calmer here and the lightning has moved out to sea. She walks the vacant stretch of the promenade called Fondamente Nuove until she reaches Vaporetto N., the night ferry to Torcello.

Standing on the open deck, she ignores the sea spray splashing her legs as the *vaporetto* cuts across the winter waters. Her thoughts run turbid as the seas beneath her. Her emotions keep rhythm with each heave of the boat across the open lagoon. *First, Faith in her watery grave. Now, I am abandoned also.*

CHAPTER ELEVEN

Burano

Crimson, cerulean and lime. The fishermen's houses, painted in vibrant hues, draw tourists and their cameras to Burano. Massimo directs Kat to snap these images too. She agrees they might lend themselves to Franco's emerging impressionism. But then, who knows anymore. The artist is silent.

Sometime into the new year Franco sends an email stating that Mateo was delivered and that the baptism will be in April at San Gimignano. This is all the artist writes. What am I to do with this, Franco? Scream at the monitor of her laptop.

Minutes later an email from Massimo enquires after the Burano shots that have not yet materialized. He wants Franco to consider them now. He also mentions the arrival of his grandson, adds that she's invited to the baptism. Being Massimo, he's already made arrangements for her stay at an inn in old town.

Burano, a ten-minute *vaporetto* ride from Torcello, is an entirely different type of island. Actually an archipelago of islands linked by foot bridges and, unlike Torcello, populated. When Kat steps off the ferry, the silence and birdsong of Torcello is replaced by the rumbles of everyday living. Folklore says that Burano became a beacon of colour to help drunken fishermen find their way home. Squinting through the dreary March drizzle, Kat agrees that the colours are visible even in a winter fog. The chartreuse and scarlet guide the fishers home.

In Venice, only a few Italian and German stragglers remain after *Carnevale* ends. In Burano there's significant foot traffic. True, the outdoor stalls, stripped bare, wait for better weather, but the shops remain open. In contrast to Venice, the *calle* are a riot of colour. The one to her left is painted in marine blue from one end to the other, even the brickwork and the paving stones. Kat shoots the Lego-coloured street scenes Massimo demands.

Moving closer to a storefront window, Kat captures the delicate lace and linen. Italians prefer a delicate palette of ivory for their fine linens. These aren't photos she'll forward to Franco. They're for her own pleasure, a stark contrast to the motley-coloured village.

A woman in a black linen sheath appears in the window, holding out a scarf for Kat's inspection: a swatch of beige linen with three-dimensional black roses rimming either end. It's dramatic. In Vancouver, a twenty-something fashionista would vogue such a scarf, but in colourful Burano it doesn't seem showy at all. The woman beckons and Kat finds herself entering the lace shop.

Between tables stacked with fabric, the woman in the black sheath holds the rose scarf shoulder height and with practiced movements demonstrates how it might be worn; as a shawl, draped or tied. "Always show the black roses to their best advantage," she counsels in perfect English. "For you, a suitable transition piece from American to Italian style."

Transition piece. Kat averts her eyes, taking in oversized napkins and tablecloths lined with delicate fretwork. Collars, cuffs and even umbrellas. She dislikes being confused with American tourists and blurts out she's Canadian. She knows that to most Italians there's no difference. She's from the new world. The place of chrome and glass, of northern light.

The shopkeeper shrugs. Offers Kat the scarf. It's fragile, almost weightless and the roses are sculpted in satin. It's not what she would choose, but then neither is the life she's living.

"*Quanto?*" The scarf is artfully folded and readied for sale.

It comes to Kat there's another purchase she needs to make. She describes what she has in mind to the clerk. The black sheath disappears through a curtain of red beads to the back of the shop. Low hum of voices and rummaging noises. The beads part and she returns, joined by a roll-shouldered ancient whose creased face reminds Kat of the rings on first-growth trees near Port Renfrew. A memory for every crevice. Over the lace-maker's arm, she's draped an ivory gown. Beckoning Kat to the window, she holds the gossamer material close, caresses the skirt on her tea-brown cheek. Kat fingers the downy softness, follows the exquisite tracery on the collar, cuffs and hem. She's found what she wanted, a baptismal robe for Franco's son.

Anna wraps the azure box containing the baptismal gown in brown parcel paper, while Kat prints the address. *Piazza della Repubblica, 6, Florence.* Vittorio carries the package across the waters to the main post office on San Marco. The gift will arrive in Florence within the week, he assures her.

Kat emails to accept Massimo's invitation, then forwards the Burano jpegs to Franco. Will it be Burano's flash of colour or San Marco's Byzantine architecture that inspires him? The question's moot. To paint any of it the artist must be in the Veneto. She's refrained from calling him, not wanting to influence a decision to end the marriage. If that is what he chooses to do. The pregnancy is over, yet his silence continues. She fears calling Franco, but she needs to know what has transpired between husband and wife since she left Florence. The only way to find out what her painter thinks is to speak with him.

Grabbing a chilled bottle of Prosecco by the neck, she climbs the stairs and stands in the doorway of the artist's studio. No need to ask for permission to enter. It's as silent as the painter. A sip of wine. *Breathe, Kat.* She speed dials the Florence number. Four tones and a low male voice. *Pronto.*

A sip for courage. Her heart races, her chest tightens. "Franco, *sono io.* It's Kat."

The brusque pronto is replaced by boyish laughter, or is that sheep-ish guilt she hears? After all, he's barely communicated since the last time she crawled out of his bed.

"*Complimenti* on your son. Mateo, *un bel nome.*" A gulp of wine this time.

"Grazie, Kat." His voice lowers, the way she remembers it when they were alone.

"I've accepted Massimo's invitation to the baptism." *I'm coming to San Gimignano, Franco. What do you think of that?*

"*Che è meraviglioso.*" Marvellous.

She catches the surprise in his tone. Is he being polite or is her lover's mind racing, taking in the new facts, new possibilities?

"There's a gift in the post for your boy. I found it in Burano. I hope you and Chiara like it." Kat takes a long swig of Prosecco this time.

"Grazie. I look for it. I look for you in San Gimignano too." The feral cries of a newborn invade the background, followed by Chiara's soprano coos. A draft runs through the studio in Torcello. Kat feels the distance of her exile.

"Check out the Burano pictures. Tell me what you think of them."

"We talk of that when we meet. Easier to explain." Chiara's voice comes closer.

Kat's chest tightens. The photos don't interest him. Has he jettisoned the move to Venice for his new Madonna project? *Push him, Kat.*

"Massimo says you have another Madonna painting. Is that your next canvas, Franco?" Kat stops breathing. But his response cannot be misinterpreted even across language barriers. A derisive grunt, followed by a plaintive rush of words.

"You say keep busy, so I paint another Madonna. Three months you say, but now five months pass. I wait, Kat." Irritation laces his words. "You never tell me when. Because Massimo invites you to San Gimignano, for this you call me?"

Twilight shrouds the studio. Kat remembers when they last lay together. She told him he'd know when it was right to leave. While she waited on her painter to find the moment, to make the decision, she realizes now that he understood the sign would come from Kat. This separation was her idea, after all. A farcical communication failure, Kat. She'd laugh at the error except the months apart have been so painful. Finishing off the wine, she realizes Franco's future is in her hands, that it always was. "I agree. It's been too long. In three weeks, in San Gimignano, we will be together again. *Presto, mio caro, soon my dear.*"

Her name is whispered low. A caress across cyberspace. This is what her painter was waiting to hear.

Vittorio guns the motorboat across the open waters towards Giudecca, the island south of Piazza San Marco. In San Gimignano, Kat will be the woman Franco captured on his canvas, *La Donna al Chiaro di Luna*. No longer willing to hide their intimacy under bedcovers, Kat will return as her painter's muse. To prepare for her arrival she seeks the services of the Casanova Wellness Centre in the five-star Hotel Cipriani.

Amid orchids, marble and gilt, specialists scour, polish and embellish Kat in preparation for her journey. Near the end of the second day, she begins to tire of all the hands on her. Balks at the suggestion she wear her hair at shoulder length. Too old, she admonishes the man in the mirror. The stylist shakes his clean-shaved head. In Italy, the age barriers so common in America don't exist. A man is considered *un giovane* long into his middle years, celebrates his masculinity even when he is a *vecchio* with a cane. *La bella donna* enjoys her femininity throughout her lifetime. Leaning close to her ear he says: *So do the men around her.* The stylist fashions her hair into a chignon, then pulls it sleek in a horsetail and finally loosens it for what he calls *quei momenti intimi.* Kat regards her mirrored self and offers a faint smile. This is Italy after all and his deft hands are persuasive.

The esthetician likewise ignores Kat's protests that she keep her makeup simple, Instead instructing on the use of brushes, shadow and blush. She explains that a violet eye shadow will enhance Kat's green eyes. Unconvinced that any of this really matters, Kat climbs back onto the launch. *Madama, ooh la la!* Vittorio's energetic wolf whistle changes her mind.

She arranges the black-rose scarf across the top of her bureau as a talisman. The transformation continues. Italian designers and labels. Kat has no sense of what is appropriate, so she places herself in the care of upscale shop keepers along Calle Vallaresso. Anna unpacks and arranges the garments, delights in each item as if it were her own. Unbidden, she creates a list of what Kat still requires, directing Vittorio to take her back to Venice. Several shopping expeditions are needed to acquire the lacy under-garments, silky sleepwear that will be discarded more than it will be worn, soft leathers and sparkling accessories.

The gold-flecked eyes of a jeweller at Procuratie Nuova blink in *simpatico* as she explains her preference for Nick's garnet drop earrings to glittery gems. Like the others who have guided her, the jeweller sets aside her point of view and presents a blue velvet tray of jewels set in sterling silver. There's an unadorned cuff, a double-braid necklace and an eternity band embedded with garnets. Dramatic ornaments more suitable for Franco's next masterpiece than everyday wear. Kat purchases the entire contents of the tray. At last, she feels no doubt. The muse of Torcello pronounces herself *pronto.*

CHAPTER TWELVE

San Gimignano

The lobby of the Hotel Cisterna resembles the tasting room of an upscale wine cellar. Vaulted plaster ceilings, old-stone pillars and smooth marble underfoot. Kat's informed that everything has been arranged. No need for a credit card on file, although there's a legal requirement to document her passport.

Her first trip to San Gimignano was for the baptism of Franco's daughter Katerina. The occasion of his clumsy incorporation of Kat into his family by naming his child after her. Proof of how far Franco will push limits for her. From the terrace of the farmhouse, she glimpsed the stone towers of the hilltop town that keeps watch over the Ghibellini. This time Massimo has placed Kat in the centre of that medieval town, inside its 13th century ramparts. The Ghibellini are beyond her reach, but the balcony off her Florentine-styled room overlooks the Tuscan countryside. Franco's down there somewhere.

The porter places her suitcase on the folding rack and asks if she requires any services. Kat shakes her head. He backs out of the doorway with a nod and Kat's tip in his left hand. It's still confusing, knowing when to tip in Italy, when not. Faith argued with her in Rome. *Not taxis, Kat.* And that cheap bastard Gerhard never tipped anyone.

There's an envelope on the credenza by the bed. Her name hand-written in black ink on heavy stock.

Katerina, I trust your travel was uneventful and that you find the accommodation to your liking. The hotel is situated in a building

surviving from the twelfth century. Please enjoy the facilities this eve-
ning. I will arrive at 09:00 to accompany you to the basilica where the
baptism of Mateo Massimo will take place.
A note of interest: If you look to the west from your balcony, you will
view the five red-roofed buildings of the Ghibellini Farm. The family will
host a celebration in the afternoon to which you are an invited guest.
Cordiali saluti,
Massimo Saverio Alighieri

Kat drops the note on the table and opens the French doors. Twilight, but
she can make out the shapes in the distance. There! The clutch of buildings where generations of the Ghibellini family have lived and worked
their land. Kat scans the hilly countryside where Franco grew up. What
was it in the making of her painter that allowed him to see this landscape
so differently? What accident of fate gave him a painter's eyes?

On the hillside, the vines stand neatly, row after row. Was it the
rhythm of these repeating motifs? Was that the beginning of his understanding of beauty? Even from here she makes out the Chinana cattle
grazing in the hilly meadows. Did the contrast between their cream-
coloured coats and the grasses on which they fed lead the boy to ponder
light and dark?

He painted *L'Elefante* barely in his manhood, passion fueling his
unlikely dream. Kat had recognized that spirit that night in Piazza della
Minerva. She remembers his hand in the moonlight, an artisan's hand.
Square-palmed with slender fingers, paint embedded beneath the nails.
She aches for his touch. Franco's hand in her own. Smooth, a shade of
umber, warm. Hands that translate the pictures in his mind's eye onto
canvas or paper; exquisite images fashioned with rudimentary tools of
brush, charcoal and paint. Massimo's words return to her. Ordinary men
can be a husband and father. Artists like Franco are few and must be
nurtured. Kat would go further. She would say Francesco Ghibellini is
a gift from the gods.

Morning light finds her caught in a tangle of bedsheets. Sleep has fled,
so Kat rises early and takes her coffee by the balcony window. From the
surrounding red tile roofs, doves still hidden in their nooks and cran-
nies coo into the morning mists hanging over the valley. She assembles
her wardrobe with purpose. The cream-coloured silk sheath is awash in
impressionistic flowers of rust, mauve and indigo. Pairs the dress with an

unlined black linen jacket, sleek long-nosed Italian stilettos and a clutch dyed the shade of indigo in the gown. What would Vancouver Kat think of this get-up? She prided herself on a minimalist approach to fashion; after all, there were more important items on her agenda. She lived in pantsuits and tees, flats for comfortable walking. No jewellery beyond her garnet drop earrings. A gift from Nick in the first days of marriage, when they were keeping up the pretense of romantic love. Why was it such work, when with Franco feelings flow unbidden? If anything needs feigning, it's detachment. Today, that will be Kat's challenge.

Applying her makeup as she was schooled at the Casanova Wellness Spa, she's almost ready. She piles her hair into a chignon, admits she likes the way it accents the curve of her jawline and neck. But will Franco like this transformation? Will she still be his Kat?

The jewellery comes last. *Remember the jeweller's finger-wagging admonishment, Kat.* Only three pieces. Today, the silver cuff, jewelled ring and the already immortalized garnet earrings for luck. Checking her image in the mirror, she's content. Time to introduce the Muse of Torcello. *Vado!* I go!

A half-dozen lounge chairs line the stone wall to the left of the lobby. Kat picks a spot which can be easily seen by Massimo, but when he strides through the glass doors, he goes straight to reception. The receptionist points at Kat; surely Massimo sees her now. Walking toward him, she offers her hand.

Kat's never seen his eyes wide open. "*La bella figura.* Kat, *sei la bella figura.*" Taking her outstretched palm, he twirls her around. The hem of her mauve and purple floral skirt lifts in the breeze.

Extricating her hand, she straightens her dress and tidies strands of hair that escaped during the pirouette. "You're in fine spirits today!"

Perfunctory air kisses and then Massimo leads the way out the portico to the centre of the Piazza Cisterna. He pauses, gives her a long look and asks if she's familiar with the concept of *La Bella Figura*? Kat shakes her head.

According to Massimo, it is an Italian concept of how to live one's best life. It begins with presenting oneself in the most pleasing manner possible. "As your stay in Venice has taught you," he notes, his eyes softening. "That's a good start, but it's only part of the philosophy. More significant is behaving well, knowing the rules of etiquette and being aware of the nuances of proper Italian society."

It's difficult to focus on Massimo's treatise while being challenged by the cobblestones. Instead, she concentrates on retaining her balance in the needle-nose stilettos, thankful for Massimo's outstretched arm.

"We'll speak later about *La Bella Figura,* but now let me tell you about what is about to happen inside the church."

Entering the Romanesque Basilica, they pause, allowing their eyes to adjust to the dimly-lit interior. At home in the glass and steel architecture of Vancouver, Kat's overwhelmed by the space before her. Stone columns, gothic striped arches and sacred murals line the arcades on either side of the central aisle. Further into the nave, hushed groups of people are seated.

"Shall we?" Massimo proceeds at a slow pace. Kat draws close to him, hears the click of her stilettos on marble and observes heads turning their way. Massimo nods to those seated. He's on familiar ground. As they reach the front row he releases Kat's arm, gestures to a space beside Franco. Her painter's on his feet, plants warm kisses where he shouldn't until Max places a hand on each of their shoulders and commands an almost inaudible *basta,* enough.

With a wooden kneeling rail between the pews, it's tricky navigating in her stilettos. Franco tugs at her hand and seats himself next to his older children, who wriggle in response to seeing Kat again. Beside them, Chiara cradles the newborn in the crook of her arm. Mateo Massimo sleeps in the delicate baptismal gown Kat bought in Burano. His downy head is covered with a matching bonnet so tiny that it fits in Chiara's palm. Their eyes meet, wife and interloper. No. This time they will be mother and muse.

Smoothing the folds of her skirt, she catches Massimo's enigmatic smile. Franco leans closer, whispers *ti amo.* Whatever Max thinks doesn't matter. Kat's with her painter.

Massimo drives a late model Pagani, which resembles a low-slung arrow. Black exterior with quilted cowhide interior, it's immaculate except for the faint whiff of cigarette smoke. He insists that Kat ride with him to the farmhouse. Climbing into the passenger side of the two-seater, she's careful with the placement of her limbs in this compact space. Max watches her, searching, for what?

This automobile is like nothing in Kat's experience. It's called a Huayra after a South American god of the wind. Custom built in Modena.

Diamond-patterned leather, suede-covered steering-wheel and a constellation of shiny instrumentation. His pride in his vehicle is evident in Massimo's voice as he describes his purchase. His gaze keeps landing on Kat's bare legs.

"What do you call this material?" Kat points to the console.

"Carbon fibre." Massimo caresses the stick shift. "*Bellissimo*. Don't you agree?"

"I've never seen anything like this."

Massimo engages the ignition with the press of a silver button and turns to Kat. "This vehicle is part of *La Bella Figura*. It's essential you understand this concept. Especially for the future, for Franco …" He pauses and lights a cigarette "… and your future also, Katerina."

How does Max think she can grasp the nuances of Italian society when she barely understands any more of the language than his grandson?

Reading her concern, he says: "Don't worry, I will guide you."

Trusting Max with one's future seems a foolish act but she has no one else.

The Pagani races down the dirt road, at one with the curves, diffusing centrifugal force as if it no longer exists. Massimo grins, his shark teeth on full display as he shifts gears. He comes gut-churningly close to a muddy pick-up truck and then bolts into the oncoming lane and throttles down. His movements are abrupt but the pace remains steady. Kat checks the side mirror. The truck is lost from view.

On the grassy patch beside the tool shed, Massimo shuts down the engine and takes Kat's hand; a cigarette burns in the other. "Italians have an intense sense of loyalty to family, friends and business partners. Behaving respectfully is crucial to maintaining *La Bella Figura* with family, as well as in the business world. Proper conduct is essential … if Franco is to meet with success. *Capito*. Understand, Kat?" Max finishes his smoke. Kat follows its trajectory as he tosses the smouldering butt out the window.

"Kat, Kat, *vieni,* come." Tugging her arm, Franco leads her down a pale yellow corridor of the farmhouse. Passing a cavernous kitchen, she glimpses women in grey dresses and white-bibbed aprons deep into meal preparation. There's a pot so large it takes two people to move it from stove to worktable. The sounds of repetitive chopping, a male voice hollering in a doorway. Franco opens a door and draws her in. Daylight streams through the casement window, reveals the tiniest bedroom Kat's ever seen. Her walk-in closet in North Vancouver was more spacious. The bed along the farthest wall is skinnier than a twin-sized. There's a roughhewn cross above the iron headboard and a crisp white coverlet drawn tightly over the bed and tucked under the mattress. Beneath a window stands an unpainted wood table and chair, probably borrowed from the kitchen.

"My room from childhood." Franco shrugs. "Still my room." He shuts the door behind Kat, pulls her into the centre of the clay tiles. "*Si piccolo Franco*? Very small."

"I don't share." He turns towards the window. "And I sketch."

Kat understands. With four older sisters, this minute space was Franco's private refuge.

"*Alora, che bella!* How wonderful!"

But he isn't listening. He's unzipping her dress.

She steps out of the pool of silk and kicks off her stilettos.

"Ooh, la-la." Franco appreciates lacy underwear. Releasing the bra's catch with nimble fingers, he places the garment on the cot. Then her painter starts a trail of kisses along Kat's neck to her breasts. Kneeling on the terra cotta tile, his mouth moves down her torso, kisses her navel. Shutting her eyes, her hands barely rest on Franco's shoulders as she concentrates on his moist breath, his heat.

A quick rap on the door and it opens. Arms crossed, Massimo takes in every inch of the scene before him. Franco on his knees with his back to the doorway, continues his kisses, unaware. Massimo watches his son-in-law, his mouth set in an angry line. He spits out a string of Italian curses that Kat doesn't understand. Realizing Massimo is in the room, Franco leaps to his feet and steps in front of Kat. But beyond etiquette at this point, Kat wraps her arms around her painter's waist, feels she's the one protecting him.

"Katerina, Francesco, in five minutes I make my speech." Ignoring Franco, he addresses Kat in English. "Get dressed and fix your hair." The door thuds heavily behind him.

Franco shrugs. "*Non si puo piacere a tutti.* You can't please everyone."

Slipping back into her clothes, Kat retrieves her compact from the clutch lying on the table.

"Let me fix, Kat." Pulling a comb from his pocket, Franco rearranges Kat's chignon.

"You do hair?" Kat lets her body relax, finding the absurdity in what just took place in the tiny room. "Four sisters. I know many things that please women. Sit."

Kat sits. With a few deft moves, Franco arranges an elegant twist. Taking her lipstick from the open clutch, Franco coats her lips and proclaims her as *perfetto*.

The stone terrace behind the Ghibellini farmhouse overlooks their vineyards and the rolling hills below the medieval towers of San Gimignano. Nicknamed the Manhattan Skyline to entertain tourists, who imagine the stone campaniles as office towers in 20th century New York. But San Gimignano is as ancient as the land beneath, where remnants of Etruscan civilization remain buried. During the Renaissance, the town flourished as a crossroad on Christian pilgrimage routes. Later, the Guelph, medieval citizenry loyal to the church, warred with the Ghibellines, who sided with the state. San Gimignano and the lands surrounding the tower town were the prize each side desired. Franco's family are the present-day descendants of that ancient history. Ghibellini today work the land their ancestors fought for and bitterly won. No wonder, when an only son abandoned their world for life as an artist, the family was left reeling.

But today is a day for feasting and thanksgiving. Twelve tables on the terrace, dressed in white linens. Three bottles, red and white wine and a blue bottle of sparkling water, anchor either end. Platters of *antipasti carpaccio di bresaola*, roasted sweet peppers, *bruschetta* and black olives. On trays, a bottle of extra virgin olive oil, another of balsamic vinegar and a salt cellar. Franco informs Kat, with quiet pride, that all the produce and wine on the table comes from the farm.

A wave of Massimo's manicured hand sends Franco to the chair beside his wife and Kat to the one on his other side. Book-ended by his women.

The clang of a cast iron bell brings guests streaming onto the terrace. After finding seats to their liking, the women share the platters of antipasti while the men uncork the wine. Ting, ting, ting of a fork against a wine tumbler. Massimo rises and begins the toast. Guests fête the husband and wife for producing three offspring. Cheers, clapping and Italian songs at the far table. *Drink up Kat, you're going to need it.*

Chiara's sheathed in the palest pink silk. Her blonde curls trail past her shoulders, delicate features so exquisite any painter would be blessed to have her as his model. Franco's wife leans towards him and kisses his cheek. The guests demand more. More, more! Emboldened, she kisses Franco hard on the mouth causing an eruption of laughter, clapping and general noisemaking until the newborn wakes and begins to fuss.

The well-wishers consume the *insalate e zuppe* but Kat, still unused to so many courses, sips the homegrown wine instead. She notices Franco's sisters' easy ownership of his children. She realizes that there's probably 25 years between Franco and the eldest, Mariola. The painter's accustomed to the company of older women. It's not improbable that he find comfort in her arms.

The servers she glimpsed in the kitchen arrive with plates of the *pasta al forno*, a baked casserole of pasta, tomatoes, cheeses and garlic. Massimo, ignoring the food in front of him, is on his feet again. *What now?* Kat gulps her wine. *Can't the man sit long enough for one course without interrupting?*

He begins with a discourse on Franco's career. *Reminding everyone that Franco turned his back on the family farm seems an odd choice for your opener, Max.*

"One painting raised great interest in the media both across Italy, Europe and even in America. *La Madonna di Levi.*" Polite applause. "The inspiration." Chiara stands. The applause gains momentum. Kat notices that pearl drop earrings have joined the baptismal gifts that Franco, with Massimo's help, purchased after the birth of each child. First, there was a single strand of pearls for Antonio, then, a double strand bracelet for Katerina and now, the earrings for Mateo. No matter what the state of the marriage, the mother receives traditional gifts on the birth of her children. *La Bella Figura.*

"The work of our painter was revealed to the world. *La Madonna* travelled across Italy and is about to embark on a European tour." He motions to Franco as if commanding a dog. The painter rises. "*Salute, La Madonna* and her painter."

The guests do as they are bid. On their feet, clapping as one. *Salute.* Franco shouts that there's a second Madonna coming, more provocative than the last. The men at the back table hoot. The painter shoots Massimo a look which Kat interprets as a challenge. Chiara reaches to kiss him on the cheek, but Franco pulls her closer and delivers a full-mouthed buss. The men break into a raucous chant. Kat can't make sense of it but Max's distaste is clear. Caught up in the moment, Chiara returns Franco's ardour by grabbing his crotch. The terrace is awash in bawdy approval. Kat won't look at Franco or his *pantaloni.* Doesn't want to know the state of his pants. Tells herself this is foolish ribaldry fed by too much wine.

Massimo hisses Chiara back to her seat. Kat bets he wants a cigarette, soon. Regaining his composure, he motions to Franco to remain standing. The painter stares at the table, his face unreadable.

Tink-tink-tink. *What now, Max?*

"Calm yourselves, *prego*. I have important news." He smiles and the crowd settles.

"Franco painted a second great painting. His *capolavoro*, his masterpiece, *La Donna al Chiaro di Luna*. Serious art collectors started a bidding war." The terrace is silent except for the guttural lowing of the Chianina cattle grazing in the fields. Kat leans forward, rests her chin in her hands. She's curious. To whom did Max sell her likeness?

Massimo places his hand on his son-in-law's shoulder. "Franco decided that he would not sell *La Donna al Chiaro di Luna*. Instead, she will go on loan to a prestigious gallery, The Guggenheim in Venice." Why not sell? Shrugs and murmurings as the gathered attempt to decipher the news. From Franco, a grin. He knew this but didn't tell her. Kat's beginning to feel uneasy. What else hasn't Franco told her?

"Like *La Madonna, La Donna al Chiaro di Luna* was inspired. *La bella musa* ..." He pauses, "Katerina, please stand."

What's next? Ghibellini faces, ten tables deep, stare. Kat searches for a smile, a nod. Finds none.

"Katerina is the namesake and godmother to my granddaughter." He points to the blonde child who never has and probably never will show the slightest interest in Kat. "Katerina e Franco, *salute*."

The terrace guests are on their feet again but it's a muted salute, mixed with queries and glances. As the meagre applause fades, Franco reaches for Kat's hand. Warm lips press her skin. "*La bellissima musa*." He bows slightly and holds out her chair. The terrace goes silent. Eyes fix on the painter. Beside him, Massimo is smiling, a full lipped smile. *This is what you want, isn't it, Max? The passion you witnessed in Franco's childhood cell transformed to canvas. Franco's next masterpiece.* Kat knows she's the pawn, Massimo's unwitting accomplice, as he masterminds the painter's destiny.

"A final announcement and then I will be silent." Sporadic clapping. The servers begin distributing the second dish, platters of steamed seafood. Focused on their task, they've interrupted Massimo's presentation. Realizing that the *vongole* and *gamberetto, clams and shrimp* are stiff competition, he hurries on. "Franco will accompany his masterpiece to the Guggenheim Museum. He has accepted a one-year internship as painter-in-residence."

Surprise registers as gasps, mainly amongst the sisters. It's Kat's turn to stare. *Franco planned to come to Venice all along. Why didn't he tell me?*

"Katerina will accompany him as his assistant and *musa*. *Grazie*, Katerina."

Smattering of applause. The seafood is winning audience share. Chiara's mouth twists, a smirk reminiscent of the one so often seen on her father's face. The faces of the sisters resemble mourners at a funeral pyre. There it is then, for all to know, Franco's joining her in Torcello. Formally announced at a family celebration.

The guests plunder the platters and Massimo excuses himself, unnoticed. Two cousins, workers on the farm, pull up chairs on either side of Chiara. She tosses her blonde curls as she joins their conversation. Kat sips on the endless supply of Vernaccia.

Brigitte takes Massimo's chair and leans in close to her brother. They share the same brown eyes and thick swath of lash. "Are you certain, Franco?" Remembering another time her brother went away in the company of the *Canadese*. "Is this best? For you and your children?"

Franco turns to Kat, slips his hand in hers. "It's what I want."

Bri pats his shoulder as she rises, but she shoots Kat a woeful glance.

CHAPTER THIRTEEN

Dorsoduro

American heiress Peggy Guggenheim purchased an unfinished palace on the Grand Canal of Venice in 1949. It's the palazzo that caught Kat's eye on her first ride down the canal on arriving. Known as *Palazzo Venier dei Leoni*, the long and low limestone façade promises visitors something unusual is in store. What Vittorio shrugged off as being American is the home of the heiress's permanent collection of 20th century art. As Kat now understands, it's also a showcase and source of practical opportunity for emerging contemporary artists. Kat takes a deep breath and pushes open the wrought-iron gate, on Calle San Cristoforo, just as she has every day for the past week.

Vittorio will ferry Massimo and Franco along the Grand Canal and dock at the Marino Terrace below the Guggenheim Garden of sculptures. This will be her painter's formal introduction to *La Serenissima*, the beloved nickname for Venice. Already, Venetian and foreign guests sip Prosecco from grapes grown in the Veneto region and admire the avant-garde statuary as they await the artist's arrival. What will Franco make of the angular figures by Henry Moore or Giacometti? For Kat, Marini's *The Angel of the City* gives reason to pause every time she lays eyes on it. A naked male straddles a horse while standing in the stirrups. The animal's head elongates, reaching into the future as the man's erect phallus echoes its mass and trajectory. With arms wide open, the rider embraces the travellers on the Grand Canal. If Franco imagines his Madonna controversial, wait till he meets up with the works of the Guggenheim. Kat ruminates on his immersion into this avant-garde art world.

Smoothing the lines of her scarlet sheath, she tugs at the thin belt of deep mauve and checks her stilettos for scuff marks. The outfit was arranged by one of the boutiques of the Merceria district during her Italian shopping spree. She hopes her hair resembles the twist Franco fashioned for her. Of course, she wears Nick's earrings which Franco captured in his *capolavoro*. She swallows hard. Her mouth's dry. If she is nervous, how must Franco be faring as Vittorio jets the outboard along the Grand Canal toward the installation of his masterpiece?

The delicate strings of a quartet in the garden add another layer of elegance to the evening. Eva, the administrator overseeing Franco's residency, welcomes Kat with air kisses.

"Everything's ready," she whispers. "*La Donna* was installed this morning and she's *bellissima*. I think you'll be pleased."

Kat's grateful for Eva's open manner. Her enthusiasm for this project has made it possible for Kat to morph into the role of painter's assistant in this Venetian galleria.

It's been a month since Massimo's limo delivered her to the train station in Florence. Franco remained at the farm. Despite rudimentary written English skills, he sends an email every morning. Brief and sometimes awkwardly amusing, they're certainly better than her attempts to respond in Italian which almost always includes a search of Google Translate. Yesterday's email was simple: "I come tomorrow." Kat feels the thrum of his presence whenever she reads his words.

A lull in conversation in the garden gives way to laughter and applause. Kat quickens her pace as Eva leads her through the knots of waiting guests. Vittorio's moored the launch to a wooden timber. Massimo, a man comfortable in any environment, climbs the steps with hand outstretched in greeting. Franco hangs back. The painter in residence, his back to the Guggenheim, takes in the Grand Canal. Moorish windows, Gothic arches. Glints of gold play off the waters below. Architecture in varying stages of decay. The palazzos on the Grand Canal seduce the untrained eye. Surely the images mesmerize her painter.

Massimo's impatient gesture jolts Franco from his reverie. As always, when Massimo commands, Franco obeys. Welcome kisses and handshakes. Franco's warm palm in her own as they make their way among the sculptures to the waiting guests. The artist is in residence.

Massimo cautions that their time is limited, that he and the artist have other commitments. Max is covering for the fact that Franco isn't comfortable in crowds. According to Max, his simple charm detracts from the appreciation of his art. Massimo nods toward Kat in a subtle reminder that her role is to keep the English-speaking guests engaged and give Franco moral support. Eva announces the appointment of Painter in Residence and introduces Massimo, who in turn introduces Franco. Venetian art lovers who pay a hefty annual fee for access to such events, along with the mayor and other civic-oriented citizens, form a semi-circle around the pair. A group of Texans on an art tour vie for floor space.

Massimo speaks first in Italian and follows with brief comments in his careful English. He's the embodiment of a successful Italian with his tailored silks, monogrammed shirt and burnished leather shoes. Beside him, Franco appears as up-and-coming as he ever has, in his pressed black suit, crisp white shirt and polished loafers. His curly locks have been tamed with scissors. None of the Italians wear ties. Neither do any of the Texans, but for a different reason. They're on vacation and underdressed, many in shorts, and the women wear slacks, even jeans.

There's a move to the temporary gallery to view the installation of *La Donna al Chiaro di Luna*, led by Eva. She stops outside the Alcove Studio where Kat's been occupied all week in preparation for Franco's arrival. The painter peeks his head around the corner. Encouraged by Eva, he enters the space. Kat watches as he takes in the solid wooden worktables, the sleek glass desk by the window with a computer where she will catalogue his projects, the light streaming in from the floor-to-ceiling windows. He throws Kat a questioning look. *For me? What do I do here?*

They continue into an exhibition room. There hangs *La Donna*. Positioned on a central column, she's visible from several angles, dominating the space even though she's one of the most diminutive paintings in the gallery.

"*Perfetto.*" Massimo rubs his hands together. "The Francesco Ghibellini master work, *La Donna al Chiaro di Luna*." With a small bow, Massimo offers the floor to the artist. Scattered applause as the guests draw near.

Eva says: "Tell us about this work, *signore*." Franco swallows hard, his Adam's apple bobbing. He's thinner than when Kat left him in Florence the previous autumn.

Kat doesn't understand his words, but the earnest set of his features leads her to believe that whatever he's saying speaks to the artist's intention. The Italians are attentive and when he finishes there's vigorous applause. Massimo registers his approval and, Kat thinks, his surprise.

Eva reminds the painter that there are English speakers present too. He throws Kat a look of wide-eyed panic but somehow finds a way to begin. He asks those who understand English to come closer. The Texans elbow forward. Their sturdy footwear, more at home on hiking trails, squeaks on the wooden floorboards.

Clearing his throat, he says: "My lady is a symbol of feminine wisdom. A learned woman." He points to the leather-bound book in her hand. "We find her as she communes with the goddess mother, the moon." Franco stops and swallows again. Kat holds her breath. She knows none of this. The Americans eye him and his painting. "Her robe is black, to remind us that without the moon, without wisdom, there is darkness. Her earrings are silver, the goddess moon's metal which shines with truth." He pauses again, wipes his mouth with the back of his hand and when he looks up, it's directly at Kat.

"People mention that *La Donna* has an air of sadness. This is true. Feminine wisdom knows the world's sorrow and makes it her own. I try to honour this in the painting." Franco steps back, looks to Eva. The Americans respond with resounding applause.

"That's mighty interesting. Your work sure beats those drop cloths that pass for paintings that we saw this afternoon." An oversized Texan speaks on behalf of the group. "We appreciate you taking time with us Mr. Gibell ..." He stumbles over Franco's surname. Massimo articulates it slowly, as you would to a toddler. *Fran-ces-co Ghi-bell-ini.* Undeterred, the Texan continues. "It's this kind of get-together that makes our trip worth it. Yes, sir." He towers over Franco, pumping the artist's hand. The Americans form a line, grateful to pay homage to an artist whose imagery is accessible and nothing like those Jackson Pollock paint splatters.

Massimo interrupts the Texans with his announcement of Franco's imminent departure, apologizing for conflicting schedules. He thanks the Guggenheim, the gathered guests and the painting's donor, who so generously agreed to loan *La Donna* to the Guggenheim.

"Katerina is the muse for this masterpiece. In fact, if you look closely, you will see that tonight she's wearing the earrings portrayed." Massimo gestures towards Kat. "More important, she's the owner of the painting." Kat looks from Massimo to Franco. *What?* "There was a bidding war among serious collectors, but Katerina wouldn't sell to a private collector, no matter how prestigious." Massimo focuses on her. "In *her* feminine wisdom she chose to share *La Donna* with the world. *Il capolavoro* is on loan to the Guggenheim for the duration of the painter's residency."

Massimo points to the label besides the painting. "*Brava Katerina e profondo graziemento.*" His manicured hands lead the polite applause.

Kat peers at the small, printed block and reads *On loan from the private collection of* and then her name. Franco leans in and whispers, "See Kat, I don't always do what Massimo wants."

As they cross the timbered Ponte dell Accademia, Massimo stops to light a cigarette. Kat and Franco, arm-in-arm, stroll a few paces behind. Franco is fascinated by the ornate facades, the play of shadow in the narrow streets called *calle*. Kat recalls his reaction to Vancouver, taking in its modernity. Massimo is correct. The new surroundings stimulate the painter's creativity. It's six in the evening and the streets overflow with tourists. Massimo leads them across Campo Santo Stefano, a wide square lined with pink Gothic style apartments, street cafés under white awnings and kiosk vendors selling cheap Venetian masks and postcards imported from China. At the far end, La Chiesa di Santo Stefano houses significant works by masters Vivarini, Tintoretto and Bambini. Venice is a trove of precious art housed *in situ*. Much to study beyond the modern works of the Guggenheim.

Entering a narrow *calle*, they discover micro markets and coffee bars sharing cramped quarters with boutiques and art galleries. They walk single file to allow foot traffic to move in the opposite direction. Massimo pauses to buy *La Repubblica* at a kiosk selling papers from around the world. Kat remembers that it was on a nearby street corner where she first saw the photo of Chiara and Franco with their newborn. She shakes off that memory, much like a dog shakes away rain. She's with Franco now, his arm in hers. Once they see Massimo to the dock where he'll take the launch to the Hotel Cipriani, they'll be alone.

"There's Harry's Bar." Massimo points out the bar made famous by Hemingway and where the Bellini Cocktail was invented. "Visiting Harry's Bar is a rite of passage for Americans," he says. "But they are often turned away due to improper adherence to dress code." Massimo pulls the last of the nicotine from his cigarette and tosses the butt into the street. "Probably the crowd from Dallas will try to get in tonight, but with no trousers, no jacket, there will be no admittance." He laughs, clearly pleased at the prospect. Franco's more intrigued with the bar's undulating gilded wrought-iron grates hanging over the diminutive windows of opaque glass. Privacy is a luxury afforded the bar's clientele.

Finally, they reach the Hotel Cipriani's private dock. The yellow canopy emblazoned with the hotel's name is visible a hundred paces away. Massimo picks up the house phone and requests a launch while Kat rings Vittorio on her cell.

Franco wanders up the pier, taking in colours and textures. Lighting another smoke, Massimo declares the installation of painting and painter a success, noting that Franco's public speaking has improved since the roadshows with the Madonna.

"He was tongue-tied then but tonight he was almost eloquent. But then this painting evokes different emotions for the painter than *La Madonna*." Massimo stares at Kat, sun-blinking. *That's why I'm here, Max.*

"Keep me informed of his progress, Katerina. Don't let anyone see that detestable new Madonna. If we're desperate for media attention, perhaps, but only then. Let's hope our painter will prove himself to be the master we promised the world this evening."

A sleek motor launch glides into its designated mooring just as Franco sprints down the promenade towards them. Quick air kisses for Kat and a handshake between the men, then Massimo climbs aboard the outboard and is gone. Franco snakes his arm around Kat's waist, kisses her in the fading heat of the Mediterranean sun. They wait for Vittorio to arrive.

As they near Torcello the sun dips behind the trees, re-inventing their shades of green. The timing's off. Difficult for Franco to appreciate the views or the light in his studio this late in the evening. Vittorio moors the boat and Franco scrambles out and offers his arm to Kat. At the bridge she notes that once he crosses the devil will take his soul in payment, according to the folklore of Torcello.

"Don't be so superstitious, Kat," he says. "Take my hand. If we walk together the devil will be too confused to take either of our souls."

"Oh, you're not superstitious." She laughs but gives him her hand. "Still, you can't be too careful."

Kat leads her painter along the side of the property to the entrance. Anna's in the great room setting a cold supper of *antipasti*, salad and seafood. As with the houseboat, now that Franco is in residence the townhouse feels like a home. Taking him from room to room, she notices his muted reaction. It's dark outside and she wishes he could see the gardens and canal views.

Anna unpacked his valise earlier in the day and his clothes hang in the wardrobe beside Kat's. The bed has been turned down. A low-wattage lamp bathes the room in an amber glow. Franco looks from corner to corner, then nods. They mount the steps to his studio, Kat first. The pit in her stomach deepens with each step.

The painter enters the studio, walks its periphery and touches every item: The palettes containing his canvasses, the tools Kat's carefully laid out on the worktables, the bench under the window facing the town and the floor-to-ceiling crate housing his Madonna in progress.

"You'll find the views diverse, Franco. The skyline of the old town, the boats in the canal, the marshlands and meadows. The light of the Veneto's unique." She's still in the doorway, reticent to enter this space until he claims it. Franco stares at her from across the studio, his generous lips drawn into a thin line reminiscent of Massimo, his eyes dark.

"I'm hungry. Let's eat." He moves past Kat and down the stairwell.

Kat hears the scrape of a chair across the plank flooring. *Oh Franco, what are you thinking?* She's lost her appetite.

They consume Anna's meal in silence except for Kat's occasional comment or question. She tells him Massimo's pleased with the installation and with his public speaking. Franco answers *bene,* unsmiling. She offers him a glass of wine but he opts for water. There'll be no toasts, no celebratory moments tonight. Pouring herself a glass, she picks at her plate.

After the meal, Kat suggests they take a stroll to the village. It's not far, ten minutes, but Franco's tired, wishes to shower and get some rest, if she doesn't mind.

Franco rises, kisses her cheek. His slender shoulders round as he walks away. The pipes rattle to life in the shower. Kat pours herself another glass, this time to the rim. She collects their dishes. He ate well, so he was hungry. Beyond that, it feels like Franco's spirit collapsed when he entered this house.

When did his mood change? He was entranced with the sights of Venice, amorous after Massimo departed. The Ponte del Diavolo. That's it. Did the devil steal his soul? Kat drains her glass, pours another and paces. Don't be ridiculous, she tells herself. That's superstition, just as Franco said. Then she remembers the white pebble and its power. No, no, not possible. The devil's bridge is just a folktale. The pipes have stopped clanking. Franco's probably in bed. *Finish your drink, Kat. Go join your painter.*

Kat hangs her dress in the wardrobe, placing the purple stilettos beneath it. Laying the silver drop earrings on the scarf of black roses atop the bureau, she remembers the morning's excitement. Franco was coming to Torcello at last! It all feels like an old memory. At the bedside, she regards Franco in sleep. In the bathroom she turns the shower on hot, enduring the pin pricks until they become intolerable. It's a futile effort to wash away her aching disappointment.

Kat pulls Franco's towel off the rail. She presses its dampness to her face and breathes in his scent. Life with Franco demands her body, her soul, her all, and tonight this feels cruel. Franco was upset, yet he turned away from her. Of what value is she to him if she cannot help her painter? Returning his towel to the rail, she knows that traces of her perfume have mixed with his scent. Padding barefoot across the boards, she climbs into bed. Hip-to-hip, thigh-to-thigh, she lies with her sleeping painter. Synchronizing her breathing with his, somehow she falls asleep. Kat awakes to find Franco above her, whispering his undecipherable phrases. Wrapping her legs around his torso, she guides him. His is a frenzied passion, as though he's trying to lose himself within her. Kat holds him tight until the storm passes.

"What's wrong? Why are you so troubled?" She strokes his unlined forehead, reminded of how young he is.

"When I work at the university Massimo tells me what to do. Here, I'm alone." He rolls towards her. "Guggenheim's painter in residence, what if I fail?" Burying his head in her breasts, "Kat, help me."

A sea of time separates their life experiences. He's been thrust by Massimo into a complex world and Franco's terrified. Using her body as ballast, Kat holds Franco steady while he sleeps. In the daylight everything will look less daunting. Tonight, she has her man in her arms at last. For this, Kat is grateful.

As the morning sun creeps across the window ledge, Kat rouses from sleep. Alone. The bed linens are cold. Pulling on her robe, the one fashioned into a gown on his canvas, Kat searches the townhouse. There's an espresso pot and a used demitasse on the counter in the great room. At least he had presence of mind to have coffee. A hopeful sign.

She hears movement in the studio, so Kat climbs the creaking stairs, which announce her presence. Franco has his back to the door. He's dressed for work. Jeans, sleeveless tee, old sneakers. He turns her way. Shadow beard, uncombed hair.

"May I come in?" Franco's studio is private domain, a pictorial diary of his thoughts, his soul. Even in Torcello, Kat knows entry is by invitation only.

The artist nods while pushing a worktable into a corner. The room's a jumble. Dismembered wooden pallets form a precarious pile by the doorway. Stools, worktables and benches await their destination. Canvasses, mostly bare, lean against walls. The tallest rests on an easel and is covered by a drop cloth. The second Madonna.

Kat goes to the east window, the canal's quiet in the early morning before the tourists.

"What do you think of the light?" Judging by the look on his face, Franco's unmoved. "Massimo picked this studio because he imagined you might enjoy the differing landscapes, the access to light from dawn till dark."

Franco drops a handful of brushes onto the worktable where they clatter and roll onto the floor.

"He isn't here, is he? Massimo's abandoned me, Kat. He knows I'm not a canal artist. I don't paint the countryside. Look at my Tuscan work. It's shit." Franco's eyes are almost black.

Kat retrieves the brushes, sets them in a cup. Franco faces her, silent. She wills him to say whatever is on his mind, get it out.

"You know what I am, Kat? I will show you." He waves a packet of charcoal sketches ready for the art shop in Florence in her face. "I make line drawings of old buildings for tourists who think they buy art." He shoves the packet into her hand and strides to the veiled canvas. Pulling off the cloth, he reveals the second Madonna.

"I paint outrageous icons to send the media into a frenzy, the idiots celebrate this as talent." His hands chop the air, underscoring his words.

Kat would like to tell him he's wrong but her eyes are fastened on his Madonna. It's early in the work, more impression than painting, but clearly it depicts a woman giving birth from the perspective of the crowning fetus, the woman's head thrown back, her face in a grimace of agony. Refine the image, adorn the Madonna with symbols. Kat knows when this painting is made public the media will go wild.

"Massimo said this painting is your back-up, for when you need media attention."

"What Massimo means is, if I fail as a master painter, this is all I have. Don't you understand?" He flails his hands about. "Massimo abandoned me to this island and a residency for which I'm not prepared. Meeting art critics and Texans." He spits on the floor. "*Vaffanculo!* Chiara will divorce me, take my children. I'm finished." Smashing his fist into the cup of brushes that Kat re-assembled, he sends them flying, where they bounce across the uneven boards.

Kat jumps. She witnessed Franco's panic in Vancouver after Faith's death but never his rage. Still, she's always known it lay beneath. Here in Torcello, it frightens her. Surely the gods of Rome didn't bring them together for this. Kat grabs Franco by the arms, holds him so tight that he ceases his rant and shivers.

"Franco, *caro. Per favore.*" She loosens her grip and the artist's response is to turn away from her, retreating to the far side of the studio. Kat's first instinct is to counter his irrational fury with reason but she felt that shiver. Enfolding him in her arms, she begs that he hear her out. His back is to her; he's rigid, but his breathing slows as she whispers: "*Caro*, it's your fear that shapes these feelings." Laying her head on his shoulder, she says: "Massimo pays for everything: your lodging here, your studio, your children's clothing." Franco stares straight ahead, his face unreadable. "Beyond that, Massimo foots the bill for sending *La Madonna di Levi* on a road tour through Europe." Kat edges closer to the window to speak to Franco directly. He stares beyond her, does not blink. "*Caro*, Massimo's time and expertise guide your career, but it's *your talent* that secured the residency and the installation of *La Donna.* Massimo believes in you."

Franco wilts, leans against the window frame. Kat takes his hand and the warmth of him calms her own ragged emotions. An artisan's hand. She presses her lips to his flesh.

"As for your marriage, Massimo's a pragmatist. He's aware of what brought you and Chiara together and that she's tired of motherhood. He understands that I am your muse, Franco. He knows that I am your love."

The studio is silent. Franco finally returns her gaze. She still can't read him. "There's something I want to show you." Kat moves towards the door. "Come Franco, it's time to see the future."

From the *vaporetto* the foot path into town passes by Kat's bedroom window as it snakes along the edge of the canal. Constructed in a herringbone pattern of pink and blonde brick, it's a new structure so tourists can walk without fear of twisted ankles on ancient cobblestone. Often the passers-by stop at the Devil's Bridge to drape themselves on the steps and take selfies for Facebook unaware of the bridge's foreboding power. The water traffic in the canal is composed of the few outboards that are moored outside the residents' home awaiting their next trip to Burano or beyond.

Linking their arms, Kat gestures toward the town. They walk without speaking. Franco focusses on the passing scene. He can't help it. He's a born painter.

Crossing a white stone bridge they arrive at the edge of Torcello. The street vendors sell cold drinks, bags of chips and frozen ice cream bars. To the right a low-slung building painted deep yellow announces that it is La Locanda Cipriani. The only inn on the island, it is a storied place. Princess Elizabeth and Ernest Hemingway were guests. Some day, tourists will note that the renowned artist Franco Ghibellini lived in the pink cottage beside the Devil's Bridge.

In the centre of the village Kat points to a remnant of brick wall which acts as backdrop to a collection of heraldic crests carved in stone. Portions of ancient columns dot the grasses, some standing, others recumbent. An outdoor *museo*. The town cistern, gone dry centuries ago, and a crudely-carved throne complete the collection. The marble chair is an immediate attraction for children who race to climb onto the weathered seat. It's from the 5th century, according to Vittorio. "Everything in Italy is old, Kat," Franco says.

She motions that he follow her through the arcade on the far side of the basilica to the dirt path beyond the church. On this grassy pathway, they're alone. Only songbird warbles reach the painter's ears in the overgrown meadows of Torcello. Kat stoops to admire a clutch of wild poppies up close. Wishes she'd brought her camera.

"Where are we going, Kat?" She feels his agitation even in this peaceful setting.

"To the future, darling."

His face remains guarded.

At the top of a hillock, they arrive at their destination overlooking the lagoon. This is where Kat glimpsed their future, it's where Franco needs to find it too.

"Shut your eyes." She places her hands over his eyes.

Franco's generous smile returns. "Games, Kat?"

"More important than that, *caro*. Think of the Ghibellini farm. What do you see when you look around?" She steps back a bit, gauges his mood.

"The farmhouse, the outbuildings, the vineyard. Up on the hilltop, there's the skyline of San Gimignano." His eyes still shut.

"Exactly, the skyline they call Manhattan, but it's not, is it?"

"No, that's an insult. A name to amuse tourists. That skyline is ancient, the skyline of the Ghibellini." He's still, waiting.

"Yes! When you look toward San Gimignano you're viewing the past. A past you know well. A past you walked away from to pursue your dream." Kat positions herself behind Franco, wraps her arms around his waist. "Now, open your eyes. Tell me what you see."

The light of the Veneto bathes the lagoon in a silver glow. The wide horizon trick the eye into believing that sea and sky merge into a luminous ether.

"How is that? I can't tell where the sky ends, the water begins." His voice almost a whisper.

"Exactly." Kat sighs in triumph. "You're looking at the future. Undefined, unknown, even to a man like you who examines life in detail."

Franco cocks his head. "But a pilot must see the horizon. Otherwise he doesn't know where he's headed. He's doomed. I am the same, Kat."

"That's why you need a navigator, Franco. Someone familiar with the dangers and opportunities ahead. It's why you depend on Massimo and why you feel his loss here." She pulls him closer. The muscles of his abdomen tighten. "You're the artist, Franco. This elegant vista represents your future."

Stepping back, she gives Franco space. "When you need me, I will be your navigator. I'm just as capable as Max." Franco considers the silver and verdigris, the trick of light in the shimmering lagoon. After a time, he speaks.

"All right, Kat. You be my navigator." Turning, he takes her hand. With an intake of breath and a voice so soft she struggles to hear him: "*Andiamo.*" Let's go!

CHAPTER FOURTEEN

Torcello

It's been five years since they shared the blue houseboat in Vancouver. Although they were not yet lovers, there was plenty of flesh in view. Faith and George were so careless in their intimacy and casual nakedness that, in such close quarters, it set Kat's teeth on edge. Surely young Franco felt the same. And in the Florence apartment, his questioning wife tracked Franco's every move. Hiding their stealthy midnight visits and stifled moans. Not wanting Chiara to hear what she must have known was occurring in the bedroom next door. On Torcello, they're alone. At last.

Franco requests a meeting with Massimo's caretakers, the second appointment with the husband and wife in five days. Initially, Franco focused on his studio. There was no sleeping cot for late nights. Did Massimo forget? Vittorio's brows rose at the request for a bed in the studio. Essential, the artist insisted. Also, a good-sized mirror to lean against one wall, but lightweight enough to move around. Where to purchase quality paints, brushes, charcoal and canvas? For these, Kat suggests they ask the Guggenheim staff.

The demands for his studio exhausted, Franco turns to their domestic scene. When Kat arrived on Torcello the discussion around the management of the townhouse took less than ten minutes. Does Franco care which fruit and vegetables Anna purchases at the market? The list in his square handwriting says he does. Pomegranates, pears, oranges and figs. Preparation for a still-life composition? Perhaps he's more particular about what he eats than she'd understood.

Vittorio and Anna step over the stone threshold and move into the great room as one unit. Tentative, as though they've never been there before. To set their minds at ease, Franco allows that the schedule and details of household upkeep should remain as originally agreed upon with Kat. Anna gives the painter a quizzical look, opens her mouth to comment and then thinks better of it. Sensing her irritation, Franco paces, hands stuffed in the pockets of his jeans. Hands better served by holding a paintbrush than ordering fruit. "But the wine, we want to change the source. Kat enjoys these more." He hands Vittorio a list of whites, reds and Proseccos from the Ghibellini Winery with his brother-in-law's contact information at the bottom. "Same price, better grapes."

Scrutinizing Franco's list, Vittorio grasps Franco's intent. Although Massimo underwrites the costs of the townhouse, decisions going forward will be made by the painter. The two men meet eyes, Vittorio nods and they shake hands. Anna stomps out, shaking her head.

It doesn't take much time to establish their own workday routine. Franco rises with the first hint of morning light, while Kat pulls the linen sheet over her head, trying to ignore his movements as her painter prepares their espresso and morning meal. Fruit for him, cheese or prosciutto for her. By nine, the first sputters of the outboard interrupt their conversation. Grabbing her canvas tote filled with necessities like her ballet flats, iPad and camera, Kat steps into her *Bella Figura* stilettos and follows Franco out to the launch.

As they glimpse the low-lying profile of the Guggenheim, Vittorio slows the engine and searches for a vacant mooring. At the stern, the painter leans into Kat, his hand resting on his muse's waist. She's reminded how much he still resembles the boy she knew in Vancouver. The painter who found the sky too cold, the city of glass and steel impossible to capture on canvas.

Today, the artist is intimidated by the wild array of works hanging on the walls of the Guggenheim and the expectation that he produce a painting worthy of permanent display among them. A work which represents the magnitude of his talent. Another *capolavoro*, a new masterpiece.

Inside his glass studio Franco stands stock still. He stares at the light streaming through the clerestory windows and leaves the worktable untouched. Instead, he hovers over Kat's desk as she catalogues his sketches and organizes the photos taken under his direction.

At first, the staff appear receptive to the new painter in residence, but Franco soon delegates all social discourse to Kat. Her Italian isn't up to the task of communicating his goals or even to identify the tools she needs at her workstation. Franco watches her flounder but makes no attempt to rescue her.

By day's end her neck muscles knot and even Franco's ministrations don't relieve the pressure across her shoulders. When she complains, he wails: "I don't know how to be their painter in residence!"

Beside her in bed, his hands glide over her torso, stop to caress her breasts. "I'm not a monkey in a zoo. I create alone, you know this." Kat does know this. His head nuzzled in her armpit; he weeps. "How to do this thing, Kat?"

While Franco struggles to make his art at the Guggenheim, she obsesses over how he's being perceived. Kat knows the staff are keen to fête their new artist, but they need something to work with. A small win. Franco has given them nothing beyond sullen looks and silence.

Outside the director's office, Kat smooths her hair and checks her posture.

She's become careful with her dress and accessories (*tre, signora*). This morning, she asked Franco to do her hair. Italians, and Venetians in particular, are quick to judge appearance, social station or age. That the staff at the Guggenheim have formed an opinion of her, she's certain. If she makes a good impression, she has a better chance of navigating her painter's success.

"Eva, may I have a moment?"

Settling into the chair across from the Guggenheim's director, Kat's mindful of how to present her thoughts. She's practiced Italian phrases but Eva's grasp of English is solid and she has kind eyes, so Kat's encouraged.

"Franco's on *un avventura scoraggainate*." A daunting adventure. Memorized last evening.

Eva nods. A trace of amusement crosses her face. "*Vuoi parlare in inglese?*"

Relieved, Kat leans forward and rests her hands on the lacquered desktop between them. "Everyone wishes for Franco's success, but certain things need to occur for this to happen."

Kat explains the artist's creative process. Early on, there's the research. Choosing the subject to be painted. She explains that she accompanies Franco, takes photos he desires from many angles, in light and shadow.

When he is ready the artist paints, often for long stretches of time, all night even. And always alone.

Eva places her hands over Kat's. "Ah! This could prove a problem, couldn't it?"

"If there's some compromise, I think the painter can adapt. If he's free to research and plan off site, if he can block out his canvas privately, I think he could be convinced to continue the work in the public studio." Kat watches Eva's reaction.

"And the administrative duties? The weekly management meeting to update the board, the speaking engagements, greeting visiting dignitaries?" They're getting to the crux of the contract.

"These I will do. Except for the speaking engagements in Italian." They both laugh at the possibility of that happening. "Franco will prepare those himself. However, I can greet the dignitaries and introduce Franco to keep disruptions to a minimum. As for the administrative tasks, I have a background in marketing. I believe I can be useful in presenting his works."

Eva sits back in her chair, waiting to be convinced. "How so?"

"Franco makes numerous sketches before he puts an image to canvas. Postcard size and then progressively larger drawings. His sketches sell commercially in Florence. I think a series culled from his research could be made into serigraphs to sell in the museum gift shop." There it is, the small win. Is it enough to buy Franco freedom to create?

"Kat, this is wonderful news." Eva claps her hands in anticipation. "How soon do you think we could see some sketches?"

It's Kat's turn to be amused. No doubt Eva's already envisioned the spot to display Franco's prints, already heard the sound of the cash register ringing up sales.

"Give me a couple of weeks, then we can look at possibles. I'm thinking groups of three and singles."

. Eva nods. "*Si, si.*" Picking up her mobile, she keys in a meeting two weeks hence. "Together, we will decide what to present to the board." She claps her hands again. "*Va bene.*"

"Franco, *vieni,* come to bed. I've wonderful news, *caro.* Come lie with me and I will tell you what I've done."

The republic of Venice is formed by an archipelago of 117 islands in a shallow lagoon. Traditionally known as *La Serenissima,* she is linked by 127 canals and connected by 409 bridges. It is the bridges that have captured the painter's imagination. He will make a bridge the subject of his masterpiece, but which one? There are 409 to select from, after all. Free to choose his own schedule, Franco relaxes into his search for his model. His purchase of a guidebook is too reminiscent of Nick for Kat's liking.

Vittorio's intimate knowledge of the waterways of the lagoon proves more useful. His antipathy toward Franco fades with this opportunity to showcase his own knowledge. He charts a marine map of the lagoon's islands, identifying the bridges and plotting routes that will make the best use of their time.

Franco approaches the bridges from land and sea. Kat follows a pace or two behind, awaiting his clipped commands for photographs. Sometimes, he stops to make sketches. Not every bridge deserves this treatment but a surprising number qualify. When Franco settles into his line drawings, Kat retreats to the Guggenheim to plant vignettes of Franco's progress in the director's mind. The artist is producing as many sketches as she'd promised. Bridges, *cosi tanti ponti,* so many bridges! Kat sighs. It's been a month and Eva asks when may she see the drawings? Her formal Venetian demeanour gives Kat little room to manoeuvre. The painter will deliver the sketches very soon. Kat hopes this to be true.

"I've changed my mind. *Niente ponti piccoli.*" Franco, head down, forks Anna's handmade *spaghetti al limone* from plate to mouth.

"No bridges?" Kat sets her fork aside. They've been researching bridges for six weeks. *Is this some artistic temper tantrum?*

"No small bridges, not no bridges, Kat." Franco grins and shakes his head. "*Scusi,* I speak too fast for you."

This jibe at her language abilities sets off an ache in her temple. She's the one taking the flak at the Guggenheim for this extended research and the artist's absence. She's the one tripping over vowels and consonants in staff meetings or mangling gender and tenses with visitors. She's the one whose head aches.

"I talked to Massimo today. He says one bridge, up close, that's easy to recognize, but not yet seen from the vantage I paint." He resumes twirling his spaghetti, fork to mouth in a fluid motion. "A huge canvas, like the bridge itself. It's *perfetto.* So, I do it."

"Do you know which bridge, then?" Kat's lost her appetite. Between photographing bridges and attempting to meet the administrative demands of the Guggenheim, she's bone tired. Massimo makes a decision in Florence between sipping his caffè and aperitivo, and Franco embraces it. "Did Massimo tell you which one to paint?"

"Rialto. Dei Sospiri. Scalzi." Rising from the table, Franco places his hands on her shoulders, massages the unyielding muscles. "Don't worry. I choose. I'm the painter, not Massimo."

She leans into his torso. "Which, one then?"

Franco returns to the table, plates the mixed greens, drizzles them with olive oil and passes a bowl to Kat. She tops up their tumblers with the family's Vernaccia. They crunch and sip. But no words.

"I review my sketches and your photos, make a choice."

"Tonight?" Please say tonight, Franco.

Greens consumed, his tumbler emptied, Franco kisses Kat's cheek. "Yes, tonight, Kat." He climbs the noisy wooden stairs to his studio. The scent of his kiss remains. Sweet and pungent.

Kat's well past REM sleep when she becomes aware of the warmth of his body. She's forgotten about the bridges. What surfaces is the joy of living with Franco in Torcello. The freedom to share a meal undisturbed, to shampoo his hair as they shower, to laze away a Sunday afternoon with her head in his lap as they listen to his favourite musicians. Unknowns with names like Nicolosi, Spadi or Galiazzo. To come together naturally, no need to guard against a betrayal of their liaison. No more longing for her man as he mounts his wife on the other side of a shared wall. For Kat, Torcello is delicious reward for the years of wanting.

Their sex is languid. Before, there was always the fear of detection. In Torcello, it seems that Franco's appetites are never satisfied. Kat realizes how often Chiara was the woman who met those needs. Now, it is Kat he reaches for at dawn, halfway through their sleep, or when they arrive home with empty stomachs, or as he's watching his soccer games on the television. But Kat's a willing partner who imagines herself greedier than he.

"Ponte dell' Accademia."

Responding to his persistent mouth, his cool hands as they seek to bring her closer, Kat ignores his words. It's only as she guides him inward that Franco's message registers. Kat's painter has decided on his bridge. Tomorrow, she'll tell Eva and then she'll deliver the promised sketches.

Tuesday nights are not Kat's favourite. It's when Franco dials up his family and sometimes, his estranged wife. The *Madonna di Levi* did not flee to Florence untethered as Massimo predicted. It seems Chiara never left the Ghibellini farm. It seems she's not estranged after all.

The children, in matching cotton pyjamas of predictable pink and blue, are ready for sleep. Mariola and Bri perch on a chintz sofa in front of a computer in a room Kat doesn't recognize. The children tuck in between them. Sometimes Chiara joins the scene with the infant Mateo. Franco leans in toward the screen. He relates fanciful stories about living by a canal on a remote island. Kat's never heard a rooster crow outside their bedroom window but Franco tells them it's their alarm clock. And that the rooster is bright blue! Nor has she seen the green-haired troll who sleeps under the bridge and begs for sweets as payment for safe passage. Kat feels anxious during these attempts to connect with the babies. If it weren't for her, Franco would be with his family.

Franco urges Kat to read a bedtime story. He wants her to bond with his children but Kat's certain she'll never be anything more than a stranger in their lives. Still, for Franco's sake she does her part, selecting children's books at Libreria Toletta or sometimes the Guggenheim gift shop. When she holds up a brightly-coloured book, there's squirming and excitement on the screen, but Kat can see Mariola and Brigitte prompting the children.

Tonight, she reads about the adventures of the puppet from Lucca named Pinocchio and his wood-carving papa, Geppetto. Franco stands behind her where, out of camera range, he's stroking the small of her back. When she stumbles over a word, he's quick to correct her. And some words are easy to mess up. *Asciugamano*, for instance. It means towel. Such errors wouldn't bother her except she knows Chiara lurks nearby. When Kat blunders, she's certain his wife has a laugh at her expense.

"Where's Mateo? I'd like to see my baby son sometimes."

Just as Kat suspects, Chiara's in the room and moves into range with the nursing Mateo camera-ready. The husband and wife converse about their boy's progress. He's gained half a kilo in the past month, his diet includes strained peas and carrots, some fruits now. Chiara assures the painter that the baby is being fed fresh produce from the farm, no bottled purée.

"He's a good baby, Franco." Chiara caresses the downy head as Mateo suckles. Kat stares at Chiara's breast, feeling she's time-travelled back to Florence. His nursing wife, their growing family. This is Franco's world. Kat will always be a spectator, even as he caresses her back in Torcello while he skypes his family in Tuscany.

After the kisses have been blown and the good-byes waved by tiny fingers, mercifully, the screen goes black. Kat heads to the fridge. It's time for aperitivos and Kat needs this drink.

"It's hard to connect with them this way." Franco accepts a flute of wine and sips, focussing steadily on Kat. She knows that look. He has something in mind and he's contemplating how best to reveal his thoughts. Usually, it's a plan already set in motion, leaving Kat no choice but to agree. "Let's go to the farm. Friday, I think." Franco's expression pleads that she go along with this idea.

"Better you go alone, Franco. I'll stay here. That way the children will have their papa to themselves." *Remember Chiara's crotch grab, at the Christening feast? This way you two can fuck your brains out.* She pours another drink. Franco's still on his first.

"Not without you, it's never good when we're apart." *Skyping is hard enough. Don't make me live under the same roof as your wife again,* her silent plea. Slow kisses, his hands trace patterns over her body, the painter knows what pleases. "We go together on Friday for a few days, yes?"

Kat closes her eyes. Answers with the only response her painter will accept. "*Si.*"

CHAPTER FIFTEEN

San Gimignano

"First door on the left at the top of the stairs." Franco's sister directs Kat to her room. "The nursery is next door."

Kat takes in the excess of white pillows piled on the queen-size bed. There's a view overlooking the vineyards and the medieval towers in the distance. From her hotel room in San Gimignano, she had wondered what went on here and now she's in the middle of the family.

"And Chiara?"

"Across the hall." Brigitte points to the door directly opposite. "To be near her babies."

Franco mounts the stairs two at a time, carrying their bags.

"You like it, Kat?" He sets their bags down on the bench at the end of the bed. "There's a huge bath and spectacular views. I love this space." He throws himself onto the bed. Pillows tumble to the floor.

"Are we sharing it?"

Franco stares at her. "Of course."

"Chiara's across the hall."

Brigitte is still standing in the doorway.

"It's OK, *cara*. My family knows we share a bed in Torcello. Chiara knows this too." A faint smile on those curvy lips. "Did you think they did not?"

Brigitte coughs, or more likely, she chokes on Franco's words. Kat's quite used to interpreting Ghibellini signals. His sister isn't fond of their relationship.

"Do you wish a different room, Franco? There's the one at the back of the house, the one we shared as girls but it's a proper bedroom now." Bri looks from her brother to Kat. She betrays her uneasiness as she shifts from foot to foot. "More privacy?"

Franco ignores his sister. "Come see the bath, Kat." Hands on her waist, he steers her into the spacious, white-tiled room with a free-standing cast iron tub under a wall of windows. It's as lovely as Franco says, but Kat would still prefer some distance between them and Chiara.

"Couldn't we use the room in the other wing?"

But Franco is adamant. There will be no room changes. "That one looks out on the driveway. It doesn't have a tub. This one is much better. You'll enjoy it."

Brigitte shrugs and disappears around the corner. Kat listens to her footfalls on the stairs.

Franco hangs his shirts in the wardrobe but Kat takes her time. She's in no hurry to join the family gathered in the kitchen below. Franco is energized. First, he wants to visit the barn. With the death of his father, Mariola's husband is the oldest family member on the farm. It's important to pay him respect.

"But you inherited the farm from your father, didn't you?" If Franco is the sole proprietor of the vineyard and its winery, why is the brother-in-law so important?

"It's true, I inherit this." He locks eyes with her. "I am the *padrone*, although I leave things for others to decide. For me, being a painter is what matters." A gentle smile. "Luigi, he's *capofamiglia*, head of the family. I give him respect for his age, his wisdom. It's important I go to him first."

How little she understands this country, this culture. Massimo's lesson on *Bella Figura* was an inadequate introduction. She still views Italy with the eyes of a Canadian. In Italy, respect is a prime social motivator. Respect for appearance, for status and for age. It's the opposite in Canada, where anyone over thirty is old. Where you're only as good as your last win. And where tending to an extended family is considered an impediment to success, a burden.

"I meet you in the kitchen." A kiss on the cheek and he's gone.

From the window, she follows his path. Shirt sleeves rolled, slim legs striding along the gravel road to the red roofed barn. With her index finger she traces his silhouette on the glass. *Mio amato pittore*, my beloved painter. Mine. An incantation to the receding figure.

Mid-June and the Tuscan countryside heats up. Even with the windows open, the air is warm and still on the second floor. Kat strips off her jeans and blouse, slips into walking shorts, whisper-thin tee and strappy leather sandals. Pulling her hair up into a ponytail, she feels the damp at the base of her skull. She repairs her lipstick. It's time to get down those stairs.

Even during preparations for the main meal, the kitchen feels much cooler than the second floor. The terra cotta tiles underfoot and an industrial fan whirling overhead effectively reduce the heat. Mariola, the eldest sister, cuts pasta on the wooden counter along the back wall. A giant pot of water boils on a nearby burner, its steam sucked away by a commercial oven fan.

Two oversized tables take up most of the space. Stacks of ceramic bowls and an array of cooking utensils lie within easy reach of the cook. At the table near the door, Brigitte and Chiara supervise Franco's children at their noontime meal. Penne with tomato sauce, which Antonio and Katerina fish out of plastic bowls with their fingers. The infant sucks at Chiara's breast. There's another child-sized bowl and spoon filled with goop. Mateo's taking semi-solids. Kat marvels at how quickly this newborn is morphing into a child.

When he sees Kat, Antonio yells "*Nonna*," and waves. His hand is covered in sauce well up his arm. Kat mimics his finger wave in return.

Brigitte gestures at a chair. "Once the children are finished, we'll eat. Ma's preparing the *prima*." Mariola nods her acknowledgement in Kat's direction and continues rolling pasta. Kat spies the magnum-size pitcher of iced water in the centre of the table. Her mouth feels like sandpaper.

"Would you like some? It's hot in Tuscany. I imagine the weather is cooler in the lagoon." Kat nods. Brigitte pours her a glassful.

Glad for the ice water, Kat pulls out a chair at the far end of the table, facing Chiara. This is getting awfully familiar. First the bedrooms in close quarters, now sharing the table with Franco's wife. Will she never escape this scenario?

"Where's Franco?" Chiara rests Mateo on her shoulder and pats him firmly to extract a baby burp.

"He went to the barn to see Mariola's husband." Kat sips her ice water, eyes Chiara. The Madonna looks quite at home in the Ghibellini kitchen. Barefoot and with her blouse unbuttoned.

Mariola turns and smiles. "Bene." Respect. Franco is doing what is expected of the returning *Padrone.*

"And leaves you to welcome his family." Chiara shifts Mateo to her other teat. Kat looks away, doesn't want to be reminded of the intimacy of Chiara's hold on Franco.

"He'll be here momentarily." Kat takes a hard swallow of the ice water and then a second, lifting her face to the overhead fan.

"I'm surprised you're here, Kat. I understood Franco wanted to spend time being papa to his children, not take a holiday with his mistress." Chiara spits this out in accented English.

Ah, is this how it is going to be, Chiara? Public insults and in my language, too. Kat glances at the others. Mariola's back is to the room and she doesn't miss a beat with her rolling pin. But Brigitte, wiping tomato sauce from Antonio's hands, stops mid-stroke.

"I'm not his mistress." *Not much of a comeback but what else is there to say?* Mistress is an antiquated term but not surprising in a country that honours ancient traditions whether they make sense or not.

"No? There's another word that's more accurate, I agree." Chiara casts her eyes in Mariola's direction and in that familiar soprano voice asks: "Are we having *Sugo alla Puttanesca* today in honour of Kat's visit?"

Rising to her feet, Kat knocks her chair askew and it clatters to the floor. "You bitch!" is all she manages. And then a quiet "*scusi,*" uttered to the sisters. Kat rights the chair, then retreats, letting the screen door slam behind her. She runs to the end of the terrace and takes refuge in a wicker chair tucked in the corner, where she's suddenly cold. She shivers, attempts to calm herself. Failing, she lets the tears come. *So unnecessary Chiara, I didn't ask for this any more than you.* She sees him from a distance and her stomach knots. How to tell him of the mess his women made while he was being the good *Padrone.* But there's no need. As soon as Franco gets closer, he knows something's amiss.

"You're crying, *mia amore.*" On his knees in front of her, he wipes her tears. "Kat, what's wrong?"

She could tell him it's her own fault, that Chiara felt threatened, that she shouldn't have responded to his wife's barb, but she doesn't. Instead, she rats Chiara out.

"I know the word *puttanesca* means slut or whore! It's stamped on bottles of spaghetti sauce, even in Canada. Chiara knows that." In the end Kat doesn't feel any better for the telling. "I'm going to the hotel in San Gimignano. It's best."

"No one insults you in my house. No one." He's on his feet now and his voice is low and hard. "Chiara lives here because I permit her but if she cannot behave, she will leave, not you." He turns to go and then stops. "*Mi scuso,* but I'll make it up to you. Please wait here." Dark eyes beseech Kat. He needn't worry, she has nowhere else to go. Franco disappears into the farmhouse.

She's fearful when Franco's pushed to his darker side, wishes now that she'd kept Chiara's words to herself. She listens hard, hears his voice. Forceful. Then a female voice but not Chiara's. Franco shouts become louder and then other voices chime in, all angry. One of the children is crying. She caused this chaos. Kat covers her ears until the silence returns.

She counts the rows of vines as the noonday sun beats down on the grapes and the heat rushes the terrace in waves. A man with a stiff gait and a wide-brimmed hat appears on the road from the barn. Luigi's home for lunch. Her appetite's vanished. No matter what Mariola ladles onto the pasta this afternoon, for Kat, it will be Whore's Sauce.

Franco at their bedside, kisses Kat awake. "We're going swimming, *cara mia.*"

Rousing from sleep, Kat orients herself. It wasn't a nightmare after all; they're still at the farmhouse. She retreated after a lunch where all eyes were on the Madonna and the *puttana*. Under Franco's watch, his wife managed to keep her thoughts to herself. Exhausted from her morning with the Ghibellini family, Kat fell asleep to the shrieks of the children as Franco ran circles around them in the garden below. Now they're going for a swim.

"I didn't bring a bathing suit." Kat wants to lie low, would still rather retreat to San Gimignano.

"We swim naked." In response to the incredulous look on her face, he says: "It's Italia, Kat. I swim naked my whole life."

"And who, exactly, is swimming naked with you, Franco?"

"Ma, Luigi, Bri, the children, of course. Everyone."

"You're serious." Kat's wrapping her mind around the multi-generational image that pops up in her mind's eye.

"Come on, Kat. You wear a robe to the pool. No one needs to see you naked, except me." He grins. "Besides, *i bambini* are excited to show how they swim." Taking a fleece robe from the wardrobe, he holds it up for her.

"Is Chiara swimming too?" She has had enough of the Madonna for today.

But Franco's not listening, he's calling to the children below. "We're coming, *ragazzi*, my children, wait up."

The pool is in a clearing between the vines and the out-buildings. Beyond the rolling hills in the distance stand the towers of San Gimignano. As they approach, Kat makes out the swimmers. Mariola, Luigi, the worn old man whom Kat met at lunch today, Brigitte and the children. No Chiara in sight.

Franco drops the towel knotted at his waist and cannonballs into the middle of the pool. The effect is as he hoped. Water everywhere. Shrieking children and scolding adults. Franco bobs to the surface and stretches out his hand, a broad grin on his face. "Come on, Kat. It's wonderful." He looks every bit the Tuscan farm boy.

Luigi methodically laps the length of the pool, undisturbed by Franco's arrival. The sisters tread water, watchful of the children in their water wings.

"*Vieni*, Kat." Franco dives, surfaces under Antonio who whoops in delight. With Antonio clinging to his neck, his papa swims towards her. "*Nonna*, come on in. No one's looking."

It's only a swimming pool in a vineyard in Tuscany. This is what Kat tells herself as she unties the robe and it drops to the ground. Franco's eyes follow as she walks to the shallow end, descends the cement stairs and glides into the deep. The water's cold but she's already doing laps beside Luigi, enjoying the push of her limbs against the water.

Franco swims up and gives her a chlorine-scented kiss. He dives beneath her, swims away and then returns, beside her again. The farm boy enjoying his summer. It's no surprise he wants his children raised here. Kat reaches the shallow end and leans against the wall, keeping her nipples below the water line.

"*Guardami!*" Chiara prances on the diving board. When did she arrive?

Naked and poised to dive. Her blonde curls shimmer in the sun, but it's her groin Kat notices. Her mound is shaved clean to showcase a tattooed star. When did that happen? There's no tattoo in the painting of *La Madonna di Levi*. She had a full crown of blonde pubic hair when she posed for the painter.

Mariola dips Mateo in and out of the water. He coos his delight. Franco and Brigitte keep the older children near, but Luigi's finished his laps. He climbs the cement stairs and towels off his private parts which are purple from the cold.

"*Guardami,* watch me 'Tonio! *Guardami 'Trina!*" Chiara arcs into the pool, glides the length of it and surfaces next to Kat. "*Ragazzi,* no arm bands. Let's show papa." She removes Antonio's floaters. The three-year-old flaps his arms and legs, motors across the pool toward Franco who raises him high in triumph. Cheers erupt as Antonio swims to Chiara and then Brigitte. He stays afloat so long as he kicks. Franco turns him on his back and instructs him to float. Antonio gives it a try but begins to sink. Franco plucks him up and sends him swimming toward his aunt again.

Katerina turns out to be an adept swimmer. Face clenched in concentration, she works her arms and legs methodically. Franco turns his daughter on her back and she floats on her first try. You'll give your brother a run, Kat thinks as she watches Franco's babies.

"Now watch Mateo swim." Chiara holds the infant above the water.

Franco's alarmed, but Mariola smiles. "He swims, Franco."

Chiara lowers the infant into the pool and propels him forward before letting go. Holding his breath, Mateo makes froglike motions with his arms and legs. Swims. Just as he did as a fetus in an amniotic sac, Kat imagines. When he raises his head, Chiara lifts him from the water. "See, he swims too." She kisses her baby's head. "*Bello* Mateo." Kat wonders if the Madonna's every caress is meant to make up for her past intention?

Kat reads the regret on Franco's face. He's missing out on moments like these. In Torcello, Franco sacrifices fatherhood for the sake of his art. Skyping isn't enough. Massimo thinks it's a fair trade, but he doesn't know Franco's pain.

Ma and Bri lure the children back to the farmhouse on a promise of strawberry gelato. Luigi's disappeared. It's just the three of them now. Chiara takes another showy dive off the board and swims close to Franco, yelling: "He's hard! Who's he hard for, Kat?" Franco grins and swims away. Kat isn't playing their games. Hoisting herself out of the pool, she pulls on her robe. Wringing out her ponytail, she settles on a chaise.

Husband and wife silently swim laps. It's all too tame for Chiara, who climbs out and wriggles into her shift. Tossing a *ciao!* over her shoulder, she flounces back to the farmhouse.

Franco pats the mattress of a chaise that he's moved to the ground. "Down here, for privacy, Kat."

Hauling her own mattress to the grass, they lie side by side on their bellies, bare butts to the sun. The steady heat eases Kat's tension.

"You like this?" Franco's skin is bronzing in the Tuscan sun and his teeth gleam white against his skin. Two days' growth of beard, his curls in disarray, he peers into Kat's face. Nose to nose.

Oh, what's not to like here, my love? Lying naked under this Mediterranean sky with you by my side. There is that pesky issue of your wife of, course. But … Franco interrupts her reverie.

"Being with my family, the children." He leans closer, drapes his arm across her back. "You like this?"

Kat deflects the question. "You miss the children. I see it." His frenetic excitement whenever he's with his babies arises from his need to make up for his absences. *Is it enough?*

Franco moves closer, burrows his head under her arm. "How to make it work, Kat? I am too far away."

"After the residency, we could live closer, San Gimignano perhaps." Kat imagines herself in the hilltop village, enjoying the thought of all that distance from Chiara. She thinks she could settle in quite well behind the ancient walls.

"What if they lived with us?" He raises his head. "Would you do that?"

"If that's what you want, but we'd need help. Who else would live with us?"

"You could learn to be their mother, it's not hard to love them, I think." He whispers this into her ear, as if to seduce her, but Kat's already won. The months alone in Torcello were gut-wrenching. That separation was for the benefit of the children as much as it was for Franco. She gave them a chance to be a family without her.

"*Mio caro*, I already love your babies." Franco kisses her neck. "In Torcello, all of my time is for you. I support you at the Guggenheim, take the photographs you need. It doesn't matter what time of day or night, I'm there for you. Now, if I had the responsibility of the children too …"

"It would be like when I live with Chiara." Franco heaves a sigh. Defeated.

Kat wants no more words. Today has left them both in need. Rolling onto her back, she mouths his name with her breath on his ear and wraps her legs around his torso. Musk clings to their damp bodies in the Mediterranean heat. She tangles her fingers in his curls, draws his pelvis closer. Kat hears only his breathing. Feels only his mouth seeking and the reach of her painter's hands. Knows only the moment he enters her. Knows that, when they make love, they're one.

With his towel knotted at his waist and the laces on his sneakers undone, Franco enters the kitchen. Kat, feeling naked despite her fluffy robe, hangs back in the doorway. Brigitte's husband Martino has joined the adults from the swim. Martino, is the town notary. He and Luigi read newspapers spread out on the table and chain-smoke cigarettes. Paolo joins them for the smoke, but he's engaged in conversation with Chiara. The sisters prepare aperitivo at the back of the kitchen. No sign of the children, they're asleep upstairs.

Franco edges his naked torso between Luigi and Paolo to grab two tumblers, filling them with ice water from the pitcher on the table.

"You worked up a thirst, Franco." Chiara abandons her conversation with Paolo and rises to her feet. Except for the hum of the ceiling fan, the room is silent. "I want to thank you for making it so clear to me and your family that you're committing adultery by fucking Kat in public." Her hands on her hips, her chin held high, Chiara challenges her husband. "So many witnesses. Not just here, but the workers in the barn, in the fields. Very gracious of you to give us such a vivid picture of your whoring, *Padrone*." Her eyes come to rest on Franco's crotch.

A trickle of semen slides down Kat's thigh and she can't look at Chiara, or anyone. Isn't this the point in an Italian film when somebody pulls out a gun, while somebody else digs the pit and checks the lime supply? She knows she's thinking like a TV crime-show fan. This is Italy, they do things differently but she has no other frame of reference.

Franco goes rigid as his wife speaks but he makes no defence. Instead, the Ghibellini son picks up the tumblers and bows slightly in Chiara's direction. He gives a glass to Kat and drains the other in one long swallow. Handing the empty to Luigi, he sends his wife a long, hard stare. Kat's certain that Franco's wordless message to Chiara is *vaffanculo*, fuck you.

"*Vieni*, come." Franco's places his hand on the small of her back, a familiar and reassuring gesture.

Halfway up the stairs, he whispers: "Massimo sends the limo tomorrow morning. Chiara needs a change of scenery. She'll stay with her papa for a few days and we can have some peace."

On the top step, in a voice meant for the ears in the kitchen: "The view from the bath is *fantastico*. You'll enjoy it. *Vieni con me, mia cara.* Come, my darling."

CHAPTER SIXTEEN

Venice

Franco's wearing his expensive Luzli headphones. Aluminum gizmos that collapse into a stack of metal squares and fit in the palm of his hand. More likely, they'll be tucked in a jacket pocket for easy transport. The headphones, with their hand-stitched leather ear cushions, arrived shortly after their return from the farm. A gift from Massimo, the only person Kat knows who would purchase such extravagant headgear.

Lounging on the sofa in shorts and a tee-shirt, Franco rests his bare feet on the coffee table and watches replays of Gli Azzurri, Italy's national soccer team, which trains in Florence. A lazy Sunday afternoon. Kat needs his help, but the painter ignores her. Undeterred, she stands in front of the television screen. Irritation flutters across his face as he sets the video on pause and removes the headphones. Why is she interrupting the beautiful game?

"We need to pick the line drawings for Eva. I can't do it alone." Kat points to the stack of sketch books on the dining table.

"*Spazzatura*, garbage, Kat. Give her whatever you want, except for the Accademia sketches." He reaches for the remote but Kat's not satisfied with that answer. This is too important.

"They're not trash; some are quite lovely." Kat approaches the sofa, raises her bare leg over Franco's thighs and faces him. He's stopped looking at the television screen, at least. "The line drawings of the Old Masters are as valued as their paintings. Da Vinci, Raphael, Michelangelo." He's listening.

"Michelangelo's are studies, not quick sketches like mine." He rubs her inner thigh, his other hand still on the remote. She guesses that for Franco it could go either way. Football or sex. She's not giving up. This time she will get her way.

"For me, line drawings are a glimpse into the artist's psyche, even into his soul." Hitching herself out of his lap, Kat plops down beside him but snakes her bare leg over his. The artist's fingertips travel up and down her thigh in slow motion. "They're the artist's first ideas, before he interprets them for the world." She places her hand on his thigh, close to the heat of him. "I love your line drawings, Franco."

Abandoning the remote, he pulls her close. His mouth comes closer. She has his attention.

"When I live in a home of my own, do you know how it will be?" She pulls back to gauge his reaction.

Franco's confused. "That's a strange question, Kat."

"There will be alabaster walls with ivory-coloured sofas and linens. The furniture would be weathered like driftwood found on a beach or whitewashed like an old barn To contrast, a chandelier of crystals or perhaps Murano glass. One thing is certain. I'd collect line drawings, Ghibellini line drawings. Mounted and framed in ebony wood. The only colour would be the on rim of the secondary mat. Red, green or indigo. It would be my Francesco Ghibellini line-drawing galleria."

"This …" he gestures to the room bursting with Tuscan colour. "It's a *carnevale* in comparison to what you dream." This time he runs his hand along her cheek. "Does it make you unhappy, living here?"

"Nothing here is mine. Apart from my books, which are becoming side tables, it seems." She gestures to his empty beer bottle perched on her pillar of art history tomes. "There is *Il Elefante.*" Franco's first commission rests on the mantel above the fireplace. "And of course, you." Franco resumes the kissing phase of their lovemaking.

"I am the most precious?" A parade of kisses, each one deeper and slower than the last.

Before Kat can think of a smart retort his hands up race up her legs, removing her underwear. A quick unzip and he's entered her.

"Does everything come down to sex, *mio amore*?"

Franco positions her hips. "*E calcio*, soccer."

As the silvery sky darkens above the lagoon islands, Franco agrees to review the drawings. Discussion, fervent and prolonged, follows. Kat hasn't lost her eye for what sells and pushes her point when it comes to what's marketable. Franco worries that unfinished images with his name attached will not represent the quality of his art. In the end, urged on by empty stomachs, they come to agreement.

The most evocative drawing is a triptych of the Bridge of Sighs, with exterior and interior perspectives. After the copies are made, Kat will have these originals framed just as she described. She's determined that these line drawings will be the start of her galleria.

Different in appeal is a comical sketch of Anna, hands on hips, standing on the Devil's Bridge as she chats with Vittorio in the outboard below. Wife giving husband his daily chores. Kitschy enough for the casual tourist, it will sell in the smaller sizes.

Lastly, a delicate rendering of Ponte Rialto, the white bridge every tourist traverses, will also do well. People like to be reminded of their travels.

Securing these sketches in his leather portfolio, Franco asks Kat which day she thinks would be best to transport the canvasses for the Guggenheim project. The gallery is closed on Tuesdays, so would that be a good day set up his studio? Does she think Eva can organize a delivery boat for the canvasses that quickly? He grins, knowing he's surprised her.

"You're ready!" Giddy, Kat hugs her painter. "*Mio caro*, we'll make it happen. Eva will be so excited. First the line drawings and then your canvasses. Tomorrow, I bring my first group of visitors to you as well. What a splendid week this will be!"

This is Kat's first presentation for an English-speaking tour. Her mouth is dry as she pats down the skirt of her red linen shift more times than necessary. Stepping into her purple stilettos, she's ready for The Friends of the Royal Scottish Academy.

The major collection of the Scottish gallery is made up of the paintings by its members. Works that illustrate the artist's talent, similar to the project Franco is creating for the Guggenheim. The difference is that paintings in the Scottish Academy are vetted by member artists. They determine whether or not the newcomer is acceptable. She imagines Franco's reaction if the artists on the walls of the Guggenheim decided if his work would hang or be rejected. *Idiota. Barbaro. Stupido.* Although Jackson Pollock or Salvador Dali might have found a Ghibellini project of interest. Franco's completed work will be judged by the artistic committee that has already vetted his portfolio and found his work to their liking.

The Scots are prompt and expectant. Nine pairs of eyes peer into Franco's glass-walled studio. These visitors aren't artists, they're donors to the Scottish Academy. Kat hopes their interest in art will make them a bit more simpatico than the Texans. Eva, impeccable in business black, introduces the group to the painter-in-residence's assistant, as Kat is officially known, and then moves out of the way.

Worldwide, critics have already had their say about Franco's work. The media argued he's a Warhol genius or a sycophant of religious tradition. Kat's confident she understands her artist and his work more intimately than any of the critics. Perhaps even more than Massimo, but this is her first opportunity to represent her painter in public and Eva's presence is reassuring.

The highly-organized Massimo made certain that a laminate copy of *La Madonna di Levi* arrived in time for the display. The 40x32-inch image is much smaller than the original but the quality of the reproduction is good. He also forwarded a dozen magazines featuring articles about Franco's opening show, the painting, the artist and his naked muse. These glossy images stoke painful memories of her time in Torcello but Kat is sure they'll be of interest to the tour.

She invites the group to enter the studio of resident painter Francesco Ghibellini, explaining that the artist's work-in-progress would be installed tomorrow. Kat describes the research that precedes the artist putting paint to canvas, explains the unoccupied workspace. Nine pairs of eyes keep watch.

Directing their attention to the laminate of *La Madonna di Levi*, she suggests some may have heard of this work. This results in a chaotic outburst of commentary in heavily-accented English from the Friends of the Scottish Academy. Kat's next suggestion is that they have a look at the journals. They need no further encouragement. One man, a head shorter than Kat, describes the group's interest. Franco's Madonna was a topic of debate among the artists of the academy: Would they admit a painting like *La Madonna di Levi* into their gallery? Would they even paint such an image? There's much discussion around the subject matter, religious content being a daring topic to some, outdated and irrelevant to others, in the non-Catholic country.

The Scot elaborates: Did the rules of the academy function as a censor to their own artists? Did they paint what they thought would be acceptable or were they brave enough to paint like the Italian? It seems

Franco's *La Madonna di Levi* generated brouhahas over the very process by which the Royal Academy of Scotland adjudicates its own works.

Eva and Kat listen carefully. Eva because the Scottish brogue is thick as glue to her Italian ear; Kat because she wants to remember every word for Franco. She thought he'd be especially interested to hear that the artists didn't know if they had the courage to paint as the Italian paints.

Eva leads the Scots down the white-walled corridor, past Mondrian's block compositions in red and grey, to the alcove where Franco's other painting hangs.

"While *La Madonna* made news worldwide, another rendering is his masterpiece, *La Donna al Chiaro di Luna*," she tells them. The painting, framed in pale antique gold at Massimo's request, is the smallest in the room. At Eva's invitation, the Scots move in to get a better look. "You've never heard of this work, but a bidding war ensued among serious collectors. It's our good fortune that the owner decided to share the *capolavoro*, or masterpiece, with our gallery. *Grazie,* Kat."

The tour group scrutinizes *La Donna* and her patron. A woman with a halo of red twist curls points to Kat's earrings. Is she also the model? Kat admits that she is, although she didn't sit for the painting. It was a surprise. She describes how *La Donna* symbolizes feminine wisdom taking on the wounds of the world, but suggests their time will be better spent asking the painter about the meaning behind his art. *Andiamo,* we'll meet him now.

It's a ten-minute stroll from the Guggenheim to Ponte dell Accademia where the artist's working. At least she hopes he is. Vittorio was to have him there by two o'clock. It's coming up on three.

Kat leads the Scots along Calle San Cristoforo, a canal street lined with red brick walls and wrought iron gratings. Two women from the group pause before a jeweller's atelier featuring unique designs of amethyst and mother-of-pearl. They catch up as their colleagues snake past the *cicchetti* bars, tiny stand-up restaurants where customers nibble on seafood delicacies and wine. Just as it appears she's taking them down a dead end, Kat turns onto Rio Terre Foscarini. The Scots, a nimble lot, keep pace. The broad thoroughfare, flooded with sunlight, leads them back to the Grand Canal.

"There he is." Franco has set his folding chair on the wooden dock of a gondolier station. Wearing a straw hat against the sun, his back is to them. He's wearing a white shirt with sleeves down today, beige trousers and is barefoot in his runners. Italian men favour bare feet in summer shoes, unlike the Scots who choose socks and sandals just as Nick preferred. Head bowed and pencil in hand, he's probably forgotten she's coming. Motioning the group to follow her across the bridge and down the embankment, she comes up behind him. She places her hand on his shoulder. Of course, he knows it's her.

"*Ciao, mia amore.*" Standing, he greets Kat with formal air kisses and then a brief touch of lips. "*Senore e senori, benvenuto. Sono Francesco Ghibellini.*" Her painter introduces himself to the group, then offers Kat his folding chair and his hat. *C'e troppo caldo* to be bareheaded in this sun, especially near water. The Scots are transfixed. Nine pairs of eyes track his every move. Kat suggests he explain why he chose Ponte Accademia, what the work symbolizes. Running his fingers through his curls, Franco warms to his subject.

"The bridge represents transition." Kat knew Franco was talking about his life as much as his career. He pauses to smile at her before continuing. "Of the bridges on the canal, this is the only one made of wood, although it's reinforced with steel." The rustic quality of the wood calls to him, reminding him that, from humble origins there comes great beauty. He takes the Scots to vantage points below the bridge. Then, they troop after him onto the deck. A few tourists gather to eavesdrop.

"The intricate pattern of the wooden trusses allows glimpses of changing vistas as you travel its boards. Look how the perspective shifts. In life this happens also, our point of view changes as we journey."

Kat, perched on his stool, her eyes shaded by the brim of his hat, watches her painter. The Friends of the Academy send a steady stream of questions his way. When he's excited his hands move faster than his lips. He motions broadly. His English is holding up well; he hasn't needed to draw her in once. Instead, she's a blissful spectator to Franco's performance as he describes his passion. Her cell trills. It's Eva. A reminder that it's time to gather the Scots and wrap up the tour.

Re-entering the narrow Calle Santa Agnese, the Friends of the Royal Academy are deep in conversation about Franco's decision to produce the image of the bridge on three panels in distinctive styles. The redhead with the corkscrew curls keeps step with Kat, a sly grin crossing her face.

"How did a woman of your vintage ever snare a gorgeous laddie like Francesco Ghibellini? He's quite delicious." Raising her pencilled brows, she expects an answer.

Kat forgets to watch the cobbles, loses her footing as her heel catches between two stones. Her shoulder lands hard against the brick wall.

"Are you alright?" The woman helps Kat to her feet and retrieves the stiletto from the cobblestones.

Kat's ankle feels strange, full. She's about to put her full weight on it when one of the Scots intervenes. He's a first responder back in Glasgow.

"Let me have a look. Sprains and breaks can be tricky, disguise themselves." He's down on one knee, manipulating her foot and ankle before she can protest.

The foot and ankle seem sound. "Hairline fractures do occur but you didn't actually fall on it, so probably less chance of that. Try bearing weight, but slowly." Kat's embarrassed that her ankle is derailing the tour when it was going so well.

Attempting to bear weight on the offending foot, she cries out in pain. Without hesitation, the first responder and a volunteer link their arms around her waist and instruct her to put hers over each of their shoulders. Locking their free hands with hers, they secure her position. She objects to the fuss. The first responder says: "It's this or we make a human chair and carry you back." Kat agrees to walk assisted.

Behind her, a sing-song voice says: "I've your shoe." Twisty-curls dangles the purple stiletto like she's won a prize.

To Eva's surprise, the Scots deliver Kat to the director's office and elevate her foot on a chair. The pain subsides. Kat would like to go back to her office but Eva won't allow it. She dispatches a staffer to the cafeteria for ice chips. Placing the bag of ice in a linen towel, the Scot wraps around Kat's ankle. He leaves Eva to watch over the wounded assistant.

"It was my own fault. That redheaded woman with the crazy curls asked me a rather rude question. She shocked me, so I wasn't paying attention to the cobbles. Lost my footing."

"What'd she say that would upset the enigmatic Kat?" Eva refreshes the ice chips, rewraps her ankle.

"How did a woman my age attract Franco, or as she describes him, a gorgeous laddie. Called him delicious. That's when I lost my footing."

Eva's grey eyes meet Kat's and she laughs. "Bold, isn't she?"

"In Canada, they're called cougars. Women who prey on desirable younger men. Is that what people think, Eva? I'm a cougar with a young lover? That's not how it is." It's so unfair. In Venice, is she considered a predator? This, after being labelled a whore in San Gimignano. Tears threaten to overwhelm Kat's composure. It's the shock of the tumble, or is it because she's beginning to understand how the world sees her? Franco is, after all, twenty-four years her junior.

"I meet people from many cultures. Make judgments sometimes. Perhaps gain insights." Eva shuts the door to her office and perches on the edge of her desk. "What I observe is that English-speaking people value two things: money and sex. That's how they measure everything. How much money will that painting fetch on auction? The young woman marries the older gentleman. His money buys her body."

Kat agrees. Before meeting Franco, those would have been her thoughts. That's the reason she hid her feelings, her desires, even from herself. She wouldn't be that kind of woman. Until he came to her that awful night, and she believed they were equals.

"Italians, on the other hand, value passion and family." Eva interrupts Kat's reverie. "We have a passion for our work—making pasta or painting a work of art—it doesn't matter what. It's the respect for the craft that counts. More important is love for family. Between a man and woman the greatest fusion of passion and love can happen. *Delizioso sesso*." Eva screws her index finger into her cheek and laughs again. Kat knows this means the meal tastes good.

"But no one worries the age, Kat. In Europe there's a tradition of seasoned women and their protégés. The woman is wise enough to appreciate the young talent, his fresh spirit. The artist feels secure, knows he's loved and wishes to return that caring. *È fantastico* when that happens. Everyone's content. Everyone who understands. Twisty-curls doesn't understand. You're English too, Kat. Perhaps you feel ashamed of your passion, but don't. *Non e necessario*."

Kat's ankle feels better. In fact, her soul feels better. Eva's words have come when she needed to hear them.

"You're in a place most *simpatico*, this gallery. Are you familiar with the life of our benefactor, Peggy Guggenheim?"

Kat admits her knowledge of the woman is scant.

"Peggy was a great lover of men, especially beautiful men." Eva lets out a girlish laugh. "She married one husband just because he was so lovely to look at! Peggy adored young artists. She had a great appreciation for them, for their work. You see proof of that on our walls." Eva turns to the shelves behind her desk, retrieves a worn book and leafs through it for pictures of Peggy Guggenheim. She slides the book across the desk to Kat. "Even though she was an American, she wasn't ashamed of her choices. Once, she was asked how many husbands she'd had. She answered: "Do you mean mine or other women's?" *Appassionato*. She was passionate, our patron."

Kat stands with some difficulty and hobbles toward Eva with arms outstretched. She embraces her Venetian colleague, whispering: "*Grazie, grazie mille.*"

"You're where you belong, Kat. I know this from the first day I meet you."

CHAPTER SEVENTEEN

Torcello

Her ankle recovers with the help of Franco's ministrations. Ice, long after Kat thinks it's needed, elevation of her foot every time she sits and frequent massage, where his nimble fingers soothe her aches. The painter's a born caregiver, it seems. His brow furrows as she tries the stilettos but when her ankle proves fit, he relaxes into a grin, gestures with his thumb and index finger under his chin. *Perfetto.*

Since housing his canvasses at the Guggenheim, the artist works there most evenings. Kat eats plates of Anna's prepared pasta alone or, if she returns to Venice, shares a quick meal with Franco. It's tiring trekking back to Venice but then she knows that he eats a meal. When she's not there he works until a security guard sets the gallery alarms at eleven. Doesn't bother with the snacks Anna prepares for him. Kat thinks Franco pushes himself beyond reasonable limits, but this is how he creates. The work becomes the focal point of his being until it is complete.

His Guggenheim studio is transformed. A trio of floor-to-ceiling canvasses occupy the wall below the clerestory windows. The long table, now protected by a drop cloth, is positioned in front of the glass wall. Paints, brushes and oils, rags and utensils end up on that table. Kat and her workstation are relegated to the farthest corner to allow the artist room to move about.

Kat's not complaining. Now, she's privy to the subtle processes of Franco's art. He works on his feet. Painting, reviewing his canvasses, peering at her bridge photos on his oversized laptop, or revisiting his sketches. Wearing Massimo's hand-tooled leather headphones, an iPod clipped to his belt, he moves to the beat of the music from laptop to canvas or brush. Kat hadn't known he listened to music as he works. When she inquires what he prefers, he shrugs. Vivaldi, Puccini, Spadi.

"Spadi?"

"Street singer in Florence, a friend from secondary school. I introduce you sometime."

So much she doesn't know about her painter, his life before.

Tuesdays are different. Arriving at the gallery late after lingering over breakfast, they work side-by-side until Kat leaves in mid-afternoon. Franco stays on until six, careful to return to the townhouse on time for the skype session with the children.

It's almost seven and Franco's just walked through the door. Kat prepares an antipasto plate for him since he's missed their aperitivo snacks. Hands him a flute of Prosecco. He kicks off his runners as she dials up the farm. Every Tuesday Kat endures this ritual of connecting with the farmhouse in San Gimignano. She's never certain if Chiara will appear and what injuries she will inflict.

Franco apologizes for eating while talking but he's hungry. Mariola worries that he's looking thin. Kat agrees with her. Franco's always lean, but he's become angular.

The skype sessions follow a pattern. Franco enjoys being papa to Antonio and Katerina, chatting about their day, enjoying their perspective of life on the farm.

"The cow chews on the hay, papa, and then it turns into milk and comes out of her tummy."

At Franco's insistence Kat reads a bedtime story to the children. She grits her teeth and complies. Tonight, it's *The Dancing Water, the Singing Apple and the Speaking Bird*, an Italian tale of trickery in which three children are kidnapped and replaced with puppies. At first the king, their papa, doesn't seem to notice he's raising puppies instead of humans. In the end he realizes the puppies aren't his children and goes in search of his offspring. Franco assures Kat that his children will love the crazy story, just as he did.

Mariola and Brigitte can be counted on to keep the children engaged and the conversation flowing. Chiara's absent. Franco's wife hasn't appeared since calling him out six weeks earlier. Usually, one of the sisters brings Mateo to the camera but tonight the baby isn't with his siblings.

Kat stumbles through the first part of the fairy-tale, but the vocabulary is wicked. "There are too many vowels in Italian," she moans in her defence.

Her painter leans in beside her, reads along silently and helps with pronunciation when her tongue tangles around the sounds. He's right, the children enjoy the story. When Kat holds up the picture of the papa with his puppy children, Antonio breaks into a loud guffaw. Points to the screen with chubby fingers, *cucciolo*, puppy. Katerina's as amused by her brother's reaction as she is by the story.

Kat's about to sign off when Franco asks after Mateo. A glance passes between the two women. Hesitation and then Brigitte responds: "Chiara's with him, he's not been well."

Franco sets aside his half eaten antipasto. "What's wrong with him?"

"I'll get Chiara." Mariola disappears from camera range.

Chiara appears, hair carelessly pulled back and without makeup. She strikes Kat as no more than a child herself, except for the shadows under her eyes. She explains that Mateo is feeding poorly, that his body is damp with perspiration each evening.

"Why are you hiding this from me?" Franco yells at the screen.

Chiara flinches and replies that she was bathing him when Franco's skype came through. Unable or unwilling to bear Franco's anger, she turns away from the screen.

The artist paces the great room. He hasn't stopped since the screen went black. "Three women, all with experience raising children, are looking after Mateo. True?" Kat tries to reason Franco out of his over-the-top reaction to a sick child. Franco continues to pace.

"It's like this for a week, Kat. Not right. I should go to him."

"Is that necessary? You have responsibilities here, too. You can't leave every time your child gets a cold. You're an artist, you have a reputation to consider." The attempt to re-focus his thoughts backfires.

"Be practical, be rational. That's most important to you, Kat." Franco's oft-kissed lips curl into a sneer.

His words sting. They're not even true. If Kat was being practical or rational, she'd hardly be in Torcello. But she knows Franco's words are rooted in before, in Vancouver. *Yes, I sent you away, but you're wrong. It was my love for you, the kind you feel for Mateo that exiled you. I'm not heartless.* She tries again.

"Remember when Antonio was ill, you stayed up all night, bringing his fever down and singing sweet songs to your boy. Such a good papa.

I remember, Franco. You showed me how to bathe him. In the morning Antonio was better. The illness passed."

Franco stares at her from across the great room, from across the divide in their thinking.

"It's true, children get sick." He concedes. "Always, it seems bad and then they recover." His shoulders relax, he shrugs out the tension.

"It'll be that way this time too, Franco. You insisted that Chiara take Mateo to the doctor in the morning. If it becomes serious, we'll go to the farm." Wrapping her arms around him. "You need to be calm, Franco; your children need their papa calm."

Franco splashes wide arcs of grey paint on the middle panel. Then smaller distinct arcs of brown. Kat sips a *caffè Americano*. He chooses to be silent today. Even their lovemaking this morning was wordless. He's still irritated with her for not agreeing to head to the farm yesterday. But Kat doesn't buy into his panic. Hers is the reasoned response. It's possible she'll never see family the way Franco does. *Never become that Italian in her thinking.*

Still, when Franco's cell buzzes, her gut knots. It's Chiara. Franco turns his back as he answers. Gestures like this shut Kat out, remind her of the temporary nature of their relationship. Much as she wishes it different, he is hers only for the moment.

"We need to go to Torcello, Kat. I want to skype the farm. See Mateo and understand better what the doctor said."

He insists they board the *vaporetto* which means taking two separate boats and trekking over several foot bridges, but Franco won't wait for Vittorio to arrive from the island. Standing on the outer deck, Kat wraps her arm around Franco. He stares at the expanse of water between them and Torcello.

"The doctor noticed a rash on Mateo's chest. He found a purple shadow in his groin. Chiara said he cried when the doctor explored the area." Franco turns to Kat. His eyes are dark with worry. "The doctor took some blood but wouldn't make a diagnosis. He suggested that further investigation was required." Kat shares his worry. The baby's illness is more complicated than the common cold she'd predicted.

Mateo lies naked on Chiara's lap so that his father can see for himself what the doctor found. The bruising, if that's what it is, in the groin area is minimal, perhaps confused with chafing. The same could be said for the pinpoint rash on his trunk, a form of prickly heat perhaps. That's what Mariola thought. But the one discovery that can't be easily explained is that Mateo has a thickening under his rib cage, a swelling. Chiara didn't notice it until the doctor pointed it out. When she feels for it, as the doctor showed her, it's there. When her fingertips trace the edges of the mass, the baby mewls.

"I think that hurts him, Chiara. Please stop." Franco's so close to the screen that it feels to Kat he might disappear into it.

"When will we know the blood test results?"

"Tomorrow." Chiara wraps a cotton blanket around her son, who seems content to be cradled in her arms. "Mateo's refusing the nipple, sometimes. He's lost weight in the past month. Just a few grams, but it's not good." Mateo's mother stares at her digital husband. Exhausted and fearful.

"You didn't notice any of this before? The rash, the bruising?" His voice louder with each query. Placing her hand on Franco's thigh, Kat motions him to stop. None of this is Chiara's fault.

"Just the sweats and not feeding. Maybe the rash, I don't know, Franco. Babies get heat rash in the summer. Antonio did, also Katerina." Her voice thins and Chiara turns away from the screen. Mariola offers to hold her nephew. A tiny foot escapes the blanket as she places the baby on her shoulder. Kat hopes it comforts Franco that the sister he thinks of as his mother is caring for his son.

Mateo isn't alone in his night sweats. The first week of August, the warmth of the Mediterranean sun lingers in the dark, even in the Veneto. Franco's restless, disturbed by unwanted dreams. Kat wakes, comforts him in the way she knows will best settle the artist. Afterwards, she rests her arm and leg over his damp body, anchors him so that he sleeps.

Come daylight they look shopworn despite their attempts at grooming. They could take a day off, but Franco follows Kat's suggestion, keeping to routine as they wait for Mateo's test results. After all, as she suggested, this may end up being nothing at all.

On the boat to the Guggenheim, he seems himself again. The distance between them evaporates. He's explains why the recent art installation on the island of San Giorgio Maggiore is all wrong. It's part of the International Biennale, an exhibition that draws artists from around the world. Their works are placed throughout the Veneto. Kat's captivated whenever Franco shares his thoughts on the art. Another glimpse into the painter's psyche.

The work at the mouth of the Grand Canal is a 30-foot-high, inflated statue in white latex. It's a naked, stylized dwarf with Thalidomide limbs and a pregnant belly. At night, the statue glows pink or purple. To Franco's classical sensibilities, the piece screams "inappropriate!"

"The placement of this joke, at the entrance of the Grand Canal in front of San Giorgio Maggiore—a classical Renaissance basilica—is disrespectful," Franco says. Kat reminds herself that *La Madonna di Levi*, the naked mother of Christ, appears against the backdrop of the Duomo and wonders how that's a lesser crime against the church.

"Imagine, Kat, you're a visitor to Venice and this is your first view of the celebrated Grand Canal. You are greeted by this neon monstrosity glowing purple in the night. *Orribile*, hideous!"

Hearing Franco discuss the perils of art installations gone wrong, a sense of gratitude wells within her. This talent, this gorgeous light, is part of her life … she pulls him closer. Franco stops mid-sentence. A tender kiss from those full lips erases any vestiges of yesterday's sneer. Her painter has returned.

Franco executes a delicate brush stroke reminiscent of the work he was doing when Kat first met him. His cell vibrates on the worktable. His paint-smeared hand motions Kat to pick up the phone. She looks at the number and recognizes it's not from Chiara. It's Massimo.

"Shall I put Franco on speakerphone, Massimo?"

"Yes, you both need to hear this. Take care of him, Kat." Massimo sighs and then inhales deeply. He's pulling on a smoke.

"I spoke with my daughter an hour ago. The news is troubling, Franco. Mateo's blood results aren't normal. Too many white cells. He needs more tests."

Franco doesn't bother to wipe the paint from his hands before grabbing the cell from Kat.

"Why did Chiara not call me? I'm Mateo's father." Panic and anger roughen his voice.

"Because she knows I can help. *Ascoltami*, Franco, *listen* to me." A command.

"*Si, si.* Continue, Massimo." Franco's fingers tremble.

"I was able to speak with the head of oncology at Ospedale Pediatrico Meyer. Mateo has an appointment at eight tomorrow morning with *Dottore* Ricci. He comes well recommended. You need to take the train tonight, stay at the apartment and meet Chiara at the hospital.

I've sent the limo to San Gimignano. She and Mateo will stay with me tonight. And if Kat can join you, that would be helpful. I'm sorry to bring you this information, but I'll find the best care for our boy. I promise you that, Franco."

Visibly paler, Franco stares wordlessly at his phone. Kat responds.

"Massimo, we'll get the next train. I will call you when we're on our way. *Grazie per tutti*. Franco appreciates your help."

Franco finds his words, his pain reducing them to a ragged whisper. "Oncology? Does he have a diagnosis? What's making my son sick?"

"Not yet. Dr. Ricci's the one to make that call, but Mateo's ill, Franco. He's seriously ill. *Mi dispiace*. I'm sorry." There's a catch in Massimo's voice. Another draw on his cigarette and he disconnects the call.

CHAPTER EIGHTEEN

Florence

It feels like she's living among ghosts again. Alone and without purpose, that sense of dislocation she endured on the houseboat after Faith's death has returned. Except in Florence, everyone's still alive, they're simply absent. Franco spends his day at the hospital accompanying his son to tests, then waiting in hallways for results. Drinking too much cafeteria *espresso*.

She tried going with him. It was clear that all Franco's energy went to his son and to helping his wife get through the crisis. Kat's in the way of their need for rapport. Instead, she kills time walking familiar streets, browsing through the art history books in the apartment or surfing the Internet looking for information about Mateo's illness. They have a diagnosis: acute lymphoblastic leukemia. Survival rates for infants are in the twentieth percentile, according to several sites. Kat keeps this to herself.

Agnes appears each morning for the same old routine: laundry, cleaning and prepping their evening meal. Today, she adds a bowl of pears to the table. The fruit is for Franco who, if he had an appetite, would devour the lot. Of course, there's plenty of cold Prosecco for Kat. Just as when she lived there, the two women communicate with an occasional *grazie* and *prego*. After chores, Agnes delivers fresh pasta dishes to the hospital and replaces Chiara's soiled clothes with clean ones.

The humid air is stale in the apartment. Kat roams from room to room, opening windows in search of cross ventilation. In the end she gives up and retreats to the terrace where there's a faint breeze. Leaning back on the chaise, she listens to the cathedral bells toll and waits for her painter to return.

Franco rearranges the fruit as if planning a still-life, chooses a golden pear and sinks his teeth into the ivory flesh. Juice streams through his five o'clock shadow. Kat takes in his slender fingers, his square palm as he wipes his chin; wishes she could photograph this moment and all the other ordinary moments. Photograph his hands, his eyes, his lips, and the naked shape of him. Keep him.

"Tomorrow, we meet with the doctors, learn what can be done." Franco stops chewing. "I'd like it if you were there when we get out of the meeting. Chiara's asked Massimo, too."

"*Certo*. We'll both be waiting." Kat busies herself plating their meal of mixed greens with cold seafood pasta. "What time?"

"We meet at one. Mateo has another indignity to endure in the morning. They wish to put a needle in his testes. How can they, he's so tiny? The doctor says it won't hurt him but come on … he *feels* things, for Christ sake." Franco's voice breaks. "I insist to be there. I'll hold him myself. *Il mio povero bambino*."

Kat embraces Mateo's papa. Holds him until his sobs subside into silent tears, which seems worse, somehow. "Oh Franco, *mi dispiace*, I'm sorry." Right now, if Kat could take Mateo's place for Franco's sake, she would. She has, after all, lived her life. Made her choices. The baby is an innocent.

Dinner proves futile, neither have an appetite. After a time, Franco turns on the television. Kat watches him while she tidies. He can't sit still or focus. Irritated by the national news from RAI-TV, he calls Berlusconi an idiot and shuts down the television.

"Let's go out to the terrace. It's cooler there." Franco leads her to the farthest wall where the view of the Duomo is best. He envelops her in his arms. Together they take in the sooty Florence sky.

"She refuses me to stay overnight with Mateo. Chiara says I abandoned him and now I don't get to be alone with my son."

"Chiara's wrong." She tangles her fingers in his curls. "In the four months you've been away you've been a most attentive father." Runs her hands along his neck. "Can you say every man who must be away from his family has abandoned them? Every truck driver, salesman or pilot?" A rigid cord of muscle runs from his neck into his skull. She caresses it, keeps her touch light for fear that pressure will cause him pain. "What is it you hope to do by staying overnight, Franco?"

He lays his head on her shoulder. His breath, hotter than the August air around them, warms her cheek.

"Be alone with my son. It's not really alone because the nurse checks on him every hour. But just Mateo and me, just for a few minutes." His voice breaks with emotion. "I want to hold him, sing to him, tell him things he needs to hear from his papa." Kat imagines Franco alone with his infant son in the antiseptic hospital room.

"I want to pray with him." He weeps. Kat wipes his cheek.

"I'll speak to Massimo. You'll be with your son, *mio amato.*"

Chiara's latest cruelty is too much, even for her. *Basta!* Enough. Isolated from his beloved son, Franco is forced to watch Mateo's fate play out from the sidelines, creating unbearable pressure. He needs relief, if only for one night. "Do you remember the first time we made love in this apartment?"

Kat feels his smile against her cheek. Perhaps she can distract him from his pain.

"Yes, I remember it was the end of my third day here. I lay in my bed, hardly able to believe I was with you. But I was also confused. By the Italian language, Chiara's pregnancy, baby Antonio so tiny and most of all, your intentions."

They've never discussed their decision to become lovers. "Three nights I waited. We were together only one time in Vancouver, so I thought I must be wrong. I thought: 'Maybe he wants me here to be *nonna* to Antonio.'"

"I stood outside your door for two nights, afraid to enter your room." Franco kisses her mouth.

"Afraid?"

"Si. I did not want to be a brute. You might refuse me, be insulted and leave. I'd just found you." More kisses. "But you did something the third day. I knew then, Kat."

"What did I do?" She's curious. Kat knows she hides her feelings well.

"There." He nods toward the dining table where the family congregated when Franco was home. "Chiara was speaking to me in Italian and you were at the far end. I turned to explain the conversation and I caught you." Grins at the memory. "A look of *amore* on your face, *lussuria*, lust so strong that I could feel it here." He touches his cock. "When you realized that I understood, you blushed and turned away." Tracing his hand along her cheekbone. "I knew then, Kat wants me in her bed." Franco surprises her by tickling her ribs. "And I was right. " Surprised again, this time by the pealing of her own laughter, Kat finds the courage to ask: "Just for tonight, can we be those people again? Be the Franco who made such tender love but was so diligent that I figured you'd planned your moves in advance?"

He guffaws, not unlike Antonio only deeper. "I did plan many times in my mind and here." The cock again.

"We made passion all night. It was …" Kat doesn't have words. Besides, Franco knows.

"You want this tonight? *La passione e il cazzo*, the passion and the fucking because we did both?" He grins, ear to ear. Oh, her painter remembers.

"Franco! *Bruto*." She kisses him hard. "*Si, voglio tutto*, yes, I want it all."

The August heat is oppressive. Her sweat mingles with the remains of their lovemaking. For Kat sleep is futile. The ghosts have invaded her dreams There's a price for every action and Franco's already paying, they remind her. Abandoning any notion of sleep, she listens to her painter's breathing, synchronizes hers to his. Outside the bells chime sporadically in the night. Kat prays to the ancient gods of the Pantheon. Protect Franco once again.

Kat makes her way down the glass-domed corridor of the pediatric hospital where families congregate. She spots Massimo at an Arborite table, his long legs stretched out in front of him. He attempts to lounge in the unforgiving plastic chair. Immaculate in his pin-stripes, he could not be more out of place. He checks his watch, probably wonders where she is and when he can duck out for a smoke. The hospital rules are hard on Massimo's habit.

"Ciao, Massimo." Air kisses and a quick embrace. "Have you been waiting long?"

He shrugs and checks his watch again, peering down the corridor. "Can't be long. Even doctors are on the clock."

Mateo's workup has been comprehensive. Extensive blood work, X-rays and yesterday a cerebral spinal tap. This morning he endured a needle aspiration of his tiny testes. His metrics have been tabulated and ana-lysed. The diagnosis is clear: acute lymphoblastic leukemia. Today his parents learn his prognosis and, from what Kat's read online, this will not be a good day.

Taking the seat across from Massimo, Kat tells him to go for a smoke. She'll watch for Franco and Chiara.

"I should be here when they come out, but *grazie*." He speed-walks to the nearest exit, cigarette in hand.

When Massimo returns, Kat's still waiting. Massimo consults his watch again, offers Kat a breath mint.

"I discussed Mateo's diagnosis with two of my medical contacts. It doesn't look promising, Katerina."

"I've been surfing the Internet, Massimo. The Mayo clinic, for instance, suggests his chances for recovery are poor."

Massimo repositions himself in the red plastic chair, failing again to find a comfortable position.

"Then we both understand what's mostly likely being discussed in that conference room right now." Kat touches his wrist.

"Massimo, Franco needs to spend some nights alone with his son, just as Chiara does."

"Of course." Massimo searches the hallway. Empty.

"Your daughter won't hear of it." Kat fixes her eyes on Massimo. "He must be allowed to care for his son as he wishes."

Massimo's tired eyes return her gaze. "*D'accordo.*" Massimo nods. It will be done.

She sees them at the far end of the hall long before they see her. Franco's hunched, listening intently to something Chiara's saying. She stands and waves. As they draw nearer, she sees Franco's eyes are bloodshot and Chiara's crying.

Massimo draws his daughter close. Kat reaches for Franco, searching his face for news.

"We signed the papers for the doctors to perform palliative care." Franco walks past her to the wall of glass, stares into the garden beyond.

"His cancer's advanced, it began in utero. The doctors say some incident, that's what they call it, occurred which led to an infection. As a fetus, his immature white cells misfired in response." Franco turns back to Kat and Massimo. "He's been sick with cancer his whole life."

Chiara looks hard at Kat. "When I was pregnant, that's when this started. What happened then made Mateo sick. He was born with this disease growing in him."

What incident was that, Chiara? Your botched abortion attempt with Franco's paintbrush? Your retribution for his infidelity on the other side of the bedroom wall? Kat returns Chiara's stare. Franco grimaces at his wife's words. "The doctors can't treat his cancer. It's everywhere and his body wouldn't survive the chemotherapy or the radiation. They gave us no choice, papa." Chiara collapses in her father's arms, sobs wracking her body.

To Kat she looks more child than woman, skinny arms and legs, narrow torso. Her mop of blonde curls needs to be brushed.

"Everywhere. His spine, his chest, even his testes." Franco turns to Kat. "That biopsy this morning, it hurt him, but now no more pain. That's what palliative means. No one will hurt Mateo anymore."

"Franco." Kat reaches for him. Perhaps if she holds him tight enough, maybe she can keep them both from falling apart.

Chiara lays her head on the table and continue to weep. Massimo caresses her shoulder, looking as bewildered as a little boy. This is uncharted territory for everyone and they are all lost.

Finally, Massimo speaks. "We'll make Mateo's time with us as comfortable as possible. There are things we need to do."

Chiara lifts her head. "Papa?"

Franco and Kat seat themselves across the table. What does Massimo have in mind?

"Starting tonight, Franco needs to keep watch over his son, just as you do."

Chiara opens her mouth to protest but Massimo swiftly mimes cutting his throat. "Stop. Mateo has two parents. You'll stay with me, let Franco say his goodbyes to his son. You will alternate nights for as long as Mateo is with us."

Chiara acquiesces, as always, to her father's commands. Franco's shoulders slump in relief and he thanks Massimo while squeezing Kat's hand. She returns the pressure: *prego*, you're welcome.

Massimo continues: "Since Mateo has lived his short life in the company of Franco's family, it's time for them to be with him." Franco volunteers to call the farm. Massimo directs him to invite the aunts, uncles, his siblings, anyone who can to come to the hospital tomorrow.

"And the priest who baptised him." Chiara's request. "For his *ultima riti,* last rites."

Franco agrees to speak with the priest when he returns to the apartment to pack his overnight bag.

"And Kat, a favour from you." Chiara again. "Ask Agnes to take Mateo's christening gown out of the storage. The one you gave him. He'll wear it at his service."

"Will it fit?" Mateo is seven months old. But it was a loose, flowing garment.

"Agnes will know what to do."

Massimo will confer with Agnes over the menu for this farewell gathering. Kat cannot imagine a sadder meeting anywhere in Florence at this moment.

Franco packs his leather weekender, eats a healthy portion of pasta salad and calls a taxi. The relatives arrive tomorrow around ten. The priest will deliver last rites to the baby he welcomed into his parish only months ago. Agnes and some local caterers will keep stomachs and bladders full. Mateo Massimo will have a final feast day with his earthly family.

Alone in Chiara's apartment, the one her father gave the bride and groom as a wedding gift, Kat feels like a thief. She pours herself a generous amount of the Ghibellini Vernaccia and switches on the CD player, recognizing a teen group called Il Volo, a favourite of Chiara's. Three young men singing with the skill of men twice their age but without the wear that age brings. Unlike Rosanna in Roma, they have not really lived. Their sound is still pure. But compared to Mateo, their lives are already filled with adventures. The baby has only begun to swim.

On the terrace the light of the moon wanes in the dark Florence sky. Can Franco see the moon from his vigil? Last night he told her how she appeared to him: a woman so obvious in her love and lust that he felt confident to come to her bed. Knew he'd be welcome. He wasn't wrong but his words shocked Kat, firm in her belief that she hides herself well.

If that's what Franco saw, what of Chiara? Did she sense that this plainly-dressed woman of "a certain age" would lure her husband out of their marriage? Surely at first Chiara was confused, unwilling to believe that Kat was competition. Chiara, a stunning woman by any standard. Chiara, her papa's darling.

Kat refills her glass, glad there are no prying eyes, glad that she's drinking alone. Kat doesn't know why her painter wants her, loves her. Why he has done horrible things because of her. The only truth she knows is her own, that she'll do anything for him. It's a terrible truth because she's proven herself capable of unspeakable acts.

Kat lifts her tumbler, toasts the fading moonlight. *This love of ours, it's a frightening power, Chiara. You don't want to get in its way.*

Kat wanders about the apartment, free to enter any room, open any cupboard. She tries Franco's studio, it's locked. Top up the wine. How arduous to be forced to paint in public at the Guggenheim when he's such a private artist. Massimo wanted him in Venice, so she lured him there. If she'd patted his cheek in Genoa and took the next flight home, would that have been better? She was used to being alone, used to the endless longing. If she'd turned away, might Franco and Chiara be here with a healthy son named Mateo?

The Vernaccia drained, Kat uncorks another bottle. She didn't eat much at dinner but no matter, she's not hungry for food. Instead, she plans on drinking away all the bad decisions, all this pain. She stands at the threshold of Chiara and Franco's bedroom. A chill shoots down her spine as she trespasses, walks to the end of the empty marriage bed. The room's been stripped of personal items except for Franco's painting of his naked bride. Opening the armoire, only unused outfits sealed in plastic bags remain. A tuxedo. A lacy white—oh, it's the wedding dress.

Kat strips the gown's packaging. A floor-length silk with an intricate overlay of flowers in heavy guipure lace pools on the carpet. She drags the dress across the floor, holds it up and peers into the floor-length mirror. Even after all the Vernaccia, Kat has no illusions that Chiara's gown will fit her. Chiara's shorter and one of those impossibly low-digit sizes. Still, she holds the wedding dress under her chin, imagines being Franco's bride.

Her cell chimes. Dropping the gown, Kat runs to catch the call.

"Hello." Breathless.

"You alright, Kat?"

"Si, I was at the other end of the apartment, didn't want to miss your call. How's it going?" She stands straight, tries to sober up. Too late.

"He's sleeping. I'm naked to the waist, the doctors suggest this, and Mateo's naked too. I wrap a blanket around us so he gets not only my heat, but the cover also. He likes it, sleeps with his ear to my heart." Franco's voice breaks. "It's hard, Kat."

"Of course, *mio amore*. You're a good papa and your son is safe with you. He feels your love."

"*Mille grazie*, Kat. I need to hear this." Franco says his good nights.

Kat returns to the kitchen and finishes off the second bottle of Vernaccia.

Part way through the third bottle she curls up on the chaise on the terrace, falls asleep. Not even the heat of the morning sun wakes her. Agnes shakes her to consciousness.

"Katerina, Kat. You must ready yourself. *Il signore* expects you to meet the family at the hospital." Agnes looms over Kat, blocks out the sun.

"God, I feel like hell." She claws her way to an upright position and winces.

"Considering this," Agnes says, holding up the two empty wine bottles, "I suppose you do. Get cleaned up. I make you *la prima colazione*, a breakfast that will fix you." She collects the bottles and disposes of the evidence in the recycle bin.

Kat pads barefoot down the corridor, groggily wondering what to wear, but Agnes is ahead of her.

"I lay out your clothes. Now prepare yourself; you don't have much time."

She turns the shower dial to as hot as she can tolerate. God-awful headache. It's when she brushes her teeth that Kat realizes how hungover she is. She can't brush her lower teeth without gagging. Tries again, ends up puking in the toilet until there's nothing left. Then she retches on mouthfuls of saliva. *Jesus, Kat.*

Self-reprimand proves futile. With extreme focus she manages to put on the black linen slacks, ivory silk shift and linen jacket. Thankful that Agnes chose black ballet flats. Kat and stilettos aren't a good pairing today.

"*Mangi. Il signore* counts on you to help him today." Agnes hands her a glass of orange juice spiked with Prosecco. "*Si, bevi.* It'll help, you'll see."

Too fragile to argue, Kat drinks, then starts in on the omelette.

"Salt it. You need *sale* too." Agnes takes a seat across from Kat, arms folded on the table and watches her eat.

God, could she feel worse?

"Eggs, cheese, prosciutto. The *frittata* will fix you."

Agnes, satisfied with Kat's progress, gets up and pours them both an espresso.

"I don't drink espresso, it's too strong." She will vomit up this whole concoction if espresso is added to the mix.

"You need this after the frittata. *Si, bevi, pronto.*" Protest requires too much exertion. Kat drinks.

Agnes sips on her espresso. She's got something on her mind and it's got nothing to do with Kat's hangover.

"At ten the Ghibellini arrive but the Alighieri are already at the hospital." In response to Kat's confusion: "Chiara's family. Her father, her aunt."

It hadn't occurred to Kat that Massimo's people might want to say their goodbyes too. Massimo shows up at formal Ghibellini gatherings and pays the expenses of the artist, but Kat was under the impression that Chiara's family was disinterested in her private life.

"I didn't know Chiara's family was involved with her children."

"The Alighieri family are of a noble rank. The Ghibellini are not. They don't mix." Agnes finishes her coffee and removes Kat's dishes. Apparently, that was what she had on her mind.

"Franco's family goes back hundreds of years. The Ghibellini are part of the history of Tuscany." Kat feels the need to defend her painter despite her pounding head.

Agnes gives her a crooked smile. "Dante Alighieri invented the Italian language. The Ghibellini were warring peasants. Chiara's lineage is one of culture and education. *Il Signore* is director of …"

Kat cuts her off. "I appreciate Massimo's credentials, his connections in places of power, but Massimo himself told me he was pleased with the union between the Ghibellini and himself."

"It's because he loves the boy, is the son that was never born. *Il signore* has a dream for him, would do anything in his power to make it come true. Sorry if I offend but if you understand everyone's place, then you can make things simpatico today."

"We're saying farewell to a dying baby. I guess in Italy that's a social event. Myself, I dread it." Agnes lets out a sigh. Kat heads to the bathroom. Taking deep breaths she manages to brush her teeth and keep the frittata down.

She remembers the christening robe and asks Agnes to prepare it as Chiara requested.

"Of course, *signora*. I have to take care of this. Like the wedding gown, already hung up. No need trouble yourself about it." Agnes gives Kat a long stare.

Fuck. She forgot about the damn wedding gown crumpled on the bedroom floor.

"*Grazie.*" Kat's certain she's made an enemy today. Agnes is another pipeline to Massimo. Spies everywhere. She heads down the stairwell. Her poor head doesn't need a talking elevator today.

By the time she reaches Mateo's hospital room, the *festa* is underway. She's too late to greet the family with Franco. The room is crowded with Ghibellini. Mariola cradles the sleeping Mateo with Chiara at her elbow, while Katerina straddles Bri's lap, softly singing a tune of her own making. The other sisters hover nearby. The men gather on the other side of the room. Their deep tones act as counterpoint to the women's hushed voices.

Easy to find Franco; the unruly head of curls gives him away. Before she can apologize for her lateness, she feels a hand on her elbow, smells a whiff of tobacco. Ah, Massimo.

"So glad you could join us. You look well, considering." The thin lips masquerading as a smile. In the twenty minutes it took for Kat's taxi to cross town, Massimo's spy had managed to get a full report to her employer.

"*Grazie.* Agnes makes a mean frittata, Max."

Massimo nods his amusement at her discomfort. "Now that you are here, I wish to introduce you to my sister, Antonia."

Kat turns to see a woman who not only has the Alighieri eye colour but could pass as a mature version of Chiara. The resemblance is so strong that Kat finds herself staring. Massimo abandons them to claim Franco from the huddle of men hovering over the buffet table.

Sombre Alighieri eyes take her in. Kat doesn't flinch but braces against the worsening ache at the base of her skull.

"We can speak in English. I studied in England … at Cambridge." Antonia's clipped diction is like her brother's. Every syllable is precise and consonants are clearly pronounced, especially at the end of a word. In shantung silk, taupe, with pearls at neck and ears, she clearly shares Massimo's sophisticated taste. She's his height and her deceptively simple black pumps are of supple leather, the most luxurious cut. Chiara's bountiful curls, at first glance, seem slightly inappropriate on a woman of her age and bearing. But Kat quickly sees that with her exquisite bone structure and the golden curls pulled up in an artful twist, Antonia is, simply, stunning.

"I understand now where Antonio got his name." On hearing her voice, Franco's son trots over to greet his *nonna*. Kat scoops him up, pudgy arms cling to her neck. "*Il mio bello ragazzo*, my handsome boy." Antonio nuzzles into her shoulder. His great-aunt looks on.

"He's a miniature of his father, isn't he?" Antonia examines the child as though considering the purchase of an expensive bag.

"I guess that's why I find him so lovely." Giving Antonio a kiss on both cheeks Kat lets him down to race back to his mother.

"This is such a sad time. Massimo's so full of sorrow. His namesake dying so young." Antonia releases a deep sigh. "He had such dreams for the child. I haven't seen him this mournful since Chiara's mother left."

A comment that Kat is unable to ignore.

"When was that?" Head pounding, she silently curses Vernaccia, and all wine.

Antonia reaches back into memories, gazes over at her brother.

"When Chiara was the age of Mateo. I think at first he wondered if the child was even his, but of course that is no longer a concern." Antonia examines Kat's reaction to her words. "Katerina, I share this so you're aware that the Alighieri family knows the passions of the heart, their power to seduce and to destroy. My brother, he understands you." After a long pause Antonia gracefully excuses herself.

Senora Alighieri says her farewells to the Tuscan family to which her niece is aligned, then a word in Massimo's ear and she's gone. Kat doubts they'll ever cross paths again. Antonia is the kind of Alighieri Agnes spoke about. Massimo accommodates Franco's family because he adores the artist, but Antonia's message was clear. Max understands human weakness and betrayal, having experienced it firsthand. More significantly, he's accustomed to manipulating people, their passions, and their allegiances in ways that meet his needs. Even a woman as clever as Kat.

La Bella Figura, my ass. Agnes, these people are not noble.

The priest arrives. Kat has a vague memory of him being the officiant at Mateo's christening in San Gimignano. What she remembers best is Franco, how excited he was to be with her, knee to knee in the church. In contrast, she's been here for two hours and they haven't spoken. He watches her as she moves about the room. She knows this because she's doing the same.

Father Anselmo prepares the last rites of his faith for Mateo. The priest, vested in black with an oversized crucifix dangling from his thick neck, lays the tools of his trade on the stark white table usually used for patient medications and sundries. The Ghibellini form a semi-circle. Chiara takes her place beside the priest and Franco joins her. The baby, eyes closed, is on medication to free him from pain. He's already slipping away, transitioning from earth to space.

Each parent places a hand on their son's head. Father Anselmo anoints Mateo's tiny forehead with oil blessed in San Gimignano. He marks the sleeping baby with the sign, the one Kat forced Chiara to make when she promised not to harm the children. *Only it was too late even then, Chiara.* Franco and his family make the sign across their chests. Chiara follows. Even Massimo. Kat wishes she could disappear. She lied to Franco; she knows nothing of their rituals. Believing her Catholic, he chose her as godmother to his daughter. The priest incants over the baby and the room whispers amen. Everyone except Kat. Massimo notices. He lifts his eyebrows in an indecipherable expression that Kat doubts is friendly.

The priest turns to the small table and readies the sacrament. Kat recognizes this part of the service from the christening. Knows the faithful will queue to receive a wafer. She moves to the back of the group, wanting to blend with those who've already received, but Franco has a different idea.

"Kat. Kat, come." Takes her hand. That cool palm, those graceful fingers wrap around her own. She has been hungry for this touch. Franco's intent on moving her to the front of the line behind Chiara. Kat panics. She'll be revealed, bring shame on herself. Her head pounds.

"Go ahead of me, Franco, after Chiara. It's right … as Mateo's father."

Franco acquiesces but pulls her close behind him. "I want that we do this together, Kat."

Fear concentrates the mind. Kat carefully observes Chiara and Franco. Slight bow of the head, hands raised to receive the wafer, hands to mouth and then the sign. It's a cross, she realizes. Mimicking their movements, she pulls it off. No one pays her the slightest bit of attention. Massimo joins the line, takes the sacrament with a practised movement of head and hands. When he turns, his eyes find hers. As he intones his amen, a smirk settles on his lips.

CHAPTER NINETEEN

San Gimignano

Her cell chimes. Kat almost drops the phone as she fishes it out of her jacket pocket.

"Please come, I think it's soon." Anguish.

Abandoning her half-empty *caffè Americano*, Kat bolts for the elevator. It's been eight days since Mateo's farewell *festa*. Hours stuck in amber while faithful eyes watch the baby's life force drains away.

Mostly, she waits with Massimo in the atrium or the cafeteria while Chiara and Franco minister to their son. Massimo says it's the couple's path to take with their child, that neither he nor she have a role to play, but Kat won't back away completely. She's still needed when Franco comes to her in the night.

As the elevator opens, she spies Massimo in the corridor outside Mateo's room. Looking gaunt in his bespoke finery, his expression announces his thoughts.

"The doctor just went in. I think he's gone, Katerina."

Shoulder to shoulder, they stare at the closed door. An unearthly scream. Chiara. Massimo pulls Kat to him; her tears blur the texture of his jacket. She smells his tobacco and aftershave, but she's unaware of the doctor's presence until he speaks.

"Give them a few minutes. They're in shock. *Mi dispiace*, Massimo. I'm sorry we couldn't do more." The healer's footsteps recede.

Kat wants to barge in, fold Franco's pain into herself, but she knows it's not her place. So, she waits with Massimo in the margins of her painter's life.

Chiara's keening evolves into a low, agonized moan. Unable to tolerate being relegated to the corridor any longer, Kat ignores Massimo's hand on her arm and pushes open the door to Mateo's room.

The nurse spreads a white cotton sheet on the long table which held Mateo's feast last week. Mateo's shroud? Beside an empty crib, Chiara sits, bare to the waist, her child swaddled to her breasts. Franco's on his knees beside her. He too is stripped to the waist. They've been cuddling this child, skin to skin, right up to the last.

Chiara rocks Mateo as tears flood her face. Franco, his head bowed, has one hand on his son's brow, the other on his wife's bare shoulder. Kat remembers the newspaper photo she happened on in Venice when she learned of Mateo's birth. Franco stood behind his wife in the grainy black-and-white, his hand on her shoulder then too. Such a different moment from now.

He speaks to Chiara in words meant only for her ears. The nurse approaches. Mateo, still and doll-like, rests in the crook of Chiara's arm. It's clear the nurse wishes to take him, to prepare the body for transport and burial.

"Franco don't let her touch him. Make her go." Chiara pulls Mateo closer. Franco kisses his son's head, more indistinguishable words. "No! He's hungry, I need to feed him first." Chiara moves to place her nipple in the dead child's mouth, but it's Massimo who intervenes this time.

"He's gone, Chiara. You can't feed him any longer. Please child, his time with us is finished." Massimo's on his knees in front of Mateo's mother. Chiara starts, peers at her father as if at an apparition.

Franco leans across his wife and lifts the dead baby from her arms. Chiara tilts her head, peers at Massimo. "Papa?"

"Let his spirit go, Chiara." Massimo gathers his daughter's flailing hands into his own and kisses them.

Franco pauses.

"Kat, Massimo, would you say goodbye to my son?"

Massimo rises, leaving Chiara to stare at her empty hands. He puts his lips to his grandson's dead eyes.

"*Andare con Dio mio piccolo*, go with God my little one." Whispered and laced with tears.

Franco's eyes, so filled with agony that Kat can barely meet his gaze, offers his son's body to her. What to say to the dead child, for his father's sake?

She places her palm over Franco's and with her other hand covers Mateo's tiny fist. The bandage from the intravenous is still in place. He's already waxy, like Nick when she last saw him in the emergency room. Mateo, like Nick, is no longer with the living.

"Take your place among the stars, Mateo. I'm so glad to have met you."

Tears stream down Franco's face as he nods his *grazie*. Laying his infant son on the white cloth, he kisses Mateo's forehead and then nods to the nurse. The keening soprano of the dead child's mother fills their ears.

Kat thinks it best to check into the Hotel in San Gimignano while the Ghibellini bury their dead, but Franco's having none of it. "Kat, I need you with me." She finds herself once again sleeping beside him across the hall from his wife. So many emotional tripwires: coping with Franco's grief and evading insult from Chiara's tongue. Kat takes refuge in the background.

But she needn't worry because Franco's wife has become a recluse. She picks at her food while her children eat, naps when they lie down and retires for the night with them. Their only interaction is when Kat's roused in the night by the mother's weeping.

Franco wraps himself in family. Insists the children be at his side during their waking hours and spends hours in conversation around the kitchen table with Mariola and Brigitte. Kat watches him from across the room. Head bowed, he listens to his sisters' words of comfort and clings to their hands like a frightened child. He sleeps poorly and startles when Chiara begins her nightly lament. Then it's Kat's turn. Their sexual connection becomes her painter's comfort.

During their third night in San Gimignano, when the sky over the farm is at its blackest, Kat rouses to find Franco at the open window. Chiara is silent.

"Do you really believe Mateo's one of the stars, Kat? That he's in that starry night somewhere?" Kat crawls out from under the covers and shivers. It's a cool September. What does she think? Remembers the stone at de Sade's ruins, his evil energy. She took it with her to Canada, and then Faith gave it to Franco. At the Pantheon in Rome, she could feel the presence of the ancient gods, even though Franco's Catholics had turned their temple into a church. Energy transforms, but it doesn't extinguish, that's what she knows to be true.

"Franco, I believe the spark that is Mateo, his spirit, still exists in this universe. I like to think he's part of the stars because that way we can look up at the sky wherever we are and know he's with us." In the dark, Kat tastes Franco's tears.

Paolo drives Franco to the mortuary where they will greet the hearse carrying Mateo's casket from Florence. Massimo insists the child be cared for after death by a firm that caters to his social strata. Mateo's casket arrives. The preparations for his farewell are complete.

Brigitte and Mariola choose the children's attire. A miniature morning suit with short pants for Antonio and an inky black chiffon dress, trimmed at the neck and wrists with white lace for Katerina. Their boots and ballet slippers await their chubby feet. Chiara will wear a brimmed hat with a crepe veil for privacy. Her black sheath and elbow-length kid gloves arrived by courier yesterday. Franco laid out his suit, the one he wore to his installation at the Guggenheim, before he climbed into Paolo's truck. Kat's mourning outfit hangs in the closet, a sleeveless black linen dress with a short jacket purchased in Florence while the baby lay dying. The last funeral she attended was Nick's. Then she wore the suit she'd bought that Saturday afternoon while Faith was seasoning his deadly omelette.

It's just after ten, plenty of time to waste until three, so Kat retreats to the lounge chairs by the pool. Soaking up the waning September sun, she plans to stay out of the way of the grieving family. The heat of the day reminds her of the last time she lay here when Franco made love with her and gave his wife proof of his infidelity in front of witnesses.

"Kat, may I join you?" It's Chiara. Always showing up when she's not wanted. *Tell her no.*

You've interrupted my daydream, I was fucking your husband. Go away.

Instead: "Suit yourself." Kat's long past watching her tongue when it comes to Chiara. That ended the moment Chiara called her a whore in the Ghibellini kitchen.

"Papa wants you to know he'll escort you to the basilica. He's arriving at two this afternoon."

Kat opens her eyes. "He could have called. He has my number on speed dial." *What do you really want, Chiara?* Shuts her eyes. *Just go.*

Chiara fusses as she settles into the chaise beside Kat.

"I don't know how to live with this idea in my head."

Kat examines Chiara. She's used to the pinched, white face and bloodshot eyes. But the chapped lips send a spasm of pity through her chest.

"Maybe I killed Mateo. The doctors say the cancer started in the womb, from an infection." Chiara gnaws at a hangnail. "Kat, do you think I'm responsible for his death?"

Swivelling to sitting position, Kat faces Franco's wife. *How to answer, when I disposed of Franco's paint brush, its handle caked in your blood. You chose a cruel implement to destroy Franco's child. But you failed and now the oncologist says an infection in the womb triggered the cancer. Yes, Chiara, I do think you killed Franco's son. Not as you originally hoped, but in time. It would have been more merciful to seek an abortion.*

"It doesn't matter what I think. It changes nothing." Kat stares hard at the grieving mother. Feels not an ounce of pity. None.

"You deal with your guilt so well; I wonder how to do that." Anger flashes in Chiara's eyes.

So that's where this is going. Save your energy, Chiara. I'm way ahead of you in the blame game.

"In this world every action has a price, Chiara. You have to be prepared to pay the toll, that's all." Kat rises. "Speak with your priest or a grief counsellor, they can help you." She makes the pause a long one. "I can't."

Chiara grabs her arm. "No. I can't go to a priest. It's a mortal sin what I did. What counsellor will feel simpatico to the mother who tried to abort the infant now dead? Only the two of you know why I did it. Only the two of you know who's really to blame."

She's heard enough. Kat pulls her arm free. She makes her hand a knife and mimes slashing her throat, the Italian gesture for enough. "*Basta!*" Kat strides up the stone walkway to the terrace. Enough.

Paolo and Luigi lift the tiny white coffin from the sleek hearse in the Piazza del Duomo. Light enough for Paolo to manage alone but there's a protocol to follow, so together the men carry it into the church. Behind the casket with her veil flung back, Chiara walks with Franco followed by Mariola, Brigitte and the children. Massimo guides Kat by the elbow. *Déjà vu.* Massimo was her escort into the basilica for Mateo's christening. The extended Ghibellini family follows behind them.

The musicians, an organist and a soloist hired by Massimo, arrive from Florence. Father Anselmo directs the driver to park at the bottom of the hill. Only the hearse has right of way in the restricted zone. He points the musicians to a side door, then turns to the family. Greeting Chiara and

Franco with a blessing, the priest takes his place in front of the casket. On the sounding of a bell, the procession enters the sanctuary.

The casket is placed on a table shrouded in white linen and surrounded by alabaster pots of day lilies, interspersed with carnations and roses, all white. Centre front stands a heart shaped wreath of red roses, with a handwritten centre: *Mateo, mio amato nipote*, my beloved grandson. Massimo's flowers for his namesake.

Immediate family, including Massimo and Kat, occupy the first row. Kat and Franco bookend the pew. The pallbearers unlock the casket and remove the top. Mateo Massimo Ghibellini joins his funeral *festa*.

When Kat asked Franco what type of service Mateo would have, the answer was no surprise, a Catholic funeral mass. If she were the Catholic Franco imagines her to be, she wouldn't need an explanation, so Kat let the subject drop.

"*Agnello di Dio, che togli i peccati del mondo: concedi la pace.*" Massimo's contralto singer repeats the refrain as Franco and Chiara lead the line of believers to receive the Eucharist.

"You go first, Kat. I'll follow your lead." Massimo's hand touches her waist, his lips curl in the familiar sneer. But Kat isn't worried about Massimo's thoughts on her religious practices. *Pay close attention to your daughter, Max. She's the one who is steeped in deceit today.* Kat receives the wafer, makes the sign of the cross and whispers *amen*. Max's smooth contralto repeats the refrain. "Lamb of God, you take away the sins of the world: grant us peace." With that sentiment, Kat agrees.

Chiara takes a seat by Mateo's head while Franco stands solider-straight behind her. Some mourners kiss or touch the child as they pass, others nod their respect. They offer the parents murmured words of affection. The aunts hold Antonio and Katerina up to view their brother. Solemn little faces, what do they understand? Mariola whispers and the siblings wave with tiny fingers. *Arrivederci*, Mateo.

Kat stands in front of the casket. Mateo's in the christening gown she purchased in Burano, with a tiny silver cross resting on the cross-stitching. A white teddy bear is tucked next to the arm that endured so many needles. She can feel Franco watching her. How to help her painter through this awful moment? Massimo's close behind her. Remembering his floral arrangement, she kneels and removes a bud from the wreath. Pressing the rose to her lips, she leans forward to kiss Mateo's forehead. A porcelain doll, except that he feels dense. Kat places the rose next to the infant's clenched fist. "Goodbye little one."

To Chiara, still bristling from this morning's accusations, she offers air kisses. In Italian, tells her that Mateo was a lovely boy. *That's all you get from me, Chiara.* Moving past the mother, Kat's eyes meet Franco's, his bloody from too many tears. She pulls him into a fierce embrace, moans *mio amato, my love,* under her breath. Franco offers a bare flutter of a kiss. *Grazie.* The line presses forward; Kat returns to the pew. When Massimo rejoins her, his face's unknowable, except that there's no sneer to be found.

The eulogy is intimate. Franco names each member of the congregation, thanking them for their love and support.

"He was loved. We grieve because we have lost opportunity to know him better. Is everyone aware that already he'd mastered swimming?" Franco surveys the pews. Heads nod, smiles loosen tight lips. "What an amazing life he would have lived, but he's moved on ahead of us." Pausing, Franco steps out in front of Kat. "Our new relationship with Mateo was explained to me like this." His eyes lock with Kat's. "Mateo's still with us, only his energy is transformed. If we wish to be with him, all we need is to look to the night sky, find the star he's resting on. You will feel him." Kat nods assurance. "So please, when you're missing Mateo, look up to the heavens, he will be there. Thank you for this, Kat." Franco bends down, his mouth to her cheek. Then to Mateo's mourners: "We share Mateo with you in the night sky. *Grazie mille.*"

The pallbearers prepare the casket as the congregation rises to follow Mateo Massimo on his final earthly journey.

The cemetery's a few hundred feet past the parking lot, at the bottom of the town. It overlooks the hilly terrain that leads to the Ghibellini farm. Forgoing the hearse, the procession descends on foot, led by the priest. Past the Duomo and down the ancient, cobbled Via Giovanni, the mourners trudge. Chiara walks directly behind the casket, leaning heavily on Massimo. She's pulled down her veil. Kat and Franco, arms linked, walk behind them. Tourists thronging the popular thoroughfare stop and gawk. We aren't a show, Kat wants to shout. These people, this misery, it's real. For the first time since she arrived in Italy, Kat feels she's crossed the divide. No longer an outsider, she shares in the Ghibellini grief.

Two men in pressed overalls stand sentinel beside a mound of dirt and an open pit, their shiny shovels upright like rifles held at ease. The Ghibellini gather in the folding chairs that ring the gaping hole. The priest approaches Chiara, who appears rooted in place, swaying. Franco's quick to take her arm, whispering to the face under the veil. Leaning into the men, she manages the steps to her son's casket. Chiara drops to her knees where she removes her gloves and tosses them on the grass. Bri offers her a spray of roses. Grasping the stems with her bare hands, she drops each rose on her son's casket. In a whispered version of her soprano she repeats: "*Perdonami*, forgive me," as each flower drops.

On the priest's signal, workmen lower the coffin into the ground. Franco lifts a handful of dirt and throws it into the grave. One after the other, the men do the same. They join Franco and likewise stare into the hole. A bird warbles in the distance, competing with Chiara's sobs and the clods of dirt hitting the casket.

Mariola leads the women to the grave. Kat chooses a chunk and throws it gently onto Mateo's casket, which is now covered by a mess of roses and soil. More women come forward until all who wish have taken part in the ritual.

"*Provengono tutti dalla polvere, alla polvere tutto il ritorno.*" Father Anselmo reminds the mourners that all come from dust and to dust all will return.

Rhythmic thuds mark the labours of the gravediggers, until the baby's entombment is complete.

"*E finiti.* Amen." The priest signs the cross.

The crowd disperses. Silent until they reach their vehicles where the chirping of remote locks interrupt the solemnity of the moment. Only Franco and Kat linger.

"What do we do, Kat?" Franco squats beside the mound of soil. "Leave him here? Alone?"

Kat falls to her knees, wraps her painter in her arms and lays her head on his neck. "We are the living, Franco. It's time for us to return to living."

With an anguished sigh, he takes her hand and turns away from the grave.

"*Andiamo.*"

Franco stands on the grassy path that cuts the vineyard into halves, his eyes heavenward. The night sky is filled with stars.

"Which one, Kat?"

Kat breathes in the cool air, moves closer to Franco. "The one that calls to you. Breathe and wait."

Franco looks for more instruction, some proof that this will work.

"Try it." A deep intake of air and a slow exhalation. His breath's scented with herbs from tonight's lasagne. Crooking his neck, he scans the Tuscan sky.

After a moment: "There, Kat! That one!" His voice lowers. "I know, I feel him." Kat follows his finger's trajectory but there's no way of knowing which one he means. Still, there's a starry point that speaks to her too, so she says: "*Si*, that's the one.".

They watch Mateo's star until Franco has no more need of it. The only sounds breaking the silence are the relentless crickets. Franco plucks a handful of claret-coloured grapes, tastes one and offers them to Kat.

"*Quasi perfetto.* They'll harvest within the week." He explains that the vineyard to the left holds red varietals. "They're Sangiovese." To his right he picks another handful. These grapes are golden, even in the moonlight. "Try these, I bet you like them better."

Kat does like the golden grapes better, they're sweeter.

"Vernaccia for your favourite wine." All the vines to the right are Vernaccia. It's an ancient varietal, even Dante drank Vernaccia. "We harvest the whites first except for the Trebbiano, they take longer to ripen."

"I didn't realize you knew so much about the vineyard, Franco." Kat pulls another handful of Vernaccia from a vine. They are delicious.

"Not an expert like the workers, but I learn. As a teenager I worked with my cousins and my uncles. When my father was alive, I work the fields in the summer, but I paint also." He takes the last of Kat's grapes and pops them into his mouth.

Kat slides her arm around his waist. Always the painter, even as a boy working his father's farm.

"When do you want to return to Torcello, to your studio?"

"Tomorrow, the one o'clock train." He grins.

His eagerness takes her aback.

"I miss my work. And I need it now." His countenance darkens. They've been on this death watch for over a month. "Like you said, Kat. We return to our life."

A figure appears on the path, Paolo. A woman, long-legged in a short skirt, stands behind him. Chiara.

"*Buona sera.*" And in English: "May we join you, cousin?"

"Franco tells me the grapes are near ready to harvest." Kat addresses Paolo. She has no desire to speak with Chiara.

"Let's see." Paolo tastes a red and then a white varietal. "Three days for the Vernaccia."

"Four," Franco says. He explains that he and Paolo used to bet on the first day of harvest as boys. "I was best." Smiles at a long ago memory.

"Franco was better at figuring the harvest day, but it's the vintner who decides and he uses instruments, not his tongue," Paolo says amiably.

The foursome walk a ways in the moonlight, not saying much until Franco reveals their intention to return to Venice.

"Can you give us a ride to Firenze tomorrow after breakfast?" His cousin nods.

"Take me with you, Franco. I need to get away." Chiara, silent until now, enters the conversation. "It upsets the children that I'm so sad."

"You have other places to go, Chiara," Kat says. This is one house-guest she doesn't want or need. "Franco's going to be working. You remember the hours he keeps when he paints." She faces Chiara down. "Day and night."

"Our apartment is where we lived when Mateo was born ... where he lived. I need a place without memories."

Kat gets her point. The Florence apartment is where Chiara attempted to abort the pregnancy and where the child lived much of his short life.

"You'd be on your own in Torcello." Kat won't be a tour guide, or worse, Chiara's counsellor.

"Papa gave you a boat with a driver. He can show me around." Chiara links her arm with Franco's, "I won't be any bother. Promise."

Disengaging his arm, Franco reaches for Kat's hand. His thumb caresses her palm.

"It's true, the children get upset when they hear their Mama crying. They need calm, a chance to heal." This addressed to Kat. "Perhaps Chiara should go away for a time, where there are no memories."

Franco's wife is going to get her way, she can feel it. At least she can contain the damage.

"How long?" Chiara doesn't blink.

"A week or so. Not long, Kat."

Kat heads back to the farmhouse, attempts to outpace Franco, but he keeps step with her. Neither speak until they reach their bedroom.

"I don't want her in Torcello, in the home we share." *Don't make me share you again, caro.*

Franco lies on the bed but keeps hold of her hand.

"How can I say no to a woman who buried her son today?" His eyes brim over. He's worn out, ragged. Kat has no fight in her for this discussion. "Okay, Franco. Rest." She kisses his fingertips and then his forehead. "We'll be fine, *mio caro*." How can she argue with a man who buried his son today?

After her shower Kat finds him sleeping, his left arm across the empty space in the bed. Kneeling beside him, she's captured by her painter's beauty as the moonlight plays off his features. Tousled hair, dark lashes, his lean jawline defined by his shadow of beard and full lips. His mouth, the taste of which lingers in her own. *If you were ugly, Franco, I might be gone by now.* Perhaps Eva's right, she's more like Peggy Guggenheim than she knows.

Crawling under the duvet, she kisses his mouth. Franco murmurs but doesn't waken. His delicate fingers curl around hers, even in sleep. Kat lays her arm and leg across his torso. Ballast. She matches her exhalations to his. *I won't lose you, mio caro, I won't.*

CHAPTER TWENTY

Torcello

"*Un momento per favore.*" Kat calls after Vittorio as he strides toward the village centre. "May I walk with you?" He's tall. She only reaches his shoulders, whereas she and the painter are the same height. She lengthens her stride to keep pace with his.

How to explain to Vittorio that she wants him to keep Chiara away from the townhouse as much as possible. He's Massimo's employee. Can she even trust him? *Go slow, feel him out.*

"*Miseria.*" Her response to the question of how they are faring. "We're miserable, but Franco finds refuge in his painting. Myself, I'm content to support him. It's Chiara who's adrift. She's come to the lagoon to heal before facing motherhood with one child gone." She searches Vittorio's face. He's darker in colouring, more rugged and sturdier than Franco. Is he buying her pitch? His eyes are black. Barriers to his interior world.

"What is it you wish me to do, Kat?" As always, he cuts to the point.

"The townhouse is small for three adults. Especially these three. Imagine. Massimo's distraught daughter, her estranged husband who is also Massimo's *protégé* and me, the painter's lover." Kat peers straight into those black eyes. "I need you to keep her occupied."

"Take her to various islands, stay away until late afternoon at least?" He pauses at the edge of the village. The *piazzetta* is empty, too early for the first tourists.

"I need you to do whatever is necessary so that the artist may paint undisturbed in his studio. I don't want Chiara to hijack his time." Vittorio pulls a cigarette from his shirt pocket, a lighter from his trousers. His hands are square and blunt-fingered compared to Franco's. "Massimo gave me specific instructions to make life for the painter as comfortable as possible. His welfare is also my concern. The daughter …" He lights his smoke and exhales with a smile on his lips. "I can be charming if need be."

Agreement in place, Kat leaves Vittorio to his errands and heads for the townhouse. Franco and Chiara will wake soon, time to put on the espresso and face them both.

When Vittorio shows up at the back door a short time later, he's changed into the tight black tee and slacks favoured by the captains of the canals. His head closely shaven, his beard neat, his appearance is sleek. His only embellishments are the silver wristwatch and thin chain around his neck. Kat notices a scent of bergamot as she closes the door behind him.

Vittorio offers his services as tour guide. There are more than one hundred islands to explore. Chiara's lounging on the couch, flipping through one of Kat's pictorial guides to Venice. Franco, at the table finishing his melon and espresso, raises an eyebrow at Vittorio. At first Chiara's blunt responses to Vittorio's questions border on rude but as he describes the pleasures of exploring the lagoon waters, she warms to his offer. Collecting her purse and sunglasses, she follows him to the boat moored in front of the townhouse. Franco watches their departure at the window. In his sleeveless white tee, paint splattered jeans and bare feet, Franco stands on the bottom step of the stairs leading to his studio.

"I paint now." But he doesn't move. Instead, he watches Kat tidy the kitchen.

"Go then." Kat wipes the countertop. Franco remains on the bottom step. "What is it, Franco?"

"I'm sketching you in my mind. That's how I capture you for the canvas."

A prick of guilt. She's been on edge since Chiara's arrival. Walking to the stairs, she slips her arms around her painter. "Sketch away, *mio amore*."

"I can't go up there, Kat. If I touch my projects from before, my brush will ruin everything. I'm not ready for them. All I wish to paint is the second Madonna but it's the one Massimo calls a joke, so I will sketch you instead."

"Massimo isn't the artist. You are. The second Madonna is Mateo's painting. If you wish to work on it, then you should." Kat knows it's useless for the painter to rail against his own creative impulse. She also knows her words hold as much sway as Massimo's. Freed to make his own choices, Franco climbs the stairs and returns to his studio.

Kat sets the table for their evening meal. Anna has prepared a favourite dish for Franco. *Scialatielli con pomodore*, thick Neapolitan pasta with tomatoes. The painter's been holed up in his studio all day. It's past eight. He should be down any minute now. Pouring herself a glass of Prosecco, Kat waits at the table. No need to rush the evening; it will happen at the proper time. Another half hour passes before Kat hears him in the shower. Another glass of Prosecco. He returns damp and refreshed, just as Chiara appears in the doorway of the makeshift guestroom set up in their office.

It's a familiar act, at the table. They've shared so many meals seasoned with double entendres and tension. Florence, San Gimignano or Torcello. Location doesn't change the dynamics between the three of them. Kat chooses to sit at the end with Franco to her right, their usual arrangement. Chiara plants herself across from her husband. Wearing cut-off shorts and a tee shirt that barely covers her breasts but doesn't make it to her navel, she flops into her seat.

Her day was unremarkable. A hint of complaint in her voice. Vittorio travelled up and down the canals until she lost all sense of direction, then they lunched in Murano, watched the glassblowers at work. Tomorrow, Vittorio takes her to Burano. This, relayed with a stretch of her arms above her head, allowing her tee to travel higher and expose the lower lobes of her breasts.

Kat passes the bowl of *scialatielli*. Chiara spoons a modest portion onto her plate, while Franco takes a hefty serving. Anna was right, he enjoys this dish. It's good that he's eating. He's grown thin like the hungry boy he was when they first met.

"Don't you miss Canada? Aren't you going back, Kat?" Chiara pulls this incendiary question out of the blue Veneto sky.

Kat ignores the taunt, offers the bubbly to Franco instead.

"What about you, Franco, what did you think of Canada?" Chiara is not about to let go of the topic.

Kat notices Franco's shiver. *What's the woman up to?*

"It's the new world; we live in the old. We have thousands of years of history; they have a couple of hundred." He shrugs and adds: "Vancouver's a city of glass and steel, of northern light. Difficult for a painter born in the Mediterranean."

"Is that why you came back, why you left Kat behind?" Chiara leans forward. Her breasts, now bare, rest on the tablecloth.

"No." Franco bows his head over his pasta, concentrates on his meal.

"Why then?"

"It's done, in the past." He frowns at his questioner. "Besides, Kat's with me now." Franco gives Kat a long look. She takes his hand and kisses his fresh-scrubbed fingertips.

Thwarted, Chiara pushes her food around her plate. "What are you painting?"

Franco admits he's working on the Madonna.

"I like that picture. I got to pose like this, Kat." She moves her chair away from the table, leans back, pulls her legs up and into an eagle spread. A glimpse of blonde pubic hair escapes the cut-offs.

Franco shoots a look at her and returns to his pasta.

"I don't need a model." His lips thin to a straight line.

"I want to be your muse then. I've pretty breasts; they're soft now like Kat's." Though her breasts are already on display, she lifts her tee, pushing her chest toward Kat. "Franco's never seen my breasts like this. I'm always making milk." To her husband: "You like them still, don't you, Franco?"

Addressing Chiara's non-lactating breasts, he tells her in a flat voice: "Cover your titties. Kat's seen them before."

"Franco loves when my *tette* are heavy with milk. He sucks my nipples while we fuck." The same smirk so often found on Massimo's face.

The painter's head jerks, his complexion as red as the *salsa* he's just consumed.

"*Basta!*" He rises and rushes at Chiara. Kat fears he'll strike his wife. Is his dark temper a part of their marriage bed? Instead of the violence she imagines, he glowers. His mouth close to Chiara's, hissing: "*Finito!*"

Another smirk. Chiara hands him her plate and utensils. Franco stares at the dishes and then at his wife before he decides they belong in the sink. Retrieving the *insalata misto* from the fridge, he forks out a portion. He hands the bowl to Kat, then digs into his greens.

Kat reaches for the Murano glass cruet. From birth until death, olive oil plays a role in Italian life. A blessing at Katerina's christening, to massage the children's bodies after their baths, for Mateo's last rites. Rubbing the golden liquid on her elbows and feet, she realizes how Italian her habits are becoming. She removes her makeup with oil and softens their communal baths with a few drops. When Franco introduced olive oil into their lovemaking, he promised it would intensify her pleasure. He was not wrong.

Tonight, her lover lies on his side, one arm under his head while his free hand draws circles around her nipples.

"Do you think I lost Mateo because of what I did in Vancouver? Sins of his father visited on the child?" His fingers cease titillating.

God doesn't colour her world view. Kat knows the Roman gods of antiquity were vengeful. Earthquake destroyed the colosseum. Volcanic eruption vanquished Pompeii. Pestilence threatened the people of Torcello. The ancient citizenry experienced the wrath of their gods. This is well documented. She's uncertain about Franco's God, though. An eye for an eye? Was Mateo sacrificed for his father's mistakes? Kat can't answer that question. She searches instead for a way to explain his son's death that will give Franco peace.

"I don't think of punishment, Franco. Instead I think of time. That it's composed of particles like the molecules and atoms that make up our physical world. When we act, there are reactions, like ripples or perhaps dominos. Some outcomes we know and plan, some are unseen or unexpected."

She uses his hand to trace another circle around her nipple. Franco takes the hint. "If we have intent, then we're accountable, but for events we don't anticipate, we can't be held responsible."

Franco's hand stops moving. "So, I'm accountable for that woman's ending and for loving you because those were my intentions in Vancouver. Anything that followed, I didn't expect?"

Kat nods. "*Si.* That night you didn't imagine I'd send you back to Italy."

Franco hitches up in bed, rests on his elbow. "I wanted to protect you, to love you. I thought you wanted this too. I saw the same passion on your face in the houseboat as in the kitchen in Florence, but I knew you were afraid."

Had she been that obvious? She thought she hid her desire from everyone, even herself.

"The students at Emily Carr called you a cougar. I answer, she's my *patron.* They say, are you from the 16th century? They make jokes about us. In Italy having a *patron* is normal. Massimo is my *patron.* I don't know what a cougar is, but a friend at the cultural centre explains. A woman who uses younger men. *Li odiavo,* I hated them for this. And I hated the glass buildings with the grey light." Franco's voice gets louder with each remembrance.

"Franco, I knew the painting was difficult, but not the rest ... that you were so unhappy." Kat runs her fingertips along his cheek. "You suffered at my expense. Why didn't I know this?"

He groans. "If I say what happens, then you'd never be with me. You knew about cougars; you didn't want to be a joke. I understood that." He buries his head between her breasts. "That night, I tried to show you I was a man who could protect you from that woman's threats, a man who loved you."

"I sent you away." She cradles his head.

"We made love together first. This confused me." Franco's muffled reply.

Kat remembers. A coupling forged from raw need.

"I sent you away because I loved you." Kat strokes his forehead, wishes to erase frown lines which are becoming permanent. "I was afraid you'd be found out, that I'd ruined your life by bringing you to Vancouver. I needed to fix the mistake I made. Don't you see that?" Tears. Fear of his incarceration still terrifies her.

He searches her face. She hopes he doesn't see the whole truth there. How destroyed she was by that night in Vancouver, how responsible she still feels for all that happened.

"I wanted you to be safe, but I hurt you I see that now, but I'm not guilty of being cruel to you. I'm not." Surely, he realizes that she suffered for him, without knowing the details.

"Your intention was to keep me from being arrested." Franco raises his head, he's eye to eye with Kat. She nods. "If we use your logic, I'm responsible for breaking my marriage vows when I come to your bed, but not for Mateo's death."

"That's what I believe. You never intended to harm your son." Remembering the family bible in Florence and how she forced Chiara to swear to keep her children safe, she adds: "Neither of us did."

"His death could be an unexpected domino?" Agony pierces those dark eyes.

"Yes, that's what I believe."

Franco lays his head on her breast again. "I hope it's true, Kat. That God didn't take him away to punish me. Mateo didn't suffer because of me."

"Mateo's death was not your fault. Know that, Franco."

Moments later he gets up, pulls on his robe and pads barefoot through the great room toward the door to the garden.

"Where are you going?"

"To say goodnight to my son."

When Franco returns Kat is half asleep, but rouses with the chill of his hands and feet as he curls his body around hers.

"I need to go to the Guggenheim tomorrow. I need to escape." He explains that Chiara came to the studio this morning wearing only her robe. "She wants to pose naked for a new painting."

Why is Kat always surprised by Chiara's ambushes? Because the woman's mind is a snake pit. You cannot predict what will slither out next.

"Let me email Eva, give her the heads up." Kat finds her mobile and sends a quick message. "We are back!"

Returning to bed, she pulls the covers up to her shoulders and lays a trail of kisses below Franco's navel. "It'll be good for you to paint in the *museo* again, *mio amore*." Kat's mouth moves southward. Her painter moans agreement as his fingers knead her hair.

Franco stands immobile before his triptych. The work is filled-in enough to give a sense of where the artist's taking the image. The end panels move from photographic precision outward to impressionism. The central panel will be the most detailed. There, the play of light against dark will dominate and the eye will centre.

With a deep breath, Franco squares off his shoulders and returns to the worktable. He picks up a brush coated in French blue.

"We were in a hurry. I didn't clean my brush." He moves to the middle canvas. "Mateo was alive the last time I held this." He regards the paint brush for a time.

"Soon I won't remember that was Mateo's brush. That is what happens to the living, we go on."

He turns back to the triptych with a sigh so deep that Kat forgets the email she's reading. Most of them seem to resolve themselves if left unattended, she's found. *If we ignore Chiara, will she disappear too?*

"Kat, I'm going to the bridge. I need to visit the site, feed my eyes."

"Shall I come; do you want pictures?"

"No, I need to be alone to feel the work again. I don't know how long. Don't wait lunch." His lean figure disappears down the hall, sketchpad in the crook of his arm, reminiscent of the young painter she met in Rome. How much of her painter's path did she set in motion the day she acquired *Bernini's Elephant*? Kat's grateful she'll never know.

Eva left a sheath of calendars for the autumn season on her desk. Tours and education seminars culminating in a glittery gala before Christmas. A handwritten note suggests she invite Massimo. A half-dozen English groups for Kat to greet and more opportunities for Franco to give presentations on his work. A busy season ahead.

Does he have a catalogue? Eva asks. Kat doesn't know but sees there's much she and Massimo could be doing to promote her painter. A slick catalogue for certain, and perhaps a web page or a twitter site. She'll speak to Massimo, get his buy-in and his euros. Kat wonders whether it's too soon to approach him. Even he grieves the dead.

Kat's cell warbles. Vittorio, who rarely calls.

"*Pronto*," she responds. "Good afternoon, Vittorio."

There he is, pacing the span of the bridge, counting out a measurement he needs.

She waves from the embankment but he's engrossed in his thoughts. She edges through the flow of pedestrians.

"Vittorio's on his way to pick us up. It seems that when Anna was cleaning the townhouse this afternoon she came upon Chiara in your studio."

Franco's eyes scan her face, his eyebrows knotted. Why is she always the one who delivers the bad news about his wife? A paint brush clotted with blood. Now this.

"Chiara's damaged one of your paintings. She's slashed the Madonna."

The painter sprints toward the launch which has executed an illegal stop at a nearby wharf. Once they're on board, Vittorio wastes no time, taking a sharp U-turn before speeding toward open water. Franco ignores Kat, fixing his gaze on their destination, as if that will get them there sooner. At the Devil's Bridge he leaps to the landing and heads for the back door before Vittorio's had time to moor the boat. He's already upstairs by the time Kat enters the great room. What catches her eye is a familiar blue box on the table. She lifts the lid. Inside there's a christening gown similar to the one she purchased for Mateo. *Has Chiara gone mad?* Kat climbs the stairs, filled with dread.

"How bad is it?" She's whispering, afraid to disturb what feels like a crime scene.

He motions for Kat to come see for herself and she joins him in front of the work he calls *The Madonna Cries*. There's a ragged tear about five inches long, slicing through the Madonna's head before veering right for another couple of inches. There must have been a struggle. The blunt knife had landed across the room after Anna wrestled it away from the painter's wife.

"Can it be fixed?"

Franco backs away from the canvas. "I think I can mask it from behind. See how the cut goes through the Madonna's hair, her cloak? An area I can refinish." Turning to Kat, he asks: "Does she hate me that much ... that she wishes to destroy my work?"

"Chiara is dangerous, Franco. This is not her first attempt to hurt you. She needs professional help with her anger and her grief. This is proof."

"*D'accordo.* I will take care of things."

Chiara is curled up on the couch with her bare feet tucked under her, repeating a senseless litany in her singsong soprano. Franco leans his elbows on his knees in the armchair opposite her. They've been this way for more than an hour.

Kat pours herself the last of a bottle of Sangiovese and regards the remnants of their meal strewn across the table. When Franco confronted her the destruction of his work, Chiara responded by knocking over a goblet of the Ghibellini family's latest offering. The red ran in rivulets along the creases in the tablecloth. A white linen napkin lies wine-soaked and bunched beside an abandoned plate of food. It looks like the aftermath of a bloody fight.

After Chiara retreated to the sofa, Franco left his meal untouched. He attempted to reason with her. That's when the mindless recital began. Kat watches, nursing her wine.

"Why a christening gown?" Franco peers across the space between himself and Chiara.

"For the baby you make with me." She shoots Kat a look. "You owe me this, Katerina. You move in *my house*; you take *my husband* to your bed. That's the reason Mateo's dead." Chiara wraps her arms around her chest and shivers.

"My son died of cancer, not by Kat's hand or mine!" Franco bellows. "We didn't kill Mateo. It was you who wanted to end the pregnancy. You, Chiara! *Stop* this nonsense!" Franco continues to challenge Chiara's warped logic, but Kat's beginning to understand the penalty his wife wants them to pay. *Franco, she's going to chant her poison until you agree with her.*

"I don't want you as my husband. I could not stand that situation again. You stay with *her*." She grimaces in Kat's direction. "What I want is our baby."

"He's dead, Chiara. You know this." Franco holds his head in his hands, his voice falters.

"It's easy to fix. You know if we fuck, we'll create a baby. We always do." Lowering her voice to a whisper: "You *owe* me my baby." She falls to her knees and strokes his crotch. Franco allows her to continue. Kat stops breathing. *What's happening?*

Chiara unzips Franco, grabs for his penis but he cups his hand over hers. "Not in front of Kat."

What the hell does that mean, Franco? Kat wants to scream at him, but she's struck mute, unwilling to believe what is playing out before her.

Chiara crawls onto his lap and Franco offers no resistance. She guides his hands up her bare thighs. The painter caresses the pale flesh. She sings her idiot's song over and over. *"Datemi un bambino.* Fuck me." Chiara pulls her panties to her knees.

If this continues, they'll have sex in front of her. It won't take much to complete the act. *Do something, Kat.* Rising from the table, she calls Franco's name. His eyes catch hers but it's Chiara he addresses. His wife untangles her panties. Throwing Kat the familial smirk, she disappears into the makeshift guest room.

"What's going on?" Kat reaches for him, but he backs away.

A kiss to her cheek. *"Mi dispiace,* I'm sorry." Her painter turns his back and goes to Chiara. Closes the door.

CHAPTER TWENTY-ONE

Venice

A kiss to her cheek. Mi dispiace. Her painter turns. Closes the door.
Kat jolts to wakefulness. Not a speck of light in the bedroom. She closes her eyes. No sounds next door either. An ache surfaces, so ugly she gags. *Mi dispiace.*

She's always known he wasn't hers. Even in Rome, in the beginning. A matter of when, not if. She was lulled into a fantasy of permanence here in Torcello but she's always known reality would catch up with them.

The kiss, so dispassionate. The apology, ordinary words spoken every day in the marketplace. The closed door, no need for interpretation. Kat feels for Franco's side of the bed. Cold, he's gone.

What to do? Leave, of course. In the morning she'll call Eva, ask for help with short-term accommodation while she decides where to live in Italy. Or Vittorio will take her to the Marco Polo Airport where she'll fly to a destination in Europe, then take a train to another country where Franco will never find her. It's easy to get lost in Europe. Not even Massimo will find her. Laurie will help her if she returns to Canada.

None of these solutions hold appeal. She wants her painter. That's all she's ever wanted. It didn't matter whether she or Massimo was his patron. She disregarded his gold wedding band and expanding family. None of it mattered, if he wanted her. One heart, until now. What tribal loyalty propelled Franco back to Chiara's bed? In the blackness of night Kat reminds herself that this is Italy and she's a stranger passing through. In the morning light she'll make her decisions, but for now she needs the part of Franco she can still claim. She tiptoes past the closed door, up the stairs that sometimes creak and into his studio. Ambient light seeps from the windows on all sides. Canvasses, some on easels, form a crowd of shadows. The pungent odour of paint and solvents create a heady musk that fills her nostrils. Her eyes adjust and she finds what she needs. The paint-splattered tee and jeans hang from a hook by the door.

Although they're of similar height and slimness of build, his sleeve-less tee shirt hangs from her shoulders, dips so low that it barely covers her breasts, skims the top of her thighs. It smells of her painter after a night of work, when he crawls into bed exhausted but still wanting her. Climbing under the worsted blanket on the cot where he sometimes rests, Kat bunches the pillow. Jasmine from his bath infuses the space. *Franco, tonight sei mio, you're mine. I still feel you.* Tears come. It's finished. Kat won't fight for him anymore.

"Kat, Kat. You're here. Thank God." Franco's voice rips through her sleep. Salted lashes part. She faces the barren wall and shivers in the morning air. The worsted blanket falls, exposing her bare thigh.

"Go away." Yanking the cover to her waist. "Leave me alone."

"I need to talk with you, I need you to understand what happened last night." His hand on her bare shoulder.

"No. I don't want to hear that an Italian baby belongs to everyone or what you owe Chiara as her husband." Facing him, she pushes her hair back, feels the crust of tears on her cheek. "I don't want to hear your story because I don't believe you." Pulling the covers over her head, she retreats.

Kneeling by the cot, Franco caresses her shoulder through the blanket.

"Don't touch me, Franco, I mean it." She pulls the cover tight around her shoulders.

He removes his hand quickly as if burned.

"I must tell you the truth. I went with Chiara. I am her husband. If I give her a child then I can make up for breaking my vow, for Mateo's death … even for Vancouver."

Typical Franco, he never takes no for an answer.

"We remove our clothes and Chiara kisses me hard. I kiss her breasts. When I am at her mound …"

Kat bolts upright and turns to him. "Franco, I don't want to hear this. *Sta zitto,* shut the fuck up."

"But this is important! Listen, *per favore.* I couldn't kiss her mound or make love." His words come in a rush; he wants to finish before she cuts him off again. "For the first time, my cock was asleep, but that was good because my heart wanted you. Chiara tries again and I tell her no, I love Kat, only Kat. I show her my cock; it wants Kat." He sits back on his heels. *Does he think this explanation will change everything?*

"Terrific, that must have taken a half-hour. What did you do the rest of the night?"

"We talk. Like we never talk before. I tell her what you said yesterday that she needs help with her grief, that it can't be like this. We can't create a baby out of guilt, or madness." He strokes her shoulder again.

"I tell her I thought I could love two women, but it's not possible. That I love only you. At first, she's angry. Then, she admits many things." He places his hand on the small of her back and she allows the connection. "The marriage *e rotto*, broken. Chiara confessed that she never loved me like a wife. Massimo convinced her to marry when she was pregnant, said it would work out. But it didn't." Franco massages her back with the familiar rhythmic strokes of his muscular hands. "She wishes me a banker so her papa wouldn't pay so much attention to my work. She doesn't want Franco, the artist. For me, I don't want Chiara to be my lover. V*oglio te*. I want you, only you. Hear me please. Everything I say is true. *Voglio te*."

Kat sees he's as dishevelled and sleep-deprived as she feels.

"Franco, what matters is you were willing to betray me last night. I need to go." She gets to her feet, wraps the worsted around her shoulders. Barefoot, Franco's tee hanging off her shoulder and exposing her breast, she feels like a refugee in a hostile land.

"Kat, here's the proof how much I love you." He pushes her towards a massive painting. "It's not finished, but close. *Guardalo!*"

A posterior view of a woman—of course, it's her. A long sweep of her back and legs, she reaches for a man seen only in partial view. His genitalia, his thigh and his hand reaching for her. He calls her, *The Goddess of Torcello*. Her painter directs her behind the easel where a twin painting shows the opposite perspective. Franco's derrière, his hand reaching for Kat who's featured as a full length nude. Traditional strokes with a modern approach. They're a magnificent pair, these paintings. Massimo will declare them his latest masterpieces, Kat thinks.

"*Meraviglioso*, wonderful, Franco." Her voice is small and fragile. "Massimo will want these."

"Others, I have others, look."

On the far side of the studio, beneath the windows overlooking the canal, three canvasses lean against the wall. *Oh, my.* He's painted the spot where Kat took him on his first day in Torcello when he was overwhelmed with fear. The place where she helped him see his way forward, where sky and water merge. Franco has interpreted that moment in an impressionistic style. Light silvers across the canvasses, just as it does in the lagoon. These paintings, so different from the traditional ones of the Goddess, are stunning. He's called the trio *Tomorrow*. They transcend his previous works. Truly *meravigliosa*. She weeps. These works, they're hers too. Franco knows this. Why did last night have to happen? It's so unfair. Her tears refuse to run their course.

"You're a great talent. I never doubt this *caro*. But we are *finito*." She kisses his cheek. *Mi dispiace.* Kat heads for the stairs while her courage lasts.

Franco grabs for her, but only pulls the blanket from her shoulders. Kat keeps going. Chiara's on the bottom step, blocking her way.

"Franco tells the truth. Our marriage is broken." Chiara, fully dressed in a tee shirt and jeans, stands with arms crossed. "He belongs with you, Kat."

"Get out of my way." Kat's caught between husband and wife. She rushes down the stairs and shoves Chiara aside. Slams the bedroom door behind her. There's no lock, so Kat screams out: "Leave me alone!" As if this will stop either of her tormentors.

Franco's quick, beside her before she can think what her next move is, hems her into a corner. Grasps her by the wrists.

"You're staying with me." She feels the tension in his touch.

"No, I'm leaving, Franco. It's over." She attempts to break from him but he holds her wrists tighter. His dark eyes shoot a shiver through her.

"Please, stay with me." His breath, stale from last evening's pasta, warms her face.

"Franco, you can't keep me against my will." Her eyes plead but he refuses to budge.

"You cannot leave. Franco will follow you. I know him. My children will lose their father." Chiara stands in the doorway "My babies need him."

Kat's beginning to think these two are both crazed with grief.

"It is me who will go. Vittorio is coming to take me to the train and papa is expecting me." Chiara rolls her luggage into the doorway to underscore her announcement. "Franco is with you. I don't want him. We agree the marriage is ruined."

Franco loosens his grip but captures her by the waist instead. Kisses her neck, whispers. "Give me another chance … please."

This standoff lasts for several minutes. Vittorio arrives and loads Chiara's valise into the boat, unaware that Kat, half-naked, is pinned to the bedroom wall by Franco. She doesn't call out to him. Instead, she waits until she hears him gun the engines.

"I have a deal for you, Franco." He looks expectant, ready to agree to almost anything. "I'll stay until the end of your residency at the Guggenheim." Kat won't abandon her painter, not yet. His work needs her still.

"*Grazie mille.*" He kisses her lips, her neck, rests his head on her breasts.

"When you return to Florence, I won't go with you. You broke with me last night. *Capisci?*" He's about to protest, but Kat puts her fingertips to his well-loved lips. "I need a man who belongs with me and you have a wife. I will not share you any longer. *Mi dispiace.* I'm sorry."

His hands fall from her waist. She retreats to the bathroom and gently closes the door.

CHAPTER TWENTY-TWO

Giudecca

*H*e kisses her cheek. *Mi dispiace. Her painter walks away and closes the door behind him. Abandoned, she's naked except for his paint-splattered tee shirt. Chiara's laughter echoes on the other side of the door. Franco's canvasses surround her, hem her in.* The Tomorrow Triad. Goddess of Torcello. Madonna di Levi. *No escape. A craft knife lies at her feet. Her only choice is to slash his art, but Kat cannot bring herself to pick up the knife. It's covered with blood. The laughter grows raucous. When she turns, it's Massimo who stands in the doorway.*

"Kat, Kat you're dreaming." A whisper in her ear. "I'm here, *ti amo.*"

Clawing to consciousness, Kat rolls toward the edge of the bed. The dream replays night after night.

She opens her eyes, feels her heart pound. Franco strokes her cheek, speaks words of calm in her ear. If she shuts her eyes, the images will loom. Trembling, she concentrates on Franco's cool hands.

Kat draws her coat close against the maritime chill as she exits the number 12 *vaporetto* on the north side of Venice. She exits in Cannaregio, the workers' *sestiere*, or quarter. It's a cumbersome route. She could have asked Vittorio to taxi her directly to the island of Giudecca, but it's Sunday. Why spoil his day off? She prefers to wander alone through the jigsaw of streets known as the Strada Nuova. The broad boulevard funnels tourists to the train station or past kiosks selling souvenirs made in China. She takes her time on the cobbles and foot bridges, enjoys finding her own way to Ponte delle Guglie. Beyond the bridge, Kat finds the *vaporetto* stop for number 4.1 to Giudecca.

Before the betrayal, they coveted their weekends together. Saturdays, Franco painted in his studio while Kat read through the pile of history and philosophy books she's accumulated in an attempt to unravel the mysteries of Italy's past. Mealtimes, with an iPad dictionary beside her cutlery, she tried to keep pace with a purely Italian conversation. Franco's jokes she didn't understand but she enjoyed the timbre of his laughter. Unproductive Sundays. Franco watching replays of soccer matches, Kat snugged up beside him. Their sexual connection inevitably devoured those afternoons.

Her painter attempts to return to that life, conveniently forgetting Chiara's breakdown or even that he still has a wife in Florence. Kat cannot forget. The nightmare won't let her. It has mutated into something truly frightening. She can't relax or read beside Franco while he watches his game. Nor can she bring herself to say aloud the thought that ricochets through her mind. *Get a divorce or I am gone.* If she isn't ready to leave him, she can't deliver her ultimatum. Her painter would only shrug and say, *mi dispiace,* this is how things are. He doesn't believe she'll go. Sundays are no longer a peaceful escape.

On this November Sunday the boat has few passengers. Kat stares at the water, not registering the chop of the waves or the greyness of the lagoon. Her head's a jumble. Thoughts form and fragment before they make sense. Disembarking at the first stop, she finds herself wandering through the precisely-trimmed greenery of the Cipriani Hotel where the spa prepared her for Mateo's baptism.

When Massimo surprised her with his announcement that the two of them would be cloistered in the lagoon for a year, she thought she'd won. Her painter was with her and Chiara remained in Florence. Now that idea seems a joke. Wherever they go, she is with them, until Franco divorces Chiara. But it will never happen. Theirs is a bond of tribal loyalty, with Massimo at its core. Always, she will be on the outside. The interloper. This she finally understands.

Modern sculpture akin to that in the Guggenheim collection graces the property surrounding the hotel. Kat pauses by an oversized marble rendering of a female head bound with cloth. Blind and silenced. She has no agency. Kat grimaces. Too close to home.

Retreating, she reaches the walkway along the canal's edge. The tourists have fled. Fondamenta Zitelle, the wide sea walk, is deserted, but Kat senses a cosiness in the hole-in-the-wall shops and family-run cafés. Some remain open despite the lack of custom. Giudecca is composed of eight islands laced together by bridges. Historically, it's the place of exile for misbehaving Venetians. Could she move to Giudecca once Franco returns to his studio and in all probability to his wife? Perhaps, she thinks, this island of exile is worth considering.

As she crosses a foot bridge, the architecture changes. The original Fortuny textile factory, coupled with the remains of a burnt-out woollen mill, showcases the transition from industrial to post-industrial wealth in the Veneto. The wreck of the mill is now a five-star hotel and the textile factory continues to produce fine-spun fabrics. Nearby, a 16th century building, with Moorish windows and intricate, wrought-iron bars, welcomes trade on a sandwich board. Transformed into a gallery, Giudecca 795 hosts contemporary artists from around the globe. Kat doesn't think Franco is familiar with this gallery so far removed. The work of other painters always pricks Kat's interest. Comparisons educate and often delight her. Chiara, on the other hand, is oblivious to Franco's work unless she's posing nude. No, her disregard goes deeper than that. Kat remembers the craft knife, shakes off the image.

The gallery appears deserted. Kat steps into a narrow room with a beamed ceiling. The floor tiles are classic oxblood and ivory marble. Professionally-lit pieces adorn the whitewashed walls. There are more than a dozen artists, each focused on a Venetian theme. Franco's competition. Mixed media. Sculpture and paint. Gold leaf. An artist known as Berico catches her eye. He comes from a humble fisher background and uses canvas made of sailcloth for his seafaring colours and motif. His works are considered both commercial and sacred. He's found a sweet spot, Kat muses. Another painter portrays the grey sea much as it appears today. A wall of wet grey. She shudders.

The exhibit that shocks is the work of Cholla. The abstracts in primary colours sport names like *Pink Woodpecker* and *Purple Goddess*. This artist isn't human, implausible as it seems, a horse painted the pictures. Kat reviews the equine offerings a second time and smiles. She can't imagine Franco sharing wall space with the work of a horse's hoof.

The artists of Giudecca 795 are an eclectic lot. They push the boundaries of what the eye will accept as art pairing sailcloth with gold. None are Franco's peers. This is what Kat decides as she reviews the works a second time. His Madonna and goddess portraits are in a class of their own. Classical themes from a modern point of view. His latest work moves away from his education. The triptych he calls *Tomorrow* and the Guggenheim project demonstrate the artist's potential. Her artist is unique. She's known this since she glimpsed him in the shadows of *Bernini's Elephant*. Even here, in this avant-garde galleria, the depth of his talent is clear to Kat. How can she abandon him? Leave him to an uncaring wife and ruthless patron? She is his muse and his protector. Peering past the grey sea as it laps onto the footpath, Kat bites her lower lip. Tastes blood.

He kisses her cheek. Mi dispiace. Her painter turns. Closes the door. She's in the Guggenheim studio, his triptychs stand unfinished and abandoned. Paint brushes askew on a table covered in viscous red. Franco, where are you? She feels her body lift above the canals, fly to Torcello. Kat enters the townhouse, climbs the noisy stairs. His paintings line up, one after the other, soldiers heading to battle. His tee's on the hook on the wall splattered with … blood? Franco? More stairs, marble this time. She knows they lead to the Florence apartment. Chiara stands in the doorway, raises the knife. No, it's the paint brush, clotted with her blood. Kat glimpses Franco's back, but Chiara's voice screams: Get out, my home, my husband. Vai! Slamming the door, Chiara turns the lock. Pounding her fists on black oak, Kat cries out for her painter.

"I'm here, *mia cara*. You're already with me."

Kat opens her eyes. Where is she? Franco peers down at her. "I hear you call me, a terrible cry." He strokes her hair, pulls her close. This is how he comforts Antonio or Katerina after a bad dream.

"The worst one, Franco. How do I end these nightmares?" She realizes she's chewing at the lower lip again. Licks it, but it stings.

Franco brings her black robe, the one he painted as a gown in *La Donna*. "Put this on, the night is cool." Wraps his own striped robe around him. "I've something to show you. Perhaps it'll help."

Still disoriented, she stumbles up the stairs to the studio. He flicks on the light. As her eyes adjust, she remembers the last time she was here, it wasn't a dream, that night. The canvasses have been re-arranged. Franco approaches two easels close to the window, where he gets the best light.

"I call this one *Sorrow*. I paint it to show you that I understand the hurt, the pain I caused you, Kat. I'm guilty. I know this."

The painting of a woman at the table downstairs, her hair dishevelled, her face in raw anguish, she leans forward to the empty seat beside her. Hands spread out claw-like, but there's nothing, no one to touch. Painted in quick strokes, disjointed rhythm, with empty spaces, but there's enough information for her to grasp that the woman is herself. She hates this work, its rawness. It guts her all over again.

"I did this to you." Franco's voice is low, heavy.

He directs her attention to the second painting.

"This one's *The Muse di Torcello*."

The muse, with tangled hair and wearing only Franco's paint-splattered tee, lies on the cot, where the worsted blanket leaves her more naked than covered. Her arm is across her face, protection from the dawn as it creeps through the window beyond. This muse, in day's light, is no more than a used-up whore.

"I can't look." Kat covers her eyes. Bites her lip. This time the pain feels good.

"No. Kat, look. I paint this to show you what I did. I know it is how you felt, but it is not who you are. You're not this person. You're my *Goddess di Torcello*, but I made you experience this." Sinking to his knees, head bowed, Franco weeps. "Swine, *brutta, idiota*. I'm these things, I know this. *Perdonami*, forgive me."

The painting is pitiless, a visceral portrayal of a woman both loved and discarded. It's what happened. Franco understands. She hates these works but her painter has reached for her in the only way he knows, through his images. His wounds are as ugly as her own. It comes to Kat that forgiveness happens when the need to stop the pain of the other is greater than one's own hurt.

Dropping to her knees, she cups his face in her hands. She won't contribute to his suffering any longer. If words can heal, she will heal him.

"*Ti perdono*, I forgive you." Each word a commitment.

Tears stream down his face. He searches her own in disbelief.

"*Questo e vero*, this is true?" He wipes his cheeks with the back of his hand.

"True." Her hand to his mouth.

"*Grazie*, Kat, *grazie mille*." Kisses her fingertips. "*Siamo di nuovo un cuore?*"

Kat rests her battered lips on his forehead.

"*Siamo un cuore, mio amato*, we are one heart, my darling."

CHAPTER TWENTY-THREE

Florence

It's mid-December. The Guggenheim is hosting its patrons on the terrace overlooking the sculptural gardens, illuminated against the winter skies by torchlight. The corridors snarl with noisy knots of staff, who rush to dress tables and decorate with massive floral accents. A string quartet sets up and begins a sound check.

Massimo will attend, press palms with his fellows and bestow air kisses on women whose bank balances equal his own. As soon as is reasonable, he'll excuse himself and Vittorio will transport him to Torcello where Massimo's true interest lies. He wishes to view his protégé's progress.

Kat busies herself editing the galleys for a glossy catalogue. She convinced Massimo to fund a quality representation of their painter's body of work. And a website. Eva allowed one of the tech-heads on staff to build the site. Early stages, but Kat believes the catalogue and website will prove instrumental in getting the word out about Franco's work. Unlike the artists at Giudecca 795, Franco's not emerging, he's arriving. Some quick edits and she shuts down her computer. There's enough material to show Massimo her marketing vision for their painter.

Franco insists he fashion Kat's hair in a twist to enhance the length of her neck and draw the eye down the plunging neckline which ends at her waist. To counter her nakedness the midnight-blue sheath features sleeves that end at the wrist with a half dozen covered buttons marching upward. Her painter regards her with the concentration he reserves for his canvasses. He likes that the dress ends just above her knees. *Elegante*, Kat.

She allows him to dress her hair, then steps into strappy stilettos, which also please him. *Bellissima,* Kat. Franco inserts the wires of the Murano glass droplets into her ears. Screwing his index finger into his cheek, he signals his muse is ready for the reception.

Kat takes her turn. She convinced him to leave his hair lightly trimmed for a curly, tousled look and to keep a five o'clock shadow. That request was denied until she googled Italian actors sporting this look. The toughest fight was for the manicure. Franco's long, finely sculpted fingers and hands are his tools both as an artist and when he communicates. The perpetual paint under his nails, endearing in a lover, gives the wrong impression. Tonight, Franco must be more than a humble craftsman. For the patrons of the Guggenheim Circle, Franco needs to be an artist to whom they relate as well as respect.

"Last touch, Franco." Kat loops the satin bowtie around his neck. "Now you look like that actor posing in *Maxim magazine, ma piu bello, mio amore,* but much better—my love."

Taking her hand, he moves to the mirror. Squints at the couple staring back, then grins.

"*Una coppia elegante,* an elegant couple! *Andiamo.*"

Vittorio cuts the engines and glides alongside the Marini Terrace where a uniformed footman offers Kat his white-gloved hand. She navigates the landing in the precarious stilettos and as she climbs the marble steps to the Guggenheim, Kat's arches ache in protest. So far, the weather is cooperating, but there's a damp chill in the air.

At the entrance, the Guggenheim VIPs greet the painter-in-residence and his assistant. Uniformed servers offer flutes of Prosecco, a vintage grown in the Veneto, on silver trays. The string quartet, two middle-aged men and two adolescent women, begin to play Vivaldi's *Quattro Stagioni.* Candlelight transforms the café. Silver on crisp linens, white orchids in clusters and the many carefully-curated guests combine to set a splendid scene.

Kat manoeuvres Franco into the middle of the room. Tonight, he needs to be seen. He's the Museum's Master Painter-in-Residence and the patrons wish to appraise the calibre of artist before they renew their financial commitment to the Guggenheim. One after another, guests approach, ask about his work. Franco relaxes, enjoying the interactions. Kat surveys the room; Franco's father-in-law will be here any minute.

"Did you forget to shave and get a haircut?" As he shakes Franco's hand, Massimo smiles broadly and takes in the room.

"Oh, but he's so *au courant*, Max. The gentleman by the quartet sports the same look." Kat gestures towards a thirty-something, suited in an immaculate tux with a shadow and hair length identical to Franco's. "An heir to the Ferrari dynasty." She raises a brow and meets Max's scowl. "Perhaps you should leave the university more often. You're beginning to lose your fashion edge." This time the smirk is hers.

Ignoring Kat, Massimo asks to see Franco's work-in-progress. As the two blend into the invited guests, the chair of the board gives Kat a brief nod. Octavia stands out, even in a crowded room. She's taller than most of the men, slender as patrician women in Italy often are. Her silver hair is piled atop her head, reminiscent of a Gibson Girl. Tonight, she shimmers in platinum silk which pools at her feet. Inching closer, Kat offers her hand.

"*Mia cara*, you're looking more Italian every time we meet." Air kisses. "This evening, you're *divina*. I adore that neckline."

They engage in small talk. Octavia asks after Franco, his progress. Is he enjoying the Venetian experience? And how is Massimo?

"You know Massimo?"

"*Mia cara*, he owns more property in the Veneto than most Venetians. Torcello, Lido, and Giudecca, as well as San Marco. I know him quite well." She shrugs. "I'd tread carefully, my dear." The women eye each other over their flutes.

Kat searches for Franco. There he is, listening to a guest, his head bowed and hands clasped behind him. Octavia follows Kat's gaze.

"I look forward to his presentation this evening. I hear he charms everyone who enters the museum."

It's true that Franco's made great progress with his public speaking since taking the position eight months before. Tonight, he speaks of the effect of the residency on his work. Exposure to the modernists, artists fearless in their experimentation, challenges to the boundaries of his own vision. Thank you for this.

Fixing his gaze on Kat, he relates how he chose his project, *Il Ponte Accademia*. It's a symbol of transition, of changing perspectives. Then he falls silent, gaze lowered, curls covering his eyes. Brushing them aside, he clears his throat.

"Some of you are aware that there was a tragedy in my life in September. My infant son, Mateo, died from leukemia."

Low murmuring throughout the room.

"My world smashed. I was torn in pieces, not a man." Franco gazes at an elderly woman who nods in sympathy. "When I had the courage to return to the museum and my work, I was lost. The canvasses meant nothing to me." He throws his arms open wide and looks over the heads of the crowd. "I had to start over. Go back to the bridge, I tell myself. Walk it, feel it and learn its message." He pauses, seeking out known faces. Eva, Massimo and Kat. "The vision returned, but it was different. Now, there are colours that you may not find on the Ponte Accademia itself, but they're there. I paint them because my experience reveals these colours. It's my hope that you will glimpse the colours of life in my work. *Grazie a tutti.*" A modest bow as the room roars with applause and bravos.

The string quartet resumes, this time an upbeat rendition of Coldplay's *Viva La Vida.* Franco's surrounded by well-wishers and words of condolence. Sorry, sorry, so sorry. *Mi dispiace.*

"Vittorio's outside, we're leaving, but stay if you wish. I see you and the *gran signora* Octavia are becoming friends." Massimo offers Kat a flute of Prosecco.

"I'm here for Franco, Max. I leave with him." Kat downs the wine, hands him the empty flute and goes to her painter.

Kat can hear footfalls on the floorboards above. The studio door's closed, however, so she can't eavesdrop on their conversation. Massimo's key concern is that Franco become the master painter Massimo imagines him to be. An honourable goal, Kat thinks, but his attitude toward his protégé is often ruthless, leaving the damage for her to repair. What is Massimo up to now?

Franco jogs down the stairs and shoots Kat a look of exasperation with eyebrows raised. Massimo descends with careful steps.

"Fetch Vittorio, tell him I'll be at the launch shortly. I wish a word with Katerina first."

Franco leaves. It irks her, Franco's mute obedience. Kat rises. Massimo is best met eye to eye.

"You've played a pivotal role in keeping our painter on track, even under difficult circumstances. I want to acknowledge that, Katerina." An appraising look. "A bonus, your marketing skills. The website and catalogue look to be powerful tools. I salute you."

She nods in acceptance of his praise. Waits a beat.

"Max, you need to be aware that my help is ending. I'm leaving Franco when his term here is finished." Waits for her words to sink in.

Massimo stares at her. The firm line of his mouth collapses. For the briefest of moments, Kat can see an old man. One who's afraid.

"Unless Franco divorces … I have no appetite for my present role. I won't be the muse or the whore, as your daughter labels me, any longer." Massimo's listening carefully.

"If Chiara agrees to a quick divorce …." At this, his brows shoot up in a caricature of surprise.

"You set up the marriage, now it's time to let your daughter set him free. You can fix your mistake." Massimo takes his time finding his cigarette case, which as always, rests in his jacket's inside pocket. "A pity, Kat. But there are other realities to consider, beyond your needs." Taps his cigarette on the case. "While you lower your necklines and jack up the height of your heels, my daughter comes to terms with the death of her child. Now you want her to consider the death of her marriage too." He moves toward the door. He needs that cigarette, no doubt.

"Leave my child be. She has suffered enough. Perhaps the marriage is repairable … after you leave."

Kat shakes her head.

"I will leave him, Max. You will lose my support for your protégé as well." Kat's voice is flat but she can hear her fear.

"A pity, yes. Why give up being his muse? Immortalized in his art." He makes a show of looking through the bedroom's open door. "Or give up that. I know you enjoy your painter, Katerina." He licks his lips. "Of course, if you must leave." Massimo lights up. "Where do you plan to go, anyway?" His exhalation drifts towards the overhead lamp.

"I'm not sure." Kat's lost this one, she knows it.

"Well, if you must carry out this folly, please send me the final proofs for the catalogue before you disappear. We're going to need them in Rome. His work is that good, Kat. He's ready. Too bad you'll miss his next showing. *In bocca al lupo*, good luck." Massimo closes the door with a decisive thud.

"*Bastardo!*" Kat yells. "*Usi tutti*. You use everyone but I'm not finished with you yet!"

Villa Guelfi, Massimo's home, is on the left. Four storeys, with Palladio windows separated by Corinthian columns, a symmetrical portico, ivory cladding with a grey tiled roof. Evidence of Massimo's wealth, Villa

Guelfi is in a class she's never known. Kat fights a sudden wave of nausea as the taxi stops at stone lions guarding the main door. No time to lose her nerve. Or is it? She could get on the train, return to Torcello. No one would know she was here.

Franco thinks she's taking a day off. He has no idea that she's outside Massimo's palazzo. Max was so quick to write her off. A Canadian with no social standing, who endures whatever he dictates to keep her painter close. *Not acceptable anymore, Max. It's my turn to be in charge.*

Straightening her shoulders, she mounts the wide stone steps to the entrance. A grey December day but the rains have held off. She sounds the knocker three times.

An older man dressed in grey livery opens the massive door. Kat recognizes the uniform as the one worn by Massimo's chauffeur.

Passing him a cream-coloured envelope, Kat asks that it be delivered to Chiara Alighieri and that she'll wait for a reply. An appraisal of both the envelope and Kat. The employee, probably called a footman, offers her a seat inside the entrance before he disappears down the length of the receiving room.

Gold leaf and ivory. Cornices and pilasters swirl in the plasterwork that blankets the walls and ceiling. Floor-to-ceiling windows on the right face mirrors on the left. Multi-coloured glass chandeliers hang from the centre of the ceiling. In the centre of the chamber, for this is no mere "room" Kat decides, identical glass-topped tables hold gilt and blue vases. Kat takes a deep breath, overwhelmed by the opulence.

Under the windows sit armchairs with dimensions so generous they might be mistaken for loveseats. They're upholstered in grey-purple brocade with gold fringe running along the bottom. Kat's seated in one of these chairs, feeling swallowed up in it, feet dangling above the floor. Not a position of strength. Rearranging herself so her feet are squarely on the floor, making it easy to rise, she waits. "What is it you want, Kat?" No social niceties today. Chiara appears, accompanied by the footman, in a blue pullover, grey tweed trousers and black flats. It seems Chiara's a chameleon. Elegance here; jeans and tees in Tuscany; filmy chiffon in the apartment. Which one is the authentic woman, Kat wonders.

"I wish to speak with you privately."

"Of course. Federico, please take my guest's coat. We'll be in the green room."

Kat removes her beige trench coat and hands it to Federico. Chiara's hands flutter to her mouth.

"You're wearing your mourning clothes, the ones you wore to Mateo's funeral."

Kat's wardrobe was deliberate. The black sheath and jacket, black stockings and heels. No jewellery. Chiara's response is just what she hoped for.

She nods. "It is because I've come to speak with you about Mateo and his death." Chiara goes pale. "But that's a conversation that needs to be held in private, Chiara. Don't you agree?"

The green room overlooks a garden. In December, the view is one of clipped boxwood squares filled with soil, awaiting their spring plantings. Chiara moves to the far side of the room and leans against the ornate marble mantel of the oversized fireplace. Logs and kindling are stacked and ready for Federico's match.

"What do you want of me, Kat? Why did you come to papa's home?" Chiara's voice is soft and devoid of emotion. She's thinner than Kat remembers, waif-like.

"Do you have your own apartment here?" Kat's curious.

"I have rooms here, of course. My own terrace." A shrug of bony shoulders. "The same rooms I had as a child." She folds her arms. "They are the same rooms where Franco and I lived when we first married, before Antonio was born."

Franco's lived here too. He's enjoyed the opulence under Massimo's roof, the gift of the Duomo apartment ... and yet he came searching for me in Genoa.

"Please state your business, Kat." Her tone turns brusque. Chiara's gotten over her initial fright on seeing the mourning clothes.

"I'm here to remind you of Mateo's death and to make you an offer, give you a choice." As Kat moves closer, her stiletto snags on the Aubusson carpet. Chiara watches Kat untangle it.

"What can you be talking about?" Irritation flits across her face.

"This. Begin divorce proceedings immediately or I will be forced to reveal the truth about your son." Kat pauses to be sure she has Chiara's full attention. "If you decide not to divorce, then I will travel to San Gimignano where Luigi and Paolo will be sitting at the table smoking their cigarettes, reading their newspaper. Mariola will be cooking their evening meal, perhaps pasta *di puttana* in my honour, and Brigitte will be tending your remaining children." Kat inches closer until Chiara flinches. The women are almost touching and she's trapped against the wall.

"I will tell them how on the first day of July a year-and-a-half ago I returned from taking the children to the carousel to find you bleeding in the marriage bed. In your hand was Franco's paint brush, its handle coated with your blood. The paint brush was the weapon you chose to kill the infant Mateo growing inside you." Kat hisses this.

Chiara's face is ashen. Her knees buckle. She grasps the mantel.

"I'll tell them that the diagnosis was that an infection—the result of an intrusion while Mateo was in your womb—caused his immune system to mutate, giving him leukemia. It's true, isn't it, Chiara?" Mateo's mother nods, tears filming her eyes.

"I'll tell them I was worried about the safety of *all* your children, and forced you to take a vow on the family bible. Remember, Chiara. You promised you'd never hurt any of them. But even now, I'm worried about the children. You're seeing a doctor, because you're unstable."

Chiara has folded into herself, rocking wordlessly.

"How Franco's family will hate you for attempting to murder Franco's son, Chiara. And they will fear for Antonio and Katerina."

"You must not do this Kat ... please." An anguished whisper.

"I'm not done, Chiara. After I meet with the Ghibellini I'll come to Massimo, but I don't trust your father, so before I meet him, I'll make a few calls. You see, Chiara, I keep the database of contacts interested in Franco's work ... including the press that covered the unveiling of *La Madonna di Levi*. Think of how excited they'll be to hear the inside story of La Madonna. You remember: RAI TV, *La Stampa News, Vanity Fair Italia, Closer* and in Europe, so many more. There was an international splash of publicity over La Madonna. The press loves a good follow-up story. Maybe they will ask you to pose again. More fame for *La Madonna di Levi*." Kat grins a hate-filled grin. Her anger grows with every word she spits out.

Chiara is transfixed.

"Of course, I'll tell Massimo, but he'll probably forgive you. After all, God knows what he's done in his day. Then again, if he loses access to those grandchildren, he may not. Perhaps he'd find an attempted abortion a stain on the Alighieri name. Hard to call that one." Kat leans in, circles her hands around Chiara's neck. Franco's wife opens her mouth but emits no sound.

"You've got forty-eight hours." Checking the clock on the mantel. "It's one o'clock. I'll give you an hour's grace. You have until two o'clock on Friday to get the divorce proceedings booked with a magistrate.

Massimo's lawyer will know how. This is all possible, and quite easy, to do, Chiara." Kat pauses to let her words sink in.

"Two more conditions that *must* be met. Franco will have full custody of the children and you will provide him with a monthly allowance for their care until they are grown. Whatever amount Massimo's lawyer suggests, double it." Kat places her thumbs over Chiara's windpipe. "Before two o'clock on Friday, you'll call Franco with the details of the divorce. Never speak of this visit to anyone. Otherwise, I'll tell the truth to Franco's family and the press. Chiara, I promise you, I will do this. *Mi capisci?*"

Chiara nods, her eyes wide and tearless.

"What I'd really like to do …" Kat presses her thumbs on Massimo's daughter's windpipe. Such a soft, slender throat.

"Please! Kat, you're hurting me." Chiara coughs.

Kat increases the pressure. "I'd like to strangle the breath out of you. You, who have caused so much pain. Have no doubt, if you don't do as I say, I'll carry through with my plan. I've done worse than tell the truth." Kat releases her grip on Chiara's throat, notes the blotches her hands have left behind. Abruptly, she stands. "I'll see myself out."

At the bottom of the property Kat leans on the stone wall. The what-ifs storm race through her mind like the Vespa screeching by. What if Chiara tells Massimo what happened today? What would he do? Try to silence her as Franco silenced Faith? Max wouldn't use blunt force but he'd be effective, of that she's certain. What if Chiara told Franco? Would he hate her? She worries less about Franco's reaction. Of everyone, he best understands how passion can drive a lover to despicable acts. But Chiara could call her bluff, do nothing. Then what?

Panic. Heading toward the *Palazzo Pitti,* she breaks into a run and races until she's winded. She must calm down, think about what comes next. If Chiara calls her bluff, what will she do? Rat her out to the Ghibellini, the press or Massimo? Open that ugly Pandora's Box? Kat has no heart for this. It was just a threat. Perhaps even a minor encounter with the press would be enough to unhinge Chiara. By the time she recovers her breath Kat's at the Ponte Vecchio and has conceived a plan. Set up a media interview, then tell Chiara when it will be held. Frighten the crap out of Signora Alighieri, who's looking pretty fragile right now. Tell her that Kat will cancel the interview if Chiara does as she's told. A reasonable plan B.

At the bridge Kat stops to view the Arno. In December it's a rushing grey torrent, not the serene summer flow that draws so many lovers. Their locks are still here. The last crop hasn't been harvested. Placing her hand on a bronze lock, Kat shuts her eyes. All she wants is to walk with Franco through their days. No one calling her whore or The Other Woman. Never the worry that he'll leave her and return to the mother of his children. A kiss on the cheek, *mi dispiace* and a closed door. Never again.

The sky's clearing. Kat has one more stop before she boards the train. The Piazza della Repubblica where Franco's studio sits empty. It's where he will return in May, but she won't be with him if Chiara doesn't play her part. From the edge of the square, she sees what she came for, it's still here too. The Carousel. The Picci family, their name painted above the antique merry-go-round, run the carousel year round. When Kat lived in the apartment, she'd watch children collapse in peals of laughter while adults climbed up on a fantasy steed. She brought Franco's children to the carousel, not because she was feeling maternal, but because she wanted to ride herself and was too embarrassed, a woman alone. Today, Kat has the courage she needs.

"*E aperto*, it's open?"

The operator with the peaked hat grins.

"*Per voi signora, si.* For you signora, yes."

"*Quanto?*"

"*Due euro.*"

Kat digs ten euro out of her tote. "Use it all."

The carousel vendor offers his hand and she climbs the steps onto the wooden platform, remembering Antonio running around in circles, shrieking.

"*Che e il tuo cavallo*, which is your horse?" Twenty brightly-painted ponies to choose from, but Kat knows which is hers. *Il cavallo nero*, the black horse.

Hiking her skirt above her knees, she mounts her steed. The carousel operator winks, the engine hums and Kat's horse glides upward, slides down again. Ten euro buys Kat a long ride on a cold December afternoon. Up and down, round and round. Kat wishes it was July again. With Franco, light-hearted and with his children. They'd ride the carousel together. *Why not? If I want it badly enough, why not?*

As she dismounts, the operator asks: *Sei felice ora, signora*, are you happy now?

"*Grazie gentile signore. Forse sono.* Thank you, kind sir. Perhaps I am."

CHAPTER TWENTY-FOUR

Venice

Vertical sheets of rain batter the launch as they approach the Grand Canal but Kat stays dry in the cabin. It's almost eight and Franco's waiting for her at *Caffè Florian*. In mid-December the only logical footwear in the Veneto is rubber boots but wishing to please her painter Kat will change into her purple stilettos when she arrives.

The weather's been on everyone's mind at the Guggenheim. Will it rain? Will the *Acqua Alta*'s tide flood the banks of the islands? The rains and even high tides are manageable but an ice or snowstorm would bring life on the canals to a halt. Everyone is alert for the sound of the high-pitched alarms that date back to the Second World War but now warn of an impending *Acqua Alta*.

They motor into a shroud of fog and the horns of the *vaporetto* warn other vessels to keep their distance. Exiting the craft in one fluid movement, Vittorio offers Kat his arm, admonishing her to take care as she clambers dockside. The *passarelle*, elevated narrow catwalks, have been erected across the piazza. How normal all of this has become. Vittorio, his boat, his watchful eye over her arrivals and departures; they're part of her life in Venice. She'll miss his ministrations and Anna's attention to the details of their daily life if Chiara doesn't do her part. In her stilettos, Kat proceeds with care on the slippery cobbles. Checks her watch. Eighteen hours left, Chiara. Unless it's already done. Her painter has been alone in the gallery for the past five. Did Chiara call and out Kat?

Franco has reserved a banquette in the *Sala degli Uomini Illustri*, the Room of the Illustrious Men. Marble pedestal tables and violet velvet banquettes line the circumference of the room. Above each banquette hangs a recently restored portrait of a person of significance to the city of Venice. Original selfies, she comments as she takes her place beside her painter. Franco laughs and agrees. He's at ease, so there's been no word from Chiara yet.

The *Caffè Florian* supports artists both Italian and international through the *Biennale Arte*. Franco says it's the appropriate place to celebrate his good news. Massimo intends to bankroll a prestigious show in Rome next June. With Kat's catalogue featured. She smiles. Massimo has made good on his promise. Her painter will travel full circle back to Rome. Will she be with him?

When they lunch at a *cicchetti* bar, Franco orders the tapas-like plates to share, expanding Kat's exposure to local cuisine and sometimes his own. Not surprising, Italy being a country of regional cooking. Region being defined so broadly it can mean your kitchen or mine. The region of Mariola, that's where I learned about food, he jokes.

If Nick had presumed to order a meal on her behalf Kat would have been irritated that he usurped her decision-making, but here it feels different. Franco leans across the table, grabs the bottle of Barolo, a red wine from the north, and pours Kat a glass. He knows she prefers white, mostly Prosecco, but even as he changes up her wine without consulting her, she isn't upset. His explanation makes sense. Too chilly for a white. Our bones need red tonight. If the words come out of her painter's mouth, Kat believes. She thinks herself so gentled by his loving that she no longer puts up a fight. Or is it that she finally understands what's important, what's worth fighting over?

The server places a Venetian specialty on a silver platter before them. *Tonno, salmone e baccalà Mariolantecato,* raw tuna, salmon and cod slices on baguette. The Barolo's full-bodied, tastes of berries and it's going to her head. Prosecco has an eleven percent alcohol content whereas the Barolo runs at fifteen. Franco tastes the tuna, feeds her the other half. Do you like it, Kat? It's fresh and lightly salted. There's more. He points to the platter, chooses the cod next. This one?

The Barolo's loosening the muscles across her back, untangling the knot in her gut. She inches close to Franco, hip-to-hip, thigh-to-thigh, his arm at her waist. He pulls her closer still. Berry-stained kisses that if they were alone would lead to deeper entreaties. Their server, immaculate in a white jacket, removes the picked-over platter and replaces it with Gamberetti, *cetrioli, bresaola, pomodorini, mozzarella di bufala:*

shrimp, cucumbers, bresaola, cherry tomatoes, buffalo mozzarella. This meal reminds Kat of dining in Provence. Endless red wine, fresh produce, cheeses ... and eating with the dead. *They're all dead now. Forget them, Kat.*

Emptying her glass, she motions for more. She rests her head on his shoulder as Franco decapitates a shrimp, snaps off its tail and frees up the succulent meat inside. Obedient, she opens her mouth, receives the sweet crustacean.

"We need to think of when we will go to San Gimignano." Franco peels another shrimp, this time for himself. Kat lifts her head, sips her red.

"I don't want to go back."

Franco stops chewing, stares.

"To San Gimignano, for Christmas with the babies?"

"No, tonight, to Torcello." Too many ghosts. "I want to go somewhere we've never been. Where I don't have to share you."

"Share me? We live alone, Kat."

She shakes her head. "No, we live with the shadows of Chiara and Massimo, and before the eyes of Vittorio and Anna. They're Massimo's spies. I want to go somewhere only for us. Like Vancouver." Accepting another shrimp, she sucks its fleshiness, its juices leaking from her lips.

"You want us to go to Vancouver?" Brows raised, tone incredulous.

Kat's drunk. She knows she makes no sense. She meant the Vancouver where they had no history to keep them company. She tries again.

"I want us to stay here tonight, alone."

Relief crosses Franco's face. He understands.

"Take a hotel together? Okay, we can do that." The waiter returns, Franco engages him in rapid Italian. The waiter nods as he clears away the hulls of the crustaceans.

The glass doors of the *Caffè Florian* whisk open and shut as patrons drift away. Steady rain on stone reaches their ears with each departure. The waiter returns. They've a reservation at Hotel Flora, a five-minute walk away. Franco wonders if the waters will overflow the piazza tonight. A chance to walk the catwalk, Kat. Franco grins, pleased with his joke in English. He pours more Barolo.

It's almost midnight when they emerge onto the Piazza, the rains now a mist, the fog still thick. Venice at rest. Deserted streets, the fog horns on the *vaporetto* silent. No need to walk the *passarelle*, the tides slowed before reaching the piazza.

"Come Kat, walk the catwalk." Franco can't let go of his new joke. He climbs onto the narrow boards and offers his hand. About eighteen inches above the cobbles, the footbridge snakes across the piazza toward their destination. Kat hoists herself onto the boards. They're slippery from the rain, probably more dangerous than the cobblestones. Franco insists she walk in front, his hands firm on her waist. "I won't let you fall, *mia cara*." Under the starless sky, they make their way, stopping for kisses, until they reach the narrow entrance of Via XXII Marzo with the ivy-covered Hotel Flora at the far end.

No lights inside, the door locked. Franco presses the after-hours button. Behind the glass doors, a shadowy figure moves toward them. Half asleep, the concierge welcomes them into the dim lobby. Only a few guests register at this time of year and everyone's retired for the night, he explains. Franco apologizes for the lateness of their arrival. He explains theirs was an impromptu decision as they dined at *Caffè Florian*. Such a miserable night to cross to Torcello. The man nods. Keen to return to his bed, he's already on the stairs. Two floors up he unlocks a door. "*Allora, ecco siamo*, so here we are." The men wait for Kat to enter. The concierge points out the amenities: bed, full bath and desk with Wi-Fi. Breakfast from seven until ten. Franco thanks him for his trouble with a twenty euro note. "My driver will drop off our change of clothing in the morning. Please let us know when he arrives. *Grazie.*"

Kat takes in the curlicues of the wrought iron headboard and stretches out on the white cotton duvet. She could shut her eyes and sleep until morning, but Franco's preparing a bath for them both. He has a lot of energy for this time of night.

Kat's in hot water up to her chin. Hot water and bubbles. Eyes shut, she concentrates on Franco's hands. Lathering the washcloth, he scrubs her body, taking his time. Kat relaxes, her limbs float, wait their turn to be wrapped in terrycloth. Slow movements, the pressure sensuous, everywhere he touches her comes alive.

Now it's her turn to bathe her painter. Lathering her hands with the fine lavender soap, she wants to feel his flesh. His face prickly with stubble, his lean torso, even the knobs of his ribs. Circles his nipples, delicate for a man. He lifts his legs, one by one. Watches her under heavy eyelids. She lathers his limbs, long and dark with hair, then his boney feet. He's ticklish, especially his feet. She soaps her hands again, strokes his penis. Franco's eyes, unseeing, widen and he reaches for her. Kat positions herself astride her half-submerged lover, wraps her legs around his torso. The water's getting cool, she says.

The bed's as inviting as she knew it would be. She could sleep a dreamless sleep here. Franco's intent on continuing where they left off in the tub, guides her hand. His lips to her ear, whispering Italian words that she's come to understand.

"*Ti amo, solo tu.* I love only you. *Sei la mia vita.* You are my life." And as he enters her, he moans over and over: "*Amami, amami, mia cara.*" Love me, love me, my darling.

Kat shudders, not with pleasure, but from fear. What has she done? What if Chiara exposes her and Franco finds her threats despicable? What if he banishes these perfect words from her ears forever?

"Franco, listen." She holds his face in her hands, his dark eyes search hers, he moves to kiss her, return to their passion, but she must have her say. "Someday someone might say 'she never loved you' but I do." Kat's crying, trying to explain this aching love. Franco kisses her cheek. "*Ti amo* as a parent adores her child, or a priest who abandons the world to worship his God more fully." She'd shout if it would help him know how deep her feelings run. Instead, she whispers: "*Capisci? Ti amo.* Do you understand? I love you."

Franco's mouth finds hers, draws her hips closer. His tongue, his penis; they probe deep and deeper. She wishes she were the male, the one who could be hidden inside the other. But Kat is Franco's symbol of womanhood, she opens to her painter and gives him comfort. Loves him.

Franco fiddles with the earbuds for his iPod, then adjusts the volume. Today, it's the street musician, Spadi. He picks up the thinnest brush with an equally narrow handle. It looks like the one Chiara used on Mateo. Stepping away from his canvas, his back to Kat, he observes his work. She wonders what he sees, what questions he asks himself. After some time, he turns to his paints, dipping the brush into the chartreuse. With the precision of a surgeon, he crafts a long thin line. Steps away again. To Kat, he's changed the angle with this hint of light just as in the beginning when she came upon him painting *Il Elefante*.

It's quarter past noon. Chiara has less than two hours left. Kat clicks opens the media file on her monitor, scrolls through the database. Who to contact? Print, television, the glossy magazines or the tabloids? Why won't that little bitch just do as she's told? Franco turns, searches her face. Does he sense her mood? In an effort to hide her thoughts, she asks how it's coming. He shrugs, turns back to the canvass.

A warble, Franco's cell on her desk, well within her reach. He's oblivious, earbuds still in place and the cell's volume on low. Another warble. *You can't miss this call, Franco.* Kat picks up the cell. It's Massimo.

"Can I help you?" Her stomach twists.

"Where's Franco, put him on." Flat tone, nothing friendly there.

"He's working."

"Are you in the studio?" Irritation.

"Yes."

"Then put him on the phone, now." Belligerent command.

Kat hands Franco his cell. Mouths, Massimo. Franco looks at the phone as if it will explain why his patron's interrupting his work. *Pronto.* Kat watches his face. Why Massimo, not Chiara? Has Kat been outed? She forces back the vomit tickling her throat.

"*Quando?*" Franco holds Kat's gaze. "*E il divorzio?*" Franco raises his brows.

The words, Franco said them. Did Chiara follow through? Kat feels the room tilt.

Franco reaches for Kat and caresses her arm. "*Grazie mille,* Massimo." The call ends. "*Vieni, mia cara,* I have some news."

CHAPTER TWENTY-FIVE

Vernazza

Two men in denim overalls carry the wooden pallet containing *The Madonna Cries* down the creaky stairs of the studio. Experienced in transporting precious goods along the waterway, they manoeuvre the cumbersome goods with ease along the narrow walkway to the cargo boat. Franco's focussed on their every move, as he follows close behind. Anna resumes packing Kat's books in cardboard boxes. Tomorrow, a different freight boat will load their personal effects for transit to Florence. There is not much: their computers, winter clothing and miscellaneous items in fifteen boxes destined for the Duomo apartment.

Kat and Franco will take a detour. At Eva's suggestion, they are travelling to the Cinque Terre for their first vacation and a celebration. Franco's divorce will be final later in the month. Fast-tracked by mutual agreement on the disposition of goods, the custody of children and the assertion that neither party held fault, the legal dissolution of the Ghibellini-Alighieri union is imminent. Chiara and Kat have managed to stay clear of each other by visiting the children separately. Franco has shifted his artistic view, moved to another plank on the Ponte dell' Accademia. No longer fearful of losing Kat, he pushes for doing things his way. Perhaps it's not Franco's attitude that's changed. Perhaps Kat is deeper in Italian culture. No longer a houseguest, now a resident.

Most pressing is the business of where they will live, a discussion that turned an argument into a stalemate.

"Kat, I make you a promise. If you don't like the changes Massimo made, the changes I demanded for you, then we won't live at the apartment. But just look at it." When his entreaties fail, he leans on his abundant charm, his kisses and those hands. "I promise, when you walk in the door if you hate it, then we leave. Will you do this?" More kisses. The hands make progress towards winning her agreement. Besides, what can she say that would change his mind? His studio is what matters. Where the Mediterranean light falls just so, where he believes he does his best work. Kat gives in, agrees to have a look. Still, her stomach clenches every time she imagines herself walking through the ebony door back into Chiara's home.

Goodbyes at the Guggenheim came in the shape of a glittery reception where the painter-in-residence unveiled his work, *Ponte dell' Accademia*. The massive project almost didn't have a home. With no obvious wall on which to hang the triptych, a junior intern suggested breaking up the canvasses around a corner. In reply, Franco spewed profanities, a stream of gutter words Kat couldn't have imagined emanating from that tender mouth. The triptych panels must hang side by side, shouted a red-faced Franco. Eva repositioned several pieces, offering Franco an expanse of wall broad enough to hang the canvasses to his liking. It was agreed a triptych is best viewed from a distance, as a whole. The photographic realism of the centrepiece expands outward into an increasingly impressionistic interpretation in the side panels. The resulting image is impassioned and visually stunning.

The local newspaper, *Il Gazzettino*, covered the reception. Milano-based *Flash Art* will highlight Franco's residency in its summer edition. RAI TV's cultural hour featured Franco in an interview that Brigitte caught in San Gimignano. Massimo approved of it all. The coverage generated great interest in the painter's career. Not a single rumour about the dying marriage moving through the courts or the dark reasons why. When Massimo announced the Francesco Ghibellini exposition opening in July, in Rome, the inner circle at the Guggenheim had concrete proof that their choice of protégé was a wise one. *Successo, mio amore*, Kat whispered in Franco's ear as the room broke into self-congratulatory applause.

La Donna remained at the Guggenheim. Despite Massimo's attempts to wrest the painting off the walls, Kat extended the loan agreement for another year, allowing the work to be part of the Rome exhibit. Massimo opted for graciousness, thanking Kat for making Franco's Rome show complete by including *La Donna*. "You aren't content yet, Kat? Franco tells me you have more demands." Massimo cocked his head, thinking. "I under-estimated your tenacity, Katerina." He turned and disappeared into the cabin of his launch.

Their last night in Torcello, they dine among the stacked boxes. In the morning Vittorio arrives to deliver Kat and Franco across the waters of the Veneto one final time. Below the train station Santa Lucia, they share air kisses and firm handshakes before calling *"arrivederci!"* as Vittorio pulls away from the dock. They arrive at their platform and board the Frecciabianca for Milan. From there they will ride a slower regional train to Santa Margherita Ligure on the Italian Riviera. At the end, theirs is an ordinary exit from a tumultuous sojourn in Venice.

The silver and white Frecciabianca travels at speeds up to 200 kilometres an hour. With no stops, they will arrive in Milan in two hours. At such high speed the view rolls by so quickly that it becomes a visual blur. Hills, fields, a scrap of town near the tracks, a tunnel and then more fields. They streak through Padua station without stopping. Of course, in Italy, there's always the possibility of interruptions along the track. Franco stows their bags overhead, then tumbles into the seat across from Kat. Uninterested in the passing view, Franco sketches instead. Kat's used to this. She never poses for him. Franco captures what he needs from real life and transforms her image onto canvas as it suits him. He's demanding, when he paints. The model becomes an instrument. Hold your chin just so, lift your arm there or hold for ten minutes more, Chiara. Franco understands that being his model is a role Kat's unsuited to play.

The first-class coach is at capacity. Businessmen in sleek suits of grey or blue, professional women in jackets with skirts or dresses. Different from Vancouver, where a woman had better not show her legs if she wishes to be considered professional, at least not in the competitive corporate boardrooms Kat frequented. She didn't own a dress until she decided to embrace Italian fashion for Mateo's christening. Even then, Anna had chosen the little floral number with a swirl of a skirt. The outfit Massimo so admired. Women with small babies display their motherhood. Baby gear spills into the aisles, bottles of juice topple as the train rounds a bend. Or a nipple swells in response to an urgent wail. The elderly, in various stages of decay, occupy the remaining seats.

As much as Franco prefers to paint in private, he doesn't mind sharing his line drawings, and proffers her the pad. Three sketches, already. A free-flowing outline of a woman's body in the crowded coach, a magazine on the table. Next, a sketch of Kat's hands resting on her lap, moderately detailed. The last is a portrait, captured as Kat peers out the window. A meticulously-crafted work of shadow and light. You can count the hairs on her head. Kat returns her painter's sketch pad. He returns to his pencil strokes. If she gave their fellow passengers paper and pencil they would produce cartoons, naïve art or crumpled pages of frustration. Massimo is correct. Franco's talent is worthy of their protection.

Milan Centrale remains a massive monument to Mussolini's desire for dominance. In marble and glass, the station is a melange of styles, from Art Nouveau to Art Deco to ostentatious jumble. Franco turns this way and that, takes in the shadows thrown by marble columns and the light-play off the domed ceiling of glass and steel. Forgetting the next leg of the journey, he wanders through the station, pausing to take in details.

"You can come back to sketch one day, Franco. Right now, we need to find the *regionale* before it leaves without us." She tugs on his elbow. "Follow me, *caro*." Kat locates the inter-city train to Genoa.

The compartments are worn, with inadequate space for their bags in the shallow overhead rack. Franco stacks them in the bin at the end of the car, where they'll have to keep an eye on them.

"Three hours and we are there, Kat." The train settles into its rhythm and they're lulled into sporadic naps, her head on his shoulder, her artist's hand holding her fast.

Palm trees, pink stucco villas, pastel-striped umbrellas, stretches of sandy beach and the sparkle of the ocean as they travel along the Italian Riviera on the coast of the Ligurian Sea. During a brief stop in Recco, Kat checks her pocket map. Santa Margherita Ligure/Portofino is the next station.

"Almost there Franco, best get our luggage from the bin."

It's a two-minute taxi ride to their hotel. Franco makes the trip worthwhile for the driver as Kat takes in the view in front of the Hotel Lido Palace. Situated on a promenade lined with palm trees, it faces a grand view of yellow and white-striped cabanas on the stretch of white sand beside the Ligurian Sea. A gentle breeze stirs as Kat breathes in the sea air. The hotel was Franco's idea. The artist chose well.

Theirs is a spacious top floor suite furnished in bamboo and upholstered in burgundy print. Solid Wi-Fi, which Franco pronounces as *wiffy*, but he is more interested in the generous porcelain bathtub. Deep, Kat. Opening the double glass doors to a terra cotta patio, Kat discovers a wraparound view of the seaport town.

"Franco, it's unbelievable!" Kat hears her own shrieks. She can't help it. A spectacular view. Limitless sea, towns clinging to cliffs, hillsides with ancient fortifications snugged in the park-like greens, all under a cloudless Mediterranean sky.

Franco's at her side, laughing: "Keep turning, Kat. A new view every second." He kisses her neck. "I'm glad you like it, *cara mia*."

"It's wonderful." A deep sigh, the tensions carried far too long fall away. "Let's get out of our gear, order some white wine and drink in the view." She kisses her painter and sashays between pots of purple, pink and red blossoms. Another whoop. "*Grazie mille, è meravigliosa.*"

Perched on a chaise, one of two dozen in a line along the beachfront, Kat kicks off her sandals and digs her toes into the fine-grained sand. A yellow and white striped umbrella stands unfurled beside her, but Kat's not concerned about getting too much sun. She contemplates a different hazard. Four teenagers check out Franco as he strides down the beach to the sea. Bikini clad, already bronzed and with the impossible slimness of the newly pubescent, they move in closer and call out to him. Franco stops to respond. They rush to surround him. Kat's mouth goes dry.

Chatter, giggling, hair-flipping. An Italian bevy and its prey. The boldest girl steps forward to ask Franco a question while her sisters watch. *What will you do, caro mio? Does their youthful nakedness entice you, Franco?* Kat's painter bows his head, as is his habit when listening to strangers, then shakes it in reply. The bold one shouts a challenge above her sister's laughter. No, this time spoken. A single word, but clear enough for Kat to hear him. Wading into the ocean, Franco swims parallel to the shore. The bevy flutters back to their chaises and resumes giggling.

Kat follows Franco's progress. He travels a good distance before he changes direction. She lies back on the chaise and closes her eyes. Drifts on pleasant thoughts until she feels a wet, cold hand on her inner thigh. She opens her eyes as the hand moves closer to her crotch. She bolts upright. "*Bastardo …*"

"You should swim, Kat. It's energizing." Grinning widely, he settles onto the chaise beside her, towels off. The girls on the beach keep watch. Kat rises from her chaise and tosses her towel over Franco's head.

"Let me help you, *caro mio*." She gives his head a brisk rub before he pulls the towel away and grabs for her. Landing atop his drenched torso, she feigns escape.

"You want this, Kat. I know you do." He pins her down as her thin cotton dress wicks up the sea. Deep kisses. Is the bevy watching? Yes.

He's right. She does want this. Her arms around his neck, fingers tangling in his damp hair. More deep kisses. His hands find their way into her panties. So easy to keep going.

"Franco, stop or we'll be arrested. We aren't on the farm anymore."

He protests but allows her to extricate herself. When she stands, her nipples and navel are visible through her damp dress.

"I need to dry off and you need to chill." She tosses her towel across Franco's groin. Returning to her chaise, she notes the bevy has left. *Yes, Franco I wanted that.*

"Which town, Kat? Pick one and we'll take the ferry there." Franco pours her second coffee as they breakfast on the patio.

Barely awake, Kat points towards the coastline of the Cinque Terre.

"The pink one." Sips the coffee. Leaning forward, she pushes Franco's hair out of his eyes. He hands her the map.

"Between here and here." He uses his thumb and pinkie finger as markers. "Close your eyes and pick one." He places her index finger on the map.

"There." Kat opens her eyes.

"Vernazza. Good, that's where we will go first." Franco flashes her another perfect grin. "*Andiamo, cara mia.*"

Kat reaches for the carafe of coffee.

On the ferry, Franco scrambles to find two seats with an unobstructed view. It's a forty-minute sail along the coast under a cloudless Mediterranean sky. Kat settles in beside her painter and adjusts her sunglasses. She accepts the straw hat Franco purchased for her on their way to the boat. You burn, Kat, he tells her.

The coast of the Cinque Terre is famous for an elegant riot of towns tucked into the mountainside. A jumble of houses in southern hues of pink, blue or yellow linked together by terraced vineyards, decaying churches and tumble-down towers. The latter are remnants of the military might that kept the invaders, mostly Turkish pirates, at bay. Franco borrows Kat's camera and records their voyage. Kat relaxes into her chair and concentrates on the sea breeze washing over her. The heat grows more intense as the morning progresses. She is aware of the sweat along her spine and the tingle on her arms. Franco's right, she will burn.

Tourists elbow one another to be first down the gangplank onto dry land. Kat and Franco hang back, not sure why the hurry. The shore will still be there in five minutes time. The ferry won't leave until everyone is off. Tourists. Kat still refuses to acknowledge that she's one of them.

Franco suggests they walk to the top of the town and offers her his arm. Kat scans the narrow street, the houses painted in shades of rose. This is the pink village, after all. Shops, cafés and hotels, family-owned for generations, call to the passers-by; stop here, pick our goods. Franco pauses to examine various olive oils. I think we should try some, Kat. While Franco tastes samples with a genial owner of an olive grove, Kat peruses the pedestrians clogging the street. A version of Nick, attired in beige, passes by. He reads his guidebook aloud. His companion ignores him. Kat remembers her holiday with Nick in Roussillon. She stares after the couple as they walk away. Together and yet strangers, just like Nick and Kat.

"Kat, *vieni*, come." Franco motions for her to taste three oils. "Which do you like best?" Intense brown eyes watch her as if choosing their olive oil today is the most important thing anyone could do under this Mediterranean sky. She loves this about him, this living of every moment as the only moment that matters. She's too Canadian, too ready to detach from the experience. Franco has some thirty years' practice at tasting the *dolce vita*, but she's working hard to catch up.

"This one for salads?" Olive oil has so many uses; she's not sure what purpose he has in mind.

"*Si*, it's good for the *insalata*. Maybe this one too … for the bath." He offers his tasting spoon. Ah, yes, sweeter. Franco's choice for lovemaking.

"*Si caro mio*, I like that one too."

Securing their purchases in a canvas sack, Franco thanks the shopkeeper with a *grazie mille* and a handshake. Turning everyday life into elegant moments, they are living *La Bella Figura*.

At the top of the town, they admire the view below. Brightly coloured Vernazza tucks into the hillside, while the ocean shimmers and sways around her shores, crisp blue shot through with diamonds. The noon sun beats down. The breezes don't reach this far away from the ocean.

"You're getting burnt, Kat. Let's take in the church for a while." There will be art to discover, appreciate and perhaps something to learn. Even bad art teaches a lesson, according to Franco. Hand in hand, they retrace their steps down to the shoreline.

Chiesa Santa Margherita d'Antiochia perches on a rocky outcropping on the north side of the harbour. Kat feels immediate relief as she enters the stonewalled interior. The sensation of being in a cool cavern. As in the basilica in San Gimignano, striped marble columns of Moroccan influence line the central aisle. At the far end, daylight streams through half-moon windows onto the altar. Modest wooden benches evoke memories of the Pantheon where she first considered the spirit and energy of the Roman gods. Unlike the pantheon, here there is silence, no shuffling feet along the floor. Here, they are alone.

Kat peers out a narrow aperture carved in the stone wall. Directly below her, the seas shift. Franco's disappointed that the walls are devoid of art. A human-sized crucifix by the altar appears to be the only artifact for the painter to study. An elongated and emaciated Christ, arms stretched almost straight above his head and nailed to a life-sized cross. The figure appears carved from one tree. Franco takes pictures from several angles. "It's good, Kat. Maybe not Italian. Spanish perhaps? I wonder how old." If Nick were here, he'd find the answer in his guidebook. Kat suggests they google on the *wiffy* when they get back to the hotel.

Kat's stomach rumbles. She'd take any table under that jumble of yellow and blue umbrellas overlooking the harbour, but Franco has a different idea. Wait, Kat. They cross the breakwater to the far side of the harbour, past the fishing boats bobbing at their moorings, and climb the tower steps. There's a restaurant up there. Franco promises it will be worth it.

Her painter is right. At the top of this stone tower, a bistro. Pristine white linens, sparkling cutlery and glassware. Views of the coastline from every seat. It's crowded, but Franco claims a table close to the edge, with a breeze. A server appears from behind a filmy cotton curtain, hands them menus. Franco asks after the catch of the day. The waiter warms to her painter as many locals do. Glad, she supposes, to have a break from the broken Italian or accented English of tourists.

Kat peruses the menu, asks Franco to repeat the waiter's recommendations.

"You speak English. From the sound of your accent, I bet you're Canadian. Takes one to know one."

Kat looks over her menu. A woman with hair clipped shorter than most men addresses her from the next table.

"Yes, I speak English." She returns to her menu. *Why do strangers imagine they have a right to interfere in your life just because you share the same language?*

"But you don't. You're local?" A chipped fingernail points at Franco.
Kat throws Franco a look. Don't encourage her. He answers the cropped-cut Canadian anyway.

"I'm Italian." A tone of pride or defense?

"We're from Vancouver on the west coast. You've heard of it, I suppose. The Olympics made us famous." She's addressing Franco now. *Please don't say anything.* "*Si*, I know it." He too returns to the menu.

"You live here then?" That nosy woman isn't going to stop.

"Firenze. We're from Florence."

"Your friend too, is she from Florence?" She nods towards Kat, who scowls at her.

"*Si*." Franco steals a glance at Kat who continues to scowl.

"What do you do in Florence, for a living, I mean?" The Canadian leans towards Franco; they are almost nose-to-nose.

"I'm a painter." Franco shifts in his seat. Kat nudges his knee. *Stop, please.*

"Houses or office buildings, that sort of thing?" Cropped-cut has two front-tooth veneers, reminding Kat of a beaver.

Franco's Adam's apple jogs as if he's swallowed a lemon whole.

"He's an artist, a master painter." Kat can't help herself. Why won't this biddy from British Columbia leave them alone?

"Oh, that's something. I'm only a high school secretary." She takes a sip of water and looks to her travel companion. "Robbie's job, you'd never guess. Almost as off-beat as yours." Kat figures the man to be in his fifties, big-boned and, although seated, she thinks well over six feet.

"Tell them what you're working on, Robbie. They'll be surprised."

Robbie sends a benevolent grin her way and clears his throat.

"Cold cases. I'm with the RCMP. I've been commissioned with reviewing unsolved murders in Vancouver over the past ten years." Certain that he has Kat and Franco's attention, he continues. "We've got a number of unsolved cases. I'm just getting started. I'll be looking for the killers out there, the ones who think they got away." Robbie looks from Franco to Kat and grins. His teeth are square and even. Then: "Let's order, hon, I'm starved."

Kat can't grasp which part of this revelation to manage first. Does Franco even know what the RCMP is? Does he get what the man just said? She steals a glance at her painter. His brow furrows; he's confused. No, he doesn't get what just transpired.

"Royal Canadian Mounted Police are like the Carabinieri." Her neutral tone says *hear me*.

Franco eyes fix on Kat. "Ah, *si capisco*, I understand. *Parli solo in Italiano*, speak only in Italian, Kat."

Now he gets it, but what to do? Her rib cage freezes, not enough air, even here by the ocean. She surveys the bistro, checks out the cop. What's he doing? He looks her way, smiles blankly and then stares out to sea. What now? Order her meal. That's the reasonable thing to do, but she can't catch her breath.

"Scusi Franco, I must leave, please understand." Head down, she won't look at him in case he wants to dissuade her. The chair scraps along the stone floor as she stands. Then, she bolts to the exit and descends the stairs. She quickens her pace until she's over the breakwater. The waves resemble the shore at Point No Point. The rhythmic laps. Safe only at dawn. *Hide until then, Kat.* Re-entering the church, she searches the dim space. She's alone.

You made a mistake, Kat. You spoke English. You forgot to be a chameleon. Now what?

Her cell chimes. She ignores it. *Calm yourself, Kat. You can make it out of here.* From the gap in the wall, she sees the dock. If she collects herself, she can make it. She'll watch for the next ferry and go.

Her cell chimes again. Still alone. Still safe. No priest, No cop. She returns to the slit of a window. Where's the ferry? What did Franco say? They run every hour. She tries to take a deep breath and calm herself, but her ribs won't move. She coughs and chokes on her spittle. *Think Kat. Take your hair down. Wear the straw hat. The cop didn't see you in the hat Franco bought.*

Her cell chimes a third time. She recognizes Franco's number. She picks up.

"Where are you?" He whispers. Have they arrested him already?

"In the church."

"*Non si muova. Sto arrivando*, don't move, I'm coming." He leaves his cell on. She hears laughter in the background and Franco's uneven breathing. He's running.

A shadow at the door of the church, it's her painter. He rushes across the grey stones, arms reaching for her. Gives her a long hard stare. "Kat, what happened? Are you okay?"

The chapel walls ripple. She feels her body slide down his torso until she crumples at his feet. She feels Franco carry her to the bench. If she could only catch her breath.

"Should I call an ambulance? *A dottore*?" Kisses her forehead.

"The cop came to arrest me, Franco." Tears stream down her face.

Franco groans. Now he understands.

"No, *cara mia*, not today. That guy ordered so much food he'll be there for hours."

"I'm Canadian. Canada can take me any time they want." Kat chokes on her tears, but her ribs feel looser. "I need to get out of here. Please, Franco, hide me."

"*Cara mia. Mi dispiace, mi dispiace tanto,* my darling, I am sorry, I am very sorry." He goes to the slit window. "Rest calm. There's the ferry."

CHAPTER TWENTY-SIX

Florence

The bamboo chairs scuff the terra cotta tiles as Franco pulls them face to face.

"Please, sit. You fainted. Are you feeling better? Should I find a doctor?"

Kat sits. They've made it to their hotel room undetected. Her panic recedes. He takes her hands in his. Franco leans forward, waiting for answers to his questions. When none are forthcoming: "Hungry?"

Kat nods. Now that he mentions it.

Franco scans the hotel menu, calls room service. Insalata, lasagne, a bottle of water. "Anything else, Kat?"

"*Vino*. I could use a drink."

He shoots her a look but orders the wine anyway. Compared to the fresh catch they would have dined upon in Vernazza, this is basic fare. Kat's embarrassed. She ruined the day. Worse, Franco caught a glimpse of how it was for her after he boarded the plane for Rome. That ugly maelstrom that took hold of her mind. The panic she wishes to forget has returned.

Franco takes her hands and observes her for the longest time. A twist of his lower lip.

"Kat, that police officer was on holiday. His wife was bragging about her husband's job. He wasn't interested in you. His words are precise, as if he's been practicing his lines. "You picked the town from the map. I chose the restaurant and he was seated when we arrived. Remember?" There's something worrisome in his eyes.

She nods.

"No one's going to arrest you. If someone from Canada wanted to… interview you… they'd have to go through proper channels. First your embassy and then our police system. The carabinieri are occupied with our own criminal element." He picks his words with care. "A possible murder seven years old, a cold case from another continent. That's a low priority in Italy. *Capisci?*" He cups her chin in his palm. "It's necessary for you to understand that your fear confuses reality. *Si?*"

"If he's chasing cold cases, someone will want to interview me. Faith lived with me. If George tells the police about Faith's blackmail attempts, they'll want to find me. Don't say they can't because they can, Franco. Today, he could do it. The hotel has my passport and the embassy has the Florence address on file. Even my bank manager in Victoria knows where I am."

"*Basta*, enough. Maybe Faith's case is closed. You don't know, do you? Maybe everything's finished." He holds her chin firmly in his palm.

"I wait for the *carabinieri* to knock on the door. That's what you're asking me to do." Kat twists away from him, a ragged agitation rising in her chest. She remembers the port towns of Vancouver Island and waiting for the RCMP to knock on her door.

"I'm saying that it's finished here. You're afraid, so we return to Florence tomorrow." There's an edge of anger in his words. "You search online if you must, but if there's no proof, we won't live in fear." He leans forward, nose to nose. "Hear me, Kat. We have a good life." A rap on the door. It's only dinner. "No more fear."

He doesn't get it. In Canada, there will be media coverage of the cold cases. It's a tactic used to entice old witnesses to bring forward new evidence. CBC breaking news: *Marketing executive blackmailed for her sudden inheritance from her penniless childhood friend who knew her darkest secret. Did the successful executive silence the blackmailer permanently?*

A circumstantial case to be sure, but one with enough motive to pursue. Robbie would imagine this scenario as much more plausible than the truth. A passionate Italian artist, with an over-developed sense of loyalty to his patron, defends her by bashing her blackmailer over the head with a random chunk of cinder block. Kat breathes deeply. That sounds more like something RAI TV would report. Still, no one in Italy would care if an Italian artist of his reputation murders a flower arranger on the west coast of Canada. Franco remains safe. He's on Italian soil.

The ebony door with the lion's head brass knocker. Chiara waits on the other side and blocks her entry. Only it's not the nightmare this time. Kat watches Franco as he turns the old-fashioned key in the lock.

"Walk around and look, just once, before you decide. Give it a chance." His tone is carefully neutral. Kat has walked these dark floorboards down the hall in her dreams, and in her life. This time it's different. The children's pram no longer blocks the entry. The hall has been whitewashed. A mirror framed in mercury glass hangs above a console of bleached oak. White orchids fill an ebony bowl. Her heels click on the hardwood as she moves toward the living space. Kat gasps. Everything has changed. Gone are the floor-to-ceiling bookshelves of academic tomes and the Ghibellini family bible. Instead, a dozen sketches in black frames, Franco's line drawings. Each one with a narrow ribbon of secondary matting in muted shades of rust, melon or green. On an over-sized computer screen, Kat's photographs of Pacific Ocean sea life cycle through in rhythmic flashes of colour. Gone too is the leather furniture, replaced by a low-slung sofa and chair in oatmeal tones. Franco explains the chaise is so she can read in comfort while he's catching up on his soccer re-plays. In front of the sofa sprawls a giant tree stump, lacquered and repurposed as coffee table. Kat smiles. This, she supposes, is her painter's attempt to bring the west coast of Canada to Florence.

She runs her hands across the surfaces. Varnished wood, nubby upholstery, weathered chair backs. The line drawings grab her attention. Sketches of *La Donna, Madonna di Levi, Ponte Diavolo,* framed just as she imagined them that afternoon in Torcello when she described to her painter how exquisite they'd look.

The chandelier above the table is Murano glass. "Milk white, not glitzy, Kat. You said you want understated." She barely remembers telling him this. How could he have stored it in his mind all this time? The kitchen remains unchanged other than new hardware of hammered chrome, shiny stainless appliances, white dishes and cutlery Massimo's designer found at a Milan Expo. "Feel the weight of them, Kat." Franco hands her a knife and fork. Kat lifts them. A luxurious heft. These were Franco's idea.

He points to the terrace. No changes because he knows she likes it. They made love there. No need to erase those memories.

"*Vieni*, there's more." Franco motions her along the second hallway. Kat stands outside the room she dreads most: Chiara's bedroom. Franco opens the door. "Look for yourself."

Like the marriage it served, the matrimonial bedroom no longer exists. Walls reconfigured to form a smaller room with white, wrought-iron bunk beds along one wall and a single adult bed along the other. A child-sized table. Shelves filled with the children's books she'd bought in Venice. Sketches of all three children on the walls. A crucifix over the door.

"When did you do these?" The sketches are fluid and exuberant, like their subjects.

"Last summer, at the farmhouse."

Kat doesn't remember Franco sketching, only Chiara's hateful barbs.

Franco takes Kat's hand and leads her to the next doorway. The room that once was hers is now an unfamiliar bedchamber. The new sleeping quarters have gained the footage lost from the children's room. Above a cane headboard, massive sketches of the *Goddess of Torcello*, anterior and posterior. *Mozzafiato*. Breathtaking.

Kat takes in the details. More salvaged-wood furniture. White linens and a lynx throw. Kat plants herself on the bed and runs her fingers through the fur. Where did Franco find this? Another tribute to Canada? On the other side of the room, tallboys with a ceiling to floor mirror between them. Their winter clothes hang in the wardrobe. Filmy ivory curtains float before the open window and there's a Roman shade to draw for serious sleep.

"Did you like, Kat?" He searches her face. Earnest, unsure, but hopeful.

"No. I don't like it. I *love* it, Franco. You've created the home in my dreams. Everything I said, you heard and remembered. You made this happen." She kisses him full on the lips.

"There's more, *vieni*." They re-trace their steps into the hall outside his studio. In the nightmare, this is where Chiara barred her entry. She shivers.

"I need you to give me a euro."

What's this about? She finds her purse and a euro. Just one? He nods and opens the door. The wooden pallets from Torcello are stacked in a corner. A golden light filters across the space. Franco's beloved studio.

"What's missing, Kat?"

Confused, Kat opens her mouth to speak. Then it hits her.

"*The Madonna Cries*." The massive painting is absent.

Franco grins.

"Correct! That painting, with its sister, *The Madonna di Levi*, and this coin. Together they purchased this apartment." Franco's grin expands.

He's excited. She's still confused. "I bought the apartment from Massimo with those two paintings and your euro." He kisses the coin.

"My euro?"

"You paid one euro. Together, we own this apartment ... once we sign these papers and get them notarized." He picks up a sheaf of paper from the computer table.

"That's incredibly generous ..." Kat feels her heart race. Can she allow such a gift?

"It's done. See." He points to the contract, her name beside his. "Our home now, *cara mia.*" He pulls her into his arms. "We will have a good life here, Kat."

Everyone participated in the transformation. Massimo took direction from Franco who conjured up the details based on Kat's daydreams. Vittorio oversaw the transport of the items that Massimo's designer sourced. Anna was their expert on Kat's preferences when the painter and the patron came to an impasse; an occurrence that had happened frequently. Emails, texts, phone calls. Even Agnes had a hand in arranging items as they arrived in Florence. The challenge was getting Massimo's Italian designer to agree to a neutral palette with the only colour coming from Kat's photographs and Franco's bowl of fruit. The painter persevered. If Massimo wanted the two sisters, as he now calls the Madonna paintings, then he had no choice. Franco chortles as he relates the challenges and tribulations that went into the project. "It's worth it, Kat. Yes?"

She discovers more of Franco's attempts to please her. The stone-washed linen sheets she had preferred in Torcello. The taupe and blue-striped Turkish towels she remarked upon in a market stall in Vernazza. Her every word, her every desire has found a place here.

In the days that follow Kat enjoys exploring all the details that make up the apartment, but one thought bothers her.

"Franco, do you like the apartment?" Did Franco ignore his own desires in favour of hers?

"I have my studio, a nursery for my children and my bowl of fruit." He cocks his head, gives her a full-lipped smile. "Besides, I put nothing in the apartment if I didn't want it too." He's on his way to meet his tailor for a tuxedo fitting for the Rome show. "It's peaceful here now. My eyes look at colour all the time, I like the rest." A kiss to her forehead and he's gone.

The Rome exhibit looms, one week away. She soft-launches Franco's website with the tech-head in Venice and a handful of Guggenheim staff who volunteered to give feedback on any tweaks before they go live. The consensus: intuitive navigation and straightforward access to information. *Va bene.*

But the website was an easy project compared to Kat's main pre-occupation: her search for cold case news in Vancouver. She googled police websites, relevant media and Faith's name. Nothing. If there's a cold case project, it's below the radar, she decides, while still feeling unsettled. There's information out there, somewhere.

The key in the lock. Franco is back so soon. A garment bag slung over his arm, he stands at the entrance to the great room and throws her a look. Her computer reads five pm. She's sitting where he left her.

"Testing your website." She answers his unspoken question.

Franco looks at the screen.

"The Canadian police are interested in my art, Kat? Still chasing ghosts, I see." He shifts his bag to his other arm. "I have a surprise for you." He nods toward their bedroom.

Franco carefully arranges the bag's contents on the bed.

"For you, for Rome."

Two pairs of cream-coloured trousers: One skinny-legged in soft leather and the other wide-legged *palazzos* in silk. Two pairs of shoes: soft leather slingbacks and toeless wedges, both in cream with a leather clutch of the same shade. Beside them lay a cap-sleeved, hip-length tunic covered with inverted triangles in hues of gold, melon and peach, hand-sewn. Elegant, dramatic and not an outfit Kat would consider wearing. "What do you think? You need to try, but it fits, I'm sure." Franco holds the tunic up so she can judge for herself. Kat can't envision herself in *haute couture* that is so … *haute.*

"I was planning on the midnight-blue dress from the gala. No one in Rome has seen it, other than you and Massimo."

Franco persists. "Massimo says it's not for Rome. He wishes to introduce you as my marketing manager, not my muse. It's different. He says these are good choices, Kat."

She gets the message. Less plunging neckline, more dramatic flair. She slips on the wedge heels. Of course, they fit. Franco smiles knowingly. The leather trousers feel lightweight and supple. The linen ones feel even lighter.

"You see? Massimo is correct, the tunic works. All you need is your hair up and earrings." She's been finessed. No doubt Massimo has already picked out the earrings. Kat has one leg in the leather trousers when the door buzzer rings. They're not expecting anyone. Kat hides her fear by pretending to fuss with the pants, her back to him.

"That will be Massimo. He's bringing copies of the catalogue and he wants to see the apartment. I forgot to tell you." Franco buzzes Max in. Kat chides herself for giving in to a stupid gut reaction, mindless panic.

Casual in a leather bomber jacket, Massimo carries a black attaché case and white orchids in an ebony bowl, a twin to the one in their hallway. Without asking, he places his housewarming gift in a spot Agnes had, apparently, designated. He wanders about, even opens the kitchen drawers to check out the cutlery. His eyes linger on the line drawings, assessing their treatment and placement. Massimo wishes to see his grandchildren's room. After the Rome exhibit, Massimo's grandchildren will live with Franco and Kat part-time. It's the reason they've retained Massimo's spy, Agnes. Antonio and Katerina are comfortable around her; she knows their habits and Chiara trusts her. Agnes wasn't Kat's choice, but she can only push Franco so far.

Massimo returns to the living room. Kat sits at the end of the weathered oak dining table.

"Are you content yet, Katerina?"

"Si Massimo, *e meravigliosa*."

He checks out the tree stump, now a coffee table.

"Franco insisted on this." Shakes his head. "So many things he insisted, Kat."

Franco draws nearer. She puts her arm around her painter's waist.

"He's a good man*, mio pittore*, my painter."

Massimo's had enough of the pleasantries. All business, he pulls three glossy catalogues from his valise. Kat can't wait to get her hands on the finished product, but Massimo keeps waiting. "It's spectacular, Katerina. The kind of thing a patron will leave out on their tree stump or perhaps on a more ordinary coffee table." Max's amused by his joke. "If you would indulge me, I'd like you to autograph my copy." Massimo hands her two copies, gives Franco the third.

Kat places her copy on the tree stump. The cover is a close-up of one of the *Tomorrow* canvasses. She longs to review her work in detail after Max has left.

As he pads his way to the door in exquisite loafers, Massimo calls over his shoulder: "Another thing, Kat, the Torcello paintings. What do you want to do with them after the show?"

"Massimo! She doesn't know yet." Franco is aghast.

"Well, she does now." Massimo grins wolfishly.

"I wanted to surprise you in Rome, Kat. I make you a gift of two paintings. Do you know which ones?" Franco embraces her, turning his back on Massimo who has screwed up his surprise. *Surprise*, thinks Kat.

She hopes that they aren't *Sorrow* and the *Muse*. "Tell me, *mio caro*," she whispers.

Max's social indignation takes the form of a loud cough. It infuriates him to hear their endearments, but he asked for it, this time.

"*The Goddess, Anterior and Posterior.* The paintings celebrating our love, Kat." A deep kiss.

Kat returns Franco's passion. "*Grazie, mille grazie.*"

"What do you want to do with them, Katerina?" Max's voice is loud. She stares at him. *You're still here?*

"Find a worthy museum and I will loan them out just as I have *La Donna*. You can manage that. Can't you, Max?"

"A wise decision. Milan, I think. We need exposure in the North." He offers his hand to Franco, ignores Kat. Massimo departs noiselessly in his precious leather loafers.

Almost nine, and Franco is organizing his studio for new work after the Rome exhibit. She slips into the outfit he purchased. It fits as if made bespoke for his marketing manager—her new promotion from Massimo. Clearly, she's no longer the painter's *puttana*.

She indulges in one last surf of the Vancouver websites before Franco emerges for the night. Nothing in the *Vancouver Sun*, but from the front page of the *Province* a headline jumps out. "Old Cold Cases See the Light." The article announces the appointment of RCMP Inspector Robert Kavanagh. It's the cop from Vernazza, in full uniform. There's an URL with details on the cases and a hot line for readers with information. Kat trembles, can barely type, misses keys. The link to the RCMP website pops up. An alphabetical list of hyper-linked names of victims, each one with a short biography and a case number. She scrolls down until she reaches Vogel, Faith. Kat's found her ghost.

"What does it say? Read it." Black eyes. Franco opens the Prosecco with steady hands. "Read it."

"Faith Vogel, 54, last seen alive just before midnight leaving a Christmas Party on a houseboat in the False Creek area of Granville Island on December 23rd, 2007. The deceased was 5'4" 125 pounds, short blonde hair, blue eyes, wearing a red dress, black boots. Her body was found in the creek in the early hours of Dec. 24 by a passerby. If anyone has any information on of the events of that night, contact the RCMP with file #7850."

Franco passes her a flute of Prosecco, then leans over and shuts down her laptop. He takes a long swig of his drink and stares at Kat.

"I was heading across the island after my class. I heard Faith threaten you earlier when I was on the stairwell. You never saw me, Kat. I didn't know what she had on you, I still don't." Franco's eyes search hers but she's not giving up her secrets. Another swig. "She was on the edge of the creek wall, walking one foot in front of the other, arms out to keep her balance. I could tell she was drunk. I knew she went to that Christmas party and that you stayed home. I hated her, Kat. She disrespected you, made you afraid. She demanded money like a whore. Her scraggy hair and that make-up, she was ... common." He finishes his drink and looks hard at Kat. "She never saw me. I picked up a piece of cement and smashed it hard on the back of her head." He refills his glass, hands steady.

"She just stood there. I was afraid she was going to turn around and scream at me. Then she fell forward into the creek." He turns to Kat, his eyes imploring. "No one around. No one saw me. I looked. I heard the splash, so I ran to the houseboat and let myself in. It was dark and silent. I took a shower, but the adrenalin was shooting through me and the knowledge of what I'd done. You were sleeping. I slipped in beside you, allowed myself to kiss you, to touch you at last." His voice is a plea for understanding.

Kat's memory of what happened next is vivid. "I woke up, your lips on mine, your hands on my breasts. I was shocked, but I didn't stop you, *caro mio*. I wanted you too." Kat crosses the kitchen and embraces him hard. "I love you Franco, *sempre*, always."

"You love me ... a stupid kid from the country who picks up a rock. *Gesu Cristo*. I caused you so much pain." Franco chokes on his tears, on his regret.

"There's nothing to forgive. You wanted to keep me safe." Kat remembers the white pebble, the evil she brought into their lives from the den of the Marquis de Sade. She knows who is responsible for Franco's act. She is. Kat, herself.

"I want *you* safe. If we marry, you can become an Italian citizen." He kisses her cheek. "We could fight extradition if it came to that. Massimo knows lawyers." His arms hang loose. "Or I confess."

"Have you ever told anyone else what happened that night?"

Franco shakes his head. "I have never said these words before tonight."

"You are never to confess. I brought you to Canada. I put you on that houseboat and I'm responsible for everything that happened there. You were an innocent. I'll take my chances if I need to but you're never to tell your story again. Do you understand me?" She presses down on his shoulders. "Never, Franco. I'd rather go to prison than ruin your life. *Capisci*?" Painter and muse, clinging to each other. Faith's long dead, but it's still not possible to escape her reach.

CHAPTER TWENTY-SEVEN

Rome

"**M**ay I have your business card? I'd be interested in you visiting my gallery." The gaunt man towers over Kat. He fumbles in a pocket of his tuxedo, a garment so exquisitely crafted that even Massimo would approve. "Here's mine. Your name again?"

"I appreciate your interest, but I live in Florence, so I don't think we could …" Kat attempts to extricate herself from the man's elevator pitch. Where's Franco?

"I represent several Roman artists. You have an appreciation for contemporary Italian art." He holds up Kat's catalogue. "I'm sure we could work out a beneficial arrangement, perhaps a catalogue with pages dedicated to each of my painters." The gaunt man hasn't heard a word she's said.

It's Massimo who comes to her rescue. Taking her elbow, he guides her through the crowded ballroom and delivers her to their artist. "Your marketing manager's becoming a hustler. A bit of publicity and she's drumming up business for herself." He chuckles.

Franco is not in the mood for jokes, especially Massimo's digs at Kat. He wants to escape. The open bar has made some of the guests too bold. One woman attempted to take him to her villa, immediately. Another wished him to paint her nude, also immediately, since she was wearing no underwear. Grabbing his hand to show him.

"We need to go."

"You're catnip for the women of Rome, Franco," she whispers in his ear as they enter the elevator.

"The only Kat I want nipping me is you." Another Kat joke she will hear for days.

Soft yellow moonlight silhouettes the apartments above the cafés in the Piazza della Rotunda, just as it did that night seven years before. A woman leans on her window ledge, sips a glass of wine. Kat wonders if she'd sipped her wine and watched the passers-by that night too.

Kat had arrived in Rome with the woman of Pompeii still fresh in her mind. The woman fated never to escape her destiny; her futile attempt chronicled for all time. Kat felt she was that woman too, desperate to escape from her past and a possible future with Faith. The moon rises steadily over the piazza, shedding its golden glow. Kat is still a woman desperate to escape her past and Faith.

"Is everything alright?" Franco pours the last of the Prosecco he ordered to celebrate the opening.

"I was remembering the night we met." She sips the ends of the bubbly, drinks in his features. Savours the memory of meeting him for the first time.

That night so long ago, Kat and Faith dined in the piazza, the night Faith admitted adding the poison mushroom to Nick's stew. She made her first blatant attempt to get Nick's money that night too. Rebuffed, she'd stomped off in a too-short skirt, her dangling earrings glinting in the moonlight. Kat recounts none of this to Franco, instead kisses his cheek. He's clean-shaven, at Massimo's request.

A kiss to her fingertips. An exotic act, but one she's come expect in their daily life.

"I was on my own, Franco. I didn't wish to stay with the tour Faith had booked. I spent the afternoon in the Pantheon." She remembers asking the Roman gods for guidance.

"That evening I ate in the piazza, possibly at this café. On my way back to the hotel I noticed a painter beside *Bernini's Elephant*." Franco smiles. It's their story from here on. "I watched you at work. The single stroke of yellow at the last, it changed everything. I knew then you were a gifted artist. You understood the power of light and shadow."

He kisses her fingertips again.

"*Cinque giorni* to dry. You were adamant. For five days, I watched *Il Elefante* dry. I wanted more. Your art to be sure, but more of you in my life … so I found you." She caresses his hand. "My want was fierce. Nothing I had ever known. I denied it. I thought of myself as a patron or supporter, not as a woman wanting a man. Easy to support your art, for you are the genius Massimo believes in. I knew it before he did. I refused to accept my deeper wants, though: to touch your body, to know your soul. I lied to myself for a long time." His expression is serious. What's he remembering? "When you came to me in the boathouse, finally I was free to accept what I'd desired since the night I met you. That's the truth, *caro mio.*"

"Come, Kat. I've something to show you." Franco settles with the waiter and they shake hands.

Bernini's Elephant. In the twilight, the pale marble presence stands in the piazza behind the Pantheon of the gods.

"Where we met ... yes?" Franco guides her to the elephant's base.

Kat stands back a few paces. She searches the skyline. The Roman moonlight illuminates the statue, and her painter. "A night just like this, Franco."

He scans the piazza where a few disinterested tourists wander by. He clears his throat. "I need to say something important in Italian and in English." Sheepish grin. "In case you don't understand the Italian." Hands clasped behind his back, elegant in his tuxedo, his curly mop brushed out of his eyes. "*Ti offro il mio amore, il mio corpo, il mio nome e il mio paese. Vi prego di accettare, di essere mia moglie.* I offer you my love, my body, my name and my country. Please accept me, be my wife." He drops one knee to the cobbles.

Kat's painter opens a silver case where a ring glints in the lamplight. "Kat, will you marry me?"

The world continues to spin on its axis undeterred, but Kat fears she's going to lose her footing. Passers-by recognize the moment by clicking their phones. Franco shifts position, uncomfortable on the cobbles.

How to respond to his grand and imprudent gesture? "Yes, Franco, *ti sposerò, I will marry you.*"

Franco rises, rubs his knee and reaches for her hand. As she expects, the ring fits. A band of platinum, three emerald cut stones a ruby with a diamond on either side. They're magnificent in design, weight and feel.

"The ruby symbolizes passion and the diamonds constancy and protection. Our symbols, I think?" He's hesitant but Kat can think of no better way to describe their bond.

The accidental witnesses break into applause when Franco pulls Kat close and kisses her. Someone offers to take a photo and Franco gives him his cell phone. The painter in his tuxedo, his muse in her sequined tunic and silk trousers. They pose beside their elephant. Click. Click. Click. Then, it's done. Kat and Franco will marry.

Kat insists on visiting the Pantheon before leaving for Termini train station. The Roman gods kept Franco safe and now it's her turn. Seated at the end of a bench, she closes her eyes. *Protect me, protect Franco. Protect us from harm. Bless our marriage.* A tap on her arm. Franco suggests they go or miss their train.

Getting married is not so straightforward as Franco imagines. She can't just pick out a dress and show up at the Basilica in her stilettos. Since she's Canadian, Italy needs a marriage affidavit from her embassy that certifies she's Katherine Black, a copy of Nick's death certificate as proof she's widowed and confirmation that neither she nor Franco have been convicted for the attempted or successful murder of the other person's former spouse. Kat smiles on reading this. Throttling Chiara would have precluded marrying Franco, it seems. Luckily, Kat merely blackmailed her instead.

Since she already has the necessary documentation, Kat returns to Rome the following week to swear the affidavit at the Canadian consulate and receive permission to marry at the Italian Prefecture. To avoid delays Franco hand-delivers the documents to Brigitte's husband, the notary in San Gimignano, who registers their intent in the region. Because he's divorced, Franco can no longer marry in the church, so the wedding will take place in the loggia of the Baptistery. The mayor will officiate, but Father Anselmo agrees to bless the union. After settling all that, choosing the bridal gown is simple. Once Kat finds the stylish shift, it requires a single fitting.

Nick and Kat had a destination wedding. That is, they had a brief civil ceremony with co-workers as witnesses and then boarded a flight to Heathrow. Ten days of Nick's guidebook narrative as they visited London and Oxford. Franco and Kat are having a different sort of wedding. Although a civil ceremony, the priest who's known Franco since he felt the child kick in his mother's womb will bless their union. The Ghibellini clan will be their witnesses.

Brigitte tucks a spray of red rose buds into the twist she's fashioned in the bride's hair. Kat removes a pair of diamond chandelier earrings from their grey velvet pouch and inserts them into her earlobes. Brigitte touches the delicate gems. Massimo's wedding gift.

Kat feels an inner calm. Thinking of Franco, her shoulders relax. Kat could weep with the pleasure she feels for being a part of her painter's life and, soon, his bride.

The loggia of the Baptistery is in the arcade behind a line of marble columns. The stout octagonal pillars, banded in red, gold and ivory, soar to the vaulted ceiling. A small altar covered in white linens with two padded stools in front, a dozen collapsible chairs line up behind them. Tall vases of lapis blue pottery on either side of the altar sprout roses and wildflowers from Mariola's garden.

The wedding guests are few. Franco's close family, along with Eva and three of the Guggenheim staff. Of course, Massimo's present to witness the event and to remind them of all that has gone before. The children wait on the top step of the basilica with Brigitte. In a diminutive lace dress, tiny matching ballet slippers and a pink rose bud on a grosgrain ribbon around her waist, Katerina is a constant reminder of Chiara. Antonio, with dark curls and tanned knees, jumps up and down in his black runners. His white jacket and short trousers are spotless so far. He fingers the pink rosebud on his collar. Kat reaches down and nuzzles the child who has always accepted her as his *nonna*.

Franco's photographer's everywhere, snapping candid shots. Kat ignores him.

Smoothing the skirt of her gown, she takes the homemade bouquet of red roses from her new sister-in-law. Hopes only that Franco's not disappointed by her choice of apparel. Spaghetti straps, the white silk dress falls on empress lines, has an accompanying bolero jacket with a row of covered buttons and long sleeves. Her only jewellery is Franco's engagement ring and Massimo's diamonds.

Kat joins her painter before the youngish mayor, who wears his sash of office over a smart business jacket. Franco reaches for her hand and holds it until they are officially wed. The service is in Italian. Yesterday, they practiced their vows so that Kat wouldn't get lost, but Franco and the mayor make it easy. Speaking slowly, they allow her time to understand and respond.

"*Io, Katerina, prendo te, Francesco, come mio sposo e prometto di esserti fedele sempre, nella gioia e nel dolore, nella salute e nella malattia, e di amarti e onorarti tutti i giorni della mia vita.* I, Katerina, take you, Francesco, as my husband and promise to be faithful to you always, in joy and in pain, in health and in sickness, and to love you and honour you every day, for the rest of my life."

In Canada, it's popular to write personal vows, but these traditional words capture all she wishes to convey. After the gossip and innuendo, those side glances and after Chiara's battering remarks, she's grateful for the opportunity to declare aloud in front of the people who know him best and, in his language, her commitment to Franco.

As guests speed away to the Ghibellini farmhouse, the bride and groom walk across the patch of asphalt to Mateo's grave. The intricate headstone Massimo ordered from Carrera has not yet arrived. Franco falls to his knees and kisses the ground. His shoulders heave as he weeps. Kat lays her bridal bouquet on the grave. Lifting her wedding gown above her knees, she kneels beside her husband and holds him.

They change clothing in silence. Franco's lost in thought and Kat chooses not to intrude. Hanging up his groom's jacket, he allows Kat to undo the top buttons of his shirt. On his wrist, Massimo's extravagant wedding gift to his protégé, a Bulgari chronograph watch. Taking his hand, she kisses his wedding band. Franco strokes her cheek and retreats to the bathroom. The air is warm and still on the second floor. The festivities on the lawn below are sheltered under a tent. Franco re-appears and offers his hand. *Signor e Signora Ghibellini* descend the stairs.

Eviva gli sposi. Toast to the newlyweds! Kat takes a long sip of Prosecco. Franco's hand firm around her waist.

Father Anselmo lumbers across the lawn to the tent. He wants a word with the guests.

"Our bride and groom travelled a painful road before they came to us today. For the gossips in San Gimignano, there was much to discuss." He surveys the gathered, Ghibellini kin who are also his parishioners. He addresses Franco and Kat. "Today, I suggest we consider not the Bible, but Dante. He wrote: 'If love is a sin, it is at least a noble sin, for true love can dwell only in noble hearts'."

The priest, who Kat imagines broke the letter of Catholic law to allow their secular wedding in the Baptistery, makes the sign of the cross and adds: "*Dio vi osservano, i miei figli*, God keep you, my children." As Kat embraces the prelate, he whispers that she's *la sposa piu bella*, the most beautiful bride. The Prosecco bubbles in the clinking glasses. The priest holds up his glass and intones: "Not since Cristo attended a wedding is there this much great wine."

Franco steers his bride from table to table until they've shared their meal with every guest and sampled their way through every course. With aunts, uncles and cousins at every turn, and children racing between tables with their cousins, Kat thinks that Franco's babies are experiencing the idyllic childhood Franco wants for them.

As the evening winds down, Mariola presents the traditional final course. Bowls of sugared almonds compete with *pane cotta* in ramekins accompanied by shot glasses of homemade *limoncello*. An inviting breeze brings guests to the dance floor. Elsewhere, men gather to smoke while women chat in twos or threes.

"*Potrei avere questo ballo, per favore*, may I have this dance, please?" Luigi, the senior Ghibellini, offers his arm to Kat. After a short twirl, Franco cuts in. They've been on and off the impromptu dance floor all evening. He guides Kat round and round. The guests begin to clap, shouting *bravo*, calls for the couple to kiss. Without warning, Franco stops and with a single motion hurls her onto his shoulder, fireman style.

"Franco!" What the ..."

"*Oggi, diventi mia moglie italiana. Andiamo.* Today you become my Italian wife. Let's go." Franco heads toward the farmhouse amid raucous clapping and singing of lyrics which Kat's sure are bawdy.

"Put me down, I mean it." Hairpins bounce on the ground. God knows what view they have of her legs and ass. She thumps his backside.

"*Oh la,* I like that!" He relents, lowers her right side up and gives her a boyish grin, utterly carefree.

"You are a bad man, *mio marito.*"

"Kiss me, *mia moglie,* my wife, then I apologize." Tidying her hair, he kisses her neck.

Songs, whistles, applause. The photographer captures it all. Kat and Franco mount the stairs to enthusiastic shouts and enter their bedroom, shutting out the world.

Mio, sei mia. Mine, you are mine. Kat crawls out of bed. Franco sprawls out on his back, arms akimbo in the mess of bedlinens and musk. Kat takes inventory of all the elements that go into the making of her painter, now her husband. Which part of him does she love more?

Retrieving her camera from the side table, Kat mutes the shutter and starts clicking. His tapered hands, those sun browned arms, that lean torso. She moves the bedclothes around, reveals him. His penis, flaccid in sleep. Travels up towards his bronzed nipples, his face. Shadow on his clean-lined jaw, those full lips, sleeping eyes under black lashes.

Click, click. Close-up. His ears. What man ever had such gorgeous ears? Economical shape and kissable. She leans close. Franco opens his eyes.

"*Buongiorno.*" He stares at her, unperturbed that she's hovering over him capturing his ear on camera.

"How long have you been awake?" Found out.

"Since you slipped out of bed." He grins.

"Why didn't you tell me?" Embarrassed now for having rearranged the bedsheet to reveal him. Even with his eyes shut, he must have known what she was doing.

"I wanted to find out what you'd do when you thought no one was watching." He gives her a look that says 'caught you'. "Now I know." Pulls the sheet back up to his waist.

"Do you want to see my pictures? What I see when I look at you, *mio amore.*" Kat attempts to elevate her actions to art. "In black-and-white they'll be stunning."

"Later, what I want right now is a morning kiss from my wife." His bronzed arms reach for her.

Kat crawls back into the bed and kisses her husband. Forgiven.

Paolo's driving them to Florence. Usually, he'd keep the driver company in front, but today Franco's in the back with Kat, his arm around her, her head on his shoulder. Paolo dials down the radio, opens the windows. The scent of fresh-cut grass fills the air as they speed away from San Gimignano.

Kat's having trouble keeping her eyes open. Getting married Italian style takes a lot out of a person. Still, she feels a peace she's never known.

"Rest, *cara mia.*" Franco caresses her arm. The lull of soft music, the men's voices as they talk about the winery, soccer.

Home. They arrive at number six. She apologizes for sleeping the whole way but Paolo was glad to catch up with Franco. Kisses and goodbyes, *grazie.* The massive *portone* door of the Levi swings open and the new-lyweds enter the marble lobby, buzz for their talking elevator.

Franco drops their luggage in the bedroom, heads back downstairs for the mail. She opens the doors to the terrace as the evening bells begin their medley. She breathes deeply. Thankful. She will not be the woman of Pompeii after all. She has her new life. She's Franco's wife, soon she will be an Italian citizen. The Roman gods have been kind.

She turns, he's standing behind her, but something's not right.

Franco holds up an envelope. She recognizes the red maple leaf.

"It's the embassy in Rome."

"A follow-up from my affidavit?"

"No. Forgive me, but I opened it." He hands her the letter. "They're asking you to meet with the *carabinieri* next week. They want to interview you on behalf of the RCMP about the death of Faith Vogel." Franco holds her tight.

She should be afraid or panicked, but she feels only calm. No! No one is taking her life away, not the beautiful life she's struggled to find. A life blessed by the priest in San Gimignano. No one, not even Faith's ghost. *E mio. It's mine.*

"Franco, ring Massimo. I need to speak with him."

CHAPTER TWENTY-EIGHT

Florence

"**B**uongiorno Signora Ghibellini. May I call you Katerina?" Pietro Barone, a solid man in his fifties, is a member of the law firm retained by Massimo for Alighieri family affairs. A solid handshake. She doesn't object to the use of Katerina. As far as Kat's concerned, she is Katerina. Kat Black, the individual the *carabinieri* wish to interview, is among the disappeared.

Anyone can see Katerina and Kat are not the same person. Kat Black wore a mousy bob because a woman over a certain age mustn't grow her hair, had no need to release her tresses when she stood before a lover. Kat never wore floral dresses or showed décolletage. Kat Black liked everything simple, linear and sexless. Solitary, without close attachments. A Canadian nature photographer on the beaches of the Pacific West coast at dawn, that's Kat Black.

This marketing guru, specializing in promoting Italian artists like Ghibellini and sought after by Roman galleries, is Katerina. *La padrona* of an extended Italian family, mother by marriage to a son and a daughter. Anyone can see that Katerina in her pencil-thin coral suit and grey stilettos is not Kat Black.

Kat Black was widow to a man who never moved her soul and, like his wife, never believed in anything they couldn't see or touch. Katerina knows the dead transform and can be found among the stars. She understands that the palm of her beloved on her naked back is worth more than any earthly goods Kat Black had accrued. Anyone looking at

Katerina would know she's not Kat Black and not capable of committing such an evil act as murder.

At least that's what Kat hopes Pietro Barone, with his grizzled curls, assumes. It's what she imagines the *carabinieri* will deduce during the interview today. Reassures herself: *People see what they want to see, believe what they think is true.*

Massimo was generous in his assistance when she asked for guidance in seeking legal counsel. She was careful to hide her true motive. Massimo understood that an acquaintance in Vancouver drowned several years ago and the police are reviewing the circumstances. The woman had rented accommodation from Kat, so she will contribute what information she can. She confides that, with her lack of fluency in Italian and inexperience with the law, she's uneasy about interacting with the legal system. Massimo hired Pietro Barone to accompany Kat to the *Commando Provinciale di Carabinieri.*

Pietro Barone's English is impeccable. The interview is routine, he tells her, merely an attempt to put an unsolved case to rest. With a friendly smile, he assures her it will all be over this afternoon. Nothing to fret about, *la mia signora.*

They're ushered into a plain room with a square table, four old-school wooden chairs and a tinted window. There's a landline handset on the table and a poster on the wall reminding the viewer that telling the truth is not being *una spia,* a snitch.

The lieutenant, barely out of his teens, and a female interpreter with a taste for loops of faux pearls around her neck, sit across from them. Barone explains his client's fluency problem and the interpreter nods. The report will be translated into English. All that's needed is Katerina's signature before it goes back to the RCMP. Barone asks to vet both versions for accuracy. Agreement, and the interview begins.

Katerina produces her Canadian passport, her Permesso di Soggiorno for long-term residency and her marriage certificate. So little paper for such a vast journey for Kat Black.

Kat confirms that seven years ago she lived with Faith Vogel, her boyfriend George Brodskzi and an art student on a houseboat moored off Granville Island in Vancouver.

The lieutenant reads from his correspondence with the RCMP: On Dec 23rd Faith Vogel was found floating face down in False Creek

When did you first learn of her death? Kat leans back in her chair, looks at the poster above the interpreter's head.

"In the middle of the night, when I woke to knocking on the door. My first thought was 'Faith forgot her key or she's too pissed to use it.'"

Her lawyer re-phrases. "You mean you thought she was probably drunk."

Kat nods. "I climbed the steps in the dark, was going to give her a piece of my mind, but when I opened the door there were two cops … police officers. I remember looking at their badges and wondering what was going on." What she really remembers is that she thought: *What the fuck, it's not illegal to sleep with your protégé, is it?* She reminds herself to choose Katerina's words even if it's Kat's life she's describing.

What is your understanding of what happened that night?

"I don't know what happened. I never knew. The police said she had an injury to her head that could have happened before or after she entered the water. They said the autopsy would probably show cause of death. I never heard from them again. I guess I assumed it was an accident. Faith in her spiked heels … stilettos … drinking at a party. Her boyfriend brought two jeroboams of champagne, so she planned to drink that night. She slipped, possibly on black ice. That's what I thought."

The interpreter wants clarification on the term, black ice.

"It's what we call ice that forms after the rains. It's thin and slick but not visible. It causes car accidents or bad falls. It's common in Vancouver, especially in December." The interpreter twists her pearls as she explains this to the constable.

We refer to this as clear ice in Italy.

"I would think George or the other people at the party would have a better idea of what happened to Faith. You know, how much she drank, did she leave the party alone because she had a fight with George. Strange that they didn't leave together, I thought."

You did not go to the party, were alone at home?

"I didn't go. The people were Faith's friends. I stayed home. The student was at home too."

You and the student are each other's alibis then. Was the student of age, old enough to be an alibi?

Black ice. Keep your head, Kat.

"He was twenty-six then, studying his master's degree."

His name?

"Francesco Ghibellini." Kat looks her interrogator in the eye, a small smile on her lips. Wills herself to look calm and unthreatened.

"The Italian artist? The one who painted *La Madonna di Levi*? That Ghibellini?" Even the lieutenant knows her painter.

"But he's your husband now, isn't he?" The lawyer making the connection of past and present.

"Yes, we married a week ago. Seven years ago, he was a student boarding in my home while he studied."

The lieutenant seems uninterested in this, gets back to the list of questions laid out by the RCMP. *What happened after you learned of Faith Vogel's death? Did you hear gossip in the community? Did anyone give you any information, no matter how insignificant, about her death?*

"George came by a couple of days later and gathered up her belongings, cell phone, everything. He must have re-directed her mail because nothing came after her death. There was never a funeral. It was as if she never existed. I stayed in the houseboat until the lease ran out. Then I moved to the west coast of Vancouver Island where I focused on coastline photography. Became recognized internationally for my work." Kat hopes she projects the air of an acclaimed photographer.

And the student, signor Ghibellini?

"He returned to Italy. The northern light wasn't his milieu. He paints best in the south. We lost track of each other for five years."

But now you're married?

"We married last week in San Gimignano."

How did that happen if you lost track of each other?

"Five years passed and then my photos were featured at an international conference in Genova. He recognized my name and came to surprise me." She looks from *carabinieri* to interpreter to lawyer. They're intrigued, but she doesn't think they connect the dots. She hopes George and the black ice did their job.

So, you stayed on in Italy.

"Yes. I market his work. I developed a catalogue for his latest show in Rome and created a website."

How does a Canadian do this in a foreign country. You have a work permit? The lieutenant feels for an irregularity more familiar than a houseboat and black ice on the west coast of Canada.

"I collaborate with his patron, Massimo Alighieri." Kat pauses to let the name sink in. "He funds the projects but my role is voluntary. My first husband provided for me. I don't need to be employed."

The interpreter fingers her pearls as if they're a rosary. The lieutenant scribbles notes. Kat folds her hands in her lap. Her lawyer checks his smartphone. A good sign. He's bored.

Getting back to the reason we're here today, Signora Ghibellini, do you have any information or thoughts that might help in resolving the status of this unexpected death?

Kat yawns, feigns boredom, before answering.

"When I received the notice from the Canadian Embassy, I was thrown back to that time seven years ago. I walked through that night, the days before and after in my mind. I could think of nothing." She sighs. "I know nothing more about what happened than I did before the knock on the door."

Kat and her lawyer wait in the anteroom as the transcripts are prepared. Barone checks his voicemail, returns some calls. Kat uses the public toilet, choking on the acrid smell. Almost an hour passes before the lieutenant produces two manila folders for her lawyer to read. She sits very still while Barone goes over the interview in Italian and English, line by line, separately and side by side. Kat knows why he's on Massimo's team. He's thorough.

"They're accurate, Katerina. You may sign them."

A flourish of a signature, the new one Kat's been practising.

"What happens next?" She appeals to the lieutenant, who shrugs. He's unsure if the Canadians will get back to him. Italy's fulfilled her role. He wishes them a good evening and takes his leave with the folders tucked under his arm.

As they wait for a taxi, she asks Barone the same question. "Will I ever know what happens or will it be like before?"

"The course of justice will play out, Katerina. In time, the case will be resolved. If the police track down all the people at the party, it will take a while. Perhaps her case is of less interest than others on their roster are and will be given a lower priority. They did go to the bother of locating you, though."

"I'm registered with the Embassy and my financial manager knows my current whereabouts. I'm easy to find." *Stay with the facts.*

"Strange that they aren't interviewing the art student, you never know what he might have heard."

Kat's suddenly dizzy. Where did this line of thought come from? Then she remembered who hired the lawyer. *He's good.*

"Franco spoke little English at the time and wouldn't have understood most of what went on around him. I think the Vancouver police saw that."

"You're probably right." Barone opens the taxi door. "I'll follow up with the RCMP in a month but don't expect much. In my experience, cold cases usually grind slowly to a halt."

Kat climbs into the cab and leans back. Shuts her eyes. It's a short ride to Piazza della Repubblica but it feels like she's been travelling for years.

Franco meets her at the door with the face of a haunted man. Wrapping her arms around his neck, she strokes away his anxiety. She tells him word-for-word what she said. That she considered lying about the name of her student *protégé* but realized that it's common knowledge that Franco studied in Vancouver. If she was caught in a lie, then what?

Kat neglects to relay that her lawyer finds it strange that he hasn't been asked to confirm her alibi. She can't jettison the thought until she realizes that husband and wife cannot be made to testify against the other in Canada. The RCMP won't expend resources setting up an interview to have Franco confirm the obvious. That they're together now might raise a flag but she laid enough empty ground between Faith's death and their reunion. Five years without contact, separate lives. Not a sign of two people in a plot against the dead woman. Still, Faith's ghost stays like a stain on well-scrubbed carpet. To the knowing eye, the blemish remains.

Worry wraps around them, holds them tight. Even so, they push forward. Franco starts several new projects using the Mercado Centrale as his theme. In abandoning his *Madonne*, Kat thinks he's venturing into the Dutch school with his raw portraits of butchers and farmers selling their produce. Kat busies herself researching social media. Is Twitter too unsophisticated for a painter of Franco's stature? Would it require too much time for minimal return?

Florence is hot and dry in August. Kat opens windows, chasing a cross breeze with little result. After their evening meal they often take their *passeggiata* by river in hopes of catching relief from the heat near the water. Some evenings, Franco returns to his studio, so she walks alone. Florence is a safe town for a woman on her own. With so many tourists about, it would be hard to bash in a woman's head and slip her into the Arno without at least a dozen phones clicking the deed.

CHAPTER TWENTY-NINE

Piazza della Repubblica

Kat stretches, enjoying the roughness of the linen sheets. Franco sleeps on his back, arms above his head, his face stern even in repose. He wears the strains of the day, as when Mateo was dying.

If there was only some way to reconcile the past. Her only hope is to wait out the investigation. Whatever happens Faith's death must not fall at Franco's feet. She fears that George might throw suspicion on her if the RCMP turns up the heat. As Faith's intimate, he's statistically most likely to be the offender. Did Faith confide to George that she had dirt on Kat worthy of blackmail? Would she be so indiscreet? No, Faith was wilier than that. But pressured, George might remember some detail which would send the cops scurrying back to Florence. Maybe George remembers nothing new, or maybe he's died in a traffic accident.

Wait it out, Kat. Barone said justice grinds slowly in cold cases. *Hang tough*, she tells herself in the dawn hours. She turns to observe Franco's features as daylight lights the room. Her new husband is nothing like Nick. The artist doesn't play by the rules, not a guidebook in sight. Instead, he creates glorious images, pushing the boundaries of reality. She caresses her painter's arm, takes his hand. His fingers curl around hers even in sleep.

I brought you to this. Forgive me. He stirs. How to deliver you to safety, Franco?

Her mouth to his back, she whispers: "You're a noble man, Franco. Never think badly of yourself, I beg you."

He turns toward her. "I got us in this mess, Kat." Rolls away, but she won't let him go. Rears up on her knees.

"No! Faith was a murderer, a pre-meditated murderer." Crawling off the bed, she falls on her knees beside him. "She poisoned Nick. She gave you that white pebble from de Sade's ruins because she wished to harm you, too. But she became a victim of her own evil when you tried to protect me."

Franco sits up in bed, stares wide-eyed at her.

"You're saying you lived with someone who killed your husband?" He's fully alert now.

If she says the truth aloud, will he realize he was a casualty of their heinous pact or will he come to fear, even hate her? Save herself or save Franco. Choose.

"It was her part of our pact. I put clam juice in her husband Gerhard's meal when we vacationed in France. He was allergic to it. I watched him die." Words never before spoken.

Franco stops breathing. A muscle spasms in his cheek.

"A terrible man, he beat her. Didn't seem to care that we could see the bruises as we travelled through Provence. New bruises at breakfast, that's what we dined on. They got worse over time. I saw that he would kill her someday. We happened on de Sade's ruins in Lacoste. There I learned that energy remains, Franco. De Sade's energy was still there. I picked up the pebble, a talisman, I joked. Later, I poured the clam juice in our stew. I knew he'd die." She fixes her eyes on the grain of bedsheet. "Then I gave the pebble to Faith. Told her it was her turn." She wills herself to look at Franco. When she gathers up her courage, his eyes are closed.

"You hated Nick that much?" His voice is dull.

"No. I was tired of our life together, the way we skimmed along the surface of existence and always by Nick's rule books. I didn't think Faith would keep the pact. She lived in Seattle. I thought we'd never see her again. Once we returned to Canada, she came to Vancouver and became a fixture in our home. Nick liked her and she liked our lifestyle. I found it suffocating sharing my home with her. Then, I came home one day to a scrawled note under the pebble. Even before I read her words, I knew. By the time I arrived at the hospital, Nick was dead. He'd been harvesting wild mushrooms for dinner. She added a poisonous variety to his omelette. It was wrong, Franco. But I couldn't turn her in. I'd murdered Gerhard in Provence. Nick haunted me for the longest time. I'd hear him passing, his footsteps on our gravel driveway. Later outside the Borghese

Palace where I found you, and always on the beaches at dawn. I learned to live with his ghost." She lays her head on the mattress, closes her eyes. "I wanted to escape the awful things we'd done together. Faith suggested we travel to Italy. Make a clean start as widows. I couldn't think of a reason to say no, so I went along with her plan. That's when I met you."

His palm heavy on her head, slow strokes.

Kat begins to weep. "I didn't know Faith gave you the pebble until you showed it to me at the airport. She said you thought it was good luck. I hated her for that. How could she pull you into our destruction? Don't you see Franco, none of this is your fault? We were the evil. Channelling de Sade's energy, we were the willing vessels. You were an innocent. Forgive me, my darling."

Kat bursts into sobs, head in her hands, unable to face Franco. Now he knows the whole truth, the ugliness she carries within her. "You can get an annulment or a divorce, Franco. I have misrepresented myself. I'm not the woman you thought you married." Kat gets to her feet, she'll leave him with his thoughts, but he grabs her wrist.

"You're my wife." He drags the top sheet off the bed, wraps it and his arms around her. "Always, you're my wife, Kat." His mouth to her forehead. "I'm thankful that you didn't kill Nick; that would be troubling." She stares at him. "Bad joke, *mi dispiace*." He rocks her in his arms as he might Antonio or Katerina.

"When you told me I was a victim I didn't believe you. It is Faith who is dead. Now I understand, but I see it another way. I was necessary for you, Kat. No man loved you as a woman must be loved. You never experienced the deep passion between a man and a woman. This is a terrible thing, to live and not feel this, a different kind of crime. A death sentence for the living." Kisses her hand.

"I introduced you to the passionate life. I see that now. You could say that I rescued you. Yes?"

Yes, my love. Kat reaches up and kisses his mouth.

"And you saved a life. You saved Laurie. That counts, Kat." He holds her until her heart slows. "We must bathe and then I make you breakfast."

Kat stares out the window at the Florentine streetscape. A delivery truck makes its way down the narrow alley. Her confession diffused Franco's anguish, although revealing herself has added to her own. But she's thankful. Theirs is a shared guilt now. Her painter won't carry a burden too heavy for his lean shoulders. Instead, he's recreated himself as her rescuer. The ancient gods have been merciful once again.

The doorbell sounds. Kat checks the street camera. There's Brigitte, with Katerina in her arms. Kat buzzes her in. Opening the ebony door, Kat welcomes Franco's children to her home. Antonio, adorable in jeans and white tee, scrambles up the stairs yelling *nonna!* She scoops him into her arms. Baby kisses that smell like sweet hay. Brigitte mounts the stairs with Katerina in her arms. Surprise, Chiara follows behind her. They haven't seen each other since Kat laid her hands on Chiara's windpipe. *Oh Franco, more you do not know.*

"Kat, I'd like to see the apartment now that you've made your changes. Papa says I wouldn't recognize it." Chiara, all smiles and guile.

Brigitte takes the children inside, Kat nods that she'll join them in a moment. She plants her feet squarely on the marble tile and crosses her arms.

"Chiara. You are not welcome. My home is private." Chiara flinches. Kat takes a step towards her and Franco's ex-wife backs away. "*Vai.* Go back to your father and your palazzo. Do not return." Kat looks deep into those pretty, treacherous eyes. Without all the makeup, Massimo's eyes.

"As you wish." Chiara shrugs off the affront and retreats to the talking elevator.

You're still the enemy, Chiara. No more humiliation at your hand. Sono Signora Ghibellini.

She waits until Chiara is gone. Calls out: "Franco, *i bambini sono qui, the children are here!*"

Caffè Gilli in the piazza at three o'clock. Pietro Barone has some news he wishes to share in person. Disconnecting her cell, Kat walks into the bathroom and vomits into the toilet. Her gut roils until nothing's left except spittle. She washes her face in cold water and brushes her teeth. A rap at the outer door. Agnes inquiring if she needs anything. No, *vai vai.* Go away.

Kat considers her reflection in the mirror. Pulls her hair into a sleek ponytail. No vestiges remain of the sinewy grey-haired recluse from Port Renfrew. Mahogany hair, green eyes and ivory skin. She's not Italian in looks but Kat sees something more important. There is a softness in her features that did not exist before. It is because she is finally loved. She changes into a floral sundress with spaghetti straps, the one she wore in Santa Margherita. Their single holiday cut short by her meeting with the cop from Vancouver. Kat shivers. *Is it their only holiday together?*

The children nap in their nursery with their aunt, their energy spent from riding tricycles along the arcades that surround the piazza. Franco is in his studio. He doesn't have to know where she's gone. Kat will need time to digest the news from Vancouver, figure out how best to frame it before sharing with her painter.

Caffè Gilli, on the ground floor of the Levi, retains the charm and style of its origins in the *Belle Époque*. Ivory walls, the chandeliers of Murano glass, arches linking the frescoed ceilings and a majestic stand-up bar the Italians favour over seating. Writers and painters have congregated here to discuss the critical moments of their lives since it opened in 1733.

Barone's already seated, shirtsleeves rolled, drinking a red. He stands as she approaches. A Pinot Grigio in front of her, she gives her lawyer the once-over but is unable to read his mood. Sighing, she settles in to hear her fate.

"The Canadians are methodical and willing to share the results of their review. I have two documents here." Kat leans forward. "A summary of their findings. You see the list of twenty-three witnesses re-inter-viewed. Your name is here." His stubby index finger directs Kat to her place on the list. Kat Black. Below it she glimpses George Brodski. "And here, a review of the original autopsy findings."

Kat barely glances at the report.

"Your friend drowned. That's what killed her but the question is how she ended up in the water. By accident or was she pushed? There was blunt force trauma to the occipital lobe which resulted in a non-specific contusion of the inferior surface, but there were no patterned abrasions or fractures, no trace elements which would point to the causative fac-tor." Barone pauses and checks Kat's expression. "I know this is graphic, Signora Ghibellini, but it's the way such incidents are documented."

Graphic? Hardly. What about the blood, crushed bones? Kat nods calmly.

"There were no remarkable findings, save one. Your friend had a blood alcohol reading of .26, consistent with imbibing 24 ounces of alco-hol over a five-hour period. In other words, Faith Vogel was very drunk when she landed in the water." He takes a swig of his red which strikes Kat as ironic, laughable even, but she's careful to keep her face closed. *So, Faith was pissed as a newt when Franco took a swipe at her.*

"The conclusions of the review are outlined in this second document." He passes Kat the stationery imprinted with the RCMP insignia. Kat takes a long swallow of wine and reads.

While Pietro Barone walks across the piazza, jacket slung over his shoulder, Kat orders another drink and rereads the letter. The sun's on the wane and it's easier to breathe. Franco will wonder where she is but she wants the wine first. She needs time to process this letter, to re-order her reality. Then she'll tell Franco what she knows, face to face.

"Franco, meet me downstairs at the main door. News from Vancouver."

Her painter emerges barefoot from the stairwell.

"No shoes?"

He shrugs. "Tell me, Kat."

"Let's go sit in the piazza."

They take a seat on a stone bench near the carousel. They look an incongruous pair, Kat thinks. An older woman in a fashionable sundress and spike heels with a comely younger man, clothes and hands splattered with paint and he's barefoot. Few of the passers-by would imagine they're husband and wife.

Kat takes Franco's hands in her own, her ruby and diamond ring glinting in the sun. Passion, constancy and protection. She reaches into her tote, retrieves the letter and hands it to her husband.

"Franco, this is what the RCMP found in their review. It's in English."

He stares at the folded letter in his hand.

"After interviewing twenty-three people, including me, there was no new evidence. The autopsy was also reviewed." She won't share the wording, it's too much. "Faith died by drowning. There was evidence of an injury to the back of her head, but she also had a significant amount of alcohol in her system. She was drunk, pissed drunk."

"What does this mean, Kat?" Franco tenses, as if awaiting a physical blow.

"Without witnesses and with the amount of alcohol in her system, it was concluded that the injury may have occurred as she fell into the water. She lost her balance walking home and she drowned. That her death was accidental and that the case is now closed." Choking back tears, she holds onto Franco so tightly that he flinches. "You're free, Franco. I'm free. We are free."

The carousel in Pizza della Repubblica whirls in its endless circle. Antonio and Katerina hold onto their papa and wait for their turn. Kat waits too. Brigitte will snap some photos, document new memories.

The carousel vendor remembers Kat. She gives him a ten euro note again, but this time it only covers one ride for her family. Antonio picks his pony, the white one. Katerina sits tentatively on the pink horse, her papa's arm holding her steady. Kat, a grin on her face, mounts her steed, *il cavallo nero*. The engine thrums, the carousel turns. Franco, a hand on Katerina's waist and a watchful eye on Antonio, looks back at Kat on her pony. She gives a girlish wave. He shakes his head and guffaws aloud.

Round and round they go under a sky that's brilliant with stars. The citizens and tourists of Florence mill about, making their own night music. *If you wish for it hard enough, maybe it will be so.* That's what she hoped last December.

As they dismount, the carousel vendor inquires: "*Sei felice, signora,* are you happy signora?"

Kat locks arms with her painter as he carries his children home. She shouts over her shoulder: "*Si signore, lo sono,* yes sir, I am."

ACKNOWLEDGEMENTS

This novel was crafted with love, laughter and tears. I wish to acknowledge Sandra Birdsell who shared the craft of novel writing with me at Humber College. I remember the late Ann Ireland who mentored me by close reading over 40,000 words during a 13-week mentorship program at Ryerson University and made me believe I was a writer. Robin Stevenson encouraged me to turn a short story into this novel with the caveat, I hope you enjoy spending time with your characters. Special thank you to Jill Fontaine, friend, early reader and the creator of the title, *Bernini's Elephant*. Particular thanks to Michael Mirolla and the talented team at Guernica Editions for bringing my words to the world.

ABOUT THE AUTHOR

JANE CALLEN lives in Vancouver, British Columbia and travels to Italy whenever the fates allow. When she isn't planning her next Italian adventure, she keeps Italy close by cooking *la cucina povera* and taking language lessons. Italy and her people feature frequently in Jane's writings. *Bernini's Elephant* is Jane's debut novel.

Printed in January 2023
by Gauvin Press,
Gatineau, Québec